ALISON CROGGON is a novelist, poet, thea[...] in Melbourne.

In 1989 she was appointed Melbourne [...] and since then has reviewed for the *Australian*, ABC Arts Online, the *Guardian*, *Overland*, *The Monthly* and the *Australian Book Review*. From 2004–2012 she ran the theatre review blog Theatre Notes, the first theatre blog in Australia. In 2009 she was awarded the Geraldine Pascall Critic of the Year. In 2018 she co-founded the performance criticism website witnessperformance.com with Dr Robert Reid.

She has written libretti and plays for theatre since 1994. *The Burrow* and *Gauguin*, with scores by Michael Smetanin, premiered at the 1994 Perth and 2000 Melbourne Festivals. The libretto for *Mayakovsky* (score Michael Smetanin) was shortlisted for the 2015 Victorian Premiers Prize for Drama, and *The Riders* (score Iain Grandage) was awarded the Vocal/Choral Work of the Year in the 2015 Australian Arts Music Awards. Her plays include *Lenz* (Melbourne Festival 1996), *Samarkand* and *The Famine* (Red Shed Company 1997), *Blue* (La Mama 2001), *Monologues for an Apocalypse* (ABC Radio National 2001) and *Specula* (ABC Radio National 2006). *My Dearworthy Darling*, written for The Rabble, premieres at Malthouse Theatre in 2019.

Alison has published nine books of poetry, which won the Dame Mary Gilmore and Anne Elder Prizes and were shortlisted for NSW and Victorian Premiers Literary Awards. Her most recent collection is *New and Selected Poems 1991–2017* (2017).

She is the author of the epic fantasy series *The Books of Pellinor*, which sold more than half a million books worldwide and were shortlisted for three Aurealis Awards. Other internationally published novels include *Black Spring* (shortlisted for the 2014 NSW Premier's Award) and *The River and the Book* (shortlisted for the 2016 WA Premier's Award and winner of the Wilderness Society's Environmental Writing for Children Award). With her husband Daniel Keene she is co-writing a science fiction series, Newport City (*Fleshers* 2018, and *Pinkers*, due out in 2019). Her first middle grade book, *The Threads of Magic*, will be released internationally by Walker Books and Candlewick Press in early 2020. Her non-fiction memoir/essay *Monsters* will be published by Scribe Publications in 2019/20.

www.alisoncroggon.com

For all the artists who made this book possible.

remembered presences

responses to theatre

ALISON CROGGON

Currency Press, Sydney

PREFACE

How to think like a theatre critic

First, you mustn't think.

You arrive at the place assigned for performance. It may be a theatre, it may be a shed or an underground car park. You wait for the ritual: the lowering of the lights, the hush in the auditorium, the slight unconscious holding of breath. Something is about to begin.

Even if it's a play that you know backwards because you've read it and seen it in countless interpretations, you have no idea what is about to happen. It will be different every time.

For days, or weeks, or months, or years, a group of people has been making whatever it is you are about to see. Theatre comes in many shapes, from many different processes, and is made for many different reasons. However it is done, it will end up in front of an audience. What makes theatre is the work of all those who created it – the performers, the writers, the directors, the designers, the backstage staff – meeting the unknown, which is the audience. The audience is you. They don't know what you think about it. You, ideally, don't know what you think of it either.

You watch and listen and feel. If you are a critic, it is your job to watch as hard as you can. You listen to the language, to the voices that articulate it, and you watch the bodies that move in front of you, weaving meaning out of relationship and space. You listen to the soundscape that embraces the voices. There may be music, there may be ambient sound, there may be silence so profound you can hear the actors breathing and every step on the stage. You look at the shape of the stage, how the set and lighting create their own meanings, how the shapes open and determine the relationship of this performance to you, the audience. You open your body to the rhythms of the performance and the language and the colours and movement that weave their meanings before you. You create a relationship with the work that is occurring in front of you.

At the assigned time the performance ends. It may last for twenty minutes, or for twelve hours. You, the audience, will have experienced that performance in the time allotted. Even if you went back to the same theatre to see the same show, you will never have that experience again. It is now in the past tense, stored in your memory. If you watched hard enough, you will have noticed all sorts of details, which at the moment are mixed up in a generalised mash. In the immediate aftermath, you will have a reaction; you liked it, you hated it, you were indifferent, you were bored, you were so excited or so sad or so astonished that you can't speak at all.

None of that matters very much. You are not a critic yet.

You take your memory home and you begin to prod it. You begin to translate your experience into words. When you were in the theatre, you were living in the present tense. That is now over. Now you are a mortician, and language is your scalpel. Now you drag out the books. You may read the play again. You may research some aspect of performance history you don't know enough about. You may need to look up the history of English kings, or dog-sledding, or what's going on in garment factories in Bangladesh in 2014. People make theatre about all sorts of things. You remember a quote by a critic writing in 1954. You remember a poem you love that seems apposite. You think about the shapes of everything you saw and you consider how they created the experience that is now living inside you. You let it all circle around your head.

Some experiences are easier to translate into words than others. The hardest are those which affect you most, the shows that possessed you so intensely while you were watching that their finishing is a kind of grief. You know that even if you had all the language in the world, what you write will never be equal to the experience of being there. If you were angered by the show, if you feel cheated or let down, you consider why. You write down sentences and you test them against what you remember. Is it true? Is it accurate? But always you are returning to the memory, which is the past tense of your present labour.

You will make mistakes. Everybody does. But you try to make as few mistakes as possible. You try to be true to what you experienced in the theatre.

You write what you write, conditioned by the context in which it will be published. You may have 400 words for a daily paper, or 5,000 for a theatre magazine that is asking you to remember works you saw years before.

It will be a response. You will bring to your response everything that you brought to the theatre: your attention, your knowledge, your experience, your sensibility, your life. You know that the less you bring, the less you'll have to respond with. You don't care about your opinion. Everyone has an opinion. That's not what matters. You don't want to be the kind of critic who doesn't pay attention, whose responses are crafted out of their preconceptions or vanity or ignorance. You want to be a critic who thinks with all of her body, in the present and in the past.

You want to be invisible.

You write.

Island literary magazine, No. 137 2014

First published in 2018 by
Currency Press Pty Ltd
PO Box 2287
Strawberry Hills NSW 2012 Australia
www.currency.com.au
enquiries@currency.com.au

Copyright © Alison Croggon 2018

COPYING FOR EDUCATIONAL PURPOSES:
The *Copyright Act 1968 (Cth)* ('the Act') allows a maximum of one chapter or 10% of this book, whichever is the greater, to be copied by any educational institution for its educational purposes provided that the educational institution (or the body that administers it) has given a remuneration notice to the Copyright Agency (CA) under the Act.

For details of the CA licence for educational institutions please contact CA, 11/66 Goulburn Street, Sydney, NSW 2000, tel within Australia 1800 066 844 toll free; outside Australia 61 2 9394 7600, fax 61 2 9394 7601, email: info@copyright.com.au.

COPYING FOR OTHER PURPOSES:
Except as permitted under the Act, for example a fair dealing for the purposes of study, research, criticism or review, no part of this book may be reproduced, stored in a retrieval system, or transmitted in any form or by any means without prior written permission. All inquiries should be made to the publisher at the above address.
Cataloguing-in-Publication data for this title is available from the National Library of Australia website: www.nla.gov.au

Front cover shows Ewen Leslie in *War of the Roses*. Photograph by Tania Kelley.

Cover design by Lisa White.

Typeset by Currency Press.

Printed by Ligare Book Printers, Riverwood, NSW.

CONTENTS

Preface: How to think like a theatre critic	v
Acknowledgments	xii
The Last Days of Mankind	1
7 Days 10 Years	4
Hamlet: Brook and Redding	6
Trapped by the Past	10
Subclass26A	16
Out on a Limb	19
The Yellow Wallpaper	21
The Ham Funeral / Journal of a Plague Year	24
Black Medea	30
Phobia	32
Songs of Exile	34
Lally Katz and the Terrible Mysteries of the Volcano	36
Eldorado	39
Construction of the Human Heart	43
The Skriker	45
Le Dernier Caravansérail (Odyssées)	49
The Damask Drum	54
Tense Dave	57
OT: Chronicles of the Old Testament	60
On Paul Capsis	63
Holiday / Chapters from the Pandemic	64
Meow Meow	68
Moving Target	69
Red Sky Morning	73
Blackbird	76
Patti Smith	79
The Women of Troy	81
Dust	84
Grace	85
The War of the Roses	87
Wretch	95
Peer Gynt	97

3xSisters / Spring Awakening	101
Tom Fool / Leaves of Glass	104
Poppea	108
One Night The Moon	111
Structure and Sadness	114
The Harry Harlow Project	116
Glasoon	119
Godzone	124
Ngurrumilmarrmiriyu (Wrong Skin)	126
My Stories, Your Emails	129
PropagandA	131
The Grenade	134
Moth / The Ugly One / Hole in the Wall	135
Do Not Go Gentle…	140
This Kind of Ruckus	141
Sappho… in 9 Fragments	143
Thyestes	146
The Trial	150
Peer Gynt / Elektra / Creditors	155
The Nest	161
Don Parties On	164
Song of the Bleeding Throat	167
The End	171
Amplification / Faker	173
Princess Dramas	176
The Burlesque Hour Loves Melbourne	180
Small Odysseys	183
Pina	185
Namatjira / Rising Water	188
Ganesh Versus the Third Reich	192
Return to Earth	196
Oráculos	198
Welcome to Thonnet	202
Olive as tragic hero	204
The Histrionic	213
Persona	219
On the Production of Monsters	222

Next Wave: Monster Body / Dewey Dell / Justin Shoulder	225
Queen Lear	229
Queen Lear: the perfect storm	233
Top Girls	236
Some notes on Orlando	239
Pompeii, LA	243
On the Importance of Being Seen	246
The Cherry Orchard	252
Roman Tragedies	255
Hedda Gabler	258
Hipbone Sticking Out / Team of Life	263
Cut The Sky	266
MTC Neon (Shit and We Get It) / Birdland / Love and Information	268
Antigone	273
Asking For It: A One-Lady Rape About Comedy Starring Her Pussy and Little Else.	278
Watching Xavier Le Roy: Self Unfinished at Dancehouse, Melbourne	280
Miss Julie	282
Neon Festival	286
Australia's leading Artistic Directors should embrace both positive and negative criticism	292
Assemblage #1, Matthew Day	294
The Book of Exodus: Part One	296
Macbeth	298
The Real and Imagined History of the Elephant Man	301

ACKNOWLEDGMENTS

This project has been assisted by the Australian Government through the Australia Council, its arts funding and advisory body.

Written in residence at La Chartreuse de Villeneuve-lez-Avignon Centre national des écritures du spectacle (National Centre for Performance Writing).

Ce texte a été écrit en résidence à la Chartreuse de Villeneuve lez Avignon – centre national des écritures du spectacle.

Most of this work first appeared on the review blog Theatre Notes. Other pieces were first published in *The Australian*, *The Guardian*, *The Monthly*, *ABC Arts Online*, *Kill Your Darlings* and *Island* magazine. *How to Think Like a Theatre Critic* was republished in *Theatre Criticism: Changing Landscapes*, edited by Duska Radosavljevic, Bloomsbury 2016.

The Last Days of Mankind

> Think of a real work of art: have you never had the feeling that something about it is reminiscent of the smell of burning metal you get from a knife you're whetting on a grindstone? It's a cosmic, meteoric, lightning-and-thunder smell, something divinely uncanny!
>
> Robert Musil, *The Man Without Qualities*

Every now and then, it is necessary to be reminded of the true resources and possibilities of art. Sometimes it seems that dullness is all: that we merely consume, like lobotomised laboratory rats, the enforced idiocies of mass culture. A real work of art calls up without shame the seriousness of being, the mind's restlessness, its functions as critique and rebuke, inspiration and provocation. All fiery discontent, artists are indeed of the devil's party; but, like Milton, they must sing as if they were angels.

Karl Kraus was such a malcontent. He was one of an extraordinary generation of Austrian artists who emerged after the collapse of the Austro-Hungarian Empire and the catastrophe of World War I, a period which included writers like Robert Musil and Joseph Roth, and the chilling visions of painters like Otto Dix and Oskar Kokoschka. Perhaps it is that time's unique sense of apocalyptic transformation which makes these artists seem so relevant now, and gives their writings such a bitter air of prophecy.

Kraus, considered one of the great satirists of last century, was arguably the most sophisticated media commentator of his day. He saw before almost anyone else the baleful influence of press-driven propaganda on public life. Ironically, he used the transient forms of journalism to articulate his critique, most notably in his famous journal *Die Fackel*. *The Last Days of Mankind*, a sprawling 800-page epic which is still not fully translated into English, is generally acknowledged to be Kraus' masterpiece.

The play is reportedly a melange of quotes from sources such as Goethe and Shakespeare and the Bible, a mixture of historical and fictional characters, songs, cinematic elements, polyphonic crowd scenes and scenic fragments. Justus Neumann opens with a quote from Kraus' prologue, in which he says: 'The events shown in this play, no matter how unlikely, actually took place; the words spoken in this play, no matter how unlikely, are true quotations.' In a play which features God Himself, this is hardly an appeal to documentary ideas of verity. But there is no doubt that it is an account which is bitterly, blackly true, in the way that only art can be true. And it is deadly funny.

A performance which lasts for just over an hour clearly offers a radically edited version of Kraus' epic, and I am in no position to judge either the quality of the translation (made for this performance by Neumann and Matthew Lilias) or how the redacted version compares to the original. However, I can say that Neumann's adaptation makes stunning theatre.

Neumann, an Austrian actor whom I last saw perform almost twenty years ago in a virtuosic one-man piece called *Kill Hamlet*, is an actor's actor, a performer of consummate skill who has the strange glamour of invisibility that only the best actors attain. Your attention is so focused on the narrative, the character, the performance, that the actor himself is paradoxically effaced. From the first moment Neumann shows himself, half-lit halfway down La Mama's stairs, and reads in that bewitching voice from Kraus' prologue, you know you are in the hands of a master.

The set is self-consciously a stage: a raised dais draped with a black cloth, and a table with a chair, on which lies a book. At the other end of the stage is Julius Schwing – as I found out afterwards, Neumann's 17-year-old son – who tickles acoustic melodies from an electric guitar, as Neumann walks slowly to the small stage and begins what is effectively a dramatised reading of the play. But what a reading...

To call it a reading, although that it what it is, threatens to undersell its subtleties and power. *The Last Days of Mankind* is theatre at its simplest, a matter of unadorned words, music, and performance, but the production is, within the rigors of its stern palette, astoundingly full of colour and variousness. Aside from Neumann's ability to play a cast of at least dozens (he contains multitudes), this is due to the beautiful and precise shifts of Niklas Pajanti's lighting states, the suggestive placings of Neumann's body, certain stillnesses and gestures. His performance is counterpointed with the responsive and passionate live music, which varies from gentle arpeggios to the anguished electric scream of Hendrix or Deep Purple, summoning in the tiny space of La Mama the technological apocalypse of modern warfare.

If it is true, as Heiner Müeller says, that the major political function of art today is to mobilise the imagination, then this production of *The Last Days of Mankind* is profoundly political. Without spectacular sets or casts of thousands, the atrocity and scale of world war is made palpable. The play's scope ranges from intimacies – a scene, for example, where children play 'world war' – to public utterances of all kinds: a teacher to his pupils, a disillusioned God to His creation. The most frightening, perhaps, are where Kraus strips back the rhetoric of war's glory and exposes its homicidal insanity.

In this most nuanced of writers, no linguistic manipulation is left unexamined: Kraus is alert to all the political dimensions of language, from the most private to the most public. He shows how abuse of language directly creates the realities which permit the human tragedy, the grief and piteousness, of war.

Kraus considered the press one of the driving forces towards war – a major reason his work resonates so uncomfortably in the age of Fox News. The play opens, tellingly, with the news being shouted in Vienna of the assassination of the Prince Franz Josef in Sarajevo. Neumann plays 'The Crowd', recreating the whirlpool of nationalism, racism, bellicose excitement, stupidity and bloodthirstiness which accompany a public lust for war. And one of his characters is an actual journalist, Alice Schalek, whose prurient interviews with soldiers and officers reveal an excitement bordering on the obscene.

'Satisfied?' she asks rhetorically, in raptures over being on a battlefield. 'Satisfied is not the word for it! Patriotism, you idealists may call it. Hatred of the enemy, you nationalists. Call it sport, you moderns. Adventure, you romantics. You who know the souls of men call it the joyous thrill of power. I call it humanity liberated!'

It made me go cold, to hear that familiar glorification of mass murder in the name of human freedom. Those words were written almost a century ago, but for all our dazzling technological innovations, for all our trumpetings of progress, how much have things actually changed? We seem to have learned nothing. And as a response – an intelligent, undeceived, conscious response – to a world of increasing fascistic paranoia and irrational passions, it puts most contemporary works to shame. Don't miss it.

Theatre Notes, September 19 2004

7 Days 10 Years

Flaubert said, in relation to novels, that 'God is in the details'. And equally, one might say that in speaking about a society in disastrous flux, it's the details – the 'opaque areas' rather than what are noted in conventional histories as significant events – that are most telling. They are certainly most telling in theatre, for human interaction is the life-blood of drama. And in *7 Days 10 Years*, presented by Theatre@Risk at Theatre Works, Louis Milutinovic reveals some of the realities of the Balkans wars in the 1990s by following the fortunes of a single family over the decade before the NATO bombing of Serbia.

The Balkan conflict was, for many people in the West, an obscure war of bloody ethnic hatred in a little-known place. By focusing on intimate detail, Milutinovic's lucid narrative offers another view than the lens of opaque ethnic hatred through which such conflicts are usually reported. It makes what happened in Serbia at once more legible and more alarming: after all, blind self-interest, apathy, corruption and fear-driven nationalism are the currency of our times.

In its structure and approach, this play owes a debt to Bertolt Brecht's *Fear and Misery in the Third Reich*, in which Brecht adopted small-scale, naturalistic forms to demonstrate how fascism impacts on the most ordinary of interactions. *Fear and Misery in the Third Reich* is a frightening parable which shows how easily extraordinary circumstances became normal, the incremental but deadly adjustments that people make in order to negotiate daily life under a Fascist regime.

Similarly, Milutinovic largely ignores the ethnic arguments – for example, the Serbian narrative of the Battle of Kosovo in 1389 – to concentrate on quotidian detail. The rise of Milosevic and Serbian nationalism and the wars with Bosnia and Kosovo are referred to obliquely: their effects are visible in the crippling of a young soldier, the heroin addiction of his sister, the impoverishment of the middle class, the marginalisation and final silencing of dissent, and the banal but terrifying thuggery of a violent kleptocracy.

The play moves swiftly through seven toughly-written scenes, each titled, in another nod to Brecht, by the date of the events. They chart the gradual disenfranchisement of the family; the activist mother Svetlana (Anastasia Malinoff) loses her job as a teacher and is forced to sell cigarettes on the black market; the son Ivan (Steve Mouzakis) is left crippled by the war, and his girlfriend Vesna (Odette Joannides) leaves for a job in Italy and becomes a prostitute. Even Svetlana's brother Branko (Sergio Tell), a small town official, loses everything he has gained through his petty corruption. The play ends with the arrival of the US war planes, which are greeted by the dissenters as a liberation after years of intimidation under Milosevic. But it is ironically clear in the final moments that this final liberation is only another betrayal.

What also becomes clear is that those who lose most are the small people, the petite bourgeoisie who ignored the larger picture in favour of their narrow self-interest. The middle-class characters who dissent and protest the growing fascism in their community, though scarred in obvious ways, manage to retain their self-respect; those who aggressively grab power and cash, like the captain who is building himself a new house out of war-profiteering, or the amoral folk singer/celebrity Shana (Larissa Gallagher) who switches to whatever bandwagon happens to be winning, also survive. In the bleakly riven society Milutinovic describes, the powerless who assent to fascistic authority with an eye to their own survival emerge as the most lost.

Chris Bendall's production is a good, honest presentation of the play with a high component of sheer entertainment. It features terrific singing, with a soundtrack by Philip McLeod of some bizarre Eurotrash folk music, in itself a sardonic comment on nationalistic propaganda. The scenes move swiftly and with great energy, capably managing the complex emotional twists of the writing, from comedy to violent tragedy, with no sense of false steps.

The production features an excellent set by Peter Corrigan: three trestles painted red which can be rearranged flexibly and quickly into a series of playing spaces on different levels. The back half of the Theatre Works stage is cut off by a huge black curtain, from which stage hands wearing pig masks – sinister images of the growing anonymous bestiality of society – emerge to rearrange the space. The design and lighting permit a theatrical spareness which focuses on an ensemble of excellent performances: in particular Laura Lattuada as Mila, the flaky but irrepressible aunt; Sergio Tell as Branko, the corrupt town official who betrays his activist sister to the authorities; and Simon Kingsley Hall as Bane, the drug-dealing son who, despite escaping national service, ends up as an emotional cripple.

This is far from didactic theatre, but it is a powerful political work. Milutinovic exposes, without a trace of sentiment but with a great deal of compassion for all the characters he portrays, the predatory nature of a society in which relationships are compromised and destroyed by mutual mistrust and fear. It's a timely reminder of Primo Levi's warning that the price of freedom is eternal vigilance.

Theatre Notes, November 17 2004

Hamlet: Brook and Redding

On the face of it, it may seem very unfair to compare these two versions of *Hamlet*. One is a filmed production by one of the greatest theatre directors of the past century, created in Peter Brook's gorgeous Paris base, the Théâtre des Bouffes du Nord; the other an exemplary example of poor theatre, put on by a young Melbourne director in a shopfront in High Street, Northcote.

As it happens, it is not unfair; theatre is a great leveller. Perhaps for similar reasons – a certain straightforwardness in approaching Shakespeare – both are notable for their clarity, and they share a great text and remarkable actors. Where Oscar Redding's production lacks Brook's exquisite aesthetic polish, it gains in robust irreverence and visceral power. But what strikes me most is how both these productions spin the focus on this most protean of texts, to reveal a Hamlet in whose body itself turns the sword of politics.

The great Shakespearean critic Jan Kott says of *Hamlet* that it is a play that absorbs its times. So there are, among many others, the Romantic Hamlet of the nineteenth century, wanly melancholic; the mid-century Hamlet, which Kott particularly documented, in which interpretation leans on the pitiless wheel of power; and now this twenty-first century Hamlet, at once sensuous and full of loathing, raging against the mortal trappings of his flesh.

Part of the reason for these many Hamlets is that the text is seldom performed entirely as written. It means that each production is cut according to the cloth of its interpretation. Both Brook and Redding take a broadly similar approach, removing the cumbersome opening scene with the ghost, and cutting out entirely the complicated narrations of battles and politics. They fillet out a claustrophobic family tragedy of individuals trapped in remorseless passions. In these productions, the personal is most assuredly political.

This approach rejects most modern interpretations of *Hamlet*, in which the character of Fortinbras is brought to the foreground. Fortinbras – who claims the throne of Denmark after all the corpses stop twitching on the floor – is in some versions an alter ego of Hamlet; in others, the legitimate heir to the throne, the man who restores order to the broken kingdom. 'If one wishes to place *Hamlet*'s moral conflicts into a historical context', says Kott, 'one cannot ignore the role played by Fortinbras'.

In these versions Fortinbras has disappeared entirely. But I think this is not so much a symptom of ahistorical consciousness, as a lack of belief in the possibility of the restoration of order, or even in the possibility of order itself. No king now comes to make it all right: the plays ends with the slaughter. Today's *Hamlet* is considerably darker than previous versions: it contains no illusion of consolation.

The brooding sense of claustrophobia is reinforced by the doubling, some of which is repeated in both productions: in both, Polonius and the gravedigger (Bruce Meyers in Brook's, and John Francis Howard in Redding's), and Claudius and the Ghost (Jeffery Kissoon and Adrian Mulraney respectively) are played by the same actor. The doubling of Claudius in particular throws Hamlet's revulsion against his uncle into ironic relief: we are reminded that he is importuned to kill his own kin, outraging familial ties just as his uncle did in murdering Hamlet's father.

Redding goes much further, doubling the roles of Gertrude and Ophelia (Nicki Paull), which makes the play's incestuous sexual drama even more knotted. His most audacious move is to double the roles of Hamlet and his friend Horatio: Horatio is played as a handpuppet. That you accept this without question is a considerable tribute to the intensity and skill of Richard Pyros' performance. What is fascinating is its theatrical ambiguity: part of the time, it is quite possible to imagine seriously that a ridiculous pair of pink eyes is Horatio, Hamlet's only friend; at other times, the hand puppet seems another aspect of his madness and loneliness, a crazed aspect of Hamlet's splintered self.

Adrian Lester's Hamlet is gentler than Richard Pyros', whose wit is crueller and violence more dangerous (especially when he is holding a huge kitchen knife to Gertrude's throat). Lester's performance is framed by lush, rich sensuousness: the rust-red walls of the theatre, the naked flames of lamps, luxurious crimson fabrics, the melancholy scrape of a cello. Pyros, on the other hand, is working in a bare, scruffy space lit by fluorescent tubes, with the sound of high street traffic as background accompaniment.

But again I was struck by similarities as much as differences: these Hamlets are mercurial, impelled by savage laughter rather than by dark melancholia. They describe an intelligence tormented by circumstance: that circumstance being primarily mortality, the fate of all flesh, but also its sullying, a fatal disgust at moral and fleshly corruption.

Of course, there is more to *Hamlet* than Hamlet; and these productions feature ensemble casts of great depth. One would expect that of Brook; but Redding has gathered together some very fine actors, who have created a subtlety and depth of performance which rivals, and in the case of Ophelia surpasses, that which Brook elicited from his. All deserve mention, but Adrian Mulraney's authoritative and subtle performance as Claudius – both unrepentant usurper and repentant brother – never falters.

In Redding's production at DDT Studio in High Street, Northcote, the women's roles are strong and disturbing. Nicki Paull plays Gertrude as an alcoholic, constantly sipping from a jam jar, who imperceptibly becomes more and more drunk as the play progresses, until by the final scene she can barely stand. Her announcement of Ophelia's death – told through uncontrollable fits of laughter – brings home the terror of the girl's suicide in a way that no sober rendition could. And Ophelia's mad scene is shaming and pitiable, in the way that real madness is.

It is very clear in this drama how the women are destroyed, both morally and physically, by their entrapment within male power. The single power Gertrude and Ophelia possess is their sexuality: it is their 'virtue', a commodity which belongs to the family, not to themselves, and it is not theirs to bestow freely. Laertes (Thomas Wright) and

Polonius lecture Ophelia at length about how she ought to be behave, and Hamlet likewise has no hesitation in censuring his mother for outraging the legitimate bonds of marriage. The fear of women's anarchic sexual desire lurks uneasily beneath the surface of the action, erupting in male disgust ('Frailty, thy name is woman!') or in female madness and despair.

However, it is not the women who are treacherous, but the men: most notably seen in Claudius' murder of his brother to gain the crown, the betrayal which unravels all the rest. And there is also Hamlet's feigned detestation of Ophelia, which drives her to suicide; Rosencrantz and Guildenstern's deceptive spying on Hamlet, betraying the bonds of friendship; Laertes' betrayal of honourable combat, by poisoning his sword.

Hamlet is, more than almost any other Shakespearean play except perhaps *The Tempest*, deeply concerned with the provenance of theatre itself. Almost no-one in the play is who he or she seems to be: all are playing roles, whether self-imposed or not, and this is underlain by our knowledge that the 'real' characters are played by actors, who are also not who they seem to be. Is this merely deception and betrayal? Hamlet's pretended madness is, rather, an attempt to find the truth: as he says, 'the play's the thing/ In which to catch the conscience of a King'. These potent ambiguities, the mask as a revealer of truth and as a lie, drive the fascination of the action as much as the repressed sexual passions.

There is a vital difference between these two productions: one was performed four years ago, and was watched on a screen; the other occurred live, feet away from me. No recorded performance beats the living experience, no matter how artfully filmed it might be. But they both gave me a new *Hamlet*, and reminded me that it is, as Kott says, 'the strangest play ever written'.

Both productions tear away the cultural barnacles that so often weigh down this most monumental of English icons – the deadening reverence, the fear of poetry, the stereotypical expectations – and deliver it into the present, with all the complexities and contradictions of a living thing. It's a rare experience that always leaves me elated. And such experiences are why I persist in going to the theatre.

Theatre Notes, December 10 2004

Trapped by the Past

'Those who cannot remember the past', said George Santayana, 'are condemned to repeat it'. Applied to theatre, this is a vision of terrifying sterility: some outer circle of Hell, decked out like a cross between an English drawing room and the set of *Neighbours*. And as Julian Meyrick argues in his very interesting polemic, *Platform Papers 3: Trapped by the Past: Why our Theatre is Facing Paralysis*, Australian theatre's ignorance of its own history dooms it to an endless cycle of 'forgetting and despair'.

Too right, say I: if memory is a form of consciousness, then Australian theatre, as a discrete if debatable entity, is a dead duck. We barely have a repertoire: how often do we see reinterpretations of classic texts by White, Hewett, Beynon, Kenna, Hibberd, or any other playwright who has made a mark in the past 50 years? And how many new plays have any life beyond a single four week season?

I'm grateful to Meyrick – that rare beast, a theatre historian – for his careful delineation of this problem in his paper *Trapped by the Past*. He spends some time discussing how institutional and governmental structures and assumptions have formed the present, and he chronicles a depressing history of botched or even hostile public policies and damaging internecine rivalries. But *Trapped by the Past* is, most importantly, an impassioned plea for cultural memory.

'Donald Horne's complaint that the industry's idea of cultural debate is a one-line telegram signed by twenty artists points up the lack of articulated vision coming from theatre professionals on the ground today', says Meyrick. 'At a recent public meeting on the future of Playbox, I was not the only one struck by the lack of specific knowledge about the company we had come to discuss. And when, at the end, someone stood up – as someone always does – and said "Who needs the past anyway?" – as someone always does – a vision rose before my eyes of a wheel of fire on which Australian theatre was to be endlessly wracked, our historical forgetting a constituent part of our on-going suffering.'

The Greeks said (they got a lot of things right) that Memory was the mother of the Muses, so cultural amnesia is probably about half of the thousand cuts that are currently bleeding Australian theatre dry. But Meyrick's thesis is not so much that Australian theatre has forgotten its past, as that it only remembers certain parts of it. He points out that theatre is an art form with a history that extends far beyond our sea-girt shores and into a past far deeper than the past 30 years, facts which too seldom seem to enter our theatrical conversations. But here his main concern is with local history.

His experience of finding teasing glimpses of alternative, unwritten histories echoes my own when, as a young critic, I was attempting to inform myself about Australian theatre. I remember being told about all sorts of interesting things – the international avant-garde edge in the Australian Performing Group (APG), for example, or the feminist theatre of the '70s – to which I could, frustratingly, find little or no reference in the histories and overviews I consulted. Meyrick mentions how whole swathes of experience – that of older actors trained in the 'Anglo' tradition of theatre, who remember the Tiv and music hall – have been forgotten, and how much poorer we are for this loss. The commonly accepted story is how this kind of theatre, colonial and hidebound, was swept aside in the larrikin 'New Wave' of the late 1960s and early '70s, when Australian theatre, as the myth goes, first found its 'voice'. These other, overshadowed histories made the prevailing myth – which is, of course, not entirely inaccurate – both more interesting and more complex.

As Meyrick says, 'Australian theatre is an art form in wilful ignorance of its own past, and the upshot is an industry that appears less interesting than in fact it is... the truth is fabulous, intriguing, high coloured, a story of titanic struggles, colossal achievements, massive defeats, murderous betrayals... ' Which, if it recalls one of those thrillers with raised gold lettering so prominent in airport bookshops, has the virtue of sounding more exciting than the usual unquestioning narratives of nationalism versus colonialism.

Although he focuses on generational change and, in particular, on the disastrous dominance of Playbox Theatre in the recent development of new Australian work, the true value of Meyrick's paper resides elsewhere. Meyrick does claim that a generation of theatre artists who are now in prominent positions through Australian theatre are, deliberately or not, stifling innovation in the art. But he says this is the result of a fracture that occurred when the New Wave first appeared, polarising the culture – on the one side, the conservative, authoritarian model, on the other the brash, questioning, anti-authoritarian Vietnam protesters – and the twain ne'er met anywhere. And he claims that the lack of a perception of a common ground – a recognition that, whatever their differences, they were pursuing to their best abilities a mutual passion for an abstract but real thing called 'Australian theatre' – led to an impoverishment of theatre culture that is now having disastrous consequences for younger artists.

'The real problem,' says Meyrick, glancing over the tangle of spats and rivalries which characterise the discourse, 'is that the "debate" is founded on such a fierce determination *not* to understand other points of view that any intellectual gain from the sparring of competing minds is lost'.

Bravo, Mr Meyrick: that's the underlying problem in a nutshell. What he is describing is a pervasive anti-intellectualism that has been the bane of Australian theatre on *all* sides, and a lack of disinterested commitment to theatre *itself*. As much as reducing discourse to pitched battles and skirmishes between rival interests, this often expresses itself in a puzzling incuriosity about theatre as an art form. Most bizarrely, given its often nationalistic dress, it manifests as a condition of cultural cringe which very often marginalises new or original Australian voices which (as they should) challenge prevailing mores. Meyrick, whose main concern is with what he calls 'verbal drama' (aka plays), correctly questions where that leaves new playwrights and other emerging theatre artists.

There is, in fact, a surprising number of young and engaged theatre writers; but as things stand, their outlook is fairly bleak. As Meyrick says, the lack of a well-supported middle sector of theatre, between co-op fringe productions and the major state institutions, means that it is extremely difficult for new artists, and especially new playwrights, to evolve. He fields some depressing statistics, courtesy of Geoffrey Milne, about the shrinkage in contemporary theatre. Between 1986 and 2003, the number of new productions by state theatre companies declined from 49 to 29.8 – a drastic fall approaching almost 50 per cent. And, even worse, the production of new plays by local and overseas writers in alternative companies has declined by 30 per cent in twenty years.

This situation is in part a result of the withdrawal of funding for the middle tier companies – Anthill, Australian Contemporary Theatre Company (The Church), Theatre Works, the Red Shed and others – which actively commissioned and produced new works. Australian theatre has never recovered from this policy-driven act of cultural vandalism. In Victoria, Playbox Theatre was supposed to pick up the slack, providing a greenhouse for the tender young shoots of new work; but Playbox's devastatingly poor audience figures reflect the failure of this policy. It is neither possible nor desirable to replace what was once the province of many alternative theatres with a single, corporatised entity: like all ecosystems, theatre needs diversity to survive. And it is a measure of theatre's ill-health that its diversity has been declining in both absolute and generic terms over the past two decades. Not only are fewer plays being produced, but fewer *kinds* of plays.

All the same, in the general atmosphere of gloom one shouldn't overlook the energies and vitalities that do exist. Out of the vacuum have sprung many small, independent companies which produce new plays, both Australian and international, with minimal or no funding. And one should not forget La Mama either, a unique treasure which actively supports the notion of an open and diverse theatre culture. Yet the fact remains that, however hard-working and imaginative they may be, these independent companies struggle with a paucity of resources that severely limits what they are able to achieve. The genius of Australian theatre has so often lain with 'poor theatre': great things have happened there. But as a default policy, it is no way to grow a vibrant and stimulating culture. There is a point where companies, simply, need money to make the art they should.

There's no getting away from the fact that part of the many-faceted crisis facing Australian theatre is the increasingly tight availability of funds, a complex issue in itself bedevilled by the whole problem of arts advocacy. Meyrick often refers to the 'theatre industry'; a common enough phrase, but a symptom of a deeper problem. As I said in an essay last year, picking up on Donald Horne's observations on the 'economisation' of the arts:

> I can remember when people started talking about the 'arts industry', back in the early '90s. I thought at the time it was a harbinger of doom. The argument used to lobby for arts funding was almost exclusively economic: the arts created employment, generated tourism, and so on. (There was, I think, a little discussion about social capital.) This focus seems to have

modelled almost all subsequent advocacy for the arts. And what we have created is a monster, to which all the arts must now pay tribute: the arts industry is here to stay, and arts companies are expected to function like other economic entities, and to justify their existences by making a profit for their 'stakeholders'...

Given its devastating impact, it is not surprising that the idea of the 'arts industry' has been attacked recently by several eminent Australians, including Donald Horne. Horne says the 'economisation of culture' is a fundamentalist creed. 'It's not supported by public stonings or beheadings but its effect can be pretty ruthless,' he said in a speech in 2002. 'It's the kind of language that turns our society into "the economy", our citizens into "the consumers" and our public funds into "taxpayers' money".' He described the phrase 'the arts industry' and the adoption by arts advocates of the vogue-ish terminology of the markets as a Trojan horse. 'How is it', he asks, 'that people concerned with speaking up for "the arts" and other cultural activities have been reduced to that kind of twaddle?'

Yes, we need another phrase. But that aside, Meyrick's main claim is that theatre practitioners need to overcome their distaste of the nationalistic connotations of the term 'Australian theatre', and to regain a concept of a 'whole' Australian theatre, a sense of common endeavour and generosity which admits difference (and history). Which raises two questions for me, neither of them rhetorical: when *was* this golden age, before we lost this sense of 'over-arching identity'? Might it not rather be an imaginary Eden that now must be, to mix my metaphors, forged fresh in the smithy of our souls? And, secondly, do we need the term 'Australian' at all, or could this sense of identity be found simply in the term 'theatre'? It sometimes seems to me that the term 'Australian' is so vexed that often the idea of 'theatre' gets elided altogether.

This is not to ignore, but rather to embrace, Meyrick's point about specific Australian traditions. To think of a common practice of theatre is to enfold these traditions into a wider and richer context which includes *all* theatre, in all times and all languages. Australian theatre is still overwhelmingly Anglophone, looking over its shoulder towards London and New York – even the name of this series, Platform Papers, is taken from a National Theatre initiative. And I would suggest that this linguistic parochialism is one of its problems, and one reason why such a narrow range of aesthetic is admitted into mainstream discussion.

With the Anglophone bias goes the traditional Anglo suspicion of 'intellectuals'. Meyrick digs up some classic artist-bashing, of the kind made familiar by such pundits as Andrew Bolt; but what is less easy to see and, I think, ultimately more damaging, is the anti-intellectualism within the art form itself. I remember speaking to a distinguished literary critic, then reviewing theatre, who told me airily that he never read new plays as they weren't 'literary', something that astonished me. What is sadder is that playwrights themselves, mistaking 'literary' for meaning 'prosaic' or 'untheatrical', often have a similar idea about their own work. At one stroke, this removes the art of writing plays from the entirety of experiment and argument that is imaginative and critical literature, and places it – where? In an isolated playpen with crayons and dolls?

A result of this is that much theatrical experiment in Australia has been confined to 'non-verbal drama' of various kinds, out of a feeling that 'verbal drama' is aesthetically limiting, and the writing of plays itself has desiccated into a hidebound naturalism. It is common to hear 'text-based theatre' spoken of in a dismissive way, as the conservative wing of theatrical artistry. This is inaccurate in terms of wider history, where writing has been the engine for most innovations in modern theatre, but here it has a certain self-fulfilling truth. And this raises a crucial issue, which is the lack of a critical discourse which can discuss aesthetic *qualities* in any useful manner. In the absence of this, no amount of structural institutional analysis – useful and necessary though it is – can make any sense. The mere presence of new Australian work is no guarantee of cultural health; it has to be Australian work that *matters*. But how one determines what makes it matter is another, and even thornier, question.

Trapped by the Past: Why our Theatre is Facing Paralysis, by Julian Meyrick. Platform Paper No. 3, January 2005, Currency House

Theatre Notes, February 10 2005

Subclass26A

The vexed question of politics and art is one of the fiercest debates of modern culture. Broadly the argument rages between two poles. In the blue corner (or the red, if one is American) are those who contend that art is above politics, an argument stemming from Matthew Arnold's imperial ideas about culture. In the opposing corner are the revolutionaries, who claim that art has a duty towards radical ideologies. Most artists, who are by nature sceptical of dogma of any kind, can be found slugging it out somewhere in the middle, arguing on the one hand that all art is inescapably political, and on the other that its highest duty is to its own imperatives.

It's wholly untrue to assert, as many conservative critics do, that art that engages with social and political critique compromises an essential artistic purity. Much of the significant art of the past three centuries – from Shelley's *The Masque of Anarchy* and Mozart's *The Marriage of Figaro* to the work of Brecht's Berliner Ensemble or Brazilian theatre activist Augusto Boal – has been in the tradition of political and social dissent. As well as, it must be confessed, much of the worst – we've seen agitprop, and we don't like it.

Art, after all, should do rather more than restate arguments that would be better expressed in a pamphlet. *Subclass26A*, a powerful group-devised movement piece at FortyFive Downstairs which addresses the question of Australia's brutal treatment of asylum seekers, demonstrates beautifully how this can be done.

I will describe the theatre in a moment. But first, some background, necessary because this piece employs a fragmentary text drawn in part from a variety of real sources: documents from the Department of Immigration, letters from asylum seekers, and primary research conducted by the artists themselves.

Our treatment of asylum seekers is one issue that starkly exposes the darker side of Australia's self-image as 'the lucky country'. We are the only nation in the world which compulsorily imprisons asylum seekers, a policy which calls up unsettling echoes of gulags and concentration camps. Tellingly, as Richard Ackland commented in 2003, the federal government's 'Pacific solution' demonstrated a baffling insensitivity to the grim connotations which still attend that word 'solution'.

As Malcolm Fraser and others have pointed out, our immigration policies are racist and inhumane. But those who protest the totalitarian aspects of these policies are attacked as 'bleeding heart liberals' with an 'agenda', their voices marginalised by a combination of misrepresentations or outright lies and populist xenophobia.

Asylum seekers are the only class of people who may be locked up indefinitely, beyond the redress of any court. They have fewer rights than convicted paedophiles or murderers, despite the fact that they have been charged with no crimes, and the even more appalling fact that many of them are children: between 1999 and 2003, 2,184 children had been held for varying lengths of time (averaging more than a year) in detention centres.

The suffering caused by the Howard government's policies has been widely documented and has attracted widespread international and local condemnation, including rebukes from all six of the human rights agencies of the UN. Even the horrors of the SIEV-X and the heart-rending personal testimonies of the children whose lives have been blighted by imprisonment have made no impact on the public apathy towards those the popular media dub, erroneously, 'illegal immigrants'. The sheerly brutal cynicism of our policies toward refugees and asylum seekers is an ongoing scandal of Australian society.

Bagryana Popov and her performers address these issues with intelligence and passion. They do not go down the now conventional road of 'documentary theatre': the added element of dance (three performers are dancers, three actors) gives the piece a stylised, alienating edge which, in a paradox peculiar to art, intensifies its emotional power.

While this group is deeply engaged with the issues, it is equally concerned to give these experiences the dignity of art. This work has the clarity of a high degree of moral and intellectual sophistication. The fragmentary text – a collage of individual experience spoken in English and Arabic, bureaucratic documents and dialogues – is poetically cadenced. Dramaturges Maryanne Lynch and Tom Wright create a simple narrative spine around three asylum seekers, telling a story of arrival, detention and Kafka-esque bureaucracy. Against the impersonal officialese of imprisonment, the human body speaks an anarchic tale of despair, love, anger and madness.

Popov's direction has an attentive eye to focus, creating eddies of movement and speech which rise chaotically and suddenly clear to brief vignettes, only to be caught up again in a flurry of movement. There is an emphasis on neurotic repetition, both the endless monotony of institutional life ('breakfast from 8.30 to 9am, lunch 12 to 12.30...') and the increasingly dissociated movements of mental illness. The emotional fluctuations are stringently orchestrated by Elissa Goodrich's spare, percussive score.

This approach permits a moral and political complexity often missing from theatre which has previously addressed these issues. Brutality is not confined to officials: the prisoners themselves are capable of cruelty. One of the striking elements of this piece is its focus on how such policies brutalise those who implement them as much as their targets. The despairing social worker unable to help increasingly desperate people, the guards who lose their capacity for empathy, are as trapped as the asylum seekers in a nightmare of systemic, soul-eroding sadism.

Anna Tregloan's stylishly minimalist design uses the white box space of FortyFive Downstairs to magnify the sense of human alienation, the notion that asylum seekers and refugees are infections which must be quarantined from the social body. The huge window which usually dominates the theatre is covered by a white wall into which is let a tiny, opaque window, which provides the only glimpse of freedom. The stage is divided by lighting and subtle design elements into rectangular areas through which the performers move uneasily, dark human figures in an antiseptic, inhuman universe. The audience is seated at the near end of the theatre, and the production takes full advantage of the stage's depth, creating a surprisingly rich texture of physical gesture and spatial image with a rigorously limited vocabulary.

A great deal of this production's success stems from its disciplined restraint, its refusal to press the standard emotive buttons and so diminish the complexities of the human issues it addresses. *Subclass26A* powerfully communicates not only the despair of detained asylum seekers, but the reasons for that despair; we can work out the injustice for ourselves. One of the performers, Iraqi actor Majid Shokor, is quoted in the program as saying: 'theatre is a place where justice and redemption can be found'. I don't believe that anyone involved in this production believes that this work will stop the mistreatment of those who only ask for our help; but the urgent desire to express the complexities of human experience, to redress the silencing of the powerless, is nevertheless a potent political act. An act of hope.

Theatre Notes February 17 2005

Out on a Limb

The entire emphasis of *Out on a Limb*, which took place over four evenings at La Mama Theatre, was on the process of expression. For Sarah Mainwaring, this has a special urgency. When she was six years old, she was involved in a major car accident that left her with serious brain damage. This was followed by more than a decade of rehabilitation. Her body remains damaged by the accident: her limbs will not immediately obey her, and tasks the able-bodied manage without thinking are challenges that require all her will and ingenuity. But, importantly, this is not a performance about conquering the limitations of the body, so much as about inhabiting and accepting it. Mainwaring's invitation to the audience to witness her struggle with her own body has an astonishing generosity and humility. That I might feel confronted by my own desire to watch such private struggles is, I think, my own business.

The performance takes place in an installation designed by Lloyd Jones and Mainwaring, which gives an impressionistic idea of the walls of a suburban house. There is a single, evocative sound, a constant harsh rustle, which I finally tracked to a plastic bag hung in front of a fan.

It begins with Mainwaring peering through a window. She asks in a kind of *sprechgesang*, half singing, half speaking: 'Who am I?' She then emerges, in a tight dress, shiny blazer and a startlingly red hat, and performs a series of tasks. The first is to pull out some wrapping paper from a basket, fold it, and tie it up with string. She makes about half a dozen little parcels, and the process takes a long time. When she has finished, the parcels are hung up on hooks on a trellis, to add to an evolving installation. She then plays with a drum, attempting to hit it and missing, puts it away, dances, poses herself in positions of entrapment and frustration.

All these simple actions take a long time, but induce a meditative patience which is intensely rewarding. Mainwaring's struggle to control her materials divests her – and therefore us – of any self-consciousness, and tying a knot in a piece of string, for example, becomes absolutely mesmerising. I found myself reflecting on all sorts of things: what it means to make something, what it means to watch an action, my relationship with my own body. Mainwaring's performance includes a sense of self-parody, and that it's possible to laugh without discomfort says a lot for her evolving intimacy with the audience, an intimacy which is reinforced by Lloyd Jones' gentle coaching from the seats.

Finally, Mainwaring strips to her underpants behind the back wall, visible through a doorway, which reinforces the unsettling ambiguity of voyeurism which circles around this show. An assistant helps to take off her clothes, puts goggles over her eyes and covers her in talcum powder. Then she moves to the front stage and throws blue paint over her body. The transformation is startling, from the grotesquely powdered, goggled body to a strange, beautifully marked marine creature that writhes on paint-slicked plastic with unabashed eroticism. She stands up, with assistance as the floor is treacherously slippery, wipes the paint from her eyes, and moves to a ladder, where she sings again: 'Who am I? What will I be? I hope it includes some really interesting sex.'

Writing the bare outline of what happened is manifestly inadequate to the experience of being there. *Out on a Limb* is performance art, coming out of the late twentieth century tradition in which artists have used their own bodies as art objects, framing ordinary human actions in ways which force us to see them anew; but it has its own particular challenge and abrasiveness. Perhaps I should employ some negative theology, and say what it was not. It was not 'politically correct'. It was not exploitative. It was not patronising. It was not artless.

'Yves Klein', said another audience member afterwards. And yes, indeed; *Out on a Limb* can't but echo Yves Klein's *The Monotone Symphony*, during which naked models daubed themselves with blue paint and, under the direction of the maestro, painted with their bodies. It also made me think of the album cover of Roxy Music's *Siren*, which featured Jerry Hall as an alien and beautiful mermaid. But unlike both of these things, which ward the erotic off into a distant objectivity, it put the audience in radical relationship to it, implicated in its intimacy.

Clearly it raises issues, about expectations of the body and sexuality, and about human expressiveness. And, with a peculiarly gentle insistence, it's liberating, both for the performer and those who witness her. 'The artist', says the program, 'is creating a form'. That is all this piece is 'about', and it is quite sufficient; such meanings as an audience might seek in that form are there for them to find, if they wish. For it is always possible to take nothing away. For me, *Out on a Limb* was a moving struggle towards freedom, a compelling expression of desire. Perhaps most signally, it had the unpornographic courage of artistic nakedness.

Theatre Notes, February 23 2005

The Yellow Wallpaper

As soon as Anita Hegh props herself primly on a wooden schoolroom chair and glances neurotically at her right hand, as if it were some wild animal that might escape any moment, you realise that you're in for a special performance. Nothing that follows disabuses this expectation. It's an enactment at the Store Room of a short story by the early feminist Charlotte Perkins Gilman, in which an unnamed woman who is being treated for a nervous condition is confined by her doctor husband in a room decorated with particularly ugly wallpaper. The story traces her mental breakdown through a series of snatched diary entries. *The Yellow Wallpaper* rivals Georg Buchner's story *Lenz* as a compelling depiction of the subjectivity of madness, notable for both its imaginative expressiveness and the almost clinical precision of its observations.

In a 1913 article, Gilman was very clear about why she wrote this semi-autobiographical work:

> For many years [she wrote] I suffered from a severe and continuous nervous breakdown... During about the third year of this trouble I went... to a noted specialist in nervous diseases, the best known in the country. This wise man put me to bed and applied the rest cure, to which a still-good physique responded so promptly that he concluded there was nothing much the matter with me, and sent me home with solemn advice to 'live as domestic a life as far as possible,' to 'have but two hours' intellectual life a day,' and 'never to touch pen, brush, or pencil again' as long as I lived. This was in 1887.
>
> I went home and obeyed those directions for some three months, and came so near the borderline of utter mental ruin that I could see over. Then, using the remnants of intelligence

that remained, and helped by a wise friend, I cast the noted specialist's advice to the winds and went to work again – work, the normal life of every human being; work, in which is joy and growth and service, without which one is a pauper and a parasite – ultimately recovering some measure of power.

Being naturally moved to rejoicing by this narrow escape, I wrote *The Yellow Wallpaper*, with its embellishments and additions, to carry out the ideal (I never had hallucinations or objections to my mural decorations) and sent a copy to the physician who so nearly drove me mad. He never acknowledged it... Many years later I was told that the great specialist had admitted to friends of his that he had altered his treatment of neurasthenia since reading *The Yellow Wallpaper*. It was not intended to drive people crazy, but to save people from being driven crazy, and it worked.

Gilman's passionate account here implies much of the history of female neurosis and its relationship to the medical profession; and more precisely, the difficulties faced by creative women in restrictive patriarchal societies that find such women to be, at best, oddities, and at worst, monstrous. In these contexts normal human desires, such as the wish for meaningful work or satisfying sex, are considered the province of men; when they appear in women, they are thought to be pathological or wicked.

The historical repression of intelligent and passionate women, from witch burnings to hysterectomies to institutionalisation, is not within my purview here; but it's a gruesome and sad and ongoing story. It is easy to say, in Melbourne in 2005, that those times are now long past; but the persistence of conditions like anorexia nervosa or the obsession with celebrity culture suggest that, even here, contemporary ideals of femininity might be little less imprisoning now than they were a century ago.

Hegh's performance is a compelling physicalisation of the fractures and deformations that the imposition of the 'feminine' can do to a woman's self. In the beginning, Hegh sits or stands in poses that are exaggeratedly prim, her neck and chin extended like a mannerist painting, and the strange calmness of her voice has an anxious, nail-biting edge. But there are more violent disturbances in this ladylike façade; her body does not appear to wholly belong to her. She jumps with sudden, neurotic intakes of breath; she strikes strange poses, grotesque parodies of the feminine grace of a ballerina; her eyes flicker, as if her face were a prison through which her soul fleetingly and pleadingly emerges, only to vanish into the repetitive tics of conventional womanhood.

Her right hand, her working hand, is a focus of anguish and desire. Forbidden by her husband to write, she makes her diary entries furtively, obsessively recording her observations of the 'optic horror' of the yellow wallpaper in the room where she is genteelly imprisoned as a kind of sick child. In keeping with her infantalisation, this room is a former nursery, and the windows are barred. Eventually she becomes convinced that the ghastly patterns conceal a creeping woman who is attempting to get out; but that woman, of course, is herself.

The wallpaper itself becomes a potent symbol of the inscrutable and devious social codes by which the woman is disempowered.

> On a pattern like this, by daylight, there is a lack of sequence, a defiance of law, that is a constant irritant to a normal mind. The color is hideous enough, and unreliable enough, and infuriating enough, but the pattern is torturing. You think you have mastered it, but just as you get well underway in following, it turns a back-somersault and there you are. It slaps you in the face, knocks you down, and tramples upon you...

The increasing sense of dislocation and imbalance is intensified by the cunning use of props and lighting; Hegh might put on a single high-heeled shoe, forcing her to limp, or don sunglasses that mask her face with a terrifying maenad-like anonymity. A wedding dress becomes at once the symbol of her imprisonment and the badge of her illness. When at last the woman breaks free into madness – the only freedom left open to her – Hegh growls the text through a microphone, declaiming like a rock star poet.

Peter Evans directs *The Yellow Wallpaper* with nuance and precision; it's inventively lit and the sound design, using music and pre-recorded text, is spare and effective. Without any fuss, the staging frames and focuses Hegh's performance admirably. On all levels, *The Yellow Wallpaper* is a very classy piece of work: riveting, disturbing and beautiful.

Theatre Notes, March 30 2005

The Ham Funeral / Journal of a Plague Year

As Michael Kantor's first presentation as Malthouse artistic director, this double bill is a provocative signal of intention. It offers an alternative means of imagining Australian theatre, outside the narrowly nationalistic or topical concerns which have dominated the Playbox aesthetic since the early 1990s. And although I don't feel it's an unqualified artistic success, I left feeling more hopeful about Melbourne theatre than I have for many years.

For a long time, mainstream plays in Melbourne have been presented under various aegises: as bearers of social issues, education, political commentary or, least offensively, as mere entertainment. As for theatre itself, it has sometimes seemed to be the Art That Dares Not Tell Its Name, a shameful embarrassment that has had to be decently cloaked in more palatable imperatives.

So it's a relief to be offered works that place themselves unapologetically in the culture and history of theatre itself. The paradoxical effect of this is to make theatre immediately less parochial in its concerns, to engage its tentacular ability to grasp social, literary and philosophical concerns and to thrust them onto the vulgar carnality of the stage. It's an aesthetic that is far from apolitical, but this is a politics which doesn't earnestly explore 'issues', in order to coax from them a masochistically satisfying (but temporary) inflammation of the liberal conscience. Rather, it's a politics which begins by attempting to address some of the complexities of existence.

These two productions, presented in repertory with an ensemble cast, look back to major movements in twentieth century theatre: the existential theatre of Beckett, the absurdism of Arrabal and Ionesco, the revolutionary theatre imagined by Artaud. It's a truism that Australian theatre has marginalised these influences in favour of naturalistic conventions, but it seems to me that the truth of that story is much more complex than a simplistic naturalistic/non-naturalistic division. Our theatre has also ignored naturalistic writers like Peter Kenna; and some of the significant playwrights of the '70s, Jack Hibberd and John Romeril, for example, were certainly influenced by White and his contemporaries.

I suspect that the work which has been most marginalised over the past few decades is any theatre which refuses easy sentiment and pierces, instead, to the marrow of complex emotion. Which is to say, a tragic theatre. There is something in the Australian psyche which flinches against such difficult surgeries, preferring instead the 'relaxed and comfortable' vision of life that was so attractively peddled by John Howard. All the same, I see a great and increasing hunger for this kind of work, as the world has darkened over the past few years. This cathartic emotional affect is also difficult to achieve. *The Ham Funeral* shows triumphantly how it can be done; the Artaudian *Journal of a Plague Year* how easily the grandiose gesture can flail and miss its mark.

The Ham Funeral was written in 1947 but was not produced until more than a decade later; astoundingly, this is its first professional production in Melbourne. It emerges from the formally adventurous theatre which grew out of European modernism, exemplified by playwrights like Arrabal, Beckett and Ionesco. Watching *The Ham Funeral*, it seems strange that it is not mentioned in the same breath as *Waiting for Godot* (which it predates by two years) or *Rhinoceros*. Part of the answer might be in its stubborn Australianness; from its poetic cadences to its irreverent eclecticism to its joyous vulgarity, it's a profoundly antipodean work. But in Australia, it was simply considered too odd, or too obscene. We do not have a good record with our best artists.

The Ham Funeral is a post-romantic work written by an artist deeply uncomfortable with his own romanticism. It's about a young poet (Dan Spielman), who lodges with Mr and Mrs Lusty (Ross Williams and Julie Forsyth) in a boarding house full of 'everlasting furniture'. Mr Lusty suddenly drops dead, and Mrs Lusty takes the opportunity to give a lavish feast, 'an 'am funeral', in his honour. Mrs Lusty, a woman driven by incontinent appetites, attempts to seduce the young poet, with comically tragic consequences. There's a fair bit of Jungian symbolism – the house as the self, the anima behind the door, the carnal desires in the basement – but this is merely a single strand in a play which works on a multiplicity of levels. One of its major obsessions is the insufficiencies of words in the face of life, the question of how language might escape its own imprisonments.

White's theatrical language is superbly dynamic, and imbued with a fearless vitality. It's resonant with allusion, prefiguring not only the slapstick of Beckett and the absurdist freedoms of Ionesco or Arrabal, but also echoing poets as bizarrely diverse as Arthur Rimbaud and

Walter de la Mare. Ultimately, the sophistication of White's linguistic skills works to evoke feeling at its most subterranean and mysterious. For all its vulgar comedy – among many other delights, it features a terrific fart joke – this is a play which reveals above all the anguish of consciousness, the pain and release which underlies any honest moment of self-recognition, and the price of risking the barren self to engage with the beauty and violence of the world. It's the kind of work which moves you to tears, without being quite sure why.

Michael Kantor's production is a beautiful realisation of the play. It's notable for its clarity: in one sense, Kantor has merely presented the text as simply and elegantly as possible. But this is a deceptive simplicity, gained through some thoughtful problem solving. Anna Tregloan has designed a flexible but evocative playing space: the boarding house is represented by a stage with a row of curtained windows backstage which can be lit or concealed, and fronted by the bare floor. The stairs – the liminal place between rooms where various characters pause to utter their uncertain thoughts – are indicated by bars of light. A red curtain drawn back by the Young Man foregrounds the artifice of the play, just as the text does. There are moments of memorable visual richness: a lyrical glimpse of Dan Spielman and Robert Menzies in overcoats, running through the rain with their umbrellas; the landlord's relatives, boxed behind windows, grotesquely attired in pyjamas like characters out of *Endgame*.

But ultimately the success of the production stands or falls on the performances; in particular, on the roles of the Young Man and Mrs Lusty, since this play is almost a two-hander with some extra characters. Dan Spielman and Julie Forsyth are up to the task. Spielman, always a performer notable for his emotional fearlessness, portrays the solipsistic romanticism of the Young Man and its violent fracture with scarcely a missed beat. If sometimes he subtly falls into what look like actorly habits, we can forgive him for his unfudged clarity of feeling and intelligent irony.

Julie Forsyth is a comic delight, always just this side of grotesque caricature: on the one hand in incandescent rebellion against the bleakness of her life, and on the other imbued with a touchingly innocent longing. The violent climax of the play, an extraordinary scene of miserable sexual violence between Mrs Lusty and the Young Man, is played by both of them with a raw passion that makes it devastatingly tragic. They are well supported: in particular, Ross Williams, one of the most underestimated actors in Melbourne, portrays the silent landlord with a deft tragicomic touch, and Robert Menzies has some gloriously black comic moments. Max Lyandvert's sound, a mixture of pre-recorded soundscapes and live piano music, also deserves mention.

The same cast also plays Tom Wright's *Journal of a Plague Year*. For this production, Kantor capitalises on the cavernous spaces of the Merlyn Theatre to create a huge black canvas on which he projects a series of tableaux. The cast creates a series of dramatic or grotesque images, some of which are strikingly memorable: the black-cloaked narrator (Robert Menzies) emerging from darkness, illuminated only by the lamp he is carrying; a plague victim (Matthew Whittet) crucified on a moveable panel, tormented by disembodied hands; Nell Gwynne (Lucy Taylor) in busty Restoration garb, singing '70s pop songs.

The major problem with this work is that these images, however striking, never amount to anything substantial; they are grotesquerie without emotional force, and so can never approach actual horror or tragedy. The problem begins with Tom Wright's script, which merits some discussion.

The pretext for this work is supposedly Daniel Defoe's 1722 novel *A Journal of the Plague Year*, an account of the plague that struck London in 1665. Defoe's novel is an early example of fictional journalism; it purports to be the memoirs of a pious Protestant merchant, H.F. It's a somewhat disorderly narrative, but all the same told with a meticulous attention to detail – Defoe researched the public records, and items like the death figures or public health measures are set down with an almost bureaucratic zeal. For all his piety, H.F.'s manner is free of pompous moralising or overblown religiosity: he is a practical and materialistic man, recording a tragic human phenomenon with an insatiable and sceptical curiosity.

Aside from its seventeenth century setting, its quotes from Defoe and the theme of the plague, Tom Wright's version has in fact very little to do with the original. *A Journal of the Plague Year* is essentially about survival; Defoe is fascinated by the endless ingenuity of human resistances against both the plague and its catastrophic economic effects. The novel ends with a rhyme about the plague which 'swept an hundred thousand souls / Away; yet I alive!' Wright's *Journal*, on the other hand, is about apocalyptic extremity and exploits a religious fervour that Defoe's text pragmatically eschews. Its actual genesis is the avatar of the Theatre of Cruelty, Antonin Artaud.

Some artists are perilous influences; they tend to be innovative geniuses whose work is so idiosyncratic that imitators without equal abilities can only seem mannered. I'm thinking of writers like Dylan Thomas or Gerard Manley Hopkins; among theatre artists, Artaud is probably the most dangerous. Howard Barker's Theatre of Catastrophe or the plays of Sarah Kane are successful examples of the contemporary application of some of Artaud's ideas; both are fiercely moral writers who launch full-frontal attacks on the humanistic tradition of reason.

One problem with Artaud is that *he means it*, and any artist who decides to pick up on his ideas had better mean it, too. Another problem is that the logical end of Artaud's idea of 'absolute revolt' is Pol Pot and Year Zero (Pol Pot was, it must be remembered, educated in Paris). Like Rimbaud, Artaud insisted on the collapse of any boundary between art and life: thought and act were to be completely identified. He despised empty formalism. 'If there is one hellish, truly accursed thing in our time', he wrote in *The Theatre and the Plague*, 'it is our artistic dallying with forms, instead of being like victims burnt at the stake, signalling through the flames.' He insisted on a carnal theatre, a theatre that reinstated the poetry that had been corrupted by modernity and reason, a theatre that 'recovers the notion of symbols and archetypes which act like silent blows, rests, leaps of the heart, summons of the lymph, inflammatory images thrust into our abruptly wakened heads'.

Wright, unlike Kane or Barker, is altogether too cerebral to answer this kind of visceral demand. The contrast with Patrick White's theatrical language is stark; where White is dynamic, tactile and supple, Wright is static and abstract. But the work suffers also in comparison to writers who shape the banalities of language, playwrights like Michel Vinaver or Thomas Bernhard: neither of them speak in generalities, where Wright seldom escapes them.

Oddly, for all its gestures towards unreason, Wright's text seems tame; it is much more orderly than Defoe, who is quite happy for most of his book to ignore the demands of chronology or even literary logic. The details of urban life that swarm in Defoe's text are filleted out in favour of apocalyptic religiosity, and events taken from the novel are simplified and exaggerated into Grand Guignol melodrama. One example is the scene about plague victims being nailed into their houses;

the actuality, as reported by Defoe, was both more complicated and less absolute. The victims in fact had their keys taken and a watchman set outside their door, and they often tricked the watchmen and escaped out the back. I personally find myself more attracted by the subversion of the original tale. And the constant equation of women with infection and sexual delirium has more than a whiff of misogyny. I think what bothers me most is that Wright has what poets call a 'cloth ear'; a problem closely aligned to the lack of tactility or carnality in his language. He might get away with a lot more if he had more intuitive sensitivity to the cadences of a line.

The text is organised in a kind of modular prison, with Brechtian signs traversing the stage signalling each month (it's only a matter of time before you start calculating that there are five months until December). Each month ushers in a different theme – contagion's genesis, evil visions, interpretation of dreams, the pit of death – which the actors duly illustrate. But perhaps where Wright most inverts his apparently anarchic intentions is at the end, when he encloses the narrative with a moral homily about the essential bestiality of human nature. This is, despite its crazed dress, humanistic theatre after all.

I can't say I was bored, even if sometimes I was impatient. There was enough visual interest and flashes of wit to keep me from wanting to lay violent hands on myself. I particularly liked the philosopher's chat show, where Hobbes, Artaud and others seated at microphones dispute the nature of reality. Robert Menzies as the narrator generates enough energy to keep it together, despite what sounds like an almost unperformable text, and the rest of the cast does its best, which is in moments more than enough. It's a shame that all this effort amounts to little more than a procession of images.

Despite my reservations, it is a breath of fresh air to see mainstream theatre with ambition and intellectual clout, and that takes itself seriously as an art. I have no doubt this shift in artistic direction will generate a lot of controversy; Helen Thomson's bitterly hostile reviews in *The Age* this week are probably symptomatic. I also have no doubt that this new phase at Malthouse is the best thing that's happened there in the past decade; and as a theatre goer, I am hoping that this is only the beginning of a more generous imagining of the Australian stage.

Theatre Notes, April 19 2005

Black Medea

A while back, around Nietzsche, the gods deserted classical tragedy. They were scaled back to psychological symbols: the Furies became externalisations of Orestes' guilt, and Oedipus' fate – to kill his father and marry his mother – became an expression of subconscious desires.

These interpretations are a reasonable response by post-Enlightenment culture to the questions posed by these capricious arbiters of human fate. To the rationalist West, pagan gods could seem perilously silly. But it can be argued that tragedy lost as much as it gained by the psychological domestication of the gods: the sacred and the divine are as much part of the tragic experience as catastrophe.

One of the fascinating aspects of Wesley Enoch's adaptation of *Medea* at Malthouse Theatre is that the gods are back, as potent, implacable and bloody as ever. Enoch has freely transposed the legend of Medea to Indigenous themes, and his muscularly poetic text excavates an often obscured aspect of its chthonic energy. Here Cypris (Aphrodite), the main mover of events in Euripides' play, is replaced by the vengeful ancestral spirits of Central Australia. Since the ancestral spirits are also the land, they have a literal potency that can resonate with even the most secular white.

Like the original, Enoch's Medea (Margaret Harvey) is a wise woman, a witch privy to the magical traditions of her people who betrays her heritage for the love of Jason (Aaron Pedersen). She leaves her desert home to marry a handsome, ambitious Aboriginal from the city, her 'ticket out'. By marrying the stranger she violates the complex kinship codes of her people, and she compounds her crime by selling her knowledge of the land to mining companies, leading them to the sacred places where she knows they will find ore.

Jason is, however, as much an exile as Medea. What destroys their relationship – as much businesslike pact as passionate sexual love – is the desert wind brought into his house, unwittingly, by Medea herself; a fate that howls through the front door and which speaks to him, through Medea's ancestral spirits, as his madness. His faithlessness is in some ways more profound than the original Jason's; he doesn't marry another, but instead completely loses touch with himself. He can't keep a job or support his family, and descends into a cycle of alcoholism and violence; a fate, it becomes clear, also suffered by his father.

Finally, despite Jason's deep emotional dependence on Medea, he obeys the promptings of the elder spirit (Justine Saunders) and throws Medea out of the marital home. Medea, who no longer has a home to return to, and who can see for her son only the same future as his father, murders her own child in revenge and despair, savagely ending the paternal cycle of violence.

Medea's act seems, interestingly, also a revenge on those spirits that drive her husband mad and demand that she bring her son home to the desert: she will hand her son over neither to his father nor to her own people, where he will suffer only another kind of dispossession. It's a startlingly bleak expression of the conflict between traditional and urban Indigenous cultures, offering no chink of hope. Perhaps what makes this story genuinely a tragedy is that there is no hint of moral judgement: Medea and Jason are trapped in the tension between conflicting imperatives which are both, on their own terms, in the right. The spiral towards catastrophe unravels from the wider injustice of their situation.

Enoch's production is unapologetically theatrical. As Medea, Margaret Harvey is skin-tighteningly compelling; the force of her curse literally gave me goosebumps. Harvey's full-blooded cry 'I am Medea!' stands with 'I am the Duchess of Malfi still!' as a great theatrical moment of defiance against fate. Aaron Pedersen's performance matches Harvey's, switching between terrifying violence and snivelling weakness. Justine Saunders plays a double role, as Old Medea narrating the story and the tribal spirit manipulating Medea and Jason, and her performance shifts from benign comedy to implacability.

Christina Smith's claustrophobic corrugated iron set, spectacularly lit by Rachel Burke, frames the story in brooding darkness. Among the most potent scenes are a number of swift, wordless vignettes, flashing out of the dark to a driving score, that give poignant glimpses of a disintegrating family. For all its classical provenance, *Black Medea* is powerfully contemporary. Enoch seamlessly weaves together with naturalism the hieratic, ritualised action of classical tragedy, giving the play both the intimacy of a domestic drama and the grand, extreme gestures of tragedy. It makes thrilling theatre.

Theatre Notes, May 18 2005

Phobia

> *wit 1 (wɪt)*
>
> *n. 1. The natural ability to perceive and understand; intelligence.*
>
> *2. a. Keenness and quickness of perception or discernment; ingenuity. Often used in the plural: living by one's wits. b. wits Sound mental faculties; sanity: scared out of my wits.*
>
> *3. a. The ability to perceive and express in an ingeniously humorous manner the relationship between seemingly incongruous or disparate things. b. One noted for this ability, especially one skilled in repartee. c. A person of exceptional intelligence.*

Perhaps the chief pleasure of *Phobia* is its wit. In all senses of the word.

It's a fond and deft tribute to the genre of *film noir*: the black and white world of hard-boiled detectives, blonde dames, mysterious violent deaths and high heels clicking down shadowy alleys: a Hitchcockian universe in which the key to a mystery, instead of comfortably knitting up the world like Miss Marple, opens up to existential blankness. But here the medium really is the message.

Described as 'the sound track to an imagined film', *Phobia* is set in a chaotic sound studio, in which each of the performers sits behind desks littered with various objects chosen, as becomes clear, for their sonic qualities. The narrative follows the employment of a detective by a man concerned by the erratic behaviour of his wife, whom he fears is having a breakdown. There follows a story of love, suicide, surveillance and mistaken identity, where of course the dame, under various identities, gets it (three times).

The narrative really exists to create a pallet of colours and moods, an occasion for the sound world shaped by Gerard Brophy and given life by the performers. The subcutaneous narrative, the detective story, the post-mortem dissection of film and the dissolution of identity are all familiar staples of post-modernity, but here they are given a fresh twist.

The focus of this opera is on the performances, which bring multi-tasking to a new level: the cast plays a multiplicity of instruments and performative roles with a tightly disciplined precision which gives the impression that they're all interdependent parts of a single organism. Part of the reason for this must be the intensely collaborative nature of its creation. Composer Gerard Brophy worked closely with the performers and the director Douglas Horton in creating scored elements and improvisatory frameworks.

As the credits make clear, the conventional roles of composer, director, performer and so on have been blurred, as have the distinctions between music and noise/sound (although some might argue that much twentieth century music has done this). And there's a fair bit of play with gender and identity as well, as none of the dramatic roles is assigned to any particular performer, and an individual role might switch from one cast member to several others in the space of a few seconds.

A fascinating miscellany of objects – black telephones, crumpled paper, celery, egg beaters, books – are transformed into instruments. There's something of the obsessed geek in this relentless tapping of the secret sound-life of found objects, and even a touch of the *Goon Show*. This intricate soundscape segues into lush and seedy jazz numbers or other fragments drawing on a wide range of musical influences.

Horton's direction makes *Phobia* – surprisingly perhaps, since it also seems strongly ascetic – visually lush. The lighting plays on the cavernous spaces of the North Melbourne Town Hall, creating soft, lamplit oases in a world where it always seems to be night-time. In the darkness behind the playing space, performers act out film tropes – for example, the looped image of a woman running upstairs and casting herself into darkness, or a man in a suit lighting a cigarette. This sense of chiaroscuro and distorted perspective reinforces a pervading nostalgia that is underwritten by menace.

With its sly cultural referencing and absurd gender-bending, *Phobia* has many comic moments, but often what makes you laugh is delight at its sheer ingenuity. Like that hardy production *Recital*, about to be revived again at the Malthouse Theatre, it's high camp refined through a rigorously disciplined aesthetic, a mode which best illuminates Horton's considerable talents.

Theatre Notes, May 28 2005

Songs of Exile

There's no question that Diamanda Galás is demanding. She demands your attention from the moment she walks on to the stage and paces, without pause or preamble, towards the piano. She demands that you listen and that you think. Most of all, she demands that you feel.

But the feeling she summons is no gentle waft on the airs of sentiment. For Galás, feeling is passion: the passion of unconsoled grief and longing; the passion for a precise and ethical beauty in the face of the unhealable divisions which scar human existence.

And she earns the attention she asks for. The aggression with which Galás performs contains the arrogance of a vast generosity. Galás will give us her all: and she expects no less from her audience. For those who expect or desire a lower-octane experience of art, something like what Barry Humphries calls a 'nice night's entertainment', this demand is more than confronting. It is felt as an assault, and expresses itself in tedium. But for those prepared to take up her gift, the experience is exhilarating.

Galás' voice, which can range from a deep growl to pure, enchanting melody to unrestrained ululation in the space of a few seconds, is an extraordinary instrument. She uses it to its fullest extent, ripping up the octaves like a wild animal. And there is indeed something absolutely predatory in this performance: how Galás crouches over the piano like a panther, the flexing sinews visible in her bare shoulders as she attacks the keyboard, her mouth almost swallowing the microphone. At one point she even slams the piano with her hands.

Songs of Exile, at Hamer Hall for MIAF, is a concert performance of an eclectic mixture of songs, from Johnny Cash's '25 minutes to go' to musical adaptations of poems by Henri Michaux, Paul Celan and César Vallejo. The poems are set by Galás herself, and in her settings she displays an intuitive understanding of the carnal nature of poetry, how poems foreground the material nature of language. The poems remain in their original language, as the poets wrote them (if not as they heard them). There is nothing cerebral in these musical settings, even if they show a great deal of intelligence – in how, for example, Galás echoes the Indigenous folk rhythms Vallejo exploits in his poetry in the fracturing melodies of her accompaniment. She reminds us, magnificently, that poetry is crucially an oral art.

In her book *Eros the Bittersweet*, the poet Anne Carson says that the acquiring of written language is inevitably a process of alienation. 'A written text', she writes, 'separates words from one another, separates words from the environment, separates words from the reader (or writer) and separates the reader (or writer) from the environment... As separable, controllable units of meaning... written words project their user into isolation.'

Poetry is an art form that seeks to unite the irreparably divided, to bring language back into direct relationship with experience, to overcome, impossibly, this primal isolation. Galás' performance takes this one step further, vocalising words back into raw physical reality. But of course this sense of regained unity cannot erase its original fracture and remain true to itself: hence the refusal, everywhere in this performance, of ease. The truth can only ever be an exposure of woundedness.

A real highlight for me was her performance of Paul Celan's poem 'Todesfuge ('Death Fugue')', about the Nazi death camps in which his parents perished:

> Black milk of daybreak we drink it at sundown
> we drink it at noon in the morning we drink it at night
> we drink it and drink it...

Galás' interpretation is nightmarish, a black parody of the mechanised rhythms of Nazi marches, or a broken and murderous nursery rhyme. Like the poem itself, the music shifts in an instant from one register to another, finishing on the lament: 'Your golden hair Margarete/ Your ashen hair Shulamith'.

She sings several gospel and blues songs. What is amazing about these versions is how, despite her radical treatment, she plugs right into the anguished truth of the music. As the title of the concert suggests, the theme of the evening is exile: exile from a homeland, exile from whatever one loves, exile from oneself. The divisions that mark existence are opened rawly, without apology and without consolation. Galás' piercingly gorgeous voice is the finely tuned instrument of lamentation and of pain.

The miraculous effect is joy: a reconnection with the vital currents of living. The twin of the god Thanatos, who haunts this performance, is of course Eros: Galás' aggression is a pure expression of desire. I know that I went to bed very late that night: Galás' wild voice still echoed through my being, forbidding the anaesthetisation of sleep.

Theatre Notes, October 12 2005

Lally Katz and the Terrible Mysteries of the Volcano

Lally Katz's universe points me irresistibly to Wittgenstein's remark in *Tractatus*: 'What the solipsist means is quite correct; only it cannot be said, but makes itself manifest. The world is my world: this is manifest in the fact that the limits of language… mean the limits of my world… I am my world.'

Lally Katz and the Terrible Mysteries of the Volcano, now playing at Theatre Works, might have been written to illustrate this statement. The most ambitious of her collaborations with Chris Kohn and Stuck Pigs Squealing, it generates a theatre of potent beauty, shot with the sinister clarity of nightmare.

The play makes the idiolect of an individual mind theatrically manifest in a way that I can only compare (hoping not to be misleading) with Sarah Kane. The theatrical poetics of Kane begin from literalising on stage the metaphoric workings of the psyche: as she says in *4:48 Psychosis*, 'the defining quality of metaphor is that it is real'.

In the work of both these playwrights, this process unearths terror, despair, myriad cruelties and strange beauties, unanswerable longings and, ultimately, a sense of astringent, even desolate, liberation. Like Kane, Katz is haunted by the possibility of death, and questions what meaning life can hold if it can be reasonlessly snuffed out at any moment. And also like Kane, she is deeply concerned with, and perplexed by, the question of love.

There the resemblances end. Lally Katz is not quite like any playwright I know of. Her work emerges from a theatrical universe that includes artists like Arrabal, Ionesco, Cocteau and Jodorowsky, but unlike these artists her world situates itself squarely in middle-class suburbia.

I'm beginning to wonder if this avant-garde theatre of suburbia is a uniquely local phenomenon. *Sweet Staccato Rising*, *A View of Concrete*,

Headlock, Lally Katz's *Eisteddfod* and even *The Black Swan of Trespass* all have this suburban consciousness in common, perhaps in the same way that street art – one of Melbourne's hidden or, at least, seldom acknowledged treasures – surges as a vital, anarchic energy from the 'relaxed and comfortable' order of suburban sprawl.

Lally Katz and the Terrible Mysteries of the Volcano is a concatenation of oneiric realities that, like *Eisteddfod*, circles obsessively around the terrors and desires of childhood. Again the author, as unstable an invention as any of the characters in the play, intrudes into her invention: as Mr Lally Katz, world-famous detective (Luke Mullins), or as Miss Lally Katz, child of an oppressively loving family (Luke Mullins), and even as her alter ego, Wendy (Margaret Cameron), who surely bears some familial relationship to the Wendy of Peter Pan or even, perhaps, Peter Pan himself. (To make it more confusing, playwright Lally Katz (Lally Katz) is taking the tickets at the door.)

The plot, if it can be called that, concerns Mr Lally Katz's commission, with his sidekick Lion (Brian Lipson), to investigate the mystery of a volcano that is on the verge of eruption and thus to save an alternative-universe Canberra, now a tropical island, from its destruction. Mr Katz has made, in a murderously childish game of hide and seek, a 'deal' with Wendy: he will save himself from the panther that wishes to eat him by sacrificing her. Wendy then disappears...

In another, later, time, Greg (Christopher Brown) is abject with priapic lust for Wendy: no matter what he tries to fuck – and he tries to fuck everything in sight, including theatre lights, poles, a dinosaur, a kangaroo, a sex worker 'with burned out eyes' and a doll – he cannot orgasm. He has to find Wendy, and he and Lion, who hopes to save Detective Lally Katz from a terrible mistake he made earlier, head off on a gruelling trek to the volcano. Greg's orgasm, it seems, will 'open the universe' and cause the volcano to erupt.

Meanwhile, the urbane detective and Lion catch the boat to Canberra, where they are initiated into a sinister Wendy fan club run by a mysterious South American, Sanchez (Christopher Brown). They are helped in their investigations by Miss Marple (Tony Johnson), who has her own obsession with quilts and manchester, and meet her crooning fiance (Gavan O'Leary) and Lally Katz falls shatteringly in love with Sanchez' sister (Jenny Priest)...

There are many more loops and whorls in this far from linear script, but that's probably enough of cack-handedly attempting to explain a narrative which moves by a system of metaphorical association and transformation, building up its own idiosyncratic theatrical language as the show progresses. But it gives some idea of the surrealist complexity of the world created here, and also hints at the sexual trauma that lies at the core of its dissociations and fractures.

Staging a text that constantly threatens to disintegrate under its own impulses presents challenges which ought to be self-evident. That Chris Kohn realises it with such sureness is a tribute to the intelligence of his direction as much as the imagination of his design crew and the commitment of his first-class cast.

Like Katz's text, Adam Gardnir's design both exploits and destroys the illusions of theatricality. At the beginning of the show, the audience waits before a huge red curtain that stretches the entire width of the theatre. The curtains pull back to reveal a stage space defined by floor-to-ceiling lengths of fabric, broken diagonally by white goalposts.

With the help of mini-sets unobtrusively swept on and off the stage and Richard Vabre's inventive lighting design, Kohn exploits seemingly every possibility of the space. There are constant shifts of perspective and focus, from intimate scenes surrounded by threatening darknesses to bleak, impossible distances, and text or graphics projected onto the back of the stage provide further dislocations. The effect is disconcertingly like being inside someone else's dream. The emotional intensities are heightened by Jethro Woodward's brooding soundscape, and by selectively miking the actor's voices.

A production as multilayered as this requires performers with a sure sense of theatricality, capable of creating extreme emotional realities without the safety harnesses of 'character' or sequential narrative. Kohn has a remarkable cast which includes some of the most distinguished artists in the business, and there's no point where you don't believe them. No-one is less than excellent, but the performances of Luke Mullins, Brian Lipson and Margaret Cameron stand out for their authoritative playfulness, their ability to generate naked feeling from even the most absurd of theatrical masks.

Something slumps in about the third quarter: it is as if the metaphorical underpinnings of the production, which up to then I hadn't questioned, loosen their moorings. I can't identify why; it might be only an effect of the performance I saw, though I suspect at that point the writing flies just a little too wide of itself; it is perceptible when the energy comes back. Theatre like this walks a perilously thin line: working with such displaced realities, it has to be utterly focused in every moment.

However, this by no means reduces the achievement of the show. *Lally Katz and the Terrible Mysteries of the Volcano* is remarkably accomplished theatre that plucks chords deep in the subconscious. It's a hauntingly sad, mysterious work, braced by the vulgarity that marks truly original theatre. In pushing their aesthetic to this pitch without losing their nerve, Stuck Pigs Squealing has truly come of age. It will be fascinating to see where they go next.

Theatre Notes, June 12 2006

Eldorado

When you enter the Malthouse's Merlyn Theatre under the dim house lights, you see before you a huge window built into a black wall that stretches the width and height of the stage. It's disorientating: with no lights behind, it acts as a mirror in which you see yourself and everyone else darkly reflected.

A black mirror is a fit metaphor with which to begin this riveting play, a parable about human self-destruction. Marius von Mayenburg presents a vision of humanity as desolate as that of WG Sebald in his novel *Vertigo*, when he speaks of the slow, inevitable conflagration of the earth: we consume all life on our planet with the creeping flame of desertification or the swift fire of war, leaving behind us a wasteland of ash.

Eldorado begins with a monologue murmured by the property speculator Aschenbrenner (Robert Menzies), who leans half-lit against the window, his voice artificially miked so we hear every inflection of his speech. He reports, seductively, tenderly, on the progress of an urban war. It is unsettlingly familiar: the language could be taken from any contemporary news report on the invasion of Baghdad or the destruction of Fallujah. Only, it seems, this war is occurring in the same unnamed Western city in which our suave businessman is living, not in some distant theatre of conflict in the Middle East or the Third World; this is a play which collapses perspectives of distance and time. It finishes with Aschenbrenner again, but this time he speaks as one of the dead: and now he tells us of a new life on Mars, of atmospheres artificially created by water, where humanity can find a new home. Like Aschenbrenner (whose very name conjures flame and ash), planet Earth is dead.

Bracketed between these two monologues is an epic family drama of the kind that Stephen Sewell attempted in *Hate*. But von Mayenburg, one of the new lights of contemporary German theatre, brings to this 2004 critique of post-industrial corporatism an emotional complexity and moral ambiguity that recalls the Brecht who wrote *Baal*. His spare, almost clinical poetic intensity traces a lineage from Georg Büchner to Brecht, through Caryl Churchill to Sarah Kane, who is his contemporary and whom he has translated.

Anton (Greg Stone) is a real estate agent employed by Aschenbrenner, who in the opening scenes is sacked for fraud. When his wife Thekla tells him she is pregnant, he is unable to confess that he has lost his job, and instead rips off his wealthy mother-in-law Greta (Gillian Jones) by selling her expensive speculative apartments in the 'government sector' that is currently under attack by insurgents, using the money to finance his household.

Greta is a woman who has no pity for anyone, least of all herself. She has a young lover, Oskar (Hamish Michael), whom she treats with contempt, and who openly admits that he is with her because of her wealth, and she lacerates her daughter when Thekla despairingly gives up her dream (clearly her mother's dream) of being a concert pianist. She is played with a sick relish by Jones, who invests her with a compellingly predatory sexuality that suggests that Oskar's attraction towards her is more complex than mere greed.

Meanwhile Anton is living the life of a vagrant to keep up the appearance that he is still working, hiding out in hotels or in the country so he won't be seen. Every time he attempts to tell his wife the truth, it becomes at once farcical and tragic: it's the one time she doesn't believe him. Thekla herself is dealing with a neurotic music student, Manuela (Bojana Novakovic), who at first rejects her as a teacher and then demands to return.

Then disaster strikes: the insurgents take over the 'government sector'. Aschenbrenner is ruined, and resolves the situation 'honourably': he hangs himself. Anton has a breakdown, crouching half-naked on top of a wardrobe in a nightmarish scene in which Greta and Oskar pound on the front door demanding their money, and the ghost of Aschenbrenner, locked in the wardrobe, beckons Anton towards his own 'honourable' solution.

The moral culpability of each character is exposed early on, and yet none of them is without innocence. Even Aschenbrenner, the very model of a ruthless businessman, considers himself an honourable man and values integrity, as is evident in the sadistic contempt with which he fires Anton. Secretly aware of their complicity with their own abnegation, each character is riven by self-contempt and loathing. They are all monstrous and yet, strangely, illuminated darkly by a desire to love: but it is as if this love is stillborn, a possibility that dies in the air even as it is spoken, leaving only the cinders of language, a vocabulary of cruelty and unexpressed pain.

This poignancy is most evident in the young couple, who are given particularly strong performances in a production notable for its acting. Alison Whyte is an intriguing blend of brittleness and misplaced strength as Thekla, and Greg Stone is as desolatingly good as I've seen him as Anton, a man inhabiting the hollow shell of himself. The only thing alive in him is his love for his wife and unborn child; yet it is this love which forces him to keep up the lie about his job, and the lie finally destroys his life. And yet, as Thekla despairingly recognises, he has in fact betrayed and abandoned her: if not sexually, as she imagines, then through his retreat into madness and suicide.

These behaviours are directly recognisable: von Mayenburg might be showing us the extremities of bourgeois banality, but they are not exaggerations. Greta's ruthless greed will be familiar to anyone who has watched *The Apprentice*; Thekla's paranoid jealousy and self-obsession are the grist of Dear Dorothy columns everywhere. And anyone who has seen mental illness close up will know that the madness presented here is almost clinically accurate. Part of von Mayenburg's boldness is in being quite literal about the phenomena he is reporting: he creates, as Marianne Moore has it, 'imaginary gardens with real toads in them'. The links between interior wasteland and exterior desolation are metaphorically very clear: these people consume everything, beginning with their own hearts.

Benedict Andrews, who also directs in Berlin at the Schaubühne am Lehniner Platz theatre where von Mayenburg is dramaturg, directs *Eldorado* with a brilliant austerity. The idea that human beings are fish in an aquarium, a recurring motif in the text, is literalised in both the performances and in Anna Tregloan's design. We witness the play through the massive window as if it were a giant peepshow, which gives the experience a peculiar intimacy spiced with the discomfort of voyeurism.

For all its moments of breathtaking visual flair, the production is inflected with an admirable subtlety and focuses attention wholly on the text and performances. I was chiefly impressed by Andrews' orchestration, which creates such various rhythms out of von Mayenburg's poetic text that two and a half hours seems like less than half the time. He discovers a surprising richness in the simple convention of the window: with the help of lighting and a lot of apocalyptic smoke he creates claustrophobic domestic spaces, into which we peer, or we find ourselves looking out onto imaginary streets. The actors delineate nightmarish spaces of psychic and physical desolation in which the only fixed perspective is the unremitting horizon of the window.

Most of the action occurs jammed up against the glass, although gradually unsettling depths open behind the playing space. As the play progresses the window's initially pristine surface is smeared with human fluids – sweat, saliva – literal traces of the physicality of the actors; just as when an actor eats a lobster, the amplified sounds of its flesh being sucked out of the shell is a repugnant reminder of our carnivorous natures.

Perhaps the most beautiful trick is when, around twenty minutes from the end, gold foil leaves begin to fall onto the stage, glittering in the theatre lights and making a brittle rustling sound. This continues for longer than seems bearable, graduating into a soft, insistent torture. (And here I also ought to mention Max Lyandvert's beautifully textured and atmospheric sound score, which is at once unobtrusive and evocative.)

The production doesn't escape the 'Porsche effect'. Such class throws into relief any moments that don't match its own high standards: a gesture that is a little too stagily self-conscious, for example, or a theatrical illusion (Robert Menzies, say, unhooking himself from a suspension harness) that is neither achieved nor usefully exposed. But these are just quibbles. This is a beautiful realisation of a significant play, and shows that the Malthouse is by no means resting on its laurels. Its ambitious programming is about placing this company in the front-line of international contemporary theatre, and a production like this demonstrates that it belongs there.

Theatre Notes, June 18 2006

Construction of the Human Heart

Physical pain, says Elaine Scarry in her groundbreaking study *The Body in Pain*, destroys human language. The problem is that, as Scarry puts it, 'the act of verbally expressing pain is a necessary prelude to the collective task of diminishing pain'.

Behind this is an assumption that we have a ready vocabulary for emotional suffering. And certainly, you can wave a hand at millennia of literary expressions of grief, loss and despair, or even at the stumblingly moving In Memoriam poems in the daily newspaper. But for all their expressiveness, can these millions of words really mitigate an iota of anguish?

For my part, my private nadirs have always exposed language – otherwise the DNA of my conscious being – as utterly useless. I have no doubt that the ability to articulate emotional pain is better than being unable to do so, and yet I have never quite felt either that therapeutic faith which underlies so many of our assumptions about human expression. A facility with language may even be counterproductive: language can be something to hide in, a means of denial as much as of admission.

This is the emotional and intellectual territory of *Construction of the Human Heart*, which is my first acquaintance with the writing of Ross Mueller. Where have I been? Mueller is surely one of the most intelligent, formally adventurous and emotionally brave playwrights now writing in this country.

On the face of it, a play that is about a play – worse, a play about two writers and a play – sounds like a sure recipe for unbridled narcissism. In Mueller's hands, it becomes a desolately moving meditation on human helplessness in the face of overwhelming grief.

Construction of the Human Heart is about a couple, Him and Her, who are haunted by two deaths. Her returns obsessively to the death of her mother, a relationship scored by unbridgeable absences and alienations. The other death is that of the couple's son. We never find out why he died, or even how old he was; but his death has triggered mechanisms of blame, denial and anger that only conceal the utter devastation of his loss.

The play sets up a disarmingly simple conceit which, almost by the bye, also interrogates the formal conventions of theatre and writing. The stage in the Tower Theatre is simply a raised platform, the acting area delineated by white paint. On the stage are two chairs, each with a bottle of water placed beside them. We are, it seems, about to attend an informal public reading of a work in progress.

The actors, Fiona Macleod and Todd MacDonald, enter through the side door when the house lights are still up. They clear their throats, fiddle with their scripts, smile nervously at the audience and settle down on the chairs. They begin to read the first scene.

So far, so conventional. Then Him drops his script, the two start bickering and you begin to understand that Him and Her are partners and that they are reading Her script, which is written out of their personal lives. At this point I realised that the house lights had gone down. They had dimmed so gradually that, although I was expecting them to go dark, I hadn't noticed when it had happened. The transition from a public reading, where the audience is visible to the actors and to each other, to a formal piece of theatre, where we sit in the dark witnessing the action on stage, is cunningly imperceptible.

The effect is a potent sense of complicity between the audience and the actors: they have seen us as much as we have seen them. And this reinforces a sense of voyeurism as the actors move in and out of differing imaginative realities – the relationship they are enacting before us, and the script they are reading. A third layer is added by Casey Bennetto's prerecorded voiceovers, which boom increasingly baroque stage directions. They describe powerful visual and sonic elements that never eventuate on the bare stage, becoming at once cues for the audience's imagination and sly satires on theatrical convention.

The dynamic between the read script and the 'real' play becomes increasingly more complex and more fraught. Is Her, as Him claims, really the one in control, the one who can articulate what happened and deal with her grief? Or is she as lost as Him, floundering in her grief as she uses her imaginative life to deny that her son is dead?

What becomes clear is how little these two people can help each other. As writers they both have a privileged relationship to expression, but even this doesn't help them communicate or even to understand the actuality of their own pain. Even their love is not enough. 'The land of tears', as Antoine de Saint-Exupéry says in *The Little Prince*, 'is so mysterious'.

In director Brett Adam's hands, this complex script is given its full emotional and intellectual range. The stripped-down design and Rob Irwin's unobtrusive but effective lighting frame two extraordinarily generous performances. Neither Macleod nor MacDonald miss a beat: the human weight of the play, the painful silences behind the words, rest wholly on them. They meet the challenge with performances that articulate its subtleties and emotional power.

It makes superb, thoughtful theatre, which manages to be at once astringently intelligent and heartbreaking. And this stylishly minimal production, imported into the Malthouse after a successful season at the Store Room, is as polished as any I've seen.

Theatre Notes, August 20 2006

The Skriker

One of the vexing and beautiful things about writing about theatre – one of the primary reasons I keep doing it, I guess – is that the more profound the experience is, the more difficult it is to express in words. So often when theatre resonates deeply, it's because it strikes chords that are crude and primitive and naïve. What is that quality which transforms what might otherwise be mere foolish pretence into an act that plucks at the roots of the psyche, waking out of the darkness the monsters that walk in all of us?

It is, for example, a truism to speak of theatre's 'magic'. *The Skriker*, surely one of the strangest and cruellest plays of Caryl Churchill's extraordinary *oeuvre*, reminds us what magic actually *is*. You can be sure, there is nothing benign or twee about it: this is the world of the uncanny, the cruel, the unhuman, the heartless. Almost a dystopian version of *A Midsummer Night's Dream*, *The Skriker* draws on ancient English and Irish folk and fairy tales to look at some inadmissably dark truths about fertility, motherhood and damaged nature.

Brian Lipson and his company of actors from the VCA School of Drama at Space 28 take Churchill's bleak, disturbing play and realise an entire theatrical world that is like being in an enchanting and sinister dream, a damaged world of transformation and dis-ease. This is, in every sense, demanding work: it wolfs your entire attention for three hours with a constantly inventive *mise en scène* of resonant theatrical image. Oneiric, haunting and toxic, it's one of the most powerful pieces of theatre I have seen this year.

In *The Skriker*, Churchill draws elements from folk and fairy tales about 'good' and 'bad' women and places them in contemporary urban settings. She creates a world of hallucinatory mirrors: the human overworld mirrors the Faerie underworld, the bad mother mirrors the good, the animal mirrors the human, the changeling mirrors the real child. It's perhaps a particularly English tradition of Gothic: Churchill's desolate urban world reminds me strongly of the London fantasy writer China Miéville's gritty realities – in particular, his dark tale of contemporary magic, 'Familiar', in his short story collection *Looking for Jake*.

Josie (Susan Miller) is the bad sister: we meet her in an asylum, where she has been confined after murdering her newborn baby and baking her in a pie. The good sister is her friend Lily (Julie Wee), who is pregnant. Both of them are haunted by the Skriker, a shape-shifting fairy who envies and desires their fertility – babies have high value in the sterile world of Faerie – and seduces them by granting their wishes. She turns up in various guises – as an American woman in a bar, a nasty little girl eaten up with sibling rivalry, a lover who behaves like an obsessed stalker – and tempts both of them down into the carnivalesque underworld.

Around the three major figures erupts a world infected with malign enchantments, a population of lost and dead children, lunatics, hags, kelpies, bogles and monsters. Nothing here is 'natural': environmental apocalypse is as much part of the sickness this play expresses as mental illness. It's interesting to think that it was written, to some hostile incomprehension, in 1994: as climate change becomes more urgently evident, as the World Health Organisation warns that mental illness will be the major growing health problem over the next two decades, it now seems spookily prescient. As the Skriker says: 'It was always possible to think whatever your personal problem, there's always nature. Spring will return even if it's without me. Nobody loves me but at least it's a sunny day. This has been a comfort to people as long as they've existed. But it's not available any more. Sorry. Nobody loves me and the sun's going to kill me. Spring will return and nothing will grow.'

Theatre is a place where the archaic meaning of 'glamour' – a spell, an enchantment – still hangs vapourously about its more conventional usage. In its original sense, *glamourie* was the word given to the ability of fairies – the Irish Sidhe, the Norse Alfar or the English Faerie – to transform and fool human senses. One of glamour's most common uses was to change human beings into animals. So in the *Odyssey*, Circe changes Ulysses' shipmates into pigs, or Puck in *A Midsummer Night's Dream* transforms Bottom into an ass.

The production begins with this kind of transformation: in the theatre foyer, a boy, up to this point seemingly another member of the audience, is turned into a pig. Inside the theatre, we hear the sounds of animal howls and shrieks, and the beasts begin to hammer on the door… and thus we are led inside, into a claustrophobic tunnel like a cattle race, dimly and obscurely lit by a single reddish-yellow light bulb. It is like the inside of a womb, or a limbo of the half-formed, where the audience members mill around with cast members that we can barely discern, surrounded by a cacophony of bestial noises. We emerge into a corral, surrounded by higher platforms on all sides; the lights widen, and human speech begins to emerge from the squeals and growls.

This introduces the first movement, as it were, of this production, which divides roughly into three main parts. The first is a promenade, opening with an evocation of Churchill's long introductory speech, in which language itself becomes other. Much of the text – the words of the Skriker, the damaged fairy – is a collage of word association, in which meaning is on the verge of slipping into nonsense. 'Slit slat slut. That bitch a botch an itch in my shoulder blood. Bitch botch itch. Slat itch slit botch. Itch slut bitch slit… Whatever you do don't open to do don't open the door… '

This is language as thickness, viscera, weight, saliva, sex, violence, the softness of palate and lip: language as spell and enchantment, where meaning constantly threatens to slip its noose and collapse back to animal howl and croon. Here Churchill is pushing theatre hard up against the poem, sense against nonsense, and one can only admire the force of the centrifugal will that keeps the text this side of comprehensible. Lipson divides the Skriker's speech between the actors of the company, who vocalise it as a sound poem or a spoken oratorio around the audience. Focus is constantly shifting: you might be listening to an actor standing at your shoulder and then to a figure suddenly lit in the distance, who as suddenly vanishes. It is a wholly immersive experience, at once shockingly intimate and alienating.

The first clear piece of narrative is a scene in a lunatic asylum, where Lily is visiting Josie. This is performed on four sides, the audience still standing in the centre, by four sets of actors; again the words are carefully orchestrated, so each scene is at once clear and splintered. No scene is identical, either: each set of actors moves and interprets the text differently. The effect is arrestingly disturbing, the beginning of a sense of a world without mooring or base reality from which reference can be made, and the realism of the performances – which touch precise emotional authenticities – is an edge against which the carnivalesque world of Faerie is whetted.

It's a contrast which is fruitfully worked through the evening, and which gives this show much of its richness and complexity: if it were merely clever and cruelly comic (and it is both) this production wouldn't possess its dark and urgent potency. Behind this show is an attuned attention to the emotional and psychic disturbance that occasions it, and it's reflected in the emotional fearlessness and clarity of the performances that Lipson has elicited from each member of his young ensemble.

The design is a mixture of contemporary street aesthetic and the grotesque, with liberal use of mask and costume. One wall of the theatre is piled to the roof with cardboard boxes, and the stage space is shaped by trolleys, which are used in all sorts of ways: scenes are sometimes performed on top of them, or sometimes, as in Ariane Mnouchkine's *Le Dernier Caravansérail*, the performers are wheeled on platforms by the other actors, so they can be at once still and in motion.

After the animal intensities of the opening sequences, the production segues to a series of scenes which play on mirroring: a bar sequence, for example, performed in double vision, with actors each side mirroring the actions of the others. After the interval, when Lily's baby is born and Josie escapes the underworld, the scenes are more singular, and the sense of a borderless, anarchic world narrows down to domestic gothic (although this is simplifying considerably). Among many other elements – this is a show headily rich on texture – there is witty use of Qioa Li's audiovisual material, from four television screens suspended from the ceiling: distorted news reports, nightmarish music clips, and a mixture of live and recorded images. The sense of multiple space invoked in the theatre is reinforced also by James Shuter's ingenious lighting design.

Primarily, something which really only became clear at the finish, I was struck by this production's elegant and powerful coherence. Reflecting Churchill's language, Lipson places the theatre under such imagistic and emotional pressures that the experience constantly threatens to fly apart into its disparate elements. He keeps it together by dint of acute directorial exactingness: this is a very detailed and carefully focused production. There were only a few moments where I felt the intensity and energies began to slacken, and even then, on reflection, I am not sure.

What I *am* sure of is that watching this play was totally compelling, and I will be chewing over it for days hence. Maybe for years. It's rare to see work in which linguistic, emotional and visual complexities of this order are realised with such thought and art. Some pieces of theatre stick with you, altering the colour of your mind; and for me, this was one of them.

Theatre Notes, September 9 2006

Le Dernier Caravansérail (Odyssées)

Dear Ariane
I hope you will forgive me for addressing you so familiarly, since I have never met you. Writing a letter seems, perhaps not so strangely, the only fit way to address *Le Dernier Caravansérail (Odyssées)*. I saw both parts in one long and dizzying Sunday and it makes me want to say many things that you must already know. Principally, I wish to say

that I witnessed something beautiful, a work of theatre that left me moved and shaken.

But this is already inadequate. Beauty is so often taken to mean the anodyne, the conventional; to be moved suggests a surfeit of sentiment. The work of your company is so far from the anodyne and sentimental, the deadliness of the worthy, that in writing about it I fear misrepresenting the breathtaking honesty and directness of its aesthetic.

The *Odyssées* began with a letter from you to Nadereh, one of the asylum seekers whom you interviewed for the work. It was projected across the back of the stage, like much of the spoken text, in a cursive script. It was a powerful preface: not only because of the letter itself which, pregnant though it was with unspoken stories of loss, was like many other letters – how are you? how are our friends? have you heard? It was also because the lights dimmed so slowly across the empty stage, introducing the play with a gentle limpidity that was heightened by the vast and lonely poignancy of Jean-Jacques Lemêtre's introductory music.

When the second part finished, I found that for the previous three hours I had been sitting next to Nadereh herself. She had been watching, among other things, events that had happened in her own life. I would have loved to have asked her what she felt, but sadly, she speaks no English, and I do not speak her language. Her presence reinforced what your letter had already made clear: that your company was dealing with what we call so easily 'real life'.

Your letter to Nadereh signalled both an intention and a refusal. The intention was to expose the genesis of this work, the reality of the people whose stories were turned into this work of theatre by you and your company. The refusal was of the betrayal of art, which so easily exploits the suffering of others to make a beautiful object that is nothing more than a plaything of the privileged. There are many cheap criticisms that might be made of this – isn't it, for example, hypocritical to speak of the poor in this expensive art form? – but the achievement of *Le Dernier Caravansérail* is its own answer.

Yes, this artfulness, this beautiful illusion and play that is theatre, can serve without dishonour something as humble and profound as human longing. You do not have the hubris to think that your play will change the world. A little bit, perhaps; an illumination here, a heartening of courage there. Art's work is not the same as that of the politician's, and you understand very well the limits of its power. And you love those limitations, also, as its strengths and freedoms.

Your importation of the whole Théâtre du Soleil into the Royal Exhibition Building – not only the set, but the bleachers, the actor's changing room, the dining tables where people could sit down and eat the food prepared there, the intimate lighting – prepared me for the experience of the play. As I walked up the stairs to my seat, I could peer down at the actors as they prepared for their performance. In between the shows, I saw them eating together outside in the sunshine. I could stare at the instruments in the sound area next to the stage – the various drums, the huge string instrument made of a turtle shell, the gong, the sound decks, the lovely wooden violin shapes hanging from a rack at the back. Before the play even started, the barriers between the theatre and those who came to watch it were already unstable and permeable.

In a way, I don't know how to talk about the work. It is not enough to say it was beautiful, as I have said; I don't wish to speak of it as if it were merely some aesthetic object, although a superb aesthetic judgment informed its every aspect. As everyone knows, it is about the dispossessed, those driven out of their homelands by war or persecution or poverty to seek a decent life somewhere else, and how they are treated by the countries they ask for help.

It was the stories of these 'voyagers' which you and your company collected and shaped into this work of art. They are the stories of human beings in exile – Kurds, Afghanis, Russians, Chechnyans, Bosnians, Africans... there are so many wars, after all, and so many famines of different kinds. And you know that as well as being full of grief and love and generosity, human beings can be murderous, cruel, weak, ignorant and stupid. That they might be cruel or stupid doesn't mean that they might not be also victims of forces beyond their control. We still hold an idea of victimhood as entitlement, which is linked to the 'deserving poor', the dichotomies of good and evil. But a person might be wicked, and still suffer.

It seemed to me that you made a whole world, and invited me to be part of it. From the beginning, I was aware of the sky, of the weather, of the elements: earth, water, light. And the very first story you tell is of a river crossing. The river is invoked by huge lengths of blue-grey silk that actors by the side billow frantically, the way you make the sea on stage when you are at primary school. But I believed this terrifying river. I understood when the ferryman refused to take the people across, understood their desperation when they argued with him and tried to cross despite the danger; I gasped when the ferryman fell in the water and wished frantically for him to be rescued... It is the simplest magic, made with the greatest degree of sophistication imaginable.

All the performers, all the little sets, even the trees, were on platforms with wheels. They were pushed on and off the huge stage by the other performers, who watched the actors, as we did, as they crouched by the platforms. It meant, among other things, that the actors could be at once still and in motion. The stage was always live: between scenes, people ran from one side to another, or pushed the props in readiness for the next scene. And as story followed story, the constant movement created an increasing sense of ephemerality and transience; against the blankness of sky and earth, these stories left no trace, save their resonances in those who heard them.

Many scenes occurred in small interiors, illuminated boxes wheeled from behind the curtains at the back of the stage. We peered through the lighted windows like voyeurs. And what we overheard were fragments, said in many languages: a nurse upbraiding a man for not looking after his leg, from which his foot had been amputated; an old woman remembering her grandchildren when they were little; the people smuggler speaking to his small son, who barely remembers him, on his mobile phone; an asylum seeker struggling violently and being brutally subdued as she is deported on a plane.

Some American critics – Robert Brustein, for example – claimed that this was theatre as martyrdom, intended to make you feel 'not just emotionally responsible for man's universal inhumanity to man, but physically uncomfortable as well'. And he castigated you for not working with a writer, as you have previously with Hélène Cixous, who would have shaped it into a proper 'drama'.

Mr Brustein is an intelligent man, but he seems to have grievously missed the point. You exposed the working of the theatre, to show that there were here no 'tricks'. And in the texts you used, you chose not to misrepresent the messiness and fragmentariness of the lives you portrayed by imposing upon them a false unity. The secret corners of life itself, its always unfinished stories, its fractures, its contradictions, its mundanities, its cruelties and beauties, opened up inside us their own truthfulness. I think that this is the reason for the work's overwhelming emotional impact.

Le Dernier Caravansérail makes you understand the profound importance of simplicities: things like shelter and food and love, the fragile stays that people make against the indifferences of the world they inhabit. As is very clear, it is not only the natural elements that are cruel. The voyagers have fled their homes – and who would leave their home voluntarily? – because they have lost hope of finding there the possibility of a decent life. Yet everywhere they go, they are non-citizens, people without a place, whose voices are not heard and not wanted. They are often, as here in Australia, herded into camps or prisons, deterritoralised places of exception, in which they exist outside the juridical space of legitimate citizenry. They are treated like criminals, and yet they have done nothing wrong except to ask for help.

With the new Terrorism Laws now all over the newspapers, it can't but occur to me that the space of the camp is growing all the time, that this state of exception is becoming the normal pulse of our times. Even in our democracies, for which we are sacrificing so much to protect, we could soon all potentially inhabit this space outside the law, where the State might do anything to us with impunity. If the natural justice of mercy can be withheld from any other human being, it can be withheld from us as well.

This is only to say the obvious, and to suggest that the work has a moralising effect that it does not, in fact, possess. Its politics exist outside the gross generalisations of power as understood, for example, in the public world of the mass media, reaching instead into the intimate and complex space of our own lives. It is here that we can understand longing and desire, love and hatred, hope and betrayal and despair. And it is from this place that we can begin to demand the freedoms that might make us whole, that allow us to live our lives to their potential fullness. For all of us must have this right.

You say that the theatre is part of the world, and that when it doesn't cut itself off from the world, it is 'one of those places that can make the world better, like an orange grove makes the world better'. You have no illusion about the importance of art: in the face of real loss, real grief, real atrocity, art can offer only its humility. It has no power against manifest injustice: it can express the intolerable, but it cannot solve it. This does not, however, make it a waste of time. As John Berger says, 'The naming of the intolerable is itself the hope'. But, perhaps most movingly, you do not only show what is intolerable: you also name the things that make life worth living. Companionship. Laughter. Wine. Beauty. Love.

Theatre Notes, October 18 2005

The Damask Drum

With the international richness of the Melbourne Festival still fresh in my mind, Liminal Theatre's *The Damask Drum* is a salutary reminder that we have our own visionary directors close to home. Robert Draffin has been working quietly in Melbourne, evolving his unique practice, for around three decades. And his production of Yukio Mishima's play, now on in an anonymous warehouse in Abbotsford, deserves to stand with the best of the work I saw at the festival.

In the countless productions he has overseen, Draffin has never been afraid of ambition. In 1991, for example, working with the young troupe Whistling in the Theatre, he created a magnificent six-hour adaptation of *A Thousand and One Nights* at Anthill (one of the small-to-medium theatres that disappeared in the Australia Council's last orgy of cultural vandalism). Or there was his epic 1992 Theatre Works production of Dostoevsky's novel *The Idiot*. More recent work includes a celebrated production of Genet's *Le Balcon-l'experimentation* at the VCA, where he has been teaching some of the young theatre artists who are putting so much zap into the Melbourne scene at present.

It's been a long time since I've seen Draffin's work. More fool me. Like Peter Brook or Ariane Mnouchkine, he works with a committed ensemble of artists, creating the long-term relationships that are the core of great theatre. This particular production is the result not only of short-term rehearsal but of year-long workshops. Funded, perhaps it ought to be noted, by no-one except the artists themselves.

Again like Mnouchkine and Brook, his work is deeply concerned with cross-cultural exchange: in Draffin's case, a long history of exchange with Asian theatre artists and practice. And as with Mnouchkine, entering his theatre is to be welcomed into a democratic social space where, until the performance begins, no distinction is made between artists and audience. When you arrive at *The Damask Drum*, you are ushered to a carpeted space at the back of the warehouse, behind the stage, with cushions, low tables and flowers. Where Mnouchkine provides dinner and Draffin makes you green tea.

And there, perhaps, the resemblances end. Unlike these two theatrical superstars, Draffin's company, Liminal Theatre, is not extravagantly funded; and Draffin's practice is all his own.

The Damask Drum is, in fact, the second instalment of a larger work, *Mishima in the City: Duets of Desire*, which aims to perform all eight of the plays Mishima adapted from the classical Noh canon.

Mishima's play updated Zeami's *Aya no Tsuzumi*, which tells the story of an old gardener who glimpses a princess and falls obsessively in love with her. Mockingly, she gives him a drum made of damask, and says that if he can make it sound in the palace, she will visit him. Of course, the old man can't make any sound at all from the drum, and drowns himself in despair. After this, the 'angry ghost' of the old man 'possessed the lady's wits, haunted her heart with woe'.

In Mishima's version, the woman, Hanako, lives in an apartment block opposite the old man, Iwakichi, and he has to make the drum sound above the city traffic: but the obsession, the mockery, the vengefulness of the old man's ghost and the woman's regret remain. Draffin has fused Mishima's and Zeami's texts to create a kind of collage, in which sound and song play as significantly as semantic sense.

When the plays were first performed in Japan in the 1950s, they were produced in a naturalistic style: a totally revolutionary decision in the context of the Japanese theatre of the time. Instead, in this production Draffin draws from a range of classical Asian theatre techniques, skilfully combining them with images projected from a hand-held cyclorama and an amplified sound score. Black-clad stagehands operate the projections, fabrics, mirrors, smoke and other stage business. This is certainly not Noh, but it's impossible to overlook its Noh ancestry.

The design exploits the length of the warehouse, seating the audience at one end. The set consists basically of a small stage made of black polished wood that is set immediately before the audience, from which stretches a narrow walkway to a door in the back wall. It's a free adaptation of the *hashigakari*, or bridge, by which actors sumptuously enter the stage in traditional Noh.

Jethro Woodward's soundscape is astoundingly good. It combines sometimes thunderous electronic sound with a collage of amplified voices that fill the space – mostly inhabited by one actor – with unseen people. The orchestra and chorus are embodied in Woodward himself, who stands in the performance space, to the left of the wooden stage. He plays live electric guitar, singing some parts of the story.

The opening scene demonstrates the potency of the elements Draffin is exploiting. The play begins in blackness, with Woodward bowing haunting melodies from his guitar. Very gradually, a dim light rises on the far end of the stage: a white figure is partially revealed in the distance. It seems to float in a globe of light through the darkness, like a ghost or a goddess, and moves towards us with hieratic slowness.

It is impossible to tell whether the figure is male or female until he is quite close: then you see it is a half-naked man (Alan Knoepfler), who is wearing a long, white, very full skirt that is held up on either side, like royal robes, by the stage attendants. He collapses before us face-forward on the small stage, the skirt like a foaming wave that has washed him up from the darkness.

Knoepfler's performance of the old gardener devastated by obsessive erotic love is utterly compelling. He is on stage, mostly solo, for the whole play, and maintains without wavering the physical, vocal and emotional extremity of his performance. His body is the expressive site of his ecstatic torment and self-disgust: he is in turn grotesque, abject, ennobled, despairing, tender. He is well met by Mary Sitarenos as the woman, whose entrance late in the show is almost as beautiful as Knoepfler's.

There are more than a few moments of breathtaking *mise en scène* in the course of this show. If it has flaws, they are of the kind that are hard to pinpoint: slight hesitancies, perhaps, that may manifest in an overdressed moment here or there. Its strength, as in the writing it is manifesting, is in its simplicity, the courage of both restraint and passion that underlies formal artistic beauty.

The Damask Drum is not only theatre that has poetry in it – which is one thing – but something rather more rare: a poetic theatre, working transformations rich and strange.

Theatre Notes, November 12 2006

Tense Dave

Tense Dave, a co-production between Malthouse Theatre and Chunky Move, is a collaboration between some of the most interesting minds in contemporary performance now working in Melbourne: Lucy Guerin, Michael Kantor and Gideon Obarzanek. Attempting to integrate three such individual visions – two choreographers and a theatre director – entails the risk of each of them becoming obscured, but a rigorous simplicity at the heart of its concept permits each talent to glow, as they say, with the genius of the ensemble. They've made a work of rich and resonant lucidity that authentically straddles dance and theatre.

It's essentially a meditation on catastrophic solitude that is at once witty, sad, violent, sinister, tragic and euphorically uplifting, shifting through its kaleidoscopic and fantastic variations with an unerring suppleness. The production on at the Malthouse demonstrates a deep polish, the mark of years of touring. Its track record speaks for itself: *Tense Dave* premiered at the 2003 Melbourne Festival and then toured extensively around Australia and to the US, where its New York season won it the 2005 Bessie (the dance equivalent of a Tony) for outstanding choreography.

The performance occurs wholly on a simple, quite small wooden revolve placed in the midst of a large, dark, amorphous theatrical space defined by lengths of black curtain. It turns through the entire show, its constant creaking a crucial part of the soundscape. I adore revolves: I know there's something about them which threatens arch theatrical tackiness, although it's probable that fairground quality is part of their attraction. But essentially I think it's the fascinating tension between stillness and movement that's created when the scenery is as mobile as the performer. I can promise that you will never see a revolve used more creatively than in *Tense Dave*.

The dance opens with a naked light bulb that gradually brightens to reveal the revolve. The revolve is divided like a pie by rough wooden walls, in which a kind of keyhole space has been torn to permit the light bulb to pass through the walls, sequentially illuminating several claustrophobic 'rooms'. In the first sequence we are introduced to the various 'characters' of the piece: first of all Tense Dave himself (Brian Lucas), a tall lanky man standing alone, his body the epitome of unspecific anxiety: his gestures are rigid, he obsessively fiddles with his shirt, he crouches foetally against the wall.

Gradually the other sections become inhabited: a man in a suit, talking to his patent leather shoes (Brian Carbee); a woman in a petticoat staring longingly at a red velvet eighteenth-century dress (Kristy Ayre); a woman in a nightdress on a bed, holding a huge kitchen knife (Michelle Heaven); a man with almost waist length hair, seated with his back to the audience, carefully combing his hair (Luke Smiles). I thought at first that Smiles, glimpsed in a classic pose of a female nude, was a woman; the next glimpse, revealing him as a man, is the first of several perceptual shocks that accumulate through the performance.

As the rooms move past us, we are privy to a series of vignettes, all of them comically sad expressions of private desire and loneliness, and begin to enter a series of fantasias that are explored throughout the rest of the show. The suited man photographs his shoes and argues with his telephone; the woman in the nightdress acts out scenarios of threat and terror with the knife, hiding under her bed; the other woman puts on her dress and reads from a bodice-ripper romance novel set in a fantasy Scotland (I'm almost sure I've read this novel – a genre which revels in wicked fathers, forced marriages, romantic soldiers and rape fantasies).

Gradually *Tense Dave* begins to be drawn into the other rooms: he eavesdrops on the other characters, enters their lives, and finds himself involved in a series of obscure dramas. The scenarios are like those in dreams: Brian Carbee gives him a shoebox that must be delivered somewhere, and abuses him when he doesn't know what to do with it; Michelle Heaven's character both threatens him and asks him for help; he becomes a hapless character in the romantic novel.

Perhaps because of the formal device of the revolve, which holds the fragmentary narratives together in a single, clearly coherent space, I saw all these characters as aspects of Dave himself, grotesquely flowering out of the repressed anxieties and desires his body expresses. But equally, it's possible to see in these scenes a version of Sartre's statement that 'hell is other people'. It's probably most true that in watching the dance, you oscillate between these possibilities, inner and outer realities, without ever deciding it is one or the other: *Tense Dave* is a show which brilliantly exploits the fertile anxieties of ambiguity.

The movement is for the most drawn from the ordinary gestures of vernacular life, here given formal precision and focus.

Desire – towards death, or towards a possibility of love – is enacted in all sorts of displaced ways in a fragmented narrative that becomes progressively more violent. In one very witty sequence, Brian Carbee sits in a chair, exactly as if he is ordering a sex worker to enact various sexual fantasies, ordering Michelle Heaven to act out various scenarios with her finger: her finger is lonely, meets a friend, has dinner, falls in love, murders, goes to prison. Luke Smiles makes various attempts at suicide. The bodice-ripper fantasy is read out by a disembodied voice, lip-synched by the performers, until it reaches its logical end of rape. Dave's anxieties fantastically explode into fear: he becomes the murderer and the rapist that he fears he is.

Perhaps the most moving sequence is between Dave and Michelle Heaven, in which they dance a lyrical *pas de deux*, mirroring each other's gestures until they make love, but all the time – even while lovemaking – separated by a wall. Despite their yearning and desire, they cannot actually touch each other. The aching sadness of this dance is immediately exploded by a musical number, a sardonically seductive take on the hedonistic, numbing optimism of American musicals. Dave, very briefly, forgets his troubles and gets happy.

Another peak moment is a comic satire on the butchery of splatter movies, in which the dancers are dismembered by chainsaws. For all its comedy, I squeamishly found this all but impossible to watch, although the violence is primarily generated through sound effects. I have often thought that horror movies primarily generate most of their visceral effects through the suggestiveness of sound, and for me, this proved it.

All the transitions are performed seamlessly, with the help of what must be a superlative backstage crew, and the rhythms are superbly orchestrated: there wasn't a single moment where I found my attention flagging. The dance ends as it begins, with the solitary figure of Dave. This time he's freed of his walls, freed of the other voices and bodies that have haunted and traumatised him. It's an image that's at once bleak and heartening; he is no longer trapped in the travail of his anxieties, but he is walking nowhere, his body relaxed, utterly alone.

Theatre Notes, April 27 2007

OT: Chronicles of the Old Testament

However you look at it, OT: *Chronicles of the Old Testament* at the Malthouse's Beckett Theatre is a mess. Some of it is a glorious, exhilarating, anarchic mess, and some of it feels rather like being locked inside a four-year-old maniac's bedroom. It seems to me like a show that is still gestating: but the beast is most certainly slouching towards Bethlehem to be born.

You can't fault Uncle Semolina (& friends) on their ambition. The Old Testament gathers together the foundational sacred texts of our civilisation, and that it's a timely idea to examine them hardly needs saying. The 'religions of the Book', Christianity, Judaism and Islam, all draw from these ancient writings, and all three religions bleed along the faultlines of contemporary geopolitics.

The question at the heart of OT is how much this contemporary violence is encoded in the ur-violence of the Old Testament, which, with its bloody parade of betrayal, revenge, murder, incest, rape, divine punishment, jealousy, dire moralistic warnings and straight-out misogyny, sometimes seems like ancient Palestine's version of the *Sun* newspaper. As devisers Christian Leavesley and Phil Rolfe say in the program: if God really made man in His own image, what does that say about God?

This question is explored by enacting some of the key stories of the Old Testament. Don't look for any Cecil B DeMille SFX here: this is the Bible for a post-capitalist, urban generation. Leavesley and Rolfe excavate the bric-a-brac of contemporary middle-class childhood – Teletubbies, soft toys, dinosaurs, plastic buckets – and pile it around a ramshackle cardboard set that's a kind of nightmare kindergarten. Yahweh himself is a senile patriarch in a cardigan, snoring in the corner. It's notable that there are no design credits – although it's beautifully lit by Paul Jackson, this is a kind of anti-design, there merely to be the occasion for its own destruction.

My major feeling for around the first twenty minutes was creeping disappointment. The cast fills the stage with energy, but it seldom gets beyond a feeling that we're watching a series of drama exercises in storytelling. (How do you perform all the 'begats' in Genesis? Phone calls and clowning!) A feeling of theatrical stasis is reinforced by the dramaturgy, which reels out the stories as sequential, if fragmentary, episodes: once the comic novelty of watching Biblical scenes enacted with stuffed toys wore off, I began to feel that this was a one-joke show, and to think rather wistfully of the savagely beautiful grandeur of the King James Bible. Paradoxically enough, these early scenes seem too polite.

Fortunately, OT soon gets a lot ruder, and the second half of the show is an entirely different experience. The cast begins to access an Artaudian sense of the sacred, the delirium that infects the subconscious with the self-annihilating freedom of dream. The show starts to generate its own dark poetic as the objects are infused with a strange and sinister life, and all the performances become at once more focused and less predictable. In retrospect, it's hard to pin down where the show turns, because it is partly a cumulative effect, but it certainly coincides with two things: a rougher and more anarchic dramaturgy that runs the stories together, so that they fragment, overlap, bifurcate; and the theatrical excavation of the brutality of the stories.

The show is structured around five main stories – the Creation, the expulsion of Adam and Eve from Eden, Cain's murder of Abel, Noah and the Flood, and the Tower of Babel – and given a semblance of clarity with the help of text projected on the walls. Leavesley and Rolfe eschew a chronological or even orderly narrative, but OT generally works backwards, literally counting down to the beginning.

These narratives are interwoven with some lesser known passages – the filial jealousy of the twin brothers Esau and Jacob, for example, or the horrific dismemberment of the Levite's concubine, who after being gang-raped and murdered, is cut into twelve pieces and her body distributed among the twelve tribes of Israel as an exhortation for revenge. God (Peter Snow) eventually wakes up from his slumber and is both puppet and sinister puppeteer, exacting jealous revenge and capricious punishment, but his main characteristic is divine indifference to his worshippers; in Job's case, he uses human beings as wagers to get one over Satan. And then He disappears altogether, abandoning His flawed creation to its own violent confusion.

The use of toys generates a cumulative metaphorical point about God the Father's infantalisation of human beings, but it also suggests that God manifests as a human creation. As in the imaginative play of children, God is generated by our own desires; as Blake says, 'all Gods reside in the human breast'. 'Play' in all its senses is key to this show. The cast – Amelia Best, Phillip McInnes, Luke Ryan, Peter Snow and Katherine Tonkin – performs with a physical and – perhaps more importantly – emotional fearlessness that makes the extremities they're exploring tangible on stage. And their performances are heightened by a very brilliant sound design.

As the show gets darker, it also gets funnier: among its highlights is a pitch-perfect vernacular rendition by Luke Ryan of Samson's first wedding, during which he slaughtered the entire wedding party, and a song that is (I guess) punk/Teletubbies fusion. But *OT* does much more than simply jam these ancient, bloodthirsty stories into a vernacular urban aesthetic; it creates theatrical moments that implode with a visceral, physical beauty, transfiguring its aggressively simple elements into potent catalysts of the imagination. In its best moments, it is – to use the appropriate vocabulary in all its senses – awesome.

OT explores – if, at present, a little vaguely – real and disturbing questions about the DNA of our culture which now seem especially pertinent. There are those, for example, who claim that Islam is 'inherently' violent, while Christianity is not: a brief survey of the Old Testament's jealous and punitive God laying waste to whole populations even unto the seventh generation will surely put that furphy to rest (remembering, of course, that Armageddon and the Apocalypse are inventions of the New Testament). It would be nice to think that we're past all that now but, sadly, the optimistic notion of historical progress seems currently to be as big a myth as Yahweh.

Seeing *OT* was strangely synchronous with a blogger hoohah I've been following with stratospherically raised eyebrows: *Time Out New York* theatre editor David Cote, 'sworn enemy of ignorant, paranoid, wasteful, culturally desolate, ahistorically pious middleamerican boobies', made some waspish comments about those of faithful persuasion, and straightway proved that hell hath no fury like riled atheists and believers scorned. I've been trying to imagine such a conversation in Melbourne theatre circles: perhaps I'm wrong, but I can't. I'm certain *OT* will polarise audiences, but I can't see it being picketed by outraged Christians. Sometimes I think there's a lot to be said for good old-fashioned Australian scepticism.

Theatre Notes, May 12 2007

On Paul Capsis

The other evening, as I walked homewards through the lashing rain of a wintry Melbourne night, my heart too swollen and luminous with blood to feel the cold, I wondered what it is that makes Paul Capsis great. Not good, but great: the kind of greatness that tears open your own mortality, that makes you feel so intensely present that you are lifted out of time and find yourself poised in anguished nostalgia for these moments that are falling now, like shining water, through your open fingers.

What is it, I thought, about this funny, short, skinny, ugly, beautiful man, this man who flounces onto the stage in his brown velvet suit, staring at us with the eyes of an Egyptian hieroglyph, his gaudily be-ringed hands fluttering like broken doves as he offers his fragility and grotesqueness like a sacrifice on the altar of our possible scorn, our possible adoration? Yes, he has the voice of an angel (or perhaps several angels: he is never singular). But that is by no means the whole of it.

And then the word came to me: he has *duende*.

Federico García Lorca defines duende thus: 'The duende… is a power, not a work; it is a struggle, not a thought. I have heard an old maestro of the guitar say, "The duende is not in the throat; the duende climbs up inside you, from the soles of the feet". Meaning this: it is not a question of ability, but of true living style, of blood, of the most ancient culture, of spontaneous creation.'

And further: 'All that has black sounds is duende'. And further: 'All arts are capable of duende, but where it finds its greatest range, naturally, is in music, dance and spoken poetry, for these arts require a body to interpret them, being forms that are born, die, and open their contours against an exact present.'

The duende stands on the rim of the wound, inviting death to be its playmate. Janis Joplin had duende. She was that wild, raw wind that stripped each song to its bone, and then broke the bone open to its bitter marrow. When Capsis sings a Joplin song, he does not silence us because he is giving us a perfect imitation of a dead woman. No, he is summoning the death that choked her in every song she sang, and it scrapes across his throat like a hacksaw. He is summoning the blood that raced through her body, and its crimson arc as it spilled out in her magnificent voice, he is calling up within his own flesh the ecstatic awkwardness of a body on the threshold of a blazing knowledge that can only be known in the body, glorious and bright and transient as the incandescent filament that blazes in the centre of a spotlight.

He is embarrassed by neither kitsch nor art: the duende is possible anywhere. He sings a Paul Kelly song and then a ballad from Schubert's *Winterreise*. In the taut-breathed silence the duende laughs like a demonic flame, and then it dares to tickle us. It has no respect for niceties. It likes crude jokes and naïve gestures. It lives in the fractures these crudities open within us, leaping out in the sudden gracelessness of a movement that forbids illusion. Its pretence is all fraud: all the time, it is telling the truth.

Paul Capsis is not Janis Joplin, nor Nancy Sinatra, nor Judy Garland. He is Paul Capsis, and he is a slender man with hands that are graceful white spiders climbing around his face, and he is sitting six feet away on the edge of the stage hurting us with a voice as pure as acetylene. His face is a mask, it changes all the time, it mocks us and seduces us, it says, you can have everything and nothing. His face is a mask of the most minute expressiveness; but his voice is naked.

The Coloured Girls Go... Paul Capsis and Alister Spence, Malthouse Theatre.

Theatre Notes, June 28 2007

Holiday / Chapters from the Pandemic

These two shows demonstrate the depth, range and quality of independent theatre bubbling beneath the skin of Melbourne. They represent a startling contrast in style: Doubletap's *Chapters from the Pandemic* is a full-on expressionist dance theatre work, devised and performed by the human tempest Angus Cerini, while Ranters' *Holiday* is exquisite minimalist theatre that focuses on the apparently inconsequential minutiae of human communication.

All the same, they do have some common ground. For one thing, they are part of a significant shift in the magnetic field of Australian culture. Over the past decade, many of the most interesting theatre-makers have been aligning themselves with Europe and Asia, rather than with the traditionally Anglocentric centres of London or New York.

Many significant artists in the Australian performing arts – Barrie Kosky, Benedict Andrews, Gideon Obarzanek, David Berthold or Daniel Keene, to name just a few – work between Europe and Australia, often developing significant careers overseas. We don't have expatriates any more, we have a culture of nomads. Ranters Theatre and Cerini's Doubletap are no exception; in recent years, they've both toured Europe, garnering plaudits along the way. And it's easy to see why they attract attention.

From writing to performance to design, *Holiday*, playing at North Melbourne Arts House, is a devastatingly elegant show. Using black curtains, designer Anna Tregloan has enclosed an intimate auditorium within the vasty heights of the North Melbourne Town Hall. Once you find your way through the slightly disorientating darkness, you see before you a small stage that is effectively a white box. In the centre is a blue paddling pool, on which float two huge, brightly coloured beach balls. To one side is an absurd velvet chaise lounge, and on the other are a couple of stools.

The actors, Paul Lum and Patrick Moffat, sit either side of the stage. They are wearing shorts and bathers, and they are apparently relaxing: sighing, rolling their shoulders and stretching, smiling at each other with the slight apology of strangers sharing an intimate space. It's clear that they're indulging in that strange Western ritual, the holiday.

Before long, the silence stretches into anxiety. Somebody has to speak. And somebody does. What follows is utterly enchanting: absurd, gentle and profound. It's a series of apparently artless, inconsequential dialogues, interspersed with a capella performances of baroque love songs by Schubert, Bononcini or Gluck that excavate the unspoken desires that run beneath the skin of idle conversation.

Raimondo Cortese's dialogues have an airy sense of improvisation, seemingly leading nowhere, but they are written with acutely honed skill. They create a sparkling surface that unobtrusively hints at depth: underneath we sense sadness, loneliness, vulnerability. Some have an air of comic confession (one man compulsively lies about himself; the other, a lapsed Catholic, regularly attends confession to relieve his mind of childhood betrayals). And others circle around performance, exploring the different selves we present to the world and to ourselves, the idea that we are always, in one way or another, acting.

At one point, one man departs the stage (to buy, as we discover, a chocolate bar and a soft drink), leaving the other in solitude. The lights come down: it is evening, and a sense of peace fills the theatre. We watch, with the lone man, a ship pass over the horizon (a video inspired by Simryn Gill's work *Vessel*) and for once, the awkward question of self is left behind, absorbed in contemplation.

The production is superb, backed by a subtly nuanced sound design by David Franzke, and beautiful lighting by Niklas Pajanti. But what matters in this show is the text and the performances, and Adriano Cortese has orchestrated these with delicacy and attention. Lum and Moffat are stunning performers, achieving the extremely difficult task of doing nothing on stage with apparent effortlessness. You can't take your eyes off them.

In its artful artlessness, *Holiday* reminded me of the anti-spectacle of Jérôme Bel's beautiful *Pichet Klunchun and Myself*, which was one of the highlights of last year's Melbourne Festival. Like Bel, Ranters Theatre achieves a profound and joyous lightness.

Angus Cerini's one man show, a post-apocalyptic dance piece at fortyfive downstairs, couldn't be more different: here there is minimal text, and Cerini and his collaborators create a rich stage environment that includes video projections, dramatic lighting (strobes, spotlights) and a huge set that evokes a world of human ruins. *Chapters from the Pandemic*, a project that emerges from Chunky Move's Maximised program, imagines a world in which all living creatures have been killed by humankind.

Cerini's vision isn't a million miles from Konstantin's ill-fated playlet in Chekhov's *The Seagull*:

> Men, lions, eagles, and partridges, horned deer, geese, spiders, silent fish that dwell in the deep, starfish, and creatures invisible to the eye – these, and all living things, all, all living things, having completed their sad cycle, are no more… The bodies of all living creatures have turned to dust, eternal matter has turned them into stones, water, clouds, and all their souls have merged into one. That great world soul – is I…

Like Konstantin's 'world soul', Cerini's human is the last living creature in the world, the final locus of memory within a dead landscape. When you enter the theatre, a naked man is displayed on what looks like a laboratory table. And I mean naked: he is, from head to toe, completely hairless. At first he seems to be a statue, utterly still, even breathless, but he draws in a shuddering breath, and then another. He is alive.

What we witness over the next 50 minutes is a man, but a man reduced to a state of new infancy. He is without speech, and he must relearn his body: how to walk, how to hold things, how pushing breath through his larynx permits him to make a noise. Slowly he begins to explore a frightening and mysterious world, a world of jarring edges and objects whose use he does not understand, while confused memory plays in his head in a jumble of sound and light.

Kelly Ryall's score shifts from lyrically plucked guitar to ambient animal noises (bird song, the lowing of cows) to loud, abstract bangs and howls, and fills the space as dramatically as Michael Carmody's video projections, which assault the stage, playing over Cerini's body so that its vestiges of humanity are almost dissolved in a chaos of light and shadow.

Cerini's performance – grotesque, touching, vulnerable, utterly concentrated – is astoundingly brave. His nakedness is the least part of it: he tests our patience and attention, taking exactly as much time as he needs to shift between one state and another. The movement oscillates between moments of lyrical stillness and extreme anarchy, when the body, its head engulfed in a gas mask, flings itself in ecstatic abandon. And at last, with neither sadness nor regret, the human body dissolves into the natural world.

Sometimes you feel that Cerini's vocabulary of gesture could be expanded, and that perhaps the space could be better exploited (the left hand of the stage, for example, is never visited). But these are quibbles: *Chapters from the Pandemic* is riveting, a strange elegy for a dead world that is somehow, to quote the poem in the program, a celebration of 'human magic'.

Theatre Notes, August 14 2007

Meow Meow

'What does a heart sound like when it breaks?'

Meow Meow, dishevelled kamikaze chanteuse, tired, bored and heartbroken, wants to know. One audience member suggests 'crash'. Another says 'horrible'. Several others deny having had their hearts broken at all.

'Mine', says Meow Meow, 'sounds like this'. She launches into a series of vocal acrobatics that sound like a cross between an animal being slaughtered and an orgasm.

Aside from its startling demonstration of the flexibility and power of that extraordinary voice, it's a moment when the toxic fragrance that winds through *Beyond Beyond Glamour* rises pungently to the surface.

Meow Meow's anarchic seduction is all about sex and death. I can't think of anywhere better to see her than the Famous Spiegeltent. If it weren't for the lack of clouds of cigarette smoke, you'd swear you were back in the Weimar Republic. Like another Spiegeltent favourite, Camille O'Sullivan, or the brilliant Paul Capsis, Meow Meow takes the art of cabaret and splits it open, exposing the disillusioned, yearning heart that beats under the sequins. She's a comedian of extraordinary nerve: her act is continually on the verge of collapse, catching itself up at the last possible moment.

I'm not sure I've ever seen an audience so tyrannised. From the moment she appears in incognito diva uniform of big coat and sunglasses, several beats after her introduction by pianist Paul Grabowsky, she is the model of the monstrous narcissist. In a cruelly hilarious parody of the femme fatale, Meow Meow dominates the room with her supposed frailty. She snappishly commands a series of hapless men to carry her suitcase, to lug her to the stage, to help her off with most of her clothes.

She uses them as props, even as bras; she sits on them and demands that they look at her adoringly. Sheepishly, they oblige. They also take full advantage of her invitation to touch her.

Complaining that 'the management' has forced her to perform even though her heart is broken, Meow Meow teasingly sings a series of cabaret classics – in French, Italian, German, Polish and Chinese. If she weren't so funny, you'd be wild with frustration: she never finishes any of them.

The show is really a lead-up to the final number – 'a standard cabaret number, darlings, you all know it' – Brecht and Weill's *Surabaya Johnny*.

Here Meow Meow stops the tease. Her performance of this well-worn classic – tender, aching, savagely disillusioned – is nothing less than revelatory. And yes, you really are there, in Berlin in 1920. Only it's Melbourne 2007.

The Australian, October 22 2007

Moving Target

The first thing you notice when you walk into the Malthouse Theatre to see *Moving Target* is that there is no escape for the actors. The six performers are already before you, in what appears to be a giant, open-fronted box. There are plainly no hidden doors, no moving walls. The actors could, of course, step out of the front of the stage, but the 'fourth wall', the convention that separates the stage from the audience, is as tacitly constraining as any material barrier. They are thrust before us, trapped in our gaze.

On stage there is a red carpet, a table, a couple of chairs, and a red couch. There is an assortment of props – a sleeping bag, a doll, a toy dinosaur, some rolls of masking tape. And that's it. What follows is one of the most intriguing pieces of theatre you will see this year. The result of an intense collaborative process between the actors, director and writer, it reminds you of the multiple meanings of 'play'. Some sequences are sheer genius. And yet, frustratingly, it doesn't follow through the implications of its own process.

I was so puzzled the first time I saw *Moving Target* that I went back a couple of nights later. It was no punishment to do so: this is, for most of its two hours, a fascinating, funny, disturbing and sometimes beautiful show. But each time I saw it, a little dialogue from Beckett's *Endgame* echoed in my head.

> HAMM: We're not beginning to... to... mean something?
> CLOV: Mean something! You and I, mean something? [*Brief laugh.*] Ah, that's a good one!

If only von Mayenburg had emulated Beckett's tact, *Moving Target* might have been revelatory theatre. But no, the text had to *mean* something. And as soon as this is clear, the glorious imaginative suspension of play that levitates this production crashes down to earth. Von Mayenburg is, without doubt, a poet of the theatre, and in *Moving Target* he demonstrates, sometimes brilliantly, his gift for unsettling, under-the-skin imagery and dialogue. But he needs more of the poet in his work, more of that blind, even foolish trust in the currents of process, if this work is to take flight, if he is to drop the conventions of writing a play in favour of playing.

To make things more confusing, the text on the page reads very well. But the problem with the show is not that the production doesn't serve the play. What is offered in *Moving Target* is something different and potentially more exciting: a work of theatre in which performance is an integral part of the script, in which gesture and words are organically linked, each emerging from each. And for most of the show, that is exactly what happens.

Its premise is ingeniously simple. Before us are the actors as themselves: each is called by his or her proper name, Alison (Bell), Julie (Forsyth), Rita (Kalnejais), Robert (Menzies), Hamish (Michael) and Matthew (Whittet). The performances emerge from the game of hide and seek, a game that has a certain poignancy already because in Robert Cousins' merciless white box there is hardly anywhere to hide.

The actors, who are all excellent clowns, become increasingly imaginative and absurd in their efforts to hide themselves. In these games, the stage oscillates between disorder and order: the furniture is thrown about the stage, the carpet is rumpled, the sofa up-ended and, in one case, an actor becomes almost terminally tangled up with a chair. And then, patiently, order is restored – to an extent. Part of the process of the work is the gradual breakdown of recognisable order, which is realised not only in the bad treatment of furniture, but in the heightening emotional dishevelment of the actors.

These enactments of childish pleasure and – increasingly – distress are counterpointed with the dialogue, in which the six actors become parent figures – each differentiated and yet not quite characters either – speaking about a problem daughter. It's unclear what is wrong with this child, who is at the unsettling age of pre-pubescence, at the threshold of adult sexuality. This girl, it appears, is dangerous: she makes stains appear on the carpet, she is surrounded by a mysterious energy, her touch can make metal hot. And always, everywhere, there are bloodied feathers.

The *mise en scène* is superbly choreographed by director Benedict Andrews, with a lot of unobtrusive detailing and a rhythmic authority that gives the impression that the space itself is animated, like some kind of meta-puppetry. This sense is reinforced by Hamish Michael's sound design, which uses mics embedded in the set itself and jagged snatches of music, to create a dense and sometimes punishing soundscape.

The actors have found a particular and very theatrical language of gesture, a mixture of exaggerated banality and child-like formalism (familiar hand games, for example, that, as the parent of every toddler knows, must always be played the same way) that develops into a rich texture of performance. It begins as faintly hysterical, faintly neurotic, and gradually accumulates into a highly expressive mimesis of contemporary anxiety.

This anxiety is free-floating, all-pervasive, and all the more uncomfortable for its lack of focus. It builds up to an extraordinary monologue delivered by Julie Forsyth, who is perhaps the most compelling performer in this very strong cast. She tells a story, comically punctuated by sounds from the other actors, in which the anxious parent witnesses what appears to her to be an ideal family having a picnic together. They have been hunting, and are happily seated by their prey:

> It brought tears to my eyes. And I asked my husband: when was the last time we had such a carefree picnic with our daughter? And my husband thinks about it and says: never, we were never carefree, even at breakfast, there's a butter knife and I break out in a cold sweat, how does the father know that none of his three children will take the front charger and gun him down from the back, what a happy and healthy family for them to stroll through the tall grass with unsecured weapons and him not afraid that they'll zero in on him and shoot his head from his body or follow a whistle command and riddle his thighs with bullets and leave him to bleed to death, or they plot it in advance and the best shot kills him with a single dry headshot through the silencer. No, everything is wonderful here…

As she takes us through the macabre absurdity of this vision, a sardonically twisted image of middle-class family life, Forsyth summons an increasing sense of tragedy. It culminates in a piercing cry of anguish: 'Why us and not him? Why us?' And it's heartbreaking, even though we don't know why she is so tormented, even while we register the horrific reality of the ideal family she so envies.

It's this kind of naked actorly presence that works so successfully in *Moving Target*. Andrews has assembled a brilliant ensemble of performers who are all capable of fulfilling Peter Ustinov's frustrated instruction to a method actor: 'Don't do something! Just stand there!' (Which is much more difficult than it sounds.) Rather than investigate character, Andrews exploits the individual performative strengths of each actor, and the result is richly rewarding.

Things begin to turn awry a little after Forsyth's monologue. It's as if the show loses focus: the lighting begins to be melodramatic, the game-playing begins to lose its earlier comic ease. The actors pull out paper and paints and do some finger painting, and the dreadful suspicion begins to form that this is, after all, merely self-indulgent.

Simultaneously, we begin to collide with the meaning of the text, which is spelt out for us by the playwright, and all the possibilities that have been opened up during the course of the show begin to be whittled down. We are speaking about terrorism, after all. We are examining how these public anxieties infect and eventually destroy the private sphere – or perhaps, it is the other way around – and yet, the focus of all this murderous terror is merely what a child puts into a box and throws away, the wounded bird of her heart. She is the blank doll on which the adult world projects its fear of its own damaged innocence. There are all sorts of ideas to unpack from this, of course, but they seem so much less exciting than what was promised earlier, when the possibilities of meaning existed in the imaginations of the audience.

It occurs to me that the central problem is that there are two possible artworks uncomfortably jostling in this show. They run parallel for some time – until quite close to the end, in fact – but then find themselves sadly at odds. The first is the work in which the text is integrated with the performances, in which gesture and word, physical games and language, are each relating freely. While this is happening, it is tremendously exciting theatre. But towards the end, the writing asserts its dominance and narrative becomes the controlling impulse of the theatre. And at this point the energy whooshes out of the whole thing.

Yet von Mayenburg has written a very interesting play that, if it were given a more conventional production, could make a compelling piece of theatre. The text has a poetic integrity, a delicate interlacing of mystery and revelation, that could, on its own, be more than enough. The problem with seeing it in this production is that you glimpse another possibility that is at once more disturbing, more exciting and perhaps more terrifying. The editor in me suspects that the problem in this production might be solved quite simply, with some brutal cutting. In this case, less might be much more.

Theatre Notes, March 18 2008

Red Sky Morning

I have often theorised, over various beverages (coffee, whisky, absinthe) that, while Melbourne is an exciting place to be if you like going to the theatre, with some brilliant theatrical minds and bodies, our theatre suffers from one debilitating weakness: its writing. Waxing lyrical, I'd suggest that this might have something to do with an inward-looking, parochial literary culture. Or alternatively, perhaps it's linked to a conviction I've encountered now and then among theatre artists and, sometimes, critics, that literature and theatre are activities that are not only mutually exclusive, but naturally opposed.

Writers can react in defence by turning into enormous intellectual snobs or, alternatively, dump the idea of literature altogether as an unnecessary affectation. There's often been a broad streak of anti-intellectualism in Australian theatre, that can sideline literary art as a secondary, perhaps optional, part of the theatre. Actors might train for years to discipline their voices and bodies but, hey, any fool with a keyboard can write. The other response is for playwrights to become the sterile kings of an untouchable domain, *á la* the Edward Albee school of theatre. (There's that joke: how many playwrights does it take to change a lightbulb? Answer: None. No changes!)

By the time I've reached this point, I usually have to be scraped off the floor and gently pushed home before I start dribbling. Or worse, before I begin to expound my ideas about what writing can be in the theatre, which is good for another three hours. But all this is a longwinded way of signalling that I think there is, in fact, a rich loam of theatre writing in Australia, which, despite the production of exciting playwrights like Lally Katz or Ross Mueller, remains mostly unploughed. Judging the RE Ross Trust Play Awards this year, I read a number of adventurous and intelligent texts that, above all, were clearly written for the theatre, as opposed to being transposed novels or bad attempts at poetry.

This is at once encouraging and challenging. Because if there are all these writers making interesting plays, how can our theatre culture support them? The talent out there far exceeds what our mainstream theatres, even with the best of intentions, can produce. I began to wonder if Melbourne needs a theatre specifically for writers, a theatre which exploits our sophisticated theatrical practice to realise the possibilities of this new work.

Or perhaps there's Red Stitch. (I realise this is a cue for other independent theatres to clamour that they, too, put on new writing: yes, yes, yes. And I'm not ignoring La Mama or Hoy Polloy or any others. But certainly, there's Red Stitch.) Tom Holloway's *Red Sky Morning* is the first product of Red Stitch Writers, a system of in-house play development started last year. This is a new step in Red Stitch's history, which since 2001 has concentrated on picking up and producing the overseas work that escapes the notice of the MTC, and it demonstrates that there's a world of difference between putting on a play, however well, and making theatre.

In choosing to produce Holloway's play, Red Stitch made a courageous bet. And it's paid off. *Red Sky Morning* is exciting work, which, as good theatre writing should, attempts to rethink the possibilities of theatre. And, crucially, the commitment of the director, performers and designers to realising this play shines through this production.

Tom Holloway has written what might be called a spoken oratorio, a poem for three voices that, like a piece of music, weaves through counterpoint and harmony and tonal collisions. Holloway exploits the patterns of ordinary speech, its repetitions and elisions and fractures, with consummate skill. There is, despite the year-long development, a suspicion now and then of overwriting, a mere whisper of a few words too many, but it's a solid and artfully worked script with a powerful emotional engine.

It consists of three internal monologues that follow the course of 24 hours in the life of a rural family, a Man (David Whiteley), a Woman (Sarah Sutherland) and a Girl (Erin Dewar). Each monologue is autonomous, touching the others not through dialogue, but through a complex pattern of echoes and repetitions. It's a device which reinforces not only the mutual isolation of each character but, poignantly, their unmet yearning to connect.

They are at first glance an 'ordinary' family living an unremarkable life somewhere in country Australia. It's a familiar landscape to anyone who has lived in a country town. The Man is a shopkeeper, his wife does housewifely duties, and their daughter is a schoolgirl whose major preoccupation is her crush on her schoolteacher. But, as Holloway begins to excavate their inner lives, it becomes clear that tragedy – as Chekhov understood profoundly – is not only the provenance of the large gesture. It exists in the smallest details of ordinary life: in the caress misunderstood, the moment missed, the dream unshared, despair unsaid and unheard.

In fact, *Red Sky Morning* is a play in which, quite literally, nothing happens, which is perhaps one of the hardest things to achieve successfully on stage. It begins with a missed moment of passion between the couple, when the Woman farts luxuriously in the bedroom, and their mutual embarrassment creates an impassable wall beyond which neither are able to reach, despite their longing for each other.

The Man goes to work, the Girl goes to school, the Woman waits for them to leave the house so she can begin drinking. Each moment of violent rebellion against the loneliness and tedium of their lives splutters out into impotent fantasy; the only character who can still express her rage is the Girl, and we suspect that she, too, will learn to push down her anger and despair, hiding it underneath the deadening normality of domestic routine.

The beast which haunts this family is represented by the recurring figure of a hallucinatory dog (like Les Murray's black dog, which he used, after Churchill, to describe his own black depressions). The Man is deeply, suicidally depressed, a weight which perhaps has sparked his wife's alcoholism. This profound dysfunction makes their daughter long for a 'proper' family, a family whose weaknesses don't expose her to shame and insecurity and, finally, terrible fear.

Director Sam Strong gives this complex, delicate play a production which is remarkable for its precision – very necessary, given the demands of the text – and its troubling, erotically charged darkness. Peter Mumford's design, moodily lit by Danny Pettingill, is a stylised Australian house floored with red earth, its walls defined by venetian blinds that can be snapped open and shut. Like the text, the design blurs the distinction between inside and outside, the hidden and the revealed.

The performances all rise to the challenges of the writing. Whiteley is almost the cliché of the decent, inarticulate country bloke, to the point where he is occasionally outshone by the other two actors (this might account for the odd moment of over-direction in his performance). Sutherland and Dewar give committed, focused performances, wringing out of the text its painfulness, violence and comedy.

If ever you need evidence that a production's process is reflected in what happens on stage, this is it. It certainly justifies Red Stitch's investment in Holloway, who is clearly a talent to watch. And it makes an intense, deeply absorbing hour in the theatre, a production that patiently accumulates power towards its devastating end.

Theatre Notes, September 13 2008

Blackbird

I might as well get the rave out of the way first.

I always suspected that this production of David Harrower's *Blackbird* was going to be the highlight of the 2008 MTC season. And as I hoped, this is easily the best MTC production this year. In fact, it's probably the best theatre I've seen under the MTC aegis since I started going to the theatre again four years ago. I'll wobble further on my superlatives, and claim that Peter Evans has delivered one of the best-judged productions of a text that I've seen anywhere.

In short, theatrenauts, this is an awesome production of an awesome play. *Blackbird* is a contemporary tragedy that does all the things a tragedy is supposed to do: it hammers your heart open, tears apart your moral certainties and leaves you with the pulsating mess of human damage leaking blood all over your hands. Harrower stands aside from judgment and instead places our moral capacity in conflict with our human empathy, opening out the complexities of relationship and self in a way that refuses the consolation of false annealment.

And, as director Peter Evans does in this production, Harrower manages all this with an absolute minimum of fuss. This is not just naturalism, it is uber-naturalism, and it demonstrates that this much-maligned theatrical form is far from dead. *Blackbird* is basically a dialogue between Ray (Greg Stone) and Una (Alison Bell) which takes place in real time, a fact reinforced by the clock on the wall ticking murderously through the silences. There is only one (very effective) theatrical trick in this play: for the rest, it relies on raw nerve. Its artfulness is invisible: text, direction, performance and production are presented in one seamless whole, so that in watching it the separate elements disappear, subsumed in one irresistible act of theatre.

The action takes place in a spectacularly filthy factory canteen. Christina Smith's set is in traverse, reinforcing the play's intimacy: a thin strip of floor, mercilessly lit by fluorescents, lies between the audience. On one side is a grubby white wall with a clock, on the other a door with a broken window patched by cardboard. Up-ended plastic chairs, a broken, overfilled plastic rubbish bin and a litter of half-eaten hamburgers, crushed coke cans and other detritus complete the squalor.

As is well known, in *Blackbird* Harrower investigates the explosive issue of paedophilia. Ray is man who, fifteen years earlier, had a three month relationship with Una which culminated in a sexual encounter in a boarding house, after which he panicked and abandoned her. At the time, Una was a bright, rebellious and precocious 12 year old. He was prosecuted and jailed, and has rebuilt his life under a new identity. But now Una has turned up at his workplace seeking – what? Revenge? Some kind of acknowledgement, some kind of closure?

What is gradually exposed through the play is how the past lives in the present for both of them. Ray has coped by totally erasing the past: he hotly denies several times that he is one of 'them', one of those men fatally attracted to children. No, this was a single moment of madness, a terrible mistake that almost wholly destroyed his life, which he has painstakingly built again from scratch: he will never transgress again. Una's sudden unheralded appearance fills him with panic: he shoves her into the canteen, terrified that she will be spotted by his workmates, that the shame that he has until now kept so secret will spill over his life like the trash over the room.

Una, on the other hand, has never forgotten. She thinks about what happened every day, and the events – their relationship, the prosecution and trial, her notoriety, her mother's condemnation – have warped her life. She is lonely, promiscuous, prone to relationships with abusive men. But what has most wounded her becomes less clear as they talk. Was it the abuse of her own nascent sexuality by an older man who should never have violated her trust? Was it her social isolation, as a victim of abuse? The way the language of police prosecution erased her own experience, so that she can no longer make sense of what happened? The moral condemnation of her own family?

Harrower corkscrews their conversation deeper and deeper into taboo areas, without ever tipping over into easy condemnation or exculpation. Both Una and Ray are unreliable narrators, neither able to withdraw from and contemplate this defining wound of their lives. We don't know whether to believe Ray when he says he is no longer sexually attracted to children. Una's desire for revenge is undermined by her greater desire for Ray. The ambiguities are held in suspension all the way through the performance.

The success of this sternly undecorated production relies almost wholly on the actors, and in Greg Stone and Alison Bell (leavened by a brief appearance by Georgia Flood) Evans has a dream cast. These are two great, emotionally precise performances, elegantly mediating between the said and the unsaid. What both have mastered is Harrower's truncated, spare language, the stuttering articulation that stumbles against what cannot be said, which flowers into painful monologues or equally painful silences before exploding into a cathartic moment of passion, violence and even perverse joy. The play is riveting in part because the balance of power continually shifts, and these emotional movements are faultlessly modulated. I'm not sure that I've seen either of these actors in better form.

Maybe the word for this production is unflinching. Evans' version of *Who's Afraid of Virginia Woolf* excavated, with a profound compassion, the pain embedded in Albee's play; this production has the same kind of emotional courage, but goes much deeper. The devastating ending strips away all our skins of moral protection, leaving us with the unpalatable fact of unhealed damage. We are given no maps with which to navigate it, no place in which to hide from its implications. It reminds us of the unnegotiable complexity of human pain and desire. It's brilliant, necessary theatre.

Theatre Notes, July 24 2008

Patti Smith

> Years ago, an eighty-year-old woman won first prize at a dance contest in Jerez de la Frontera. She was competing against beautiful women and young girls with waists as supple as water, but all she did was raise her arms, throw back her head and stamp her foot on the floor. In that gathering of muses and angels, beautiful forms and beautiful smiles, who could have won but her moribund duende, sweeping the floor with its wings of rusty knives?
>
> *Play and Theory of the Duende*, Federico García Lorca

Bring on your wings of rusty knives, Patti. Bring on your soaring, shamanic voice, your unbrushed hair, your face with its stern profile of an Incan priest, your skinny upraised arms. The loved dead gather to listen and the living rise up and cheer, they rise up with their shining eyes, they rise up and you smile like a little girl, or you sag suddenly, tired and 60 years old, vulnerable and needing a sip of water, needing to touch someone's shoulder, you turn away and turn back and the chords begin and from nowhere, again, how do you do it, from nowhere the duende enters and here there is no tiredness, no pain, no death, only the song of celebration, the rebellious dance of living itself, the heartbeat triumphant into eternity, for this moment, this moment only.

> All we do is for that frightened thing we call Love, want and lack—
> O but how many in their solitude weep aloud like me.
>
> 'Wichita Vortex Sutra #3', Allen Ginsberg

Or gentle in a theatre, leaning into the microphone, leaning into the music, the piano rushing like a river you can never enter twice, only now, shy and inhaling all that water, glancing over to Philip Glass who sits at the keyboard soberly possessed by his hands. And the words struggle out of your mouth and transform the air we breathe, the words are your own and you weave them into a paean, an elegy, a chant that celebrates living with all its imperfections, all its fleshly mistakes, and the girl next to me is weeping, what has she remembered, what has she touched in the soft, dark vaults of her body?

And yes, this is poetry, one flame that leaps from mouth to ear to heart and burns the living and the dead, no distance here, no mask to save us from ourselves, only the cleansing rush of laughter, that naughty Buddhist Allen, bless and forgive him for he knew what he did all the time, an old man in his old body with the soul of a damaged, hungry, joyous child, an old man who wrestled with shame until it danced as a fiery angel, an old man who lived his life and wrote it down in poems, uncensoring and tender, with a hand that smelt of mortality and sex. A simple thing, the gifts of those who loved a poet and pledge them in his name, saying this is what I can give, these things I make with my hands and my voice, unchained from the page and in flight, here they are, blazing wings and broken feathers, a body of light and music, poems, in your desiring body, now.

> The world is holy! The soul is holy! The skin is holy! The nose is holy! The tongue and cock and asshole holy!
> Everything is holy! everybody's holy! everywhere is holy! everyday is in eternity! Everyman's an angel!
>
> 'Footnote to Howl', Allen Ginsberg

Patti Smith in Concert, Hamer Hall, Melbourne Festival.

Theatre Notes, October 14 2008

The Women of Troy

Sophocles is supposed to have remarked of Euripides that, while Sophocles portrayed men as they ought to be, Euripides showed them as they are. It's an observation that goes to the heart of his drama. While Sophocles and Aeschylus wrote heroic tragedy, Euripides was concerned with the everyday: his characters were often the despised and marginalised, the women, children, slaves and functionaries caught in the unforgiving machinery of larger events. Euripides was, in fact, Western drama's first realist.

Yet even on Euripides' terms, *The Women of Troy* is an odd play. For all the archaic beauty of the original text, it has an air of unsettling modernity. It's a play of almost brutal simplicity that crystallises the traumatic shock of the aftermath of war. Originally part of a full-scale tragic trilogy that looked at different aspects of the war on Troy, *The Women of Troy* seems to have been a kind of coda, the final comment on the tumultuous events that preceded it. The other two plays are now lost, leaving us this fragment in which nothing happens because the worst already has.

The other thing to note about Euripides is that, for all his mythical framing, he was writing directly about contemporary events. When *The Women of Troy* was first performed, in 415BC, Athens was mired in the Peloponnesian War with Sparta and was about to launch its disastrous expedition to conquer Sicily, an invasion which ended with the humiliating defeat of Athens in 404BC. In the various conflicts, Euripides had ample opportunity to observe the cruelty with which each side treated its civilian captives: most commonly, the men were put to death and the women and children enslaved. Sometimes this happened to entire cities.

Barrie Kosky and Tom Wright's adaptation, a Malthouse Theatre/Sydney Theatre Company co-production, highlights this realism, bringing Euripides' steady gaze to bear on contemporary events. They've created a production which is probably as close as we can get to an experience of classical tragedy, which looks unblinkingly into catastrophe: from the beginning, its outcome is inevitable and unavoidable. It reveals that this is a play of our time as much as of Euripides, at once true to its ancient roots and opening up its contemporary aptness. And it's bleak indeed: no chink of light pierces the darkness. The emotional effect is cumulative, and ultimately shattering. It's extraordinary theatre.

This twofold vision of the ancient and the contemporary is evident from the moment you enter the theatre and see that the auditorium is shaped like an amphitheatre. Every seat is draped in white; the fabric is reflective and has a weird effect on the fluorescent lighting, which is already alienating and harsh. We look down on a naked stage, which is dominated by a huge back wall constructed of old lockers, stacked like bricks up to the ceiling.

It begins with a figure draped in black and crowned in a tiara being pushed onto the stage on a flatbed trolley by a guard. The guard is wearing a white mask, like those worn by people who deal with corpses, which is subtly configured to look like the masks on Hoplite helmets worn by Greek soldiers. The woman – for we know at once it is a woman – is standing in the pose made famous through the photograph taken in Abu Ghraib, balancing precariously, her arms stretched out, trembling with strain, on either side. The guard (Kyle Rowling) takes a photograph with his mobile phone, and then begins to strip the woman's finery – her rings, her bracelets, her necklace, her tiara – putting them in a clear plastic bag. He leaves her face draped, anonymous and blind, helpless, until he also takes her sumptuous dress.

At last she is revealed as Hecuba (Robyn Nevin), former Queen of Troy, standing in her shift on a cardboard box as ordered by the guard, her face bruised and bloodied, her hair shorn. Then the guard leaves and wheels in the other women, also cowled in black: also brutalised, anonymous, stripped of all civic rights as they are of their clothes. They are the theatrical image of what Giorgio Agamben called 'naked life', the 'state of exception' that defines the sovereign power of the State.

What follows is the summary allocation of the women – in particular, Hecuba's daughters – as spoils of war. Some have been distributed to the Greek soldiers by lot, some will be shot. The play simply consists of the women waiting to discover their fate, and finishes when we know what happens to each of them.

The adaptation hacks what is already a minimal play to its bones, hewing closely to its original dramaturgy. Tom Wright's language is chillingly effective: utterly plain, with the weight of tragic necessity in every word. Basically, three things occur: Cassandra – the virgin cursed with second sight by Apollo after she refused his advances – is taken away and given to Agamemnon. The heavily pregnant Andromache, who enters with her son Astynax (Giorgios Tsmamoudakis or William Larkin) is sent to be the slave of Achilles, who killed her husband Hector, and finds that her small son is to be murdered. And Helen of Troy, whose abscondment with Paris started the whole thing, is given a short trial by Menelaus (Arthur Dignam) and Hecuba, and condemned. These three women are played by Melita Jurisic, making the play effectively a duet between Nevin and Jurisic.

This brutal reality is punctuated by singing, a diverse range of music which includes Dowland, Mozart, Bizet and Slovenian folk songs. The music is a lament for everything that the action of the play denies and destroys – love, beauty, harmony – and is the single human expression remaining to the women.

As in conventional Greek tragedy, the violence occurs offstage, a most effective means of engendering imagination. We hear offstage screaming and gunshots, and we see the fear before it and the effect afterwards – most desolately when the half mad Cassandra is raped in one of the lockers by the guard and returns, her bloodstained pants around her ankles, hobbling and violated, babbling incoherently of her marriage to Agamemnon, or when the blood-drenched corpse of the little boy is carried onto the stage.

This production is particularly effective in how it exploits the banality of atrocity. One aspect of torture is how it transforms ordinary objects, even household items, into instruments of pain. Here there is a rather grim moment when the guard walks across the stage, fiddles in a tool box and returns with a huge awl. We have no idea what he is going to use it for, and don't want to imagine. When the women are allocated, they are put in cardboard boxes which are sealed with masking tape and wheeled off, reinforcing their dehumanised status as cargo, mere trophies of war whose identities are not only erased but irrelevant.

What carries the grief and crushing inevitability of the horror enfolding these women is the performances. As Hecuba, an old woman witnessing the destruction of her life, Nevin is the lynchpin of the play: she is present on stage all through, and she is the medium through which we experience the tragedy. This is an unmissable performance: that voice vibrates in your bones, raging, lamenting, sorrowful, utterly broken and defeated and yet stubbornly refusing to be demeaned, even in this ultimate degradation. Melita Jurisic in her three roles is a brilliant foil, the hysteric counterpoint to Nevin's stoic refusals.

Perhaps what is most impressive about this production is its refusal to reach for easy theatrical manipulations. The contemporary allusions are never gratuitous: rather, they emerge as inevitable aspects of the reality this play is revealing. It's heartbreaking, but Kosky's restraint means that the effect goes deeper than tears. His directorial tact represents the reality of war without cheaply exploiting it: this seems to me to be a production of exemplary honesty, that openly and without showiness acknowledges its own artifice and by doing so reinforces the horrific realities behind it. It's a cry of grief, a keening, that resonates in its own present and then leaves us to deal with the aftermath. Because the worst part about it is that you know that it's all true.

Theatre Notes, November 20 2008

Dust

The phrase 'community theatre' is liable to conjure images of earnest amateur thespians giving demonstrations in coarse acting. But this is hugely misleading.

Community-based companies are responsible for some of our most vital political theatre. In the hands of companies like Alice Springs–based Big hArt – who created *Ngapartji Ngapartji*, a work which looked at the impact of the Maralinga nuclear tests on the Pitjantjatjara people – it becomes a powerful conduit for the concerns of specific communities. This is work that's neither earnest nor polemic, but rather a reminder that theatre is the most human of art forms.

In Melbourne, Donna Jackson, founder of Footscray's Women's Circus, has been making exemplary community theatre for years. Recently she's been working with trade unions. Her spectacular show *We Built This City* was a site-specific work created with former Hunters and Collectors frontman Mark Seymour, and featured, among other things, a surreal ballet of bulldozers.

Dust – an exploration of the grim history of the Australian asbestos industry – is their latest collaboration. Again a site-specific work, it was made originally for the Mechanic's Institute in Ballarat and remounted in the beautiful Victorian space of Williamstown Town Hall, in Melbourne's west.

It demonstrates Jackson's talent for accessing the energies of diverse community groups. The show is backed by the Asbestos Diseases Society and its 60-voice choir includes singers from the Victorian Trades Union Choir, local Williamstown songsters Willin Wimmin and the Ballarat Arts Academy Ensemble.

The show is in two halves. In the first, the audience saunters around the huge space of the town hall visiting acts – short plays, a magician, visual installations – in booths on either side, set up as in a fair. The second is a more conventional musical, in which stories glimpsed in the booths are expanded through song.

Its major mode is comedy – James Hardie is represented, for instance, by a corporate woman (Laura Lattuada), who is having problems with her shonky hairdresser before an important address to shareholders.

What binds the show together is Jackson's sharp satirical eye and the driving guitar of Mark Seymour. Seymour's songs have the rock'n'roll power and lyricism of Bruce Springsteen, and pack a huge emotional punch.

Without a trace of earnestness, but plenty of anger and grief, *Dust* relates the corporate scandal and individual tragedy of the history of asbestos manufacturing. It's straight-up, moving and enormously entertaining. Community theatre at its very best.

The Australian, December 2 2008

Grace

Grace, a 'theatrical essay' written by Mick Gordon and philosophy professor AC Grayling, presents me with something of a dilemma. How do you respond to a perfectly inoffensive play that embodies everything you hate in the theatre?

It is, after all, honest in its intentions. It's well written, in that erudite, self-aware, slightly deprecating way that's copyrighted by well-educated Englishmen. And it's given a handsome production by Marion Potts in her MTC debut. It's carefully cast and directed, and attractively designed. Every scene is thoughtfully shaped and performed, and the dramaturgy bounces along.

There is, in the sense of watching a decent play decently done, little to complain about. The MTC delivers what it promises in the brochure: a play that discusses the pros and cons of religion, and which will provide plenty of fodder for dinner-table debate.

Grace (Noni Hazlehurst) is a female Richard Dawkins, a science professor who is a prominent militant atheist. She is married to Tony (Brian Lipson), a non-observant Jew. In Grace's view, religion is humanity's original sin, irrational and superstitious belief that entrenches ignorance and violence.

The family spirals into crisis when their son Tom (Grant Cartwright), a lawyer who at the beginning of the play is defending Islamist militants, announces that he wants to be an Anglican priest. Grace is bitterly outraged. Tony, caught uncomfortably in the middle, attempts to mediate between the two. And Tom's Asian girlfriend, Ruth (Leah Vandenberg), then announces she is pregnant.

Thus we have the major ethnic and religious points of view of contemporary Britain neatly embodied on stage through a family soap opera. And thus – sensitively, articulately, with impeccable theatrical dress and that deprecating humour – we get to witness the various arguments for and against religion.

It is so consciously shaped to its intellectual purpose that I was possessed by a screaming tedium. I wanted to grasp Mr Gordon and Professor Grayling by their ties and ask them, *Why*? Why didn't you just write an essay, instead of constructing this creaky illustrative plot? What, I wanted to know, is the *point*?

They might quite rightly retort that theatre can be anything you like, even this kind of un-theatre which reduces the possibilities of the stage to an animated lecture hall. Certainly, if you want a civilised debate about religion, this is the play for you. But if you want actual drama, you're better off reading Dostoevsky.

The Australian, January 1 2009

The War of the Roses

> History is the discourse of power.
>
> Michel Foucault, *Society Must Be Defended*

> Here's a good world the while! Why, who's so gross
> That cannot see this palpable device?
>
> *Richard III*, III, 6

> Borders are always drawn in blood and states marked out with graves.
>
> Ratko Mladi, Serbian Army Chief of Staff during the Balkan War

Beginning with King John and ending with Henry VIII, the ten works known as Shakespeare's History Plays dramatise five generations of brutal power struggle in mediaeval England. Although they were never written to be performed as cycles or as single epic works, the contemporary stage has seen a number of notable versions of the History Plays as epic theatre. Peter Hall inaugurated the Royal Shakespeare Company with a cycle of eight plays, *The Wars of the Roses*, in 1963; again with the RSC, Adrian Noble made *The Plantagenets*, an adaptation of the second tetralogy in 1988. Michael Bogdanov directed another famous seven-play adaptation, *The Wars of the Roses*, at the English Shakespeare Company in 1987. And so on.

Less illustriously, Bell Shakespeare did their own version, *Wars of the Roses*, in 2005. That production begged the question: why should twenty-first century Australians be interested in plays that are so crucially concerned with the question of Englishness, and which in fact have been formative of the fiction of English national consciousness? Can our staging these plays be anything more than a colonial gesture of defiance or obsequiousness, either being different sides of the same cultural coin? Or is there something else going on in these plays that can elicit a proper contemporary attention? Is there still something they can reveal?

Tom Wright and Benedict Andrews answer these questions authoritatively with their Sydney Theatre Company adaptation, *The*

War of the Roses. Rendering eight plays in four acts over eight hours, this is a work of massive intellectual and theatrical ambition that will be impossible to encompass properly here. Trying to think about it is rather like a pleasurable version of Hercules' adventures with the Hydra: every time I address a thought, another two spring up and demand attention. But, as Wittgenstein so comfortably says, one has to begin somewhere.

The War of the Roses is theatre of a rare and desolating beauty. It generates its startling visual richness from a poverty of illusion. Andrews strips the stage to its back walls and finds for each act a single informing (and utterly transparent) theatrical metaphor. This lyric simplicity has the effect of framing and foregrounding Shakespeare's language. It highlights the literary beauty, wit and power of the speeches, not by reverent attention to their formalities, but through excessive physical demands on the performers, which excavate the visceral truths of poetry.

In these plays, *The War of the Roses* is no longer plural. It is a single war, an Orwellian total war without end, a war in which peace is only war by other means: a war very close to that within which we live. And yes, in this intellectually epic realisation, Wright and Andrews demonstrate that there is indeed a reason to mount these plays in this day and time. Yes, they are parables that concern themselves with much more than narrow questions of British nationalism or pretty kings. Yes, in these old stories of English kings we can see, reflected in their faces, our own complicities, our own shames. They reflect for us the nightmare of our history, the blind, murderous tragedy that continues in our own time.

Power never goes out of fashion.

Power

Giving it the proper capitals, Shakespearean critic Jan Kott called it the Grand Mechanism: the eternally revolving machine of History that raises high and casts low, so that he who at first believes he makes history becomes at last history's plaything, the executioner executed. In the History Plays, the primal violence that inaugurates the State is laid bare; the illusions that conceal its bloody origins are torn roughly aside. Pomp and ritual, the notion of justice, the vision of an 'anointed king' whom God blesses, or a President with a personal phone line to the Almighty, all fly up like the painted scenery on a stage to reveal a bleak world driven by the machinery of power, in which the only thing that counts is who is stronger. In this world, the world that Shakespeare brought to artistic fruition in the dark, bestial universe of *King Lear*, history is Godless and bereft of meaning.

The wheel turns: the pretender murders the king and seizes the crown, only to become himself a victim. Thus, as Camus sardonically observed, you might witness the true meaning of Revolution. Hegel thought history had a deeper and rational purpose, the evolution of the human spirit towards freedom and enlightenment: Marx, following Hegel, thought it a mechanism that would generate freedom for the masses enslaved by capital. But Shakespeare's view of history is altogether starker.

It is, in many ways, a pre-Christian vision. As a young man, Shakespeare encountered the Latin poets, in particular Seneca, whose bloody tragedies influenced works like *Titus Andronicus*, and Lucan. Marlowe's translation of Lucan's *Pharsalia*, his epic poem about the Roman Civil Wars, was popular in Elizabethan England when Shakespeare was writing the Henry VI plays, and may in fact have been their model. In this poem, Lucan describes the cosmos as a malfunctioning machine facing inevitable collapse under its own weight, a universe without meaning or purpose. Certainly in both works, ruinous civil wars lead to the creation of a tyrant – Caesar in one, Richard III in another.

Like Lucan and Seneca, Shakespeare saw history as an endless wheel of pain, a cycle of suffering that serves no purpose but its own continuation, and whose only production is corpses. The wheel turns and turns again: blood oils the axle, its iron rim crushes the human body under its irresistible weight, the next king rises and murders and falls. And for what? For the golden circle that is without beginning or end, the empty crown of state, the beautiful delusion that, once it has seduced its victims, reveals its true face:

> ... for within the hollow crown
> That rounds the mortal temples of a king
> Keeps Death his court...
>
> *Richard II*, III, 2

Time

Eight hours, eight plays, one hundred years. Shakespeare's medium was time, his tool was language. He used language to sculpt time, revealing the sinews of History, its dynamic, dramatic form. Andrews and Wright have sculpted Shakespeare, cutting back the eight plays to their essential speeches, laying bare the bones of language and time that underlie the flesh of history.

The War of the Roses is an oratorio, a series of soliloquies made by people in agonising solitude. The protagonists are caught outside historical action, in the isolating interstices when they become conscious of the implications of their acts. As the audience, we become their silent witnesses, their co-conspirators, their allies and enemies and subjects. It's a bold reworking that seems to create theatre at its purest and most essential, and yet the result continuously demands comparison to other arts, demonstrating its essential impurity: you think it is pure music, pure sculpture, pure poetry. Pure vision, pure dream.

Wright and Andrews have loosened the self-consciousness of the Renaissance stage, summoning an earlier idea of theatre. As the Shakespearean scholar Anne Richter noted, mediaeval drama implied both audience and player in one transcendent reality: the Easter plays were originatory rituals, where time future and time past were resolved into an infinite present. Shakespeare's plays were part of a reality that splintered this holistic pageantry: his plays were the culmination of the secularisation of the dramatic stage, the zenith of the self-contained, self-conscious, articulate world that was the great invention of the Elizabethans.

Yet when the fire-curtain silently rises on the first stunning image of the cycle – Cate Blanchett as Richard II seated in a throne, surrounded by her unmoving courtiers, while an endless fall of gold leaf rains down onto the stage – what we see is not a Renaissance image, nor even a modern image. It is a mediaeval image, recalling in its hieratic formality nothing so much as the famous portrait of Richard II that is now in Westminster Abbey. And like the mediaeval pageants, this is a theatre that directly addresses us, which seeks to makes us implicit in its world. Through the four acts, we are begged, importuned, commanded, rebuked; we weep and laugh and are bewitched. We are not apart from this world. It even makes us flinch in immediate, visceral fear at the end of Part One, in an extraordinary coup of lighting: a huge shadow seems to fall from the top of the theatre as the curtain closes, as if a wall of darkness is falling onto us, a winged omen of dread. This theatre is more than a mirror. It is us.

There are of course still dialogic scenes – most notably the brilliant scene in *Richard III* when Richard (Pamela Rabe), the killer of Anne's (Cate Blanchett) father and husband, seduces her as she follows the corpse of Henry VI, whom Richard has also murdered; or the scenes between Falstaff (John Gaden) and the wild, contemptuous young Hal (Ewen Leslie) in Henry V. But these play out in relief against a frieze of grinding existential solitude, and call into question the very basis of human communication. This is what makes *The War of the Roses* a contemporary production, rather than a nostalgic glance back to a romantic history: each character here is as pitilessly exposed, as cruelly alone, as any character in Beckett.

The War of the Roses begins and ends with two tragedies, *Richard II* and *Richard III*, which between them comprehend the decadence of power. They rhyme in more than name. Where *Richard II* is accompanied for more than an hour with a rain of gold, *Richard III* is performed on a children's playground on which falls, silently and mercilessly, an endless rain of ash that blurs and conceals the corpses that accumulate about the stage.

In *Richard II*, we witness something more profound than mere regicide: we see the death of the idea of the king, the humanising of the sacred mouth of God to a mere mortal man, a foreshadowing of Lear's realisation that he is but a 'poor bare, forked stick'. In *Richard III*, we see what happens when desacralised power is put into conscious action. Richard II believes, up to the moment of his death and despite his forced abdication, that he is a king by divine right; Richard III knows he is king by right of his own malice, deception and violence. Richard II is a melancholy dream of a vain but sacred illusion that is ultimately destroyed by the concealed power that sustains it; Richard III a terrifying vision of amoral brutality.

In between the two tragedies, six plays are compressed into two acts. These follow the histories of three King Henrys, IV, V and VI. We witness the remorseless mechanism that is the engine of historical tragedy: an abattoir, an endless parade of death played out across the rich garden of the kingdom, ultimately reducing it to the final desert of ash, an endless winter of discontent.

In Part One, Act Two, a conflation of *Henry IV* and *V*, the stage is utterly bare, the only decoration to the action the guitarist Stefan Gregory, who stands by a giant amp, his back to the audience, picking out a growling lyric on his guitar. This act plays out the crisis of royal legitimacy, reminding us that the etymology of the word 'royal' is the same as the word 'real' (and that the Real was also a currency of the Spanish realm: gold and divine authority, the ultimate realities, were – and still are – closely linked). Henry IV (Robert Menzies), the murderer of Richard II, the anointed king, is haunted by doubt in the legitimacy of his power. He rules a realm riven by rebellion and is shamed by his wastrel son, Hal (Ewen Leslie), a stark contrast to the bellicose young Hotspur (Luke Mullins), who is fomenting rebellion against the monarch.

Henry IV's desired legitimacy only comes after his death, when Hal, now Henry V, forswears his debauch. The state demands sacrifice for its inauguration and legitimation, and Henry expiates the sin of regicide with French blood. Defeated France marries Henry V in the person of Katherine of France (Luke Mullins), who, in one of the more chilling images of the play, rises from the floor as a French corpse covered with blood, and is washed and dressed in wedding clothes before being offered to Henry V.

This foreshadows the mechanical violence of Part Two, Act One, which follows the conflicts between the houses of York and Lancaster, symbolised by the white rose and the red. This slaughter takes place on a ground of flowers, a garden that becomes a battlefield. Each character plucks out their assigned colour in the legendary scene in the garden, when the nobles chose the red rose or the white to indicate their loyalties. But the colours are given a darker meaning: they are echoed in the blood spat into the face of actors, to signify murder, and the flour thrown over their bodies as corpse pallor. The flour hangs in the light like the phosphorous bombs hung over Gaza at Christmas time.

The Players

A hundred years, five kings. Outside the Globe Theatre, a sign read *Totus mundus agit histrionem*: All the world's a stage. It's a sentiment as ancient as Petronius, who is credited with its invention, and it was a commonplace of the Elizabethan age, when theatre was considered the mirror of the times. No-one worked this metaphor with more variety, wit and point than Shakespeare.

This metaphor is woven through the entire production, but there are telling moments when it steps into the foreground. One is in *Richard III*, when Richard is plagued by nightmares before the Battle of Bosworth Field, assailed in his dreams by all those he has murdered. Each ghost curses Richard – Pamela Rabe in bloodied t-shirt and black trousers, her hair curtaining her face like an evil Joey Ramone – and blesses his enemy, Richmond (Luke Mullins). And then they all gather front stage, as actors do when the show is finished, and bow. And we see that the stage is Richard's mind, a macabre playground where at first he is king of the castle, the playground bully and liar murdering his way to the top of the class with macabre glee. When the ghosts bow to us, heedless of death since the worst has already happened to them, Richard discovers that he is no longer playing history. Now, like all his forbears, all those kings who thought they were the authors of their own action, Richard finds that he is merely history's plaything, after all. The role is playing him.

In this moment and others like it, we are also made pricklingly aware that Richard is an actor, a player who is, moreover, a woman, Pamela Rabe, who after the play is over will walk off the stage, strip off her costume and take a shower. This double consciousness of performance is a particularly Shakespearean trope, and Andrews has exploited it to the hilt in *The War of the Roses*. The ambiguity of the Player King – the king whose pomp is all performance, the actor whose performance is all kingliness, each reflecting the perilous illusions and realities of the other – is a constant motif through the History Plays and the tragedies, and its double meaning expands still further in this production in the ash-strewn playground of *Richard III*.

The metaphor generates its power from the compelling reality of the performances: if we did not believe in the cruel grace of Richard II, if we were sceptical of the grief opened on the whetstone of Bolingbroke's ambition, if the lewdness of Hal and Falstaff played false or Anne's tragic death were laughable instead of pathetic and sad, then the mundane reality beneath the playing would have no power to enrich our watching, and to unite our quotidian and imaginative worlds into a single complex reality.

What does it mean to 'believe' a performance? This production gives plenty of occasions to consider this question: the acting is superlative, as good as you will see anywhere, with performances of breadth and disturbing depths, with nuance and skill and delicacy and the kind of passion that hooks the heart on barbed wire. To 'believe' an actor means, I think, to become more conscious, to open the imagination to the full scope of emotional possibility. It means to understand better the meaning of our own humanity. It is not always comfortable.

This is the final production of the STC's Actors Company, the beautiful dream of a permanent ensemble that foundered on the Scylla and Charybdis of Sydney public opinion and uneven programming. To my mind miraculously, the Actors Company produced some unforgettable work along the way. And it seems to me that if it took three years to make this show, and *The War of the Roses* were all that the Actors Company produced, it was well worth the bother. After all, there are companies in Europe – much lauded by critics here who have been very quick to claim that the Actors Company was a waste of resources – who have done no more than work on a single production for three years.

Every time I've seen the Actors Company, I've been impressed by the fluidity of its performance, the depth of the ensemble's dynamic on stage. *The War of the Roses* takes this several steps further, with Andrews' direction springing off those relationships to generate the terrifying alienation that is the harsh lesson of this production. Above all else, one is watching a practised group at work, by now polished by three years' daily intimacy. The stage glows with the genius of the ensemble, which generates a lucidity of performance that you simply cannot attain in the job-to-job schedule of normal acting work.

A month into the season, I didn't see a single weak actor, and the two guest actors – Cate Blanchett and Robert Menzies – sit brilliantly within the cast. And this show features individual performances that are simply remarkable, portrayals that deserve to be lauded and remembered years hence as moments when greatness graced our stage.

Images that remain with me: Cate Blanchett as Richard II, luminous and sly, the image of arrogant wit and grace, heartless and heartbreaking, walking over broken glass to the crown; Robert Menzies as Bolingbroke, Henry IV, driven by anger, grief, regret and bitterness, surrounded by his likenesses in a macabre dance that stirred real horror; Ewen Leslie as

Henry V, a revelatory performance, charismatically sexual, violent, his body drenched with honey and oil and blood in a diabolical anointing of royalty; John Gaden, brilliant and desolately moving as John of Gaunt and Edmund Duke of York, wickedly knowing and irrepressibly lustful as Falstaff; Marta Dusseldorp, terrifying in her hatred and ambition as Margaret of Anjou, teaching Queen Elizabeth (Amber McMahon) how to curse; Eden Falk, fumblingly innocent and somehow frightening as the child king Henry VI; Pamela Rabe, wickedly juvenile, blackly witty, clumsy, terrifyingly amoral and charismatic as Richard III. But none of these moments would be possible without the context around them.

And now, having reached this pitch of real greatness, the Actors Company is to end, to be replaced by a humbler workshop version of fresh faces that, according to the 2009 program, will be mainly working behind the scenes, 'refining new work in the rehearsal room'. No doubt it is a sensible decision, given the controversy that has surrounded the Actors Company; perhaps Sydney will heave a huge sigh, to be relieved of such difficult and expensive beauty. But I can't help wishing that Cate Blanchett and Andrew Upton had held their nerve and persisted in the grand folly of the Actors Company. Having seen the brilliant work that is *The War of the Roses*, dropping the company that made it seems like nothing so much as a terrible failure of imagination.

Theatre Notes, February 15 2009

Wretch

A prison is a place where people are watched, and know that they are watched. In these spaces, behaviour shapes itself beneath the pressure of the assumed gaze. Human action becomes, in a disturbing sense, pure performance. As the Abu Ghraib photos brought home brutally by implicating all who looked on them in the act of torture, there can be an uncomfortable element of sadism in the act of looking.

It's an irony of history that the man who first theorised total surveillance, the Utilitarian philosopher Jeremy Bentham, was an influential progressive. The panopticon – the institution in which an inmate is watched all the time – has become the symbol of the repressive surveillance state; and yet Bentham opposed slavery, campaigned for the decriminalisation of homosexuality and advocated rights for women. For all his humanitarian views, the chilly intellect in the idea of the panopticon makes mere brutalisation seem almost friendly.

Plays set in prison enact this discomforting element in the relationship between actor and audience. They derive their unsettling power from a meta-theatrical consciousness of the parallels between theatre and prison, heightening the awareness of the mutual confinement of the watchers and the watched, and dramatising the predatory gaze of the audience. This is true of plays as formally various as Athol Fugard's *The Island*, Jean Genet's *Deathwatch* or Peter Weiss' *Marat/Sade*. And Angus Cerini's *Wretch* is yet another.

Wretch is in many ways a wholly uncomfortable experience. Marg Howell's confronting design transforms La Mama Theatre, almost placing the audience inside the white box of the set. The friendly stairs are hidden completely, which radically changes the nature of the space: all that is visible is a floor and overarching ceiling of institutional white tiles, illuminated harshly by fluorescent lights.

The two performers are already seated on stage when the audience enters. When we sit down, we know we are as visible to the actors on the stage as they are to us, and their exposure is a reflection of our own: we cannot conceal from ourselves that our watching is active. As witnesses, guards, silent bystanders, we are implicated in this act of theatre and, by extension, in its social meaning.

The fictional conceit of the script – the co-winner of the 2007 Patrick White Playwrights' Award – is that it is visiting hour in prison, where a mother (Susie Dee, who co-directs this piece with Cerini) is visiting her criminal son (Angus Cerini). At first, as the banal conversation unfolds into an argument about cigarettes, *Wretch* appears to be a naturalistic piece enacted in real time, but this soon shifts into another, much more heightened register. Cerini's densely poetic text attacks language at its most brutalised and grotesque, and wrings out of it a starkly lyric beauty. The play itself sculpts experience into a single, unbearable present, where the past erupts in sudden psychotic shifts, beautifully signalled by Kelly Ryall's sound design and Richard Vabre's lighting.

The young criminal in *Wretch* bears striking similarities to the 15-year-old boy in Cerini's extraordinary 2007 show *Detest*. Although they clearly ring fictional variations on each other, they are not the same man: the story in common with both is that of a young man who beats to death the killer and rapist of an old woman. Here the abjection of Cerini's brutalised character is, if possible, even more exposed: but this time it's seen in relationship to his mother, a former street prostitute who is suffering from breast cancer. She has had one mastectomy, and is facing another; but we know as well as she does that she is dying.

Possibly only Susie Dee – whom I last saw on stage 15 years ago – could match Cerini's style of extreme grotesquerie, which marries outrageous, even Hogarthian, caricature to a pitiable yet complex humanity. Slouched on stage, their bodies somehow deformed and twisted under the lights, Dee and Cerini are two tragic clowns, creatures whose abjection is so extreme, so humiliating, that our witnessing is painful. And yet they are stubborn, they make us laugh, and there are telling moments when the slyness of their understanding, their subversive humour, slide in and slash away any possibility of patronising pity.

This doomed pair confront each other, accuse each other, hate each other, humiliate each other. They reveal their brutalising histories, and we understand that both of them have always, from the moment of their births, been imprisoned: by lack, by cultural deprivation, by the inability to articulate their desires.

We know there is no redemption for either of them, just as there is no escape from our gaze. And yet, just as clearly, we see how much they love each other. There is no moral to this story (for which, more than anything, I thank Cerini); just the fact of their love, in the midst of so much ugliness. And the difficult act of looking.

Theatre Notes, February 23 2009

Peer Gynt

Peer Gynt. What a loser! Liar, narcissist, storyteller, dreamer, wild boy, arms dealer, Emperor of the Self, so fixated on his own desires that he loses himself altogether. Sinless because there isn't enough of him to sin with. He's saved by a song. (Or is he?) Saved by love. (Or is he?) Kept alive in the heart of a woman. Or was that him? Did he exist? (Do any of us exist?) What is he doing in this work of theatre? Is it a work of theatre? What is a work of theatre?

Who is Peer Gynt? He doesn't know. He jumped out of the brain of a Norwegian playwright one hot summer in 1867. Henrik Ibsen was an expatriate in Italy, then in the midst of war: as Garibaldi marched against Rome to eliminate the Papacy, Ibsen grumbled his way through various Italian beauty spots, his crazy epic poem spiralling recklessly out of the brutally hot sirocco that hit Ischia that year, so that he rose in his nightshirt sometimes because his head was so full of verse, writing down his octosyllabics and decasyllabics, the iambics, trochaics, dactylics, anapaestics and amphibrachs that all translators claim are impossible to translate into English. On a day of 46 degrees, Ibsen sent the first three acts to his publisher. After a minor earthquake sparked his famous physical cowardice, Ibsen fled Ischia for Sorrento, then Naples and Pompeii, and finally Rome, where he finished the poem in October. It was published in Scandinavia a month later.

Unlike Ibsen's previous epic *Brand*, which featured a noble protagonist, *Peer Gynt* met mixed responses. The poem was eviscerated by Norway's most influential critic, Clemens Petersen, who called it an 'intellectual swindle', and declared that it was not poetry. Georg Brandes, another critic, said: 'Ibsen's poem is neither beautiful nor true; what acrid pleasure can any poet find in defiling humanity like this?' After his fury (Ibsen was a bitter hater of his critics), his most illuminating answer to his critics is in an inscription he wrote in a book: 'To live is to war with trolls in heart and soul. / To write is to sit in judgement on oneself.'

In all its unstageable recklessness, *Peer Gynt* is a pitiless self-portrait of a man fleeing the most essential conflicts within himself, endlessly seduced by his own trolls. Ibsen wasn't admired by people like James Joyce or Sigmund Freud for no reason: he was one of the first modern writers to externalise the demons of the unconscious, and *Peer Gynt* was the first of his extended explorations of the potent truths of nightmare and fantasy, the trolls beneath the skin of mundane reality.

Its fantastic elements mean that *Peer Gynt* is, like Goethe's *Faust*, famously unstageable. (Hence the joke in *Educating Rita*: How does one solve the staging problems in *Peer Gynt*? Answer: Do it on the radio.) In fact, in his astonishing production at the Victorian College of the Arts, it's debatable whether Daniel Schlusser has staged the play at all. He has rather conducted a parallel examination to Ibsen's of himself. He delves beneath the skin of Ibsen's text, reaching into its prior impulses in an attempt to summon the demons that lurk in contemporary realities. This production of *Peer Gynt*, performed with the VCA Acting Company 2009 and VCA Alumni at the Victorian College of the Arts' Space 28, ambitiously extends the explorations begun in Schlusser's productions of *A Dollhouse* and *Life is a Dream*. Here Ibsen's nightmare becomes a fragmentary and hallucinatory haunting that spirals out of distorted, everyday mundanity.

For the first 45 minutes, the play exists only in a snatched phrase or two, a scrawl of graffiti on the wall, a jokey reference to Grieg's famous music. The set – an extraordinary over-the-top design in dayglo colours by Anna Cordingley, mainly fashioned out of dozens of balloons – stretches the length of the studio theatre. On stage are a red sports car, a combi van, a blue swimming pool, banana lounges, a table. Nothing happens for a time, aside from some outrageously kitsch music and the sounds of magpies carolling (it is morning). A man stumbles out of the combi van and shuffles about the stage. He wakes a woman who is sleeping in the sports car. He gets a beer. Several beers. One by one, various actors in a confusion of costumes – a woman in white twinset and sunglasses carrying suitcases, a man in a panama hat, women in bikinis, a man in football beanie and shorts, people on motorbikes and bicycles – enter the stage. Some leave and return, some stay and fuss about with the banana lounges, opening champagne bottles, greeting each other with squeals of pleasure, gossiping inaudibly.

Gradually we understand, from fragments of conversation that we overhear as if by accident, that people are gathering for the rehearsal of a wedding. It's a wedding in which there is conflict; the bride is unhappy and keeps bursting into tears. Still the actors' movements are mysterious: they eddy about the stage, inscrutably private. It is as if we were watching a party from an elevated angle. And this is sustained for much longer than seems possible, flirting with the edges of frustration. Always, just as you begin to lose patience, something else catches your attention: a man enters with an enormous bag of balloons and fills the swimming pool, or a fight breaks out, or a woman runs away crying.

Where, you begin to wonder, is Peer Gynt? And then you realise he is the skinny young man causing trouble at the edges of the gathering. And out of what seem like random swirls of activity, a story begins to emerge. It's the story of Peer Gynt, radically translated into contemporary symbols, barely recognisable but nonetheless present through a glass darkly. The wedding is – or is like – the wedding at the beginning of the poem, in which Gynt's sweetheart is married unwillingly to the local butcher, and runs off with him for the night, causing his banishment. Imperceptibly, we find we are watching a double reality, a mundane and ugly reality that is infected by images from a dream.

At about this point the dream begins to shift to the foreground: the lighting states shift from general to specific, and fragments from the play begin to be enacted, spiralling out of the banal event we have been watching. It's never quite pinned down, and the reality is never quite stable. But from this fascinating confusion emerges moments of strange, almost surreal clarity that reflexively are excavated from the superficial and strangely heartless social occasion we've been witnessing. Peer Gynt himself (a marvellous performance by Kyle Baxter) stands out in relief at last against the action; he meets the trolls, he is mocked by a nameless voice wanting to know who he is, and he discovers, over an epic and strange journey to material success, that he has no idea who he is. He is, he finds, as empty as the middle of an onion: beneath all the layers that he is created of himself, he is nothing.

The urgency beneath the performance is a questioning of authenticity: of experience, of art. For all its fantastic nature and bizarre incongruities, what makes this show compulsively watchable is a profound veracity in its performances and intellectual exploration which is, all the same, radically dislocated from any sense of literal truth. It's most true to Ibsen's text in its poetic vision, how it has burrowed into and exploded the metaphors in the play, returning them to a surprising and vexed sense of truthfulness. It is an excoriating expose of the culture of narcissism that is nevertheless not without compassion, attending closely to the trivial details out of which people construct meaning.

In some ways, this production seems like a defiant wrenching of richness from a wide menu of emotional poverties. The ambiguity of the ending is telling: Schlusser pushes the sentiment of the love story between Peer and Solveig to the risible, placing them next to a giant pink heart made of balloons as Solveig sings a folk song of aching loveliness. And yet out of this extreme collision of kitsch, this strange wedding of contradictions, emerges a sharp splinter of real feeling; a glimpse, however ambiguous, of salvation.

Schlusser's re-blending of *Peer Gynt* is mischievous, beguiling and ultimately haunting, demonstrating that an act of creation is always simultaneously an act of destruction. He gets away with it because of the quality of attention in the direction: the stage is always focused, always dynamic, with a spatial discipline that recalls dance. If you expect to see a respectful performance of Ibsen's text, you'll be disappointed: the text is rather a provocation or occasion for thought. What you get instead is the chance to watch the continuing evolution of a fascinating investigation, in one of the most deeply interesting works of theatre you'll see in Melbourne this year.

Theatre Notes, March 29 2009

3xSisters / Spring Awakening

In his stories and plays, Anton Chekhov is a pitilessly intelligent observer of human beings. A writer of enormous moral scrupulousness, he lets fall a cruel light on the excesses of his characters without ever losing sight of their frailties and contradictions. He's most often seen as a poster boy for naturalism, but this is inevitably reductive. A play like *Three Sisters*, for instance, can be seen as a moral tale about the decadence of the pre-Revolutionary bourgeoisie, or a nostalgic evocation of a society on the brink of collapse. But like any simple interpretation, this is far from the whole truth.

Its real fascination is in its details, how it is constructed as a kind of collage of social performance: each character's self-insight is questionable, conditioned and repressed by his or her consciousness of the presence of others, and each is ultimately trapped in a state of existential solitude. It is this aspect of Chekhov which makes him so attractive to successive generations of artists, among whom must be counted Samuel Beckett. In last year's drop-dead beautiful production of his early play *Platonov*, the Hayloft Project, one of Melbourne's most vital new companies, began an excavation of his work.

Under the restless direction of Simon Stone, they've continued their exploration with *3xSisters*, now on at the Meat Market in repertory with a remount of the Belvoir St version of their first show, *Spring Awakening* – a performance so radically changed (different script, different design, different concept, different cast) from its original Melbourne outing that it is effectively an entirely new production. Hayloft's take on Chekhov is an attractively ambitious conceit: three directors – Benedict Hardie, Simon Stone and Mark Winter – oversee different acts, effectively giving us three radically different interpretations of the play. But it's telling that the names of the writers who feature in this mini-Hayloft retrospective – Franz Wedekind and Anton Chekhov – figure nowhere on the program credits.

3xSisters is fascinating and frustrating in equal measure. The production shifts neurotically through three different sets, costumes and interpretations. Stone, who begins and ends the play, sets it in a place like a waiting room in an airport, under a row of clocks showing the time in Buenos Aires, Johannesburg or Moscow, with the characters in formal dress, as if waiting for some festive event. The actors speak straight out to the audience, their more intimate thoughts sometimes whispered through a microphone, their movements constrained by the narrowness of the stage. It suggests a promisingly stern aesthetic – Stone even inserts the famous quote ('Fail again. Fail better.') from Samuel Beckett's *Worstward Ho* – but, in the major problem that runs through this entire production, neglects to follow this promise through. The hint of Beckett remains merely decoration, and peters out in the end, disappointingly, into the borrowed emotion of Cat Power.

Hardie directs a deftly choreographed rehearsal of the play, complete with actorly interpolations. It's a reminder of the performance heritage that has so conditioned Western interpretations of Chekhov: Chekhov's first and most famous interpreter was Stanislavski, one of whose most famous acolytes was Lee Strasberg, father of the Method. In Hardie's first scene, the black slacks and casual shirts evoke the 1950s cool of the Actors Studio; in the second, the actors have evolved into brainless noughties dweebs, dressed in 'I heart Chekhov' t-shirts. This permits a metatheatrical shifting, a consciousness of artifice overlaying the moments when the actors step into character. It's not that new as an idea – David Mamet's film *Vanya on 42nd Street* features actors workshopping the play, similarly shifting between their 'real' and performative characters – but it's still effective, and perhaps in its minimalist approach the most satisfyingly thought-through of the evening.

The middle acts, courtesy of Winter, are a psychotic explosion seen through the mind of Solyony, an asocial soldier with Romantic delusions who ends up killing his only friend. Here Chekhov collides with *Taxi Driver*, with Travis Bickle's slaughter presaging the Revolution's murders of the Romanov family. This middle act is at once the most interesting and the most problematic of the lot: there are moments of genuine power, moments when the wholesale destruction of Chekhov suggests wider implications – the repressed violence and sexuality squirming beneath bourgeois social conventions, the classist cruelty that led to the Russian Revolution, even a reflection of how a production can be a forensic dissection of a cultural corpse.

But these possibilities are undermined by cheap gestures. Its excessive bath of sexual transgression and violence ends up being brutalising and boring (and sometimes – what was with the Indian head-dress? – simply baffling). As with the rest of the production it's full of quotations, most obviously from Martin Scorsese, but also from a menu of pop cultural and theatrical references. Again, a directorial quote from Romeo Castellucci will mean nothing without the aesthetic rigor that underlies Castellucci's practice: and a swipe at Benedict Andrews is simply a gratuitous in-joke which illuminates nothing except the director's insecurities. At its worst, it justifies the outraged criticisms of those who claim this kind of theatre is simply self-indulgent bullshit only interested in generating offence, in the absence of doing something more challenging (such as engaging with Chekhov); which is a pity, because at its best it has the potential to be something far more substantial.

In short, the line between intellectual provocation and gratuitous shock-value is crossed too often, and the whole production oscillates between genuine insight and shallow gesture. It's interesting to compare these explorations, for instance, with Daniel Schlusser's recent production of *Peer Gynt*, or more directly, Chris Goode's transcendently beautiful… *Sisters*, both of which radically dismantle a classic text. The difference is intellectual rigor, and an illuminating respect for the source text.

All the same, I found *3xSisters* riveting. The performers are astoundingly good (and very well cast – you can't help reflecting that a straight production with this cast would be really something), and Chekhov, tellingly, survives the rough treatment. It's well worth seeing, if only for the arguments you'll have afterwards.

Simon Stone's production of *Spring Awakening* is a far less problematic prospect. I was expecting a polished version of the show I saw at fortyfive downstairs three years ago, and found very quickly that I was mistaken: the Belvoir St version is a complete rethink, with Adam Gardnir's chicken-coop set literalising the social barriers that confine and destroy Wedekind's young characters. Stone solves some of the problems of the original text – most notably, the Man who appears at the end – by simply editing them out, transforming the play into a series of impressionistic dialogues and monologues.

The most compelling aspect of the initial production was the tension it established between sexual desire and childish innocence, a collision that was ultimately tragic. Literalising the subtleties of physical interaction between the actors, and perhaps even neatening up the original messiness of Wedekind's play, has a concomitant cost: it's undoubtedly more elegant, and perhaps more impressive, but it has lost something important. Innocence, perhaps.

Theatre Notes, April 27 2009

Tom Fool / Leaves of Glass

I keep hearing, here and there, that these days 'text-based theatre' (to you and me, 'the play') is out of fashion. The contemporary stage, the whisper goes, is hostile to the writer: in these post-dramatic, post-structural, post-everything times, the director has seized the crown in the theatrical hierarchy and the playwright is out in the cold, shivering in his underpants.

The truth is, just as the masculine pronoun is no longer a default grammatical device, so theatre's practice has shifted to a broader consideration of the semiotics of the stage: meaning is expressed through movement, design, music and performance as much as through words. On the other hand, is that emphasis really new? Meaning is an unstable quiddity, sure, but it's been unstable since modernity began to erase the certainties of church and state (and reading Lucan can make you realise that such instabilities are about as ancient as human civilisation). And after all these years, I'm still not sure what a 'linear narrative' really is: I'm not sure I've ever met one.

In any case, I see text everywhere. Even an exploration like *3xSisters* depends on a source text, however it spirals around it. And that old-fashioned concept, the play, is a hardy one. People keep writing them, and people keep putting them on stage. I saw two last weekend. They were definitely plays, done in the old-fashioned way of getting actors to remember the words and enact them on stage. They were even, in very different ways, naturalistic plays.

In fact, I think that the diversity of contemporary practice means that the grim days of default naturalism – the idea that theatre is divided into 'accessible' (meaning televisual) 'naturalism' and weird 'non-naturalistic' experiment – are well and truly over. Instead, naturalism as a formal device has been injected with something like its original energy and urgency. Recently there have been some vivid reminders of how powerful – and how poetic – naturalism can be in the theatre – Peter Evans' brilliant production of David Harrower's *Blackbird* for the MTC, for example, or Duncan Graham's *Ollie and the Minotaur*.

Perhaps this is why Hoy Polloy's production of *Tom Fool* by Franz Xaver Kroetz seems so timely: Kroetz is one of the major invigorators of naturalism in postwar theatre. Although there are more obvious reasons for its aptness: Kroetz's portrayal of the alienating mechanisms of capitalism, of how human beings are reduced to disposable cogs in a gigantic economic machine, is as relevant in 2009 as it was in 1977, when it was first written. Beng Oh's exemplary production, directed with a profound and compassionate clarity, brings this home with devastating, painful emotional force.

Tom Fool is a fable of late twentieth century capitalism. It's the story of Otto Meier (Chris Bunworth), a semi-skilled factory worker who lives in a tiny apartment with his wife, Martha (Liz McCall) and son Ludwig (Glenn van Oosterom), and is written in a series of short, titled scenes that focus on the banal domestic minutiae of their lives. Kroetz is a master at digging the tragic meaning out of moments that appear on the surface to be trivial, and this production meets his demanding poetic with an admirable honesty.

Tom Fool would be very easy to get very wrong; so much depends on the play of the emotional subtext of each moment, and that in turn depends on a larger wisdom about human behaviour that must meet the playwright's. Every decision in this production hits the right note, neither overdone nor glossed. Beng Oh hasn't attempted to update or Australianise it: Chris Molyneux's stylisedly naturalistic set is a perfect simulacrum of late '70s decor, and the actors, speaking an unobtrusive lower-middle-class Australian, refer to German currency and social conditions.

The scenes are punctuated with a sure rhythmic hand: as the scene title is projected onto the wall, the actors and a couple of stage hands arrange the props, which becomes in itself part of the texture of domestic routine. Then there is a snap, the lights come up and the scene begins. (Tim Bright's sound design and Ben Morris' lighting find a brilliant variousness in this stern aesthetic.) These structural decisions create a solid frame for the actors, which permits them to explore the emotional nakedness of the play. Bunworth, McCall and van Oosterom generate their characters with deft, accumulating touches, gradually excavating their extreme loneliness. This production is notable for its precise detail, which is particularly noticeable in Kroetz's long silent scenes – here the smallest gesture, a shrug, a glance, becomes pregnant with meaning.

They create unforgettable portraits of the fragmentation of the self in contemporary capitalist society. Otto Meier, the 'human screw-driver', a 'car-screw in-screwer, a screwologist', knows he is dehumanised by his work, but the knowledge doesn't help, as he sees no way out: it emerges in violent rages of frustration that only serve to further alienate his family. Each character becomes more alone, more isolated, although each deals with their alienation in a different way. What makes this play so painful is that their recognition of their isolation, their abandonment of their various dreams in the face of obdurate reality, collides with a heightened realisation of their yearning: the further the dream retreats, the more they desire. It is all the more painful for their inability to communicate their longings to each other.

It's a beautifully performed, tactfully produced realisation of a play that is, for all its apparent banality, a work of great poetic delicacy. The evening passes with astounding swiftness; for all its grim concerns, this production has a nicely judged lightness of touch, and is infused with moments of surprising comedy. It's a rare chance to see Kroetz done as he ought to be. Don't miss this one.

Inevitably, Philip Ridley's *Leaves of Glass* suffers by comparison to *Tom Fool*. It's another family drama, and again written in a series of naturalist scenes. Although it features some astounding writing, especially in the monologues, it doesn't have anything like the imaginative sweep of Ridley's *Mercury Fur*, a dark fantasia about snuff parties which also centred on the relationship between two brothers. Put next to Kroetz's sparely judged writing it seems fussy and melodramatic, and its social commentary – an exploration of the human capacity for denial, of how we can erase reality with language – not nearly as deeply thought.

I suppose the title, *Leaves of Glass*, is an elliptical nod to Whitman's *Leaves of Grass*, though it's difficult to make the connection. There are certainly touches of Tennessee Williams' *The Glass Menagerie* in its exploration of human fragility and damage. It's a family drama with all the expected Ibsenite elements – dark secrets, deaths, dramatic revelations, murderous sibling rivalry – given a twenty-first century twist. Steve (Dan Frederiksen) is a picture of materialist Britain, a successful, emotionally stunted businessman married to a WAG-style shopaholic wife (Amelia Best). His younger brother Barry (Johnny Carr) is an artist, traumatically scarred by the suicide of his father, and both still live in the shadow of their mother, Liz (Jillian Murray). What makes it interesting is how the writing turns on its clichés, especially in the climactic scene where language itself becomes a means for murder.

Simon Stone gives it a spare and well-judged production, with a design by Peter Mumford in which the stage is divided into parallel sections by clear plastic curtains, which are drawn back or closed to reflect the degrees of separation between the different characters. The performances are excellent; I especially liked Johnny Carr and Daniel Frederiksen as the two brothers. Although it's a bit of a disappointment after *Mercury Fur*, it's well worth seeing all the same. And certainly the best production at Red Stitch since Tom Holloway's *Red Sky Morning*.

Theatre Notes, May 13 2009

Poppea

George Orwell once remarked that if a writer says he can't write, he can't write. It's not laziness or malingering or disorganisation: it's mysterious, crippling incapacity. When allied to the desire to write, he listed it as one of the major frustrations of a writer's life; if a writer isn't writing, he enters an existential no man's land in which it's difficult to see his reason for being on the planet. (This is assuming that a writer's self is entirely defined by writing which is, fortunately, not entirely true.)

So it is that Ms TN [Ms Theatre Notes] has been thinking about Barrie Kosky's Vienna Schauspielhaus production of *Poppea* for more than a week, yet has been curiously unable to write a word. Last Saturday I stole a precious 24 hours, flew up to Sydney, relaxed enough to realise how near to burnout I actually am, and then trotted off to the Sydney Opera House to see the opera. From the overture, during which the lights slowly faded in the auditorium and the curtain rose, revealing Amor with her back to us, one garishly braceleted hand gracefully extended in silhouette, my breath seemed to stop. I left the theatre exhilarated, moved and shaken.

I thought *Poppea* was an outstanding and fearless work of theatre, which is perhaps what has inhibited my writing about it. It seemed to me to be a work about love that was for grownups, a work that enacted the darkness and beauty and amorality of eroticism with a rare honesty. It showed at once the preposterousness of lust and the dignity of love, the ruthlessness and tenderness of desire, its ludicrous obsessiveness, its corruption and its purity, the murderous seduction of power. Its ironies are savage, and yet it pierced my soul, that wounded and scratched prison of my body, with profound sorrow.

Kosky has taken Monteverdi's last opera, *L'incoronazione di Poppea*, and given it a very twenty-first century treatment. The opera is cut to the bone: all the secondary characters and all the gods save Amor, the goddess of love, are gone. He has also translated the original libretto, by Giovanni Francesco Busenello, into German, and he's interwoven Monteverdi's music with songs by Cole Porter, which illuminates both of them. I'll certainly never hear Porter's songs in the same way again; this production brings out their themes of obsession and passion, their world-weary cynicism, the black polish of their urban wit, and their contrast with the baroque intensities of Monteverdi's music is as exciting as their thematic collisions. It's a bold, dramaturgically elegant attack on the original work that brings its blood to the surface of the skin.

The opera tells the sordid story of Poppea's accession to power as Empress of Rome. Originally Ottone's (Martin Niedermair) lover, she attracts the attentions of Nero (Kyrre Kvam). With the blessing of Amor (Barbara Spitz, played as a world-weary madam), she schemes to marry him: Nero has to divorce his wife Ottavia (Barbara Frey), and in order to do that he has to get rid of Seneca (Florian Carove), Nero's former tutor and an influential moral voice in the Senate. Meanwhile, Ottavia hatches a plot to murder Poppea, blackmailing Ottone into doing the dirty deed despite his continuing love for Poppea. Ottavia is backed by Ottone's lover Drusilla (Ruth Brauer-Kvam), who was thrown over for Poppea and still seethes with jealousy. Seneca commits suicide on Nero's orders, Ottone and Drusilla are exposed, punished and banished, Ottavia is exiled, and Poppea and Nero emerge triumphant, celebrating their marriage with an achingly beautiful duet.

There are ironies here that are mostly lost on a modern audience. Busenello's libretto was based on Tacitus' account of the Emperor Nero's reign of Rome, which is by any measure a racy read. Monteverdi's audience would have been aware that Poppea came to a bad end: most Roman historians agree that Nero murdered her by kicking her in the stomach when she was pregnant with her second child. Some even say he jumped on her. (Modern historians note that Suetonius, Tacitus and others were very biased against Nero, no doubt for good reason, and that she may have simply died from complications in childbirth or a miscarriage.) Moreover, Ottone, Poppea's rejected lover, became Emperor in the end anyway.

Shorn of this context, Monteverdi's triumphant ending is disconcerting, even obscene, a blackly realist view of the effectiveness of ruthless power. Kosky exploits this ambiguity to the full, reserving easy judgment for a more sternly Platonic morality: that virtue is its own reward, and vice its own punishment, which I've often thought is one of the bleakest observations ever made.

The couple's first crime is the death of Seneca, which in the opera comes about through Poppea's urging. (It is certainly true that Nero ordered Seneca to commit suicide, but in fact it was after the Pisonian Conspiracy, a plot to kill Nero, in which the Emperor believed Seneca was involved, although it's unlikely that he was – but hey, Monteverdi was no more interested in historical accuracy than Kosky is.)

Seneca cuts his wrists in a hot bath, the favoured Roman method of self-slaughter, and so here he rises up, naked in a bathtub, from the floor of the stage. He is mute, as Nero has already cut out his tongue, and his arias are sung by another actor or, in an extraordinary scene, acted out in sign language. The scenes that show his death are the most powerful in the opera. Nero climbs into the bath with him and smears himself, with gestures like those of a lover, with Seneca's blood, before the corpse slumps heavily out of the bath in an image which is one of the most shockingly abject representations of death I've seen on stage.

Nero's spurned wife Ottavia, who first appears as a figure of grotesque comedy, writhing with jealousy and spite, comports herself in her final song as a figure of intensely moving dignity, proudly accepting her exile and proclaiming her innocence. She shows up the lack of dignity of Poppea and Nero, who prowl the stage like the grotesque, bestial creatures their power has made them into.

Likewise, the love story between Drusilla and Ottone emerges as a contrast to the self-satisfied self interest of Nero and Poppea. For this couple, their murderous adventures and their punishment lead to a sacrificial declaration of love, with Drusilla pledging to go into exile with Ottone at the height of their humiliation – both are raped by Nero, although he stops short of ordering them off to the torture chamber for a lingering and painful death. And this prompts an impassioned solo from Ottone in which he declares his happiness: a happiness, it is quite clear, that Poppea and Nero have foresworn, and which Poppea, stalking the stage like a crazed monster behind them, murderously envies.

None of this, however, takes away from the ravishing beauty of Poppea and Nero's final declaration of love. They can be monstrous and amoral and still truly love each other; after all, their victims gain their dignity through losing the power game and, aside from Seneca, are no less morally questionable than the Imperial couple. Amor, the goddess of love, is not concerned with the morality of passion: her drive is towards the orgasmic moment of excess, the primitive, unbridled nightmare of passion.

The production is realised with a simplicity of staging that mercilessly exposes the action. The set is an office-like box, white walls with doors, that throws the emphasis onto the bodies of the performers. The revealing costumes make the actors seem more naked than they would be if they were actually unclothed: here everything is revealed by what is hidden, which is the secret behind the erotics of almost everything, and especially art. *Poppea* works off contrast, turning in a trice from cabaret grotesquerie to sublime operatic beauty, from comedy to tragedy. And the cast, without exception, rises fearlessly to Kosky's demands; every performance here fully inhabits the contrasting extremities of the roles.

One effect is that it abolishes duration; you wake up at the end as if from a dream, aware only then of what has been stirred out of the dark reaches of the psyche. For me, it was mainly sorrow, which is perhaps what beauty inevitably does; it breaks open my awareness of mortality by briefly lifting me, with its gorgeous, fleeting illusion, out of time. If opera is indeed a song of love and death, then *Poppea* is, for all its impurities, pure opera.

Theatre Notes, August 17 2009

One Night The Moon

The lost child is an iconic, even obsessive, figure in Australian folklore, the subject of song, story and painting. Frederick McCubbin's 1886 painting *Lost* encapsulates the myth: a young girl stands hesitantly, almost invisibly, in bushland, on the verge of being swallowed by the trees.

The lost child focused a settler's anxiety in a land which refused to obey the known laws of European agriculture, in which even the seasons were upside down. Settlers entered an environment that faced them with climactic extremes – flood, drought and fire – and which was unfamiliar and harsh to eyes coached by the domesticated landscapes of England.

And this anxiety was underlaid by grim reality. White children commonly did wander into the bush, often with tragic results. *One Night The Moon* – originally a 2001 film – is based on one such story, when a little girl was lost in Dubbo in 1932. When the police force's Aboriginal tracker, Alexander 'Tracker' Riley, was called in, the girl's father refused to have a blackfella on his property and conducted the search himself.

It's a story which highlights how the resistance to Indigenous knowledge among Europeans led to tragic results for both black and white. And it shows how the mythology of colonisation in Australia, wretchedly similar in terms of the state's dispossession of Indigenous people, differs from the United States. There the major annual holiday, Thanksgiving, celebrates the life-saving offer of food by Native Americans to starving settlers.

One Night The Moon emerged from a collaboration between director Rachel Perkins and a distinguished creative team that included songwriters Kev Carmody, Paul Kelly and Mairead Hannan. That movie in turn inspired a work of musical theatre, adapted for the stage by one the film's original writers, John Romeril, and directed by Wesley Enoch. Here this story, transposed to the Victorian Grampians, becomes a fable of the gulfs between two cultures. And yet its very aesthetic, which knits together traditions from both cultures into a highly original work, is an expression of hope for some other way.

Perhaps what is most striking about *One Night The Moon*, now on at the Malthouse, is how Romeril and Enoch have created a work that is profoundly of its medium: this is, from the ground up, pure theatre. Enoch and Romeril have brought together their different sensibilities to create a fascinating hybrid of theatrical influences, which are fused together in a work of deceptive simplicity.

Both, in different ways, return to theatrical roots. Romeril has long been influenced by Asian theatre, most explicitly in works such *Miss Tanaka* and *Love Suicides*. This interest is perhaps an extension of the Brechtian emphasis in his work. Like other modernist theatre artists, Brecht was heavily influenced by Asian theatre: his 'alienation effect' emerged from his seeing the Peking Opera in 1935, and he adapted Noh techniques for his *Lehrstück*, or learning plays.

Likewise, the theatrical shape of *One Night The Moon* draws heavily on Asian influences: as in traditional Asian theatre, the band is on stage, and the narrative unfolds through music and song rather than dialogue.

But perhaps it is most visible in its slow, inevitable dramatic movement: this is a work that builds steadily to emotional climax, and which bypasses conventional Western techniques of affect. Character, for example, is not a major concern: the figures are symbolic and representative, rather than psychological portraits.

Enoch, on the other hand, returns to Indigenous ritual. He frames the show with a 'welcome to country' smoke ceremony conducted by Ursula Yovich, and includes sand painting – a traditional part of Aboriginal ritual – as a key visual element. When Albert, the police tracker (Kirk Page), dresses for work with the help of his wife (Yovich), it has at once the sense of Indigenous ceremonial preparation and a European echo, as if, as an arm of the law, he were being draped in the robes of a judge.

In part, this show is a dialogue between Aboriginal and European representations of landscape, just as it is a tragic fable about miscommunication between black and white. Just after the smoke ceremony, in one of its more spectacular moments, Yovich sets fire to an early drawing of the Grampians by Eugene von Guérard, and throughout the show are glimpses of a comprehensive selection of colonial landscape art. These elements are combined seamlessly with some beautiful 3D animation, which itself draws from the iconography of European fairytales, and are heightened by some superb multimedia. The music also expressively combines diverse influences.

It all sounds a lot more complicated than it is in execution. The set is a high, bare stage with steps down to the floor where the ceremonial elements take place. Anna Cordingley's flexible design permits all these different elements to come together.

The songs both drive the action and are the chief means of emotional communication, and it's in the songs that the performances find their heart. The dialogue doesn't wholly escape a vexing sense of alienation caused by the use of mikes, but the cumulative power of the four performers winds up to a shattering climax.

The result recalls most compellingly the work of Robert Wilson, but Enoch evades the sense of slickness that can mar Wilson's theatre. There's a complexity of thought in this work that lifts it beyond cliché, but it still retains the potent simplicity of fable. A fairytale for our time.

The Australian, September 18 2009

Structure and Sadness

The melancholy of modernity

There's a poignancy in looking down over a city from a plane that in certain moods can be overwhelming. The structures that dominate and shape our lives are suddenly rendered miniature by perspective and – especially at night, when the lights give it a shimmering unity – a city seems a live creature, a single organism that pulses and consumes and excretes. A parasitic organism perhaps, cankering the landscape like a feral moss or a luminous fungus, but still with its own fragile beauty.

Flying into Melbourne on a clear evening you can see human habitats with the same eye that perceives the web of an orb weaver or the scarring aridity of rabbit warrens: as functions of us. We are animals who build. The structures we make are at once intimate ('a house is a skin') and alienating, our private selves intersecting with the implacable machine of capitalism, our social beings and collective imagination exteriorised and made concrete.

We trust those structures: we will not admit our fragility, our contingency, our smallness, since if we did, if we really knew it in our bones, how would we get out of bed every morning?

The tower will stand tall. The bridge will not fall down.

Fulcrum: passion and intellect

Lucy Guerin's *Structure and Sadness* is about Melbourne, and its performance here has a particular poignancy of recognition. The collapse of the West Gate Bridge is part of our story: we all, however tangentially, know that history. From my house I can walk to the memorial for the 35 men who died when it fell into the Maribyrnong River. Many people still remember what they were doing when they heard the news. That famous tale of how the editor of the *Age* took a call in his Spencer Street office from a reporter who told him the bridge was down. 'Don't be stupid', he said, and hung up. Then he turned around and looked out of his window.

The perspectives in *Structure and Sadness* are close up and far away. Like so much of Guerin's work, it is a weaving of duets, of relationship: these six bodies meet under stress, desire and repulse each other, moving in rhythmic harmonies of yearning that dissolve into solitude. In the first half, Gerald Mair's score is an abstract electronic score woven with the sounds of materials – wood, concrete, steel – creaking under stress. It opens with a solo dance with a flexible board, the dancer at once in total control, fluidly manipulating the board, and vulnerable, his body hanging like a corpse over a deadly edge. The dancers embody vectors of force and balance; they are geometric and precise, leaning into each other, straining against each other. Objects – an elastic, a stick – are at once tools of expressiveness, extending their bodies, and harbingers of danger, capable of piercing the skin, hard against a visceral softness.

Behind these duets the other dancers gradually, patiently, build a house of cards, triangular structures made of rectangles of wood that slowly cover the stage, slowly rise into a tower. It looks unsettlingly like Bruegel's *The Tower of Babel*. We know it will fall down, that is part of the narrative before the show begins, but when it does, it is wholly unexpected: one little piece is knocked over and the whole thing folds like a row of dominoes, amplifying disaster until the whole stage is covered in litter, the potential energy of the fragile triangulations of wood dissipated in collapse.

In the centre is a bold glimpse of realism, the ethical core of the show. To speak of any event which cost 35 lives as if it is merely an occasion for aesthetic tinkering is beyond heartless. On the other hand, to be constrained in a documentary verity is imprisoning, a courting of artistic coarseness. Guerin finds the fulcrum in the centre of the dance, where she invokes the reality of grief head-on with a moment of literal domestic banality. A woman is doing the washing up, singing along to the radio, when the broadcast is interrupted by a news report about the West Gate Bridge.

The dance tips now into an elegy, an evocation of mourning that has the emotional simplicity and restraint of Greek tragedy. The three women dance with their dead men, reaching out to ghosts who vanish from their embrace: the men are summoned by their burning longing, but will never come back. It is a dance with the bitter beauty of Philip Larkin's poem *The Explosion*, an account of an accident in a mine when men went to work in the morning and didn't return. A common enough story, a common enough grief.

Coda

In the final sequence the dances of the first half are reprised, this time as a chorus work, the molten significance of grief informing the dancers' gestures. An abstract pattern of neon lights on the back wall is selectively turned off to reveal the West Gate Bridge, complete and undamaged: it is ambiguous, we don't know whether it has been rebuilt or if, in the impossible dream of return, it has never been broken.

Dance is always impure in Guerin's work, its precision intersected with the unruliness of chance and the literalness of narrative bodies; yet through a thickness of encroaching meaning it reaches moments of lyrical purity, sheerly beautiful movement that escapes itself and lifts its resonance out of its specific time and place. Celebration and elegy are two sides of the same coin, just as death is the subtext of civilisation.

The final image is breathtaking in its simplicity: the dancers lie in a diagonal line on the ground and a plank is placed on top of them. The last dancer walks over the plank, into the darkness at the edge of the stage.

Once human sacrifice was a sacred ritual, a consecration of a building. Sacrificed bodies have been found in the foundations of Roman buildings; some ancient keystones are said to be red because they are mortared with human blood, and legends of immurement are rife in Serbian history. Our modern cities still demand their sacrifices.

It is said they never found all the bodies, that some are still embedded in the West Gate Bridge. And every day we drive over them.

Theatre Notes, December 1 2009

The Harry Harlow Project

> Love is a wondrous state, deep, tender, and rewarding. Because of its intimate and personal nature it is regarded by some as an improper topic for experimental research. But, whatever our personal feelings may be, our assigned mission as psychologists is to analyze all facets of human and animal behavior into their component variables. So far as love or affection is concerned, psychologists have failed in this mission.

> The little we know about love does not transcend simple observation, and the little we write about it has been written better by poets and novelists. But of greater concern is the fact that psychologists tend to give progressively less attention to a motive which pervades our entire lives. Psychologists, at least psychologists who write textbooks, not only show no interest in the origin and development of love or affection, but they seem to be unaware of its very existence.

So begins Harry Harlow's classic paper 'The Nature of Love', delivered to the Annual Convention of the American Psychological Association in Washington DC in 1958. And so begins too *The Harry Harlow Project*, James Saunders' fascinating theatrical examination of Harlow's controversial experiments on baby rhesus monkeys.

The irony – more, the perversity – of Harlow's experiments is that, while they were driven by Harlow's almost lyrically expressed desire to understand something as unscientific as love, they were exemplary in their cruelty. He radically demonstrated the importance of maternal love – the security of physical affection – to the physical and psychological development of an infant by showing what happened to monkeys that received no affection and no socialisation. The result, unsurprisingly, was psychotic monkeys.

Then he went further, producing babies by forcing female monkeys raised in isolation – and who were so asocial they couldn't mate – into what he unblinkingly called his 'rape pack', a wire restraining device which he used to force-mate females. Finally, he created his most notorious experiment, the 'pit of despair', a cage of total isolation in which monkeys were sometimes confined for two years, with which he deliberately engineered clinical depression.

Aside from their ingenious cruelty, it's not difficult to discern a disturbing subtext of misogyny beneath some of these experiments: Harlow's 'hostile mother', a machine of teeth and spikes that shot cold air on the unfortunate babies, seems like a caricature of a pathology. Yet these experiments revolutionised contemporary attitudes towards child rearing, changing practice in orphanages and rewriting the book on infant psychology. And he initiates a theory of fatherhood – 'It is cheering... to realize that the American male is physically endowed with all the really essential equipment to compete with the American female on equal terms in one essential activity: the rearing of infants', he noted at the end of his paper – which still has reverberations today.

In Harlow's day, childrearing authorities recommended that one should never kiss a child good night, but shake his or her hand. A generation of mothers listened in anguish to their crying babies, sure that should they obey their instincts and comfort them, they would be bad mothers. Harlow changed all that, legitimising human affection as more than mere 'indulgence'. For all that, it's hard to contemplate these experiments with any sense of ease. And it's hard to escape the thought that, by scientifically proving that maternal love was necessary to develop a healthy child, Harlow convinced the men in white coats of wisdoms that women in so-called 'primitive' societies have known since, well, the beginning of time.

It's an ambiguous heritage, and James Saunders accesses much of its bleak emotional resonance in *The Harry Harlow Project* (Fairfax Studio, Victorian Arts Centre) which manages to be at once harrowing and funny without either cancelling the other out. The stage becomes a slapstick simulacra of Harlow's psyche, with some deft video work by Martyn Coutts and a subliminally disturbing score by Kelly Ryall framing a bravura performance by Saunders. The conceit – a just one, since in later life Harlow had ECG treatment for depression – is that in his increasingly sadistic experiments Harlow is enacting his own mental distress.

As a theatrical evocation of the hell of alienation, parts of this show are hard to beat. The stage – a white box scattered with minimal props – is fronted by sound and lighting boards, with the artists, their backs to the audience, orchestrating the show like lab technicians. A sequence where the actor interacts with his life-size projection – reaching out, like Michelangelo's God, to his fleshly human image, but finally unable to touch – is masterly. It's set up by an earlier sequence where Saunders is interviewed by a television, a device that works seamlessly through split-second timing but which here is comedic. Saunders' performance invokes the damaged monkeys through physical movement, which itself also presages Harlow's death through Parkinson's disease.

The narrative is told through fragmentary episodes that examine the experiments in tandem with glimpses of Harlow's personal life. At one point Saunders puts on a wig and becomes his own biographer; at another, he becomes Harlow's son. Curiously, in both these enactments he doesn't cease to be Harry Harlow: these other characters seem like mere projections. Perhaps what I found most interesting is how Brian Lipson's direction coins a kind of dramaturgy of anxiety: from the beginning the comedy is uneasy, and despite the explosive release of laughter the tension subliminally winches up, not permitting any release, until the show is over. It left me with all that anxiety still in my body, bleeding out a slow release over the following days.

Perhaps because its black and white aesthetic so successfully evokes the 1960s, it got me in personal places that I wouldn't have predicted from its set-up or subject. It made me think of how my father was sent to boarding school when he was four years old, and of my mother's unhappiness, raising babies alone in a mining village at the same time as Harlow was torturing monkeys. It made me think of the postwar scientist-god, certain that all human knowledge can be dissected and measured, sure in his march towards the ultimate good of Progress. It made me ponder again how such smart animals as human beings can get things so wrong.

Theatre Notes, December 1 2009

Glasoon

Black Lung Theatre and Whaling Firm's eight-day season of *Glasoon* is the hot ticket in town. It sold out in five days after its announcement on Facebook, so if you're not already booked, you'll have to resort to blackmail, robbery or espionage to get a ticket. To give it even more an air of samizdat, the location is 'undisclosed': you have to phone to make a booking, whereupon you're told to head for a certain bar in East Brunswick at a certain time, buy a drink, and wait, like someone out of *Smiley's People*, for the Sign.

Which is all cool enough. The actual site is a warehouse music venue scrawled with graffiti art from floor to ceiling, with rugs on the floor and battered laminex kitchen chairs and ancient sofas as seating. And then there's the performance, which won't disappoint any Black Lung aficionados. It begins with a Christ figure stumbling through a door, covered in blood, and being revived by an operatically-attired and voiced mother figure who offers him her ample breast to suckle. It continues with a vicious parody of fatherly advice to a young man and then descends into a kind of sexual hell, a dizzying, blackly funny and relentless parade of bodily incontinence, perversity and violence, where people fuck and vomit in each other's mouths and dance even though they're dead, where a zombie doll in a dress is playing an electric guitar, where God is a man with a beard in a Britney Spears wig and lace panties who lounges carelessly to expose his testicles.

In fact, there is plenty of opportunity in this show to contemplate the fact that the Black Lung fellas really have balls, some of them startlingly waxed.

You could just go ZOFMG!!!! and leave it at that, but it seems inadequate (Oh, those bad Black Lung boys!) The alternative is to flail in several different directions at once, since the show is sort of indescribable. It makes a guerrilla foray on the conventional wisdoms of rock'n'roll death art, attacking the glamour of those impeccably masculine acolytes of Thanatos, Jim Morrison to Nick Cave, fake Rimbauds the lot of them. Rebellion here is stripped back to its egocentric adolescent defiance, exposing the incontinent holes in its skin, its deadly cunt envy. What rock critic Anwyn Crawford describes as the 'bodiless despair' of the male rock god is given back its body. And it's not pretty at all.

If *Glasoon* were pretty, it would become seductive; for all the nudity and sex, it's not sexy. It's an assault, mostly on the male body. Though it certainly has a kind of beauty: that of the abject body unsexed and pinned to its mortality, like the dead Christ in seventeenth century Spanish art where the god is so embodied, so corpse-like in his meticulously rendered wounds and green-mottled skin, that it seems shockingly blasphemous and perverse.

Glasoon isn't merely sensational *épater le bourgeois*. If it were, it wouldn't be nearly as interesting as it is. It's certainly obscene, but it makes you realise that the obscene is of a different order than the pornographic. The obscene, even if it violently rejects the idea of God, is on the same spectrum as the divine, while the pornographic is monodimensionally of the order of capitalism: cummodity for the masses, rather than ecstatic nightmare. Think of the seventeenth century saint, Margaret Mary Alacoque, who wrote of licking up the vomit of her patients, a 'pleasure' she wished she could repeat every day, or of Saint John of the Cross, cleaning out the sores of lepers with his tongue.

Mere sensation wouldn't sidle into your subconscious like a slow-release toxin. It wouldn't create this riveting theatre, sharp and loose, galvanically in the present. *Glasoon* plugs into an inner urgency, a neurotic anxiety that spirals into an excoriation of the murky solipsism of the self, an unforgiving massacre of internalised social authority. It employs the vocabulary of now, but its circling gods seem to be Nietzsche and Freud: *Beyond Good and Evil, Civilisation and its Discontents*, thrown on the pyre of its malicious laughter.

❖ ❖ ❖

I googled 'Glasoon', and found no definitions, aside from it being a surname about as rare as Croggon. Warming to my search, I looked it up in *Brewer's Dictionary of Phrase and Fable* (no entry), the *Oxford English Reference Dictionary* (nothing between Glasgow and Glasnost) and a series of online maritime dictionaries (nada). Nor is it mentioned anywhere in the play itself, which is, despite all appearances to the contrary, a tightly scripted work from Thomas Henning.

Glasoon is, it seems, a word that means nothing, and refers nowhere. It's a nonsense coinage, empty of semantic meaning. It is a perfect Dada word. As Tristan Tzara said in his 1918 Manifesto: 'Dada means nothing'. Dada expresses, he said, 'the knowledge of a supreme egoism, in which laws wither away'. It's worth pursuing Tzara a little further here, from his 1922 *Lecture on Dada*:

> The beginnings of Dada were not the beginnings of an art, but of a disgust. Disgust with the magnificence of philosophers who for 3ooo years have been explaining everything to us (what for?), disgust with the pretensions of these artists-God's-representatives-on-earth, disgust with passion and with real pathological wickedness where it was not worth the bother; disgust with a false form of domination and restriction en masse, that accentuates rather than appeases man's instinct of domination, disgust with all the catalogued categories, with the false prophets who are nothing but a front for the interests of money, pride, disease, disgust with the lieutenants of a mercantile art made to order according to a few infantile laws, disgust with the divorce of good and evil, the beautiful and the ugly (for why is it more estimable to be red rather than green,

to the left rather than the right, to be large or small?) Disgust finally with the Jesuitical dialectic which can explain everything and fill people's minds with oblique and obtuse ideas without any physiological basis or ethnic roots, all this by means of blinding artifice and ignoble charlatans promises.

As Dada marches it continuously destroys, not in extension but in itself. From all these disgusts, may I add, it draws no conclusion, no pride, no benefit. It has even stopped combating anything, in the realization that it's no use, that all this doesn't matter. What interests a Dadaist is his own mode of life. But here we approach the great secret.

Dada is a state of mind. That is why it transforms itself according to races and events. Dada applies itself to everything, and yet it is nothing, it is the point where the yes and the no and all the opposites meet, not solemnly in the castles of human philosophies, but very simply at street corners, like dogs and grasshoppers.

Like everything in life, Dada is useless.

If anything is palpable in *Glasoon*, it is the solipsism of disgust. The Black Lung Theatre and Whaling Firm's reliably uninformative press release for *Glasoon* quotes writer Thomas Henning, self-described as 'a reasonably mediocre personality':

> The great dramas of my life are enacted majorly within my mind. My experience of hardship, of politics, of social change is thin on the ground. My ideas are lofty but my world is small. I retreat habitually to my mind, where the world is an exciting place… The way I convince myself to sleep, is with violence. Dreams of violence and guns. I think it's a focus for me. Death. Is this something key to a sense of mediocrity, or weakness, or failure? That I convince myself to go to sleep with war fantasies and dreams of slaughtering dozens of people? Is this a common male thing?

The focus of disgust here, as in so much of Black Lung's work, is maleness itself, projected out in a phantasmagoria of loathing. *Glasoon* is an adolescent nightmare, a solipsistic excursion through the dark edges of male desire, a murderous exorcism. It's pure, like acetylene is pure.

Does it mean anything? Does it matter?

❖❖❖

Among others, Hennings' text also calls to mind the British writer Heathcote Williams, whose 1972 play *The Immortalist* was described at the time – and from this end of things, quite justly – as 'the first play of the twenty-first century'. Williams' anarchic radicality seems, like his American poetic contemporary Ed Dorn, a darkly prescient foreshadowing of the mediated, consumerist, corporatised war machine of the twenty-first century. Like Williams, who spiralled out of the Vietnam and Cold Wars, or Tzara, who was writing in Switzerland while Europe was razed in World War I, Hennings' *Glasoon* springs from a reality predicated on war, the matrix of the petro-chemical-military-industrial-Disney-Murdoch complex.

It's a woman-hating paradigm in which the leaky, penetrable feminine body is the site of deathly denial and loathing. In *Glasoon* the female love object is, in an obscene joke, dead. (It's perhaps worth commenting here that exploring the pathology of misogyny isn't the same as being misogynistic. If this work were misogynistic, the female body would be naked and abject, not the male.)

In this reality, utopia is as extinct as the thylacine and the broad-faced potoroo. The nowhere of utopia depends on there being a place to go to: if the planet is burning up and drowning in its own waste like a plague victim, then the only refuge is inside your own head. There is no utopia even hinted here. *Glasoon* is an assault on given wisdom, on history, religion and social authority, which are minced into nonsense and funnelled into the central character's head, like a goose being force-fed to make foie gras.

Translated into performance, it's like being in someone else's nasty dream. Its insistence on now is a hatred of mediation. Its characters, or phantoms, all speak a debased language of pre-formed mass media clichés. Like a dream, *Glasoon* generates its own inescapable logic. Its power depends on the extraordinary cast, who without exception take the text and run through the pain barrier: they are not characters so much as embodiments of extremity, caricatures who joylessly fuck, bleed and die like creatures in a mediaeval depiction of hell. Only I, played with what you can only say is startling courage and honesty by Vaczadenjo Wharton-Thomas, contingently approaches the status of character: he is the subject to whom all this humiliation is happening, the passive eye in the storm.

There's a kind of hope, if it can be called hope: when his abjection is compete, when the ritual is over, I kills everybody and goes away, like the teenager in the story. Where does he go in his new suit? Into the sober disillusion of adulthood? A new, sane life? Who knows?

Like the poet said: *True, the new era is nothing if not harsh…*

Theatre Notes, December 3 2009

Godzone

At what point does politics move beyond parody? Maybe when you have a Prime Minister who looks like he belongs in a Lego set, and who ought to be reported to the Society for Prevention of Cruelty to English.

Kevin Rudd can shift mid-sentence from warning of 'incremental bifurcation' in the Asia–Pacific region (while, of course, needing to 'work within the extant political vocabulary with China's national discourse') to his notorious manglings of outdated Australian slang ('fair shake of the sauce bottle!')

Weld these together with clichés ('working families', 'decisive action', 'the end of the day'), buzz words ('synergies', 'outcomes', 'reverse engineering') and mixed metaphors ('preglacial position'), and you have a Teflon-coated PR machine that evades satire by overtaking it.

Its effectiveness can be seen in *Godzone*, Guy Rundle and Max Gillies' latest satire on contemporary politics now playing at the Melbourne Theatre Company. 'Let's go for gold!' says Gillies' Rudd. 'Let's optimise programmativity!' And it sounds just as boring and incomprehensible as Rudd himself.

It's a measure of the hyperreality of contemporary politics that satire in the noughties moved to featuring the politicians themselves. American comedians Stephen Colbert and Jon Stewart invite politicians to be interviewed on their shows. The Chasers were regulars at Canberra press conferences.

And it's a dilemma for a satirist who, like Gillies, has made his name by impersonating politicians. The humour of his mimicry of Hawke, Peacock and Howard depended on both the startle of recognition and a recognisable gap between the reality and the portrayal. The absurd exaggerations reflected back on their originals, prompting us to see them in a different light. But when impersonation can't prompt this frisson, it loses its bite.

It's why *7.30 Report* satirists John Clarke and Bryan Dawe, who don't rely at all on mimicry, still hit their targets: there's a cognitive dissonance at play that spikes their wit with the necessary unreality. *Godzone*, on the other hand, seems like an '80s TV skit expanded to the stage. It is as if theatre is where television goes to die.

The set-up is a feel-good public conference, rather like Rudd's 2020 Summit but with added religiosity, where the PM introduces a brace of contemporary political figures to address the audience. In between perorations from the lectern from Rudd, Julia Gillard, Tony Abbott and various commentators such as Andrew Bolt or Christopher Hitchens, Gillies rushes off-stage to apply a new false nose and funny wig and we are treated to a series of video sketches – 'live' interviews with Malcolm Turnbull or Noel Pearson or ads from the 'sponsors'.

The best of these was a vision of hell, or Liberal Party HQ, complete with shadowy Ku Klux Klan figures and swinging light bulbs. There was a YouTube aesthetic here – perhaps stemming from budgetary limitations – that rather undermined the effectiveness of others. Corporate PR gloss doesn't come cheap.

The blandness of the New Left – impregnably smug, impeccably coiffed and upholstered in incomprehensible jargon – creates a smooth, all-reflecting surface that simply doesn't give the purchase for this kind of satire. It's telling that the most successful sketches – Barnaby Joyce as a used car salesman, Gerard Henderson arguing with his local video store – are the rough-hewn conservatives.

Gillies' impersonations don't always hit the mark either. Rudd is reduced to a pout, Tony Abbott to a pair of Billy McMahon ears and Julia Gillard – the least successful of all – is a spinsterish school teacher with 'man hands' brazening out her secondary role as Rudd's henchwoman.

The portrayal of Andrew Bolt made me reflect that parody always includes a modicum of homage. Rundle's script made him seem the most intelligent of the lot: its scathing caricature of left-wing inner-city suburbanites possessed a wit Bolt's columns signally lack.

The most mystifying – nay, bizarre – was Christopher Hitchens, who tells a meandering Boy's Own story of meeting Osama bin Laden in the Hindu Kush (didn't I read something like that in Robert Fisk's book *The Great War for Civilisation*?) and finishes with an account of being raped by Arabs. Which is why, he declaims, it was right to invade Iraq.

Hitchens as Lawrence of Arabia? Well, maybe – at a stretch – there's something in that, but here it's just a cheap punchline. And those allusions – if that's what they are – have no force at all in the format of sketch satire.

None of this is helped by Aidan Fennessy's static direction. Rundle and Gillies' last collaboration, *The Big Con*, featured Eddie Perfect crooning a series of cabaret numbers ('Don't be so damn September 10!') and was a lot more dynamic. Here the switching from lectern to screen gets monotonous and most of the set is simply flashy décor.

For those who have enjoyed the Gillies–Rundle combo before, this is a disappointing outing. It's a bad sign when the program is funnier than the show.

The Australian, December 14 2009

Ngurrumilmarrmiriyu (Wrong Skin)

Aboriginal and Torres Strait Islander readers are warned that this review contains the name of a deceased person.

Many people will have first encountered the Chooky Dancers on YouTube. Their hilariously unlikely Yolngu version of Zorba the Greek became a viral hit, scoring 1.5 million viewers.

They come from Elcho Island (Galiwin'ku), which is north east of Arnhem Land. They live in a poverty which ought to make all Australians ashamed: 25 people share a house where the wiring is falling out of the walls, and where there is often not enough food to ensure that people do not go hungry. People die every week from the many complications of poverty: as if to illustrate this, Frank Garawirrtja, the mentor behind the Chooky Dancers and the *Wrong Skin* project, died during the process of making the show. *Wrong Skin* in fact features footage from his funeral.

In 2007, the Howard government launched the aggressive military intervention policy, which was imposed without consultation with the communities involved. This paternalism – continued under Labor – was supposedly to combat Indigenous deprivation, but its effect has only been to further disenfranchise an already scandalously deprived community. As many community leaders have protested, their rights have been taken away, and many claim it's part of a larger policy to extinguish land rights and Indigenous culture.

Nigel Jamieson canvasses all these issues in *Wrong Skin* at the Malthouse. It's a show that emerges from a community little understood in white Australia, and like *Honour Bound* – Jamieson's physical theatre piece about the Guantanamo Bay prisoner David Hicks – it is driven by a profound political anger. But what you come away with is a vital joyousness, the rebellious humour and resilience of the Yolngu people, that shows the other side of the doom-laden headlines. Indigenous people have often responded to their situations with subversive humour, and the Chooky Dancers are no exception.

This is a difficult show to write about, not least because it requires complicated explanation that the show itself manages to eschew, reaching into the immediacy and vitality of performance to make its various points. Jamieson has put together a multimedia spectacular that enacts the cultural contradictions of contemporary globalism, where Yolngu in one of the most remote regions of Australia download Bollywood and hip-hop to their mobile phones and cheerfully appropriate *Singin' in the Rain* into traditional dance. The whole is strung together by a simple Romeo and Juliet story of forbidden love between Yolngu of the same Yirritja moiety (a relationship which is strictly forbidden), illustrating the tensions between Western ideas of individual freedom and traditional law.

Very little of the narration is in English, but the action, assisted by some miraculous use of multimedia, is crystal clear. The dancers each introduce themselves, identifying their clans and moieties, and then introduce the story. The rest is a kind of patchwork of song and dance and film, woven together to enact a mimesis of life on Elcho Island: its sorrows and imprisonments – which are starkly demonstrated – and its delights – dance, fishing, play.

To the European mind, the complexities of kinship in Indigenous society is mind-boggling. Skin names or moieties and clan affiliations govern your language, your totem, your clan and every aspect of social interaction with other people and with the land. Your skin name determines who you can marry, and who you are forbidden to even speak to. To complicate things further, the cyclical kinship patterns mean that your great-grandmother can be your child, and your great-grandchild your mother.

Take, for example, the term 'Yolngu'. Yolngu means 'person', and can mean someone specifically from East Arnhem Land, or simply an Aboriginal person. The term Yolngu Matha covers the more than 100 languages spoken by the clans of East Arnhem Land. According to anthropologist Emma Kowal, Yolngu inherit their language from their father, but adults generally speak at least five languages, and often understand fifteen or more. In short, to understand what any 10-year-old Yolngu knows is a lifetime study for an outsider. I can't quite get my head around this stuff: this is a culture that challenges basic Western notions of possession and relationship, and which blurs together into a holistic and collective world view concepts that in Western traditions are clearly distinguished from each other.

Jamieson employs all the resources of the stage to communicate some of this complexity, and along the way creates spectacular theatre. There are extraordinarily beautiful scenes which seamlessly meld film and live performance, such as those set in the actual home of the Chooky Dancers. The camera climbs up the rotting steps, enters the dark hallways, lingers over the holes in the walls, and wakes up the boys, who rise from the stage floor, turn on the TV to see a Bollywood film – which they turn into their own dance routine (something really to be seen). The result is a powerful mixture of documentary realism and the joyous celebration of live performance.

Perhaps the real triumph of *Wrong Skin* is how it opens a small window on this world, while managing to avoid the falsities of worthiness or patronisation. Being there is a delight: the sheer exuberance of the young dancers carries the day. Its tragedy is enacted lucidly, although it occurs outside cultural referents I understand; and the whole show powerfully reveals the beauty of this ancient culture, its adaptiveness and curiosity, while unsparingly showing the conditions in which it survives. I liked too how the process of making this work – clearly a complex and difficult one – is folded into the work itself. Not to be missed.

Theatre Notes, March 23 2010

My Stories, Your Emails

You might have noticed that Ms TN is pretending that the Melbourne International Comedy Festival is not happening. If the Melbourne Fringe sends me into a tailspin, contemplating the MICF causes flat-out panic. This is not a syndrome that afflicts punters; it is an anxiety peculiar to crrritics, who all (the real ones, that is) start looking haggard about this time of year, as if they have been indulging in absinthe in grotty nightclubs while pondering Jean-Paul Sartre's observations on the nausea of existence. Ms TN, however, is innocent and blithe and, above all, ignorant of all this. I am wearing my novelist's hat and, as everyone knows, that means being grimly chained to a desk and having no fun at all.

This hat is not quite nailed on, however, which means that every now and then it slips off. So it happened that, in the course of my normal theatre-going last week, I saw by accident a couple of very funny shows. One – Ursula Martinez's *My Stories, Your Emails* at the Malthouse – is, in fact, part of the Comedy Festival. The second, Acrobat's *PropagandA* (of which more later), on this week at the North Melbourne Meatmarket, isn't. Both are slyly subversive and wholly entertaining works of theatre, and are highly recommended.

Ursula Martinez is best known for her magic act *Hanky Panky*. A highlight of the popular burlesque show *La Clique*, it is a witty, wickedly sexy takedown of striptease. Martinez enters in a prim business suit, her hair drawn back tightly in a bun. The one intimation of lust is a red handkerchief, which she makes disappear, and then discovers in items of clothing which she removes. At last, there is no more clothing to hide it: but she still makes it disappear. In the intimate environs of the Spiegeltent, which is where I originally saw it, I thought I had never seen such a subversively erotic act: it was notable for Martinez's sexual self-possession, how, even when she was completely naked, she was never reduced to a mere object of the audience's gaze.

However, in 2006 the act was filmed and uploaded, without her consent, to the internet. Martinez plays the video during the course of *My Stories, Your Emails*, and it's striking how filming the striptease changes the nature of the act. It remains subversive and comic, but something crucial has shifted: it removes Martinez's direct relationship with an audience. In a video, the watching eye is dominant in a way that doesn't happen in live performance, wholly overturning the feminist subtext of the original act. And into the vacuum caused by her physical absence rush the lively fantasies of the voyeur.

After the video appeared, Martinez was bombarded by thousands of fannish emails. *My Stories, Your Emails* is a consistently hilarious and often uncomfortable exploration of the gap between her idea of herself, and those projected onto her image by her sometimes deluded fans.

The show, as she explains in a straight-up introduction, is divided into two parts. The first – fragmentary, almost poetic narratives about herself and her family – consists of her stories. They build up a complex and contradictory picture of a bi-cultural upbringing in London, exploring the intricacies and brutalities of class and race, sibling rivalries and cruelties, a vexed relationship with her father, brushes with celebrity (performing at Salman Rushdie's stag night) and brief observations: a football crowd in a pub, an encounter in a lift.

The second half consist of emails and photographs she received after her act was uploaded to a porn site. These vary from the obscene ('Eric', who sent her photographs of his penis before and after watching her video, helpfully telling her its dimensions) to Niko, a young Australian whose open and naïve confession of his sexual loneliness is as painful as it is funny. There are the enthusiastic naturists who wish her good luck in all her nude activities, the Latino gentlemen seeking a discreet affair, and the Californians who practise Tantric sex and whose physical exertions should never be tried at home by anyone who isn't a Yogi.

The contrast between the two ideas of Martinez is what drives the energy of the show. Martinez lightly invokes a darker subtext – racism, familial abuse, grief and, especially in the second half, loneliness and delusion – that ensures *My Stories, Your Emails* is never merely glib, or merely cruel. Martinez doesn't moralise – she leaves that to her audience – but the show feels like a reclamation of sorts. Also, it's very, very funny.

As an aside, this show caused a bit of a ruckus when it premiered at the Barbican in the UK. As Matt Trueman reported in the *Guardian*, amid some glowing four-star reviews were others which expressed discomfort or even outrage at the show's ethics. *Financial Times* critic Ian Shuttleworth wondered about the provenance of her use of the images and words of others. 'Her own intimacies are hers to peddle', he said. 'Other people's, even if sent to her unsolicited, are not.' Others wondered whether she had permission to identify her correspondents (where they are identified, she does have permission, as is clear in the course of the show), and claimed she was 'punishing' men for expressing desire. In short, there was quite a lot of moral frothing.

There's no doubt that this show is sometimes uncomfortable viewing, and that the expressions of loneliness in those emails can be movingly sad. But it's noticeable that somehow in this argument Martinez was again erased. Nobody mentioned the dynamic that drives the show: the transformation of an empowering expression of female sexuality into the passive objectification of porn. Martinez here simply exposes the mechanics of that transformation.

In its original context, *Hanky Panky* caused exactly the effect it intended: reduced and flattened onto a screen in a private room, it became something entirely different. Without any editorialising, *My Stories, Your Emails* explores one of the major dilemmas of the age of instant celebrity and internet reproducibility: context is what you make it, and the virtual trumps the real. When Martinez strips at the end of the show to deliver the promised 'minge', she simply takes off her clothes, as casually as if she were about to have a shower, and stands naked before her audience. She is no sex bomb, simply a naked woman with the chutzpah to make fun of her own body. And most of all, you know it is her body.

Theatre Notes, March 29 2010

PropagandA

But who are they, tell me, these vagrants, a little
more fugitive even than us, in their springtime
so urgently wrung by one who – who pleases
a never contented will? So it wrings them,
bends them, twists them, swings them,
flings them and catches them behind: out of the oil-smooth
air they come down
onto the flimsy carpet worn

by their eternal leaping, this forlorn
carpet lost in the universe.

> 'Fifth Duino Elegy', Rainer Maria Rilke
> (Translation Alison Croggon)

Circus might appear to be the most ideology-free of the arts, but it has a long tradition of association with revolutionaries and avant-garde artists. In the early twentieth century, poems by writers as diverse as Osip Mandelstam and Rainer Maria Rilke demonstrated their fascination with the circus. Kafka wrote stories set in the sideshow and the ring of the big top; Picasso painted the acrobats. And Vladimir Mayakovsky, the exemplary poet of the Russian Revolution, wrote plays for it, and collaborated from his early years with the Bolshevik clown Vitaly Lazarenko. Circus was, in fact, a key arm of the Soviet Union's propaganda machine, inside and outside Russia; for many years, the Moscow Circus was Russia's most friendly international face.

More recently, our very own Circus Oz, which with troupes such as San Francisco's The Pickle Family Circus and New York's The Big Apple Circus in New York reinvented circus in the 1970s, evolved out of the avant-garde practice and revolutionary ideals of the Pram Factory. This tradition of subversive populism remains alive and well in Australian theatre, as is brilliantly demonstrated by the family troupe Acrobat, now on at North Melbourne Arts House.

Acrobat is one of the treasures of regional Australia. A husband and wife team (Simon Yates and Jo Lancaster, with appearances from their children Grover and Fidel) hailing from Albury, they've generated an enthusiastic international following with their low-tech, highly skilled theatrical circus. And no wonder: these are exceptional performers, whose mix of unpredictable comedy and astounding physical feats creates irresistible entertainment.

PropagandA – as its poster demonstrates – draws consciously on the tradition of Soviet social realist propaganda. Lancaster and Yates stand proudly in front of a green star, striding forth as the idealised man and woman of the future. Naturally, the show itself collides, sometimes violently, with this professed idealism: the first performance is a duet of acrobatics – backgrounded by one of their children playing chopsticks on an amplified keyboard – in which the two of them struggle into impossible structures which then, always, collapse.

Finally Lancaster gives up and lies stretched out on the ground. Yates drags her by her ankle off to the side, strips off most of her clothes, dresses her passive body in a kangaroo costume topped by a fluffy rabbit, and gives her a bass electric guitar. She stands bare-breasted in a spotlight wearing this absurd, slightly disturbing costume and plays a grunting riff, tonelessly singing lyrics about banal domesticity. This was the first time I got goosebumps.

The rest of the show consists of the usual circus acts – aerial and trapeze performances, the slack wire, the bicycle act, the pole, the leap from a springboard – all executed with an astounding skill that allows them to play with the idea of failure. Each act becomes a metaphor, usually of domesticity, and is given a comic spin. The absence of decoration means that the emphasis falls fiercely on the performers, and I'm not sure that I've seen any of these acts done better. They are miraculous.

The aesthetic here is anti-glamour – the costumes are all brown, and the performers often appear with white Y-front drawn up over their brown shirts. The rigger is, slightly mysteriously, dressed as an early twentieth century Eastern European Jew, complete with false beard. Sound and lighting are operated in full sight at the side of the stage, and props are arranged around the edge of the circle, to be thrown away when they're no longer needed. Children wander across the stage, performing obscure tasks. Or maybe just wandering. It's a little like being in someone's kitchen, assuming of course that a kitchen can be a circus.

The propaganda of the title is double-edged. On the one hand, this show lightly explores the insidious conditionings of consumerist, capitalist society, the sub-lunar commands that define the roles of man and woman, family and worker, imprisoning their possibilities. On the other, it has its own message: at one point a child is dressed in ragged hessian wings and lifted on a trapeze, where he shows us handwritten cards on which are written, in wonky capitals, things like BE KIND or GARDEN NUDE or USE ONLY WHAT YOU NEED. If only all propaganda were so benign.

You are most aware that this is a family performing. In the final act, Lancaster and Yates circle on a bike performing acrobatics, pursued by a remote control megaphone shouting BUY A CAR or GET OFF THE ROAD. At one point, I found myself moved to tears. It was, I think, a very small gesture of reassurance, as Yates touched Lancaster's leg as she climbed onto his shoulders. It seemed expressive of the purest trust. Perhaps it revealed what is rendered invisible by the puissant skill of these performers: the risk and danger of what they do. And I should add that for all the seriousness of this review, this is a joyous show, leaving you with the lightness of heart that is the gift of performance.

Theatre Notes, March 31 2010

The Grenade

The Grenade is the sort of play that makes me wonder why people don't stay home and watch *Arrested Development* on their widescreen. Television does this stuff so much better; and besides, you can order pizza.

It's not as if it's a bad play. Tony McNamara is an unashamedly populist playwright, a cut above a David Williamson. He sets up stereotypes in order to explode them with the unexpected, and there is a cruel edge to some of his comedy that, at a stretch, could enter an Ortonesque universe.

But this is comedy that reassures, and any promising subversion is despatched quickly. As Brecht said, 'The bourgeois theatre's performances always aim at smoothing over contradictions, at creating false harmony, at idealisation'.

The Grenade is bourgeois theatre *par excellence*, and part of me wearies of pointing out that its function is to anaesthetise its audience's anxieties about themselves and the world. After all, why shouldn't theatre have the same function as several expensive cocktails?

The conceit is simple. Tough guy political lobbyist Busby McTavish (Garry McDonald) arrives home with his wife Sally (Belinda Bromilow) after a night out with the racing fraternity to find a grenade in his living room. Busby's response is to install security screens and spy on his family. The grenade is really a device – we never discover anything more about it – that enables a farcical plot involving a cast of unlikely characters which explores the notion of middle-class paranoia.

McNamara can't seem to decide if it is a naturalistic romance or an over-the-top comedy (like, for instance, *Arrested Development*): the first half, with a baby that's growing fangs and speaking Spanish, leans towards the absurd, but then the naturalism takes hold and gives us a somewhat mawkish resolution.

There's no arguing the quality of this production. The action occurs on a revolve with some beautiful side lighting from Matt Scott that craftily slides through doors and venetian blinds. In a particularly effective touch, director Peter Evans exploits the turning revolve to allow brief, wordless glimpses of the characters.

I couldn't get enthusiastic about this, but I couldn't hate it either. It is a class above most work of its kind, and no doubt will appeal to many. I'd say it was, like the description of Earth in *The Hitchhiker's Guide to the Galaxy*, 'mostly harmless'.

The Australian, April 19 2010

Moth / The Ugly One / Hole in the Wall

If another person writes another op-ed complaining that Australian theatre is dying, beset by aesthetic crises and apathetic audiences, I will simply point them to Melbourne, May 2010, and have done with it. I can't remember a time when our theatre culture conspired so successfully to demonstrate that it's well and truly alive: and it's been happening at every level. At the MTC, *Richard III* is packing them out and *The Ugly One* has scheduled late performances; you can't get a ticket to *Moth* at the Malthouse for love nor money and *The Threepenny Opera*, in previews later this week, is officially sold out. Beyond the main stages, indie companies are posting 'full' signs all over town.

What's going on? A lot of very interesting theatre, for one thing, boosted by the Next Wave Festival, which continues until the end of the month. And also a lot of word of mouth. Many shows are selling out without the benefit of a single review. So much for the much-vaunted power of crrrritics! What counts for much more is the excited report of a friend or acquaintance: that is, the impact of the work itself. This also demonstrates very clearly the baselessness of the idea that the success of one aspect of the theatre culture comes at the expense of others. It suggests something altogether more interesting: that vitality breeds vitality, and that theatre companies ignore their interdependence with the rest of the culture at their own peril.

Out of all this richness, reports of which have reached even my subterranean ears, I've been able to see very little. What I did see gives some indication of the quality of work that is not only expected but is delivered in this city. Following are some notes on what I've seen:

Moth

At a distressingly young age, Declan Greene has carved out a reputation in Melbourne's independent scene with a series of plays demonstrating a black wit, iron nerve and a considerable lyrical gift. What's notable is the restlessness of his work: he's a playwright whose work is distinctive but never predictable. And he's learning fast. *Moth* represents yet another startling evolution: it was not at all what his previous work led me to expect, and yet is an absolutely logical progression.

It's a powerful examination of mental illness, especially in relation to young people. Greene's two 15-year-old protagonists are Claryssa (Sarah Ogden), a Wiccan emo, and Sebastian (Dylan Young), all-round oddball, who are both rejects in the merciless pecking order of high school. They are compelling portrayals of adolescents – self-centred, mocking, vulnerable and funny – who are traumatically alienated from the social lives around them. A horrific, if horribly familiar, instance of bullying unlatches Sebastian's already uncertain sense of reality, and his sense of self splinters into delusion. He has an apocalyptic vision of Saint Sebastian, embodied as a moth he keeps in a jar, and sets off on a mission to find the saved. Meanwhile Claryssa, as traumatised by Sebastian by the bullying episode, sinks into paralysing depression and is unable to help her friend.

Perhaps the strongest aspect of this script is how unsentimentally and accurately it represents not only the speech and attitudes of teen subculture (I had a 15-year-old with me who affirmed its authenticity) but the subjective experience of mental breakdown. The story is told through enactments by Ogden and Young, shifting between times and different subjective states in ways which recall the narrative of the cult film *Donnie Darko*, and Greene exploits to the full his capacity to soar from vernacular speech into pure poetry.

Chris Kohn directs *Moth* on a stage bare of everything except what looks like three lengths of underfelt, cascading from backstage to the floor, that define three different theatrical areas. Kohn's direction is absolutely simple and absolutely lucid, directing so good it's almost invisible. Jonathan Oxlade's design, Rachel Burke's lighting and Jethro Woodward's music conspire to focus the action on stage to diamond precision. Ogden and Young are remarkable, giving passionate, minutely disciplined performances that wind up to a shattering climax. What begins as a comic picture of two teen misfits ends up as a piece of theatre with the catastrophic power of tragedy. The long, devastated silence that preceded the applause was its proper tribute.

The Ugly One

Marius von Mayenburg, long-term dramaturg with Thomas Ostermeier at Berlin's Schaubühne am Lehniner Platz, debuted in Melbourne at the Malthouse in 2006 with the brilliant Benedict Andrews production of *Eldorado*, a scorching parable on the human capacity for self-destruction, and returned in 2008 with a production of a fascinating collaboration, again with Andrews, called *Moving Target*. *The Ugly One*, written between these two productions, is a play on a smaller scale, but demonstrating to the full von Mayenburg's imaginative control of theatrical form.

As an exercise in theatrical elegance, it's an exemplary text. *The Ugly One* is a painfully hilarious and disturbing satire on the contemporary obsession with appearance, in which von Mayenburg cunningly exploits a simple theatrical idea – identically named characters played by the same actors – to explore the place of individuality in an increasingly homogenised society, and how our uniqueness plays into our idea of self.

Lette (Patrick Brammall) is the inventor of a new kind of plug, but finds that when it's time to present it to the world, his boss Scheffler (Kim Gyngell) thinks he is too ugly to sell it, and instead intends to send his assistant, Karlmann (Luke Ryan). When he asks his wife Fanny (Alison Bell), she confirms, to his astonishment, that he is as ugly as everyone says. In despair, he undergoes plastic surgery. Lette emerges looking exactly the same, but finds that his world has changed. Women lust after him, and he becomes a corporate success. But now everybody wants to look like him.

Using this simple premise, von Mayenburg pulls to the surface all sorts of contemporary anxieties. The face is both more and less than a marker of individuality: it is, in the corporate world, the equivalent of a brand, through which perceptions of success and failure are filtered independently of the reality of achievement or quality. Lette's 'transformation' – Brammall is the only actor, incidentally, who doesn't play multiple roles – gives him the competitive edge in both the sexual and corporate worlds. But all too soon technology catches up and reproduces him, creating a hall of mirrors, a nightmare vision of Lettes that flood the market like generic drugs. In such a world, no human being can be anything but a product, a commodity valued by his or her exchange value. In the process, Lette's personal identity – whatever uniqueness he originally possessed – is completely lost.

Peter Evans gives this play the elegant production it deserves, directing it in the round with minimal props. The razor-sharp shifts in the text are handled with finesse and spareness, and some ingenious staging: among other effective touches, the amplified crunching of an apple excruciatingly evokes the sounds of surgery. All four performers rise to the challenge, giving nuanced and witty performances that bring out the play's comedy, and permit the darker themes simply to rise to the surface as a profound rippling of disturbance. This is definitely a highlight of the MTC's 2010 season, and not to be missed.

Hole in the Wall

Hole in the Wall is the only show I've been able to catch from the Next Wave Festival. This 45-minute show knocked my socks off, and made me even more sorry about what I've been missing. It's a fascinating multi-disciplinary theatre work that explores the experience of domestic, suburban space as lived by a twenty-something couple. Sounds mundane? As *Hole in the Wall* manages to demonstrate, the mundane is only dull if you're not looking.

The text, written by My Darling Patricia member Halcyon Mcleod, has a simple premise: it articulates the thoughts, fears and desires of a young couple (Matt Prest and Clare Britton) during the course of a single night. They would like a better house; they wonder what they are doing with their lives; they take out their frustrations on each other in bitter and violent arguments; they are afraid of dying; they are lonely. All these recognisable vignettes play out with a dream logic that ignores chronology, giving us snatches of their domestic lives.

It creates the premise for an extraordinary piece of experiential theatre. The audience is divided into four, and then put in four separate boxes that are simulacra of the average weatherboard rental house, with wallpaper up to the picture railing, a paned window (which is closed), and a painted white door with a brass handle.

Once you are enclosed with your fellow audients, the box begins to move, forcing you to walk along with it. It is difficult to describe how disorienting this is: it quite literally made me dizzy. Part of the dizziness was the necessity to reorient my sense of place. While in fact the floor is quite still, and it's the box that's moving, from the point of view of those enclosed, it's the walls that are stationary. There was a similarly disconcerting exhibit of a swaying room in the Guggenheim exhibition at the NGV recently (I'm afraid I can't remember the artist) – this was much more displacing, because it was more claustrophobic.

Once the box stopped moving, the lights went out, leaving us in complete darkness, and the first monologue – about the way a bed is like a grave – boomed out over us, accompanied by a rising growl of sound. And then one wall was thrown open, revealing the rest of the audience in the three other boxes, all ingeniously linked together to make one room, in the centre of which was a bed.

The performances played out in these intimate spaces, which were continually reconfigured in constantly surprising ways by unseen manipulators. Sometimes the boxes became a long hallway, through which the performers entered and left, in which we became guests at a party, or ghostly witnesses of private grief. Sometimes we looked out through a window at Preston walking outside in his pyjamas. Once all the walls opened and we watched a projected animation of puppets who played out the story of a happy suburban couple.

The effects were haunting, poignant, moving; sometimes (as in the terrible quarrel between the couple) confronting. Aside from the compelling performances, perhaps the most powerful aspect of *Hole in a Wall* was how the initial disorientation made us all complicit in the show. Social barriers immediately dropped in our initial surprise and puzzlement, and when we were watching the performances we were all aware not only that we were watching together, but that we were in the same intimate space as the performers, and that we were, in our witnessing, part of the show. An absolutely fascinating and beautiful experience.

Theatre Notes, May 25 2010

Do Not Go Gentle...

Patricia Cornelius' award-winning play borrows its title from Dylan Thomas' poem, 'Do not go gentle into that good night'. Perhaps the most beautiful villanelle written in English, Thomas' poem celebrates the vivid life of old age, pressed hard against death: 'Old age should burn and rave at close of day'.

Likewise, *Do Not Go Gentle...* explores the flare of vitality that reaches a desperate intensity in the face of death, through seven characters who live in an old people's home. The central character, Scott (Rhys McConnochie), is obsessed with the tragic heroism of Robert Falcon Scott's ill-fated expedition to the South Pole, a race he lost to the Norwegian explorer Roald Amundsen, and which ultimately cost him his life.

In Cornelius' hands, this expedition becomes a metaphor for the long defeat that is life itself, moving with a poetic suppleness between entries from Scott's diary and the mundane details of life in an institution. She evokes with unsentimental compassion the confusions and longings of old age, or, in the case of Bowers (Pamela Rabe), a younger woman suffering from premature Alzheimer's who doesn't remember her own husband, of tragic memory loss.

Scott's story provides a narrative spine from which emerges the stories of the various characters. Most powerfully, this double reality becomes a theatrical metaphor for the uncertain world Cornelius' characters inhabit, with the white wastes of Antarctica a potent image of desolation.

Yet, like Thomas' poem, the play is primarily a celebration of life. Cornelius' characters, like the actors who play them, are funny, angry and defiant, and out of the poverties of their situation create a richness that is its own meaning.

Director Julian Meyrick has assembled an extraordinary cast that includes some of the best known names in the business, and the production generates many moments of sheer beauty.

The play isn't wholly successful: there are scenes where the conceit of the double reality isn't sustained, and Cornelius' poetic language loses its tension, falling into the merely literal. But for most of its length it makes riveting and moving theatre, from the spine-tingling opening, in which Maria (Jan Friedl) emerges in her dressing gown and sings a glorious aria.

It recalls Walter Pater's insistence that all art aspires to the condition of music, yearning towards the mysteries of what can't be expressed in words, and is as moving an image of mortality as I have seen in the theatre.

The Australian, August 9 2010

This Kind of Ruckus

I've been meaning to catch up with version 1.0 for years. Under the guidance of David Williams, this Sydney-based theatre has established itself as one of Australia's must-see companies, redefining and, most of all, revitalising contemporary political theatre.

One of the few Australian companies that lists political engagement as its *raison d'être*, version 1.0 has developed a theatrical language that jams found texts from a variety of public sources – court transcripts, media interviews, television shows – against the personal stories of the performers. In their own words, version 1.0 'engages with significant political and social issues using innovative theatrical strategies'. The corporate-speak mission-statement vocab is off-putting, but don't let it deter you: this is a company alive to the complexities, ambiguities and, above all, the deceptions of language. Not least, one suspects, its own language. On the evidence of This Kind of Ruckus (Fairfax Studio, Victorian Arts Centre), the company's ambitions work in ironic counterpoint with the jargon it employs, takes apart and, ultimately, subverts.

Version 1.0's previous work includes shows about the Australian Wheat Board scandal (*Deeply offensive and utterly untrue*); the ethics of the invasion of Iraq (*The Wages of Spin*); and the scandal and tragedy of SIEV-X, the boat of asylum seekers that sank in 2001, killing 353 people (*CMI: A Certain Maritime Incident*). *This Kind of Ruckus* steps into the equally explosive arena of sexual politics. It's certainly the most lucid demonstration I've seen anywhere of the lose-lose deal that goes with being a woman in a patriarchal society, and I walked out of the show feeling a deep, ancient rage burning its way to the surface of my psyche.

This Kind of Ruckus is an exploration of sexual violence, beginning with the notoriously misogynist culture of leagues clubs in NSW. In the careful, intelligent hands of the five performers – Valerie Berry, Arky Michael, Katia Molino, Kym Vercoe and David Williams – this potential minefield not only makes excellent theatre, it makes its point.

It avoids simplistic portrayals of woman-as-victim, man-as-aggressor – images that permit us to avoid thinking about the complexities of sexual violence – and throws an uneasy light on the grey areas that exist between these too-easy absolutes. It makes the point that women want sex just as much as men do, that women can be filthy, ugly, rude, aggressive and criminal, just as men can be. Yet in a society that privileges the male, a woman's expressions of desire will be seen differently from a man's. Ultimately, a woman's sexuality will be used against her: her own desire can be used to violate her autonomy, to grind down and destroy her sense of self.

We all know about the famous double-standard, but this is a show uninterested in binaries, the easy hefting of blame. Instead, it seeks to make its audience more conscious of the implications of language and actions that many people never give a second thought. With intelligent repetition and juxtaposition, *This Kind of Ruckus* excavates the realities of male privilege. Patiently, without histrionics or exaggeration, it exposes how the female subject is routinely marginalised and even erased by the unexamined assumptions that place the male at the centre of legitimate experience.

And it does all this through effective, vernacular theatre, which is neither didactic nor simple-minded. From the opening moments, when each performer walks separately onto the stage in front of a drawn curtain, the performers exploit familiar images and gestures: here the men and the women parody cheerleaders, posing theatrically before the audience with their red pompoms. At a given signal, the actors perform a complicated twirl that leaves all five seated and apparently in the middle of lively conversation. Like everything that follows, it's sharp, clever and arresting.

The action weaves around a central recurring image: David Williams, a shaven-headed, heavy-set man, seated on a chair looking straight at the crotch of an unconscious woman (Kym Vercoe), who is stretched out on the floor. Her left leg is propped slightly, so the pose is exactly the same as the woman in Gustave Courbet's iconic erotic painting, *The Origin of the World*. Williams is inscrutable: he is looking, but seems to have no pleasure from what he is seeing; he is transfixed but curiously passive. Sad, perhaps; creepy, perhaps; threatening, maybe. It's an image of aftermath: the one thing we know is that something has happened.

The show itself is a collage of fragmentary narratives – a couple in therapy; a personal anecdote of a horrific unacknowledged rape; a quote from Matthew Johns' notorious shamed interview, from *Four Corners*; glimpses of a woman who is a victim of domestic violence – that are punctuated by dancing and seduction to pulsing electronic funk in a leagues club, where beer in plastic cups is lined up on a makeshift bar. Two screens dislocate the action further, sometimes projecting live action, sometimes not. The show winches up unease, cutting deeper and deeper into the ordinary, everyday self-deceits of which no-one is not guilty, paring away at the exceptionalism which permits the audience – ourselves – to claim that it's them, not us.

The point is not to drive home a lesson, which can be easily learned and as easily forgotten, but to open a scab. Scratch this kind of theatre, and it's no surprise to find Brecht. Version 1.0's practice is in fact a very smart contemporary application of Brecht's theory of Epic Theatre, which by describing an event from the contradictory angles of all its witnesses, attempts to build a truthful picture of what happened. Above all, it's a dynamic picture, that opens out of the comforts of received wisdom the uncomfortable prickling of consciousness. Yes, it reminds you of the reasons to be angry; but most of all, at various levels from the subconscious up, it provokes thought. Frankly, it's pretty rare to find theatre that so clearly and stylishly does exactly what it says it intends to do.

Theatre Notes, August 24 2010

Sappho... in 9 Fragments

As the poet Anne Carson points out, it was Sappho who first described eros as 'bittersweet'. 'No-one who has been in love,' says Carson, 'disputes her'. Desire is, after all, fraught with paradox: it is the zenith of human bliss, but its annihilating power destroys the illusion of human autonomy. As Sappho describes in her most famous fragment (translation mine), it can seem like dying:

> How like a god he seems, that man
> who sits across from you,
> who is close enough to hear
> your sweet speech
>
> and the delightful laughter
> that sets my heart fluttering –
> even a glimpse of you
> snuffs my speech –
>
> my tongue breaks, a subtle flame
> runs over my skin,
> my eyes no longer see
> and my ears buzz –
>
> a cold sweat covers me and I
> tremble all over, I am paler
> than grass, so near to death
> I feel my dying –

After two and a half millennia, Sappho's poems still speak across what would seem unbridgeable gaps of time and culture, expressing with a directness and delicacy that has rarely been matched the contradictions of 'limb-loosening' desire. In her extraordinary performance *Sappho... in 9 Fragments*, actor/writer Jane Montgomery Griffiths takes on Sappho's legacy, exploring the history of her texts and the various myths and conjectures that fill the absence of knowledge about her life. Lesbian, wife, mother, suicide, exile, tenth muse of the archaic Greek world: how can we hear her elusive voice, through the clamorous myths that cluster about her name?

Sappho... in 9 Fragments is not so much a homage to Sappho as a reanimation of the body of her work (with an emphasis on 'body') through a particular subjectivity. Most of all, it's a passionate engagement with the poetry itself, a multifaceted imaginative dance with Sappho's work brought with painful intensity into the present moment. Montgomery Griffiths does a seemingly impossible thing, and makes theatre out of an act of understanding.

Reading, listening, watching, comprehension, become – both in our watching, as audience members, and in Montgomery Griffiths' performance – acts of love: the stroking of a page is also the stroking of skin. Before our eyes she enacts the creation of meaning, which is always a collaboration, a dynamic exchange, between the artist's work and those who encounter it. But it's an act fraught with peril, with the risk of annihilating damage and pain. Eros wakes an unassuageable longing, making us aware of our incompleteness, our existential solitude. As Atthis says in Fragment 8, recalling Plato:

> Once, we were whole. A smooth, round completeness of total happiness... But we did something wrong, and the gods punished us. We were split and sundered... and our two dismembered halves were left to wander. Looking for each other. Looking for that wholeness. But when we met again, the damage was too great... And when we embraced, all we felt was our hollowness. And so we parted. Resigned to live forever with our emptiness and our lack.

First performed at the Stork Hotel in 2007, this complex, moving and powerful work has been further developed by Malthouse Theatre under the direction of Marion Potts. I missed the first production, but was very glad to see this one. The writing is sharp, witty and passionate: Montgomery uses her own free translations of Sappho which, unlike the spare renderings of Carson or Diane Rayor, spiral in intensifying thickenings of linguistic desire that work surprisingly well in performance.

Anna Cordingley's design, lit with Paul Jackson's usual sensitivity, is breathtakingly beautiful. The audience is placed on three sides, facing a tank that appears to be full of honey, which gradually empties onto the stage during the course of the monologue. Sappho's naked body is gradually revealed inside the tank, at last emerging from this amber prison to a soundscape composed of fragments of Greek, the trickling of fluid and archaic percussion. It's a bold and hauntingly lovely opening to a riveting show.

Through the performance, Montgomery Griffiths embodies several things at once. She performs the poet herself, but also becomes her poems – there's a moment where she is the fragments of papyri which have lain underground for centuries, begging to be discovered, to be read again. There are skin-tingling recitations of the fragmented poems in the original Greek, which invite us into Sappho's exquisite musicality. Montgomery Griffiths explores, with various degrees of irony, their lexigraphical adventures through the centuries, and the invented biographies of Sappho that have rounded out the few historical facts, while also adding her own projected narrative.

Montgomery Griffith's Sappho is seductive and terrifying: a potent, desirous and desirable woman, as unforgiving and vulnerable as the art she creates. She and her avatars are in fluid dialogue with the voice of Sappho's lover Atthis ('there can be no Sappho without an Atthis'), told through a contemporary story of seduction and betrayal. Sappho is figured through a famous actress playing that great victim of love's extremity, Phaedra, and a lowly chorus member who catches her eye. This sometimes painfully comic narrative twines through the other voices, enacting the passions – desire, love, jealousy, anguish, loss – of the poems.

Montgomery Griffiths' performance is outstanding; like her wit and intellect, the virtuosity of her superb physical and vocal skills do not serve as masks so much as tools to excavate the unmediated rawness of feeling. She can be spiky, predatory, even bestial, and in the next moment expose a piercing vulnerability, walking a tightrope of extremity which, if she faltered, could tip her into bathos. But her assurance and, finally, her naked honesty, ensure there is not a trace of sentiment in her performance. Anyone who believes that passion and intelligence are opposites should see this show, where each crucially informs the other. Not to be missed.

Theatre Notes, August 11 2010

Thyestes

> Their flesh is heaving
> Inside me.
>
> *Thyestes*, Seneca, translated by Caryl Churchill.

> An idea – the antagonism of the two concepts Dionysian and Apollonian – is translated into metaphysics; history itself is depicted as the development of this idea; in tragedy this antithesis has become unity; from this standpoint things which theretofore had never been face to face are suddenly confronted, and understand and are illuminated by each other… 'Rationality' at any price as a dangerous force that undermines life… Christianity is neither Apollonian nor Dionysian; it negates

all aesthetic values; it is nihilistic in the most profound sense, while in the Dionysian symbol the ultimate limit of affirmation is attained...

> Friedrich Nietzsche, in *Ecce Homo* on *The Birth of Tragedy*

Since 2007, The Hayloft Project has established itself as one of Australia's leading independent companies with a string of elegant, razor-intelligent productions. In particular, they've attracted attention for their reworking of modern classics, such as Wedekind's *Spring Awakening*, Chekhov's *Platonov* and, controversially, a fascinating version of *Three Sisters*, *3xSisters*. For *Thyestes*, Malthouse's Tower Theatre residency for 2010, director Simon Stone reaches much further into the past, to the plays of Nero's tutor and adviser, philosopher and sometime dramatist, Seneca the Younger.

He's linked forces again with Black Lung stalwarts Mark Leonard Winter and Thomas Henning. Others include Chris Ryan (seen most recently in Malthouse's *Elizabeth* and Benedict Andrews' *Measure for Measure* at Belvoir St); Hayloft dramaturge Anne-Louise Sarks, one of the brains behind Hayloft's Fringe hit *Yuri Wells*; and sound designer Stefan Gregory, who was responsible for the astonishing sound in the STC's *The War of the Roses*. The result is Hayloft's best work yet, and one of the highlights of the year. *Thyestes* is rock'n'roll theatre: confronting, transgressive, uncomfortably hilarious, obscene, horrifying, and desolatingly beautiful.

Yet it's hard to know where to begin talking about this show. Thinking about it is very like contemplating one of those breeding tangles of snakes that featured on David Attenborough's *Life*: it's an orgy of forms and ideas, each writhing about the others, which makes the mind slide distractingly from one thought to the next. I think that above all, you're dazzled by the sheer outrageous excess of it, its shockingly wasteful expense of energy. And yet this impression of excess is created by what is surely one of Hayloft's most austere productions.

The austerity begins with the design, which is stark black and white, reflecting the absolute moral world of classical tragedy. The Greeks didn't do shadows: this is a universe of darkness visible, where the hidden is dragged into the unforgiving light. Claude Marcos' traverse set – effectively a black, narrow, enclosed box, with a white interior exposed by Govin Ruben's harsh fluorescent lights – embodies this sense of continuous revelation. When the blinds that serve as curtains are down, as they are between every scene, it's impossible to see the audience on the other side: each new scene reveals the audience as well as the actors. This becomes increasingly disconcerting, because one of the paradoxical effects of this show is to erase distances: between then and now, them and us, the actors and ourselves.

A major reason for this sense of collapse between boundaries is Stefan Gregory's sensually enveloping sound design. Gregory shamelessly exploits the capacity of music to locate us ecstatically in the present: the soundtrack includes Schubert and Handel, Wu Tang Clan and Ice Cube, Roy Orbison and Queen. This connects with another convention – the use of surtitles – to make *Thyestes* seem like a kind of opera. It looks like theatre and sounds like theatre, but in its strangely abstracted narrative, and especially in its emotional excess, it works more like an operatic history.

And what of the story itself? Simon Stone and his collaborators claim their version of *Thyestes* is 'after Seneca', but it's probably more true to label it 'before Seneca'. Seneca's actual play – notoriously 'modern' in that very little happens aside from the climactic event – is enacted in a mere couple of scenes, right at the end of the show. The rest is an excavation of the bloody history of the House of Tantalus: the first and worst of all unhappy families.

From Tantalus himself, who stole ambrosia from Olympus and who most notably slaughtered and cooked his son Pelops to feed the gods, to Menelaus and Agamemnon, who besieged Troy for ten years to recover the faithless Helen, this single family constitutes the DNA of what we think of as canonical Western literature. The doings of Tantalus' descendents exercised, among countless others, Homer, Aeschylus, Sophocles, Euripides and, later, Seneca. And through his influence on Jacobean and Elizabethan tragedy, and especially on Shakespeare, Seneca is arguably the biggest classical influence on English drama. What Hayloft presents isn't recognisably Shakespearean. It's not particularly Senecan, come to that. And yet its effect is surprisingly close to both: which I think is a result of a complexity of texture on the one hand, and a primitive, unforgiving harshness on the other.

Its narrative genius is the surtitles, which flash up before each scene, describing the plot of the story, before the curtains rise on the stage, revealing another, altogether more mundane reality. It's a brilliant way of coping with the tale's anachronisms, which are mostly removed from the actual performances, and become instead a framing device. And this convention means that the dozen or so short plays or tableaux that make up the whole need not concern themselves at all with plot. When the curtains rise, we are suddenly pitched into twenty-first century Melbourne, into the unremarked spaces between larger, tragic events. What we see are overwhelmingly domestic scenes.

The story begins with the murder by Thyestes (Thomas Henning) and Atreus (Mark Leonard Winter) of their half-brother, Chrysippus (Chris Ryan), at the urging of their mother Hippodamia, who is angry that her sons have been passed over to inherit the throne. The first scene is brilliant in how it winds you into its double reality: the three actors perform with an almost documentary realism that at first almost makes you believe you're overhearing three young men passing time, late at night, at a party. Until, that is, Chrysippus turns his back, fiddling with his iPod to get a favourite song, and the two brothers stand up, suddenly full of menace, and pull out the gun, and the machinery of tragedy is activated. Oddly, not so much on stage, as in our minds.

It's clear from the beginning that this version of *Thyestes* is primarily about the relationship between two brothers. The show has a genuinely Freudian edge, and not just in its unafraid confrontations of sexuality. Its increasing sense of disturbance is in how it echoes those dark jealousies that only exist between siblings, and that can continue lifelong, coloured into adulthood by the uncontrolled passions of infancy. Chrysippus' murder is at first presented as the originatory crime from which emerges the others, but as this bloody family history unrolls before us, it becomes clear that even this is an echo of earlier crimes, that these brothers are trapped in a hell of repetition that is the curse of their family.

This understanding has both a symbolic and a literal value: we understand the story in wholly contemporary terms, in how incest, for instance, can be passed down from generation to generation, the parent visiting on the child his or her own suffering; and we also understand it as myth, as a representation of something larger than it is. This dislocatedness is why it is, at times, very funny indeed. Some of its most powerful moments are when these double recognitions, which weave a complementary dance through the show, suddenly unite into a single breathtaking image.

The most memorable perhaps is when the curtain rises on the suicidal Pelopia (Chris Ryan), singing a Schubert lieder: mother of a child who is the product of incestuous rape, she is the image of unhealable damage, lifted suddenly into an ecstatically operatic moment, pain and beauty united. In such moments – there are others – the performers embody Nietzsche's idea of the tragic: a Dionysian image of absolute negation becomes, through the ecstasy of performance, 'the absolute limit of affirmation'. It's a quality that Barrie Kosky also achieves, although in very different ways: and the secret is in the balance between restraint and excess.

Winter, Henning and Ryan are astounding, on the one hand achieving a naturalistic authenticity that locates these extreme events in the middle of the mundane present, without on the other losing a sense of heightened reality. We believe in these ancient tales of warring kings, because we also understand, through these performances, that betrayal, violence, sexual excess, greed, despair and madness are, in fact, the most ordinary of human realities. Scratch the history of any family, and you will find such behaviours lurking not far beneath the surface. I'm not the first, for example, to link Thyestes' eating of his children with incest: in Hayloft's rendering of the story, this connection is even clearer, as it becomes a mirror of Thyestes' rape of his daughter Pelopia.

There's much more to tease out, but I've probably said enough. If you can possibly get there, don't miss it. The word is out, and it is wildly good: and the critics are in unusually rhapsodic alignment. The season has been extended an extra week, so there is still a chance to see it. But I suspect you'll have to be quick.

Theatre Notes, September 24 2010

The Trial

Last week, as is our wont now and again, Ms TN and her alter egos spent some hours pondering what it is that most matters to me in art. Is there one quality, we wondered, by which I gauge how much a work matters to me, one value by which we measure the rest? Yes, I answered myself, there is. What's more, for all the hundreds of thousands of words I've written here and elsewhere, I have never really said what it is.

Why is that? Is it cowardice? Is it because it's too private? Is it that to articulate something so personal as what matters most is, somehow, to do it violence – to reduce it, to nail down a delicate and necessary silence with the crudity of words? And let's face it, when you put it baldly, it just sounds banal. What matters most to me, in any artwork, is its truthfulness.

Of course, 'truthfulness' is a shorthand term for a constellation of qualities, some of them contradictory (as Whitman says, 'Do I contradict myself? Well, then, I contradict myself... '). There is, however, one thing I unambiguously don't mean by truthfulness. I don't mean that a work of art must tell The Truth, that one-eyed monster so beloved of morally calcified politicians or right-wing columnists. The Truth – a singular, jealous god that admits no Other – is only the shiny side of a lie.

No, I'm thinking of less monumental, more profound qualities of truthfulness. True, as in when a craftsman runs his hand along a beautifully-made table, or when a dressmaker cuts a pure line. True, as when you are true to your ideals, or to someone you love. True, as in poetry. This quality of truthfulness can't be disproved; but then again, it can't be proved either. Since its foundations are, like the ladders of Rilke's lovers, 'long-since groundless... leaning / on only each other, tremulously', it is, ironically perhaps, a little like faith. It has nothing to do with being 'right' or 'wrong'. Can a life be right or wrong? Can an artwork?

'Poetry is, above all, an approach to the truth of feeling', says Muriel Rukeyser. For Rukeyser, life and poetry are very nearly synonyms. They are a dance, an exchange, an invitation. I would say that of most arts, and claim it an especial quality of the theatre. The negation of feeling, its complexities, its realness, results in waste and injury, a necrosis of denial that infects every area of public and private life. Truthfulness is beyond mere honesty: 'If we settle for honesty', said Rukeyser, 'we are selling out'. It is more complex and more ironic, more supple, more self aware. It's also more primitive. Its presence alerts the same kind of senses that make a deer startle when it smells a predator on the wind, or which reassure a suckling infant that it is safe. This truthfulness is never still, because it is a living thing. It keeps on happening, rippling out from the energy generated by encounter: artist and world, artist and work, work and witness.

So, if I have a 'bias' – as is asserted now and again by more or less anonymous commenters on this blog, or by disaffected directors, or even by professional arts journalists interviewing total strangers about stuff that has nothing to do with me – then this 'bias' tends to art that, to my mind, struggles towards the true. Equally, work that flinches from the true – especially art that makes grand gestures towards truthfulness, borrowing the weight and courage of others who have dared it, but refusing their risk – gets up my nose. Truthfulness has a price – for the poet Lorca, the price was his life – and you can't cheat it.

Are my judgments 'subjective'? Indeed they are, as are all judgments in matters of art by anyone. They don't mean that work I don't enjoy is therefore a lie – just as The Truth is almost certainly always a lie, so the opposite of a truth might be another truth. But they are certainly judgments that record my own struggle to be truthful. More, in writing down these thoughts and speculations, I seek to make reasonable judgments, because I value rationality as fiercely as I do feeling. No-one can argue with my belief, because belief is unarguable and incorrigible: but anyone can take issue with my arguments.

Well, now I've said my ideals. Which, if any of you are still reading, brings me finally to last week's theatre viewing: *The Trial*, Matthew Lutton and Louise Fox's staging of Franz Kafka's famous novel at the Malthouse. It's an adaptation, and it's reasonable, given my preamble, to begin by asking whether the adaptation is true to the original. After all, Kafka, Prague insurance clerk, is to the point of anguish a truthful artist. This fidelity is not about slavishly copying the work from one medium into another: it's more properly a question of whether the adaptation faithfully refracts in its new form the truthfulness of the original work.

Although it was first published in 1925, a year after Kafka's death, *The Trial* is one of a handful of novels – George Orwell's *1984* and Albert Camus' *The Plague* are others – which articulate with an almost sadistic precision the 'human condition' of the twentieth century. Matthew Lutton and Louise Fox have achieved something brilliant with this production: they have translated this iconic story to the stage without trivialising it, and without resorting to the romantic clichés that cluster around Kafka like flies around a corpse.

Kafka's work especially attracts this kind of thing, perhaps because of the obdurate refusals and opacities of his texts. They are more like cruel objects than stories, full of brooding significance that seems to retreat further the more you attempt to interrogate its meaning. For some commenters, he becomes a moraliser, although Kafka went to more trouble than almost any other human being to avoid moralising; to his hagiographers Max Brod and Gustav Janouch, Kafka was even a saint.

The brief essay printed in the program, by Dimitris Vardoulakis of UWS, is not untypical: Vardoulakis says the 'main objective' of *The Trial* is 'a critique of the ideal of liberal democratic freedom'. 'Instead of the logic of the law, Josef K should have followed the logic of desire that he discovered in his association with women characters... only then can Kafka's other freedom be possible.' Yet the great nightmare of *The Trial*, and the reason why it resonates so disturbingly through the history of the past century, is that it shows a world in which freedom is not possible at all.

It's fortunate that the production has nothing to do with Vardoulakis' argument, which attempts to rescue a utopic hope from a novel that is peculiarly resistant to any such illusion. The multiple seductions in the novel are far from expressions of liberation; rather, like the kiss Josef K bestows on Leni, they are 'aimless', fevered and furtive exchanges that promise nothing except another slavery, this time to the imperatives of bodily functions. Josef K doesn't just die 'like a dog'; like everyone else around him, he ruts like a dog too, only without the privilege of a dog's bestial innocence. The torment in this novel is consciousness, which is why Josef K's death comes almost gently, as a relief. One of the great virtues of Lutton's production is how powerfully it communicates a palpable sense of the sordid bodily realities Kafka evokes in *The Trial* – you can almost smell the grotesque seductions, the shabby, stuffy rooms, the sour sweat of panic.

Josef K's unavailing struggle against the law that both accuses and condemns him is uncannily prescient; it foreshadows the faceless bureaucratic violence that came to fruition in Auschwitz or Kolyma or Tuol Sleng. Nor have its insights dated: in the surveillance society of the twenty-first century it resonates with an extra chill. And yet it's a mistake to think of it as a political novel. To regard *The Trial* as merely as a critique of the state's power to inscribe itself on the bodies of its subjects is to ignore its metaphysical dimensions, which culminate in the famous and inescapably Judaic parable of the Doorkeeper at the end of the novel. Kafka is, like Beckett, a master of the precise and essential metaphor: *The Trial* might be most accurately called a portrait of the modern soul, in the same way Foucault's study of the penal system, *Discipline and Punish*, described that soul's genealogy.

The major strength of Fox's lucid script is that she refuses to lay any interpretation over Kafka's hauntingly mundane narratives, leaving them open to the multiple interpretations that resonate in the book. It's almost sternly faithful to the novel, but avoids any hint of deadly reverence. Likewise, Lutton's direction constructs a theatrical simulacrum of Kafka's claustrophobic reality that is at once compelling and, for all its nods to Orson Welles' magnificent film, totally original.

In Lutton's hands, the narrative becomes crudely theatrical, mockingly exposing the clumsiness, embarrassment and abjection of the human bodies which tumble around the raw plywood revolve that mainly constitutes Claude Marcos' set. The direction is swift, almost clinical, in how it moves the story imperceptibly from its banal, comedic opening into the logical absurdity of a nightmare. From its opening moments, when Josef K wakes up to find two police officers by his bed ('before breakfast!'), to its desolate final image, Lutton and his cast generate an irresistible cumulative power.

The action is punctuated by several changes in the set – the dropping of curtains, the activation of the revolve about an hour in, and particularly a stunning set reveal late in the show. Each change serially exposes the mechanics of the stage, making us aware that the actors are trapped in the machinery, literally as well as metaphorically. Kelly Ryall's brilliant sound design is one of the most textured and dramatically active I've experienced: it's a world in itself, paranoid and inscrutable, of half heard human voices, technological noise, irritating beeps, acoustic echoes punctuating the spoken text. In certain crucial scenes it segues gloriously into the lush romantic piano music of Ash Gibson Greig, a harsh juxtaposition that generates an almost unbearably poignant irony.

However, the credit for generating this reality must lie with the cast, who give impeccable performances, precise, comic and powerful, in a genuinely ensemble production. Only Ewen Leslie as the increasingly abject Josef K has a single role: the other six actors – John Gaden, Peter Houghton, Rita Kalnejais, Belinda McClory, Hamish Michael and Igor Sas – play differing parts as the play requires. Leslie is riveting, slumping from the entitled outrage of the wrongly accused bank clerk to a man who is more and more abject, more and more certain of his own guilt and especially of his own shame. With some clever doubling, such as the splitting of the role of Leni between Kalnejais and McClory, the recurring faces become increasingly disconcerting, reinforcing the feeling that the action is some terrible, endless dream-reality where meaning and sense infinitely regress.

I think this a brilliant and perceptive theatrical adaptation of a novel that is at once simpler and more difficult than is generally allowed, as is the case with so many books called masterpieces. And it's also first-class theatre. I went twice, to make sure. And yes, I thought it truthful. All the way through.

Theatre Notes, August 26 2010

Peer Gynt / Elektra / Creditors

The talk in the foyers of late has been that of scarred veterans swapping notes from the front-lines of culture. Never, say hardened theatrenauts (as they whittle their programs into speaking likenesses of Ibsen) has Melbourne seen such a season as this. A few years ago, you could count on the theatres going dark in November, leaving summer free for extra-curricular frolicking in front of the Wii. Not this year, they add blackly (expectorating into handy spittoons). This year, the culture has gone feral.

Some, their spirits broken, point silently to the whisky bottle behind the bar. Others lean mutely against walls, a thousand-yard stare betraying their inner turmoil. If only, they mutter into their beards, most of it wasn't so good. If only we could all stay home and watch Australia get demolished in the Ashes, secure in the knowledge that the local stages are bereft of interest…

Like some of my colleagues, Ms TN ran out of gas a month ago. Personally, I don't see a lot of point in TN if all it offers is straight up-and-down reviews; but sometimes, straight up-and-down reviews is all a gal can manage. So here goes…

Peer Gynt

Like Goethe's famously unstageable *Faust*, Henrik Ibsen's verse drama *Peer Gynt* is something of a gift to theatre-makers. A phantasmagoric parable of a man's struggle with himself, it's one of the more bonkers plays in the repertoire, leaping with its anti-hero from the mountains of Norway to the deserts of Egypt, from rural wedding scenes to lunatic asylums. It is not a play for literal minds: the only level on which it makes sense is that of metaphor. And there it makes a great deal of sense indeed, foreshadowing Freud's own grubbing about with the monsters of the subconscious.

It's easy to see its attraction for a young, ambitious company like Four Larks. This company has in fact attempted this play before, in 2008. I can't compare their stagings; despite a bunch of good intentions – and we all know where they lead – I hadn't seen their work before last week. This young, unfunded collective has been making waves for a couple of years now, and finally last Wednesday I got to its production of *Peer Gynt*, staged in a barn-like space off a back lane in Northcote, to see what all the fuss is about.

The fuss is certainly warranted. Although the theatre they produce is vastly different, the aura around the event reminds me strongly of the early days of the Keene/Taylor Theatre Project, which – similarly unfunded – staged several seasons of short plays in the Brotherhood of St Laurence warehouse in Fitzroy. There's the same sense of an audience excited by discovery, the same raw faith in theatre, the same feeling of welcome.

This adaptation of *Peer Gynt*, co-adapted and directed by Sebastian Peters-Lazaro, Jesse Rasmussen and Mat Diafos Sweeney, hovers just on the theatre side of music theatre. The text is heavily cut, and many transitions or episodes replaced by narrative or lyric songs that channel the independent folk scene – think Joanna Newsom, the Decemberists, José González, Sufjan Stevens. The six-strong band, lined up on bales of pea-straw on the left of the stage, includes a harp, double bass, violins and banjo, and the vocals feature some sublime harmonising.

But maybe the strongest aspect of this company's theatre is its design. It stretches through the building's environment – charcoal drawings of Norwegian mountains adorn the walls as you enter the theatre, and a drawing on the barn door to the left of the set, which Peer Gynt himself is extending as the audience enters, is of a man with antlers, recalling the English folk figure Herne the Hunter, but is more pertinently an echo of the deer shamans of the Sami, who would adorn themselves with reindeer antlers during their mystic ceremonies.

Reaching back into pagan folk tales, just as Ibsen did for his play, gives the text and the music a powerful resonance, a sense that this is a contemporary enactment of a story that reaches back far beyond the nineteenth century. And the constantly inventive staging, often using repurposed objects like feather dusters or bits of rope, reinforces this feeling: the ordinary is here made strange. It makes for a heart-lifting investigation of theatrical storytelling, with an unabashed intention towards beauty. There are glorious moments – Solveig (Tilly Perry), for example, appearing lamplit in a high window, singing to Peer Gynt (Ray Chong Nee), or the rambunctiously disrespectful trolls.

My only reservations are at the level of performance. Especially in the first half, its style veers, sometimes uncertainly, sometimes with unsettling sureness, from a Pythonesque grotesquerie to moments of clear naturalism. This was most successful in Ibsen's most surreal act, where Gynt becomes serially a rampant capitalist, a prophet and a scholar. The actors are clearly a talented bunch – each has a chance to show his or her strengths – and there's no questioning their commitment. This is mainly a technical quibble about voice – a complex text like *Peer Gynt* needs to sound clearly, and sometimes I was simply struggling to hear the lines. It almost seems churlish to mention it, since the theatremaking here is otherwise so exciting. But there it is.

Elektra

I wondered how the very talented young director Adena Jacobs would stage the ancient tragedy *Elektra* in a theatre as tiny as The Dog in Footscray. The answer is: with absolute simplicity. Eugyeene Teh's design surrounds the playing area in translucent plastic curtains, and the walls vanish: we are suddenly in a space without edges. Actors can be so close we could almost touch them, and yet, by merely stepping behind the curtain, are suddenly cloaked in an illusory distance, or loom behind the unobscured characters like uneasy ghosts.

In the centre of the stage is a single object, a bed covered with old bloodstains that invokes the crimes of sex and murder that shape the action of this play. This production also makes a virtue of the venue's intimacy. The lights are up on the audience for much of the play, and when the actors speak to each other, they turn and meet our eyes as well, so we are not merely witnesses, but accomplices in the unfolding action.

Elektra is the second act of the trilogy of the Oresteia. The story begins with the murder of Agamemnon as he returns from Troy by his wife Clytemnestra and her lover Aegisthus, as revenge for the sacrifice of her daughter Iphigenia. In *Elektra*, Agamemnon's daughter camps on the threshold of Clytemnestra's house, neither inside nor outside, awaiting the return of her brother Orestes. By the code of vendetta, Orestes must avenge his father's death; however, if he does so, he will commit another unforgivable crime, that of matricide.

Anne Carson's fine translation of *Elektra* is clean and contemporary, drenching the action in an unforgiving lucidity. Here it is – very effectively – cut: most notably, Aegisthus' return in the final scene is deleted. In the mouths of this most accomplished cast, around a stunning central performance by Zahra Newman as Elektra, it plays with a compelling muscularity; sometimes the language is bitten off with a contemporary, almost slangy curtness, and at other moments the keenings of the original Greek are left untranslated. These cries are spine-tingling, Elektra's purest expression of what Carson calls her 'torrent of self'. For she talks all the time, all through the play, veering between obsessive madness and a bitter rationality. All she can do is talk.

Two things are immediately striking about this production. The first is the obvious fact that this is a play primarily about women. When Clytemnestra (Jane Montgomery Griffiths) speaks of the pain of birth giving, or of her grief for her murdered daughter Iphigenia, or when Elektra savagely claims that she is the shape her mother has made her, or in the arguments with her meeker sister Chrysothemis (Luisa Hastings Edge), the play summons darkly feminine turbulences that drive it towards its grim climax.

These women writhe under their subordination to male power. Unable to act as men do, they can only take refuge in speech, plotting their actions through the bodies of their men: in this case, Orestes (Gary Abraham) and his guardian Pedagogus (Josh Price). The actions of men become in this play functions of the women's frustrated desires. Elektra's inability either to act or not to act make her vengefulness a different thing in kind to that of Orestes: her lack of control alarms and frightens him. What is for Orestes a question of male honour becomes, through Elektra's voicing, a darker and more visceral thing, inchoate hatred and love driven from the gut, rather than Apollonian justice.

The second aspect is the claustrophobic awareness of the human body. From the beginning, when Elektra squats on the bed, or strips naked, or when the Chorus (Karen Sibbing) slowly eats a cake that is a grave offering, finding inside it a bone, the sense of opaque fleshliness, of the weight of muscle and bone, is foregrounded. On the skin, all light: on the inside, all obscurity.

This culminates in an extraordinary final scene. After the offstage murder of Clytemnestra, Orestes carries her body onto the stage and attempts to lay it on the bed. The body passively flops to the ground instead, a dead weight. For the next minute or so, Orestes tries to lift the body up, thwarted constantly by its limp lifelessness. He pauses and fixes a frustrated eye on Elektra, but she will not help him. At last, after an excruciating struggle, he succeeds in lifting the corpse onto the bed. Elektra, without looking at him, seats herself on the floor next to her mother, cupping her dead hand to her cheek. Orestes sits on the bed and stares into space.

It's in these anti-climactic moments that we feel the weight of the crime that has just been committed. It is the realisation that the murder solves nothing: rather, it has orphaned them entirely, and left them mired deeper in shame and grief. They can't even take comfort in each other. Neither sibling can look the other in the eye.

Creditors

August Strindberg is one of my favourite misogynists. As with Friedrich Nietzsche, his perception of how men have shaped the femininity of Woman mitigates – to some extent, at least – his mingled loathing and attraction towards actual women. He comes close to the top of the list of Men To Avoid, especially in matrimony. His second wife, Frida, described her marriage as 'a death ride over crackling ice and bottomless depths', and there's no evidence that his first and third wives would have disagreed.

A paradoxical side effect of Strindberg's obsessive loathing (all women, even his wives, were 'whores') is his perceptiveness in analysing the war of the sexes. He could speak as an insider, a man who practised what he preached – a treatise that translates roughly as treat 'em mean, or they'll have your balls. Yet his pitiless intelligence doesn't permit him to gloss his own behaviour. For a scathing portrayal of the wounds patriarchy inflicts on both sexes, it's hard to go past Strindberg.

His three-hander play *Creditors* is a classic example. Adolph (Brett Cousins) is a gullible and highly suggestible young artist who is the second husband of the novelist Tekla (Kat Stewart). Tekla is a thoroughly modern woman, the dominant partner in the relationship. As the play begins, she has left her husband at home for a few days while she goes out gallivanting. Enter Gustav (played with Mephisphelean oiliness by Dion Mills), a stranger who perceives the young man's weaknesses, manipulating him into a state of jealous hysteria.

Gustav is, of course, Tekla's first husband. Unable to forgive the blow to his masculinity caused by Tekla's departure, he has coldly determined to destroy their marriage. Having sown the seeds of insecurity and paranoia in Adolph, he seeks to seduce Tekla into betraying her husband while Adolph listens behind a door. Adolph has a fit and dies, Tekla is distraught with grief, and Gustav finds, to his enormous surprise, that his ex-wife loved her husband, after all.

Within this melodramatic plot lurks a surprisingly complex argument about men and women. Strindberg exposes a series of archetypes – the dominated man, the dominant man, and the Woman. All are ruthlessly articulate about their desires and feelings, and all expose their weaknesses as well as their strengths, generating a darkly fascinating narrative of argument and counter-argument that builds up into a devastating tragicomic satire about marriage. Strindberg dismisses from the outset the possibility of an equal relationship in a marriage; one partner must always be dominant, and – in his view at least – it must always be the man. What's provoking is how contemporary so much of this sounds. Not a lot has changed in the past century.

David Bell's production at Red Stitch is an excellent and lucid reading of the play. It focuses, quite rightly, on the actors. Using a muscular new translation by David Grieg, the three give powerful and detailed performances, opening out the complexities of their characters. The melodrama gets its due, as it ought, and it doesn't flinch back from comedy; but what sticks in the mind afterwards is the visceral emotions that Strindberg transcribed with such troubling accuracy. My only complaint is a decorative pillar in the middle of the set that kept obscuring the performers. Why was it there? A querulous quibble perhaps; but not being able to see an actor's face for no good reason drives me crazy.

Theatre Notes, December 5 2010

The Nest

A fascinating phenomenon over the past few years has been the revival of naturalism as a theatrical force. For years, commentators divided Australian theatre into two strands: 'naturalism', the accepted form of the mainstream or proto-mainstream; and 'non-naturalism', which covered everything from mime to Barrie Kosky. Naturalism was linked to the so-called 'well-made play', in which theatre did its best to imitate the conventions of television. Non-naturalism had a suspicious internationalism about it, and was best left to the Europeans or people who dressed exclusively in black and lived in Fitzroy.

This did theatre no favours, since the art form overspills such simplistic binaries. And not unsurprisingly, this binary – which also masquerades as the division between the 'mainstream' and the 'fringe' – has been collapsing, along with many other theatrical truisms, over the past decade. It's worth remembering, however, how recent this collapse is: only three years ago, critic Hilary Glow argued in her book *Power Plays* that naturalistic, character-based drama was a defining form of the 'mainstream'.

The state theatre presence of artists like Benedict Andrews or Tom Wright is a telling symptom of this shift. Just as telling is the fact that some of the most interesting independent work around Melbourne in recent years – ranging from Beng Oh's production of Franz Xaver Kroetz's *Tom Fool* at Hoy Polloy, to floogle's production of Duncan Graham's *Ollie and the Minotaur*, to Daniel Schlusser's theatrical reworkings of classics – has been re-examining naturalism. Which brings me to *The Nest*, Hayloft's exquisite version of Maxim Gorky's first play, *The Philistines*, now on at Northcote Town Hall.

Written by Benedict Hardie and Anne-Louise Sarks, *The Nest* at once returns naturalism to its radical, poetic roots, and liberates it into the present. It's an impressive work of adaptation: Hardie and Sarks have cut Gorky's unwieldy two and a half hour drama back to a finely-honed 90 minutes, filleting out its essentials from Gorky's baggily structured original. In doing so, they have created a piece of theatre that situates itself convincingly in contemporary Melbourne, while at the same time retaining an unmistakeable sense of Russianness, an achievement which almost feels like sleight of hand.

The Nest is a scathing indictment of a bourgeois family, which in Gorky's original play is a metaphor for Tsarist society on the brink of the Bolshevik Revolution. Here it's shifted, with a surprising aptness, to middle-class Australia: a generation that defined itself through stability, security and authority is threatened by a world of bewildering global and technological change. Anti-globalisation protests are not quite the 1917 Revolution; the Revolution has already happened. And this is key to the poignancy of this adaptation, in which the shadow of the past is a dark smudge beneath the present.

The action revolves around Victor (James Wardlaw), in this version a widower, who is the miserly and viciously angry father of Tanya (Julia Grace) and Peter (Benedict Hardie). Victor is embittered and bewildered by his loss of authority over a rebellious new generation – his children and their friends, his young lodgers, even the maid. His avariciousness extends to his children: unable to let them go into adulthood, he finds he is equally unable to keep them. He is desolatingly lonely: some of the most powerful moments of the evening feature Victor alone in his house, tidying up the kitchen in rubber gloves, punching uselessly at the buttons of an iPod to turn off the music his children have left carelessly blaring through the house, or sitting emptily in his patriarchal seat in the dining room.

The Nest isn't simply about the divisions between generations; it is also about the profound connections – of habit, affection, grief, memory – between them. The young are as lost as their elders are, falling into patterns of which they are not even conscious. It's clear, for instance, that for all his rebellion against his father, Peter will follow in his footsteps. That these complexities play so beautifully is a tribute to the Hayloft ensemble: this is a strong, focused cast, each member of which deserves mention, and the various characters are played with beautiful emotional detail.

Claude Marcos' design sets the action in the round; the audience sits one deep around a wide playing area, dotted with the solid furniture of an old, middle-class Australian house representing a lounge room, a kitchen, a hallway, a bedroom, a dining room. Russell Goldsmith's sound design unobtrusively heightens this reality with ambient sound and music – passing traffic, bird calls. The imaginary walls and doors are at first meticulously observed in the performances; as the work subtly shifts into a heightened stylisation, the 'walls' dissolve, becoming a poignant subconscious metaphor for the dissolution of the family.

The audience is almost in the house, visible and invisible just as the walls are. This makes scenes like an impromptu party in the lounge room intensely direct, almost as if we are at the same party; it's this directness of communication, placing events explicitly in the same social space as the audience, that is the real strength of contemporary naturalism. Anne-Louise Sarks' direction modulates this immediacy with subtle reminders of artifice: this is not theatre that aims to seduce us into an unthinking acceptance of its conventions.

Attention constantly shifts, without apparent effort, from one space to another; as the action progresses, there are more and more simultaneous moments – a couple making love in a bedroom, Tanya swallowing poison in the kitchen, a group on the back verandah – which gives a textured, increasingly powerful sense of individual privacies crossing in a mutual space. It's one of those shows which manages the delicate balance between deep polish, the result of craft and work, and yet in which each moment glows with spontaneous discovery.

Since their first production, in 2007, I've learned to expect a lot from Hayloft: I rather suspect, after *Thyestes* and *The Nest*, that my expectation has wound up another notch. Looking over this company's body of work, what's most striking is that they have never repeated themselves, although each project has deepened what appears to be a very singular exploration. Which seems to me the very definition of exciting art.

Theatre Notes, December 11 2010

Don Parties On

Every time David Williamson writes a new play, the Australian theatre world launches into one of its favourite games. It goes like this.

There's a flurry of pre-publicity in which we hear, again, that Williamson is our best-selling playwright, a 'national myth-maker' who takes the pulse of our times and touches the receptive hearts of the masses. We hear that 'the critics' are unkind and out of touch with ordinary folk, and that the only reason people dislike his plays is because he's too popular. We hear that the theatre world is continually chanting that 'you can't have naturalism on stage'. Preferably, somewhere in the middle of this, someone mentions Barrie Kosky.

Then a good chunk of the theatre community gets dressed up to the nines and heads off to the premiere. The play occurs. Some people laugh. Some people leave at interval. A sizeable proportion of the audience applauds rapturously. Another sizeable proportion emerges in various states of crankiness and flees for a debriefing session over a stiff drink.

Then the fun begins. Some critic, bristling with righteous fury, writes a slashing review of the Williamson phenomenon. Said critic is in turn accused of general nastiness, humourlessness and elitism. Williamson fans point once again to the box office. Various right-wing pundits weigh in to opine about Williamson's leftiness. Various left-wing pundits complain about his lack of leftiness. Someone (often it's me) says something plaintive about art. And everyone, his or her expectations satisfyingly met, has a marvellous time.

Lather, rinse and repeat.

So it is with *Don Parties On*, the sequel to Williamson's 1970s mega-hit *Don's Party*, which opened at the Melbourne Theatre Company last Thursday. And here's my contribution to this particular circle of Hell.

In *Don's Party: The Sequel* we meet the central characters from the first play 40 years on, as they gather around Kerry O'Brien for the ABC telecast of the 2010 election. As Williamson says in his program note, he's doing a *Seven Up* on his fictional characters. Baby Richard (Darren Gilshenan) is now a Generation X advertising executive with marital problems. Don (Garry McDonald) is still married to Kath (Tracy

Mann), who brings up a decades-old infidelity every two minutes or so. We hear that Don finally did write his novel, which sank like a stone after offending all his friends, and is the cue for some self-referential jokes about commercial writing not being proper art.

Don's mentor Mal (Robert Grubb) and his sharp-tongued wife Jenny (Sue Jones) have divorced, and Jenny has subsequently built a political career. Cooley (Frankie J Holden), as lascivious as ever, has turned into an obscenely rich right-wing lawyer with emphysema, and is married to a patient woman with a social conscience, Helen (Diane Craig). There's a sententious granddaughter, Belle (Georgia Flood), who watches *Twilight* DVDs and calls herself a Greenie, and Richard's lover Roberta (Nikki Shiels), a redhead whose histrionics are apparently explained by her Italian genes.

At the beginning of the play, Don and Kath are, once again, preparing tidbits for an election night party. Mal turns up early and asks Jenny along, to Don and Kath's dismay, as they haven't spoken for decades after a disagreement about Twisties. Meanwhile there is much rhubarb about Richard, who has left his wife for Another Woman. Richard's daughter Belle is displeased. Richard's wife makes a suicide attempt and ends up in hospital, and is promptly forgotten until the end of the play. Cooley turns up with an oxygen bottle and mask and his wife Helen, and lusts after the granddaughter until he has to put on his oxygen mask.

The actors watch 30 seconds of Kerry O'Brien and then mute the TV for some expository dialogue about the good old/bad old days. There are in-jokey references to Play No. 1. Richard turns up and makes the entire audience wonder how a whiny, hysterical boy-man could possibly be holding down a megabuck job in advertising. There are revelations, a couple of heart-unwrenching confessions and some reheated scandal. Belle overhears it all and is displeased. Richard's lover turns up in high heels and low-cut dress and has conniptions. Belle is displeased again. And so on. And on.

Well, I practically went to sleep writing that. Williamson's great gift is that he is incapable of surprise. He is at once so popular and so reviled because he knows exactly how to meet the expectations of his audiences. It creates a dilemma for me, because I hate repeating myself; so forgive me for pointing to some earlier essays. In a 2004 piece, I discussed how troubling it is that state theatre companies, forced to make commercial decisions by their financial bottom lines, are so anxious to bruit Williamson as not only a best-selling playwright – which he undoubtedly is – but as a great playwright – which he emphatically is not. Harry Kippax did Australian theatre no favours at all when he compared Williamson to Chekhov. And this claim to artistic quality is my beef about Williamson, although the beef is smaller these days.

One of the things that seems clear in this round of the Williamson Game is that the theatrical conversation has shifted markedly. For instance, it seems (even more) ridiculous to claim that naturalism isn't allowed, when so many young companies are exploring it themselves. And I can't get too exercised about state companies making commercial decisions, given the paucity of their subsidies; although it could be I'm just tired of the argument. And really, who cares? Nobody said that people will be shot if they like going to Williamson plays. Some people merely objected when Williamson was promoted as the *ne plus ultra* of Australian theatre.

Recently, some defenders of the Williamson *oeuvre* have begun to say that Williamson is not a naturalistic playwright, à la Chekhov or Ibsen, but more a playwright of heightened social satire, a crafter of comedies of manners. This is in fact a much more accurate placing of his work, but it means that one has to assess him in the company of Sheridan or Feydeau or his contemporary Alan Ayckbourn, all masters of stage business. One of the things that has puzzled me for years about Williamson's reputation is that he is such an inept theatrical technician. Popular, as these other playwrights demonstrate, doesn't have to mean bad; but in the Dan Brown–Charles Dickens continuum, Williamson is definitely thumping the tan.

In *Don Parties On*, all his writerly clumsiness is writ large – the dire expository dialogue, the stereotypical characters, the almost neurotic repetitiveness, the constant machinations of getting people on and off stage. Much of the dialogue – the pronouncements on baby boomers, greenies, Australian politics and so on – sounds as if it's been cribbed from some of Australia's more active political blogs. The people-moving is about as clunkily done as I've seen – characters are constantly announcing that now they must go into the garden to show each other photographs of their children, or to the bedroom to check on someone hysterical, or to the study to watch a DVD, so that two or three people can be left on stage to reminisce or reveal something shocking. Alternatively, you get rows of frozen actors standing on stage watching as two or three others do their dialogue.

Robyn Nevin's direction makes as decent a fist as is possible of this stylistic rubble. I left feeling that it could have been a lot worse. The actors fail to make the characters credible, but it's hard to blame them given that they are all written as walking clichés; although Sue Jones gives some feisty life to the character of Jenny. But for me, there was no escaping the creeping numbness as the evening wore on.

Naturalism this certainly isn't. Considered as a comedy of manners, it lacks the grace, wit and formal mastery that gives the form its champagne fizz. A direct comparison with *Don's Party* starkly demonstrates how stale Williamson has become: the lively colloquialism of the original, its chief virtue, has long leached out. This really is zombie theatre, devouring the brains, not only of its audience, but of its own playwright.

Yes, some people love it. The guy next to me, for instance, was having a super time: he kept up a running commentary and walked out happily humming the Credence Clearwater Revival song that is the subject of one of the running gags. As always with Williamson plays, it will continue to please those who like his work and annoy everybody else. He's still making the box office go ka-ching, and as long as people keep buying tickets, companies will keep programming his work. And there it is.

Theatre Notes, January 16 2011

Song of the Bleeding Throat

On a mild summer evening in the ivy-clad courtyard of The Eleventh Hour's headquarters in Fitzroy, it's not difficult to think that you have suddenly been transported to a different era. The lawn is studded with marquees; a door behind the temporary bar opens teasingly to a private house with shuttered upstairs windows, which you can't help but imagine must look like something painted by Bonnard or Vuillard. Even your host, artistic director William Henderson, could have stepped out of a daguerreotype.

Maybe it's Europe circa 1912, before world war and revolution wracked the planet, when a disparate bunch of radical artists were creating something that would be called 'modernism'. Only it's Melbourne 2011: a different place, a different era. Given the present sense of social urgency, perhaps it's not surprising that so many artists are looking to the modernism that flowered as the anxieties of its times thickened and convulsed, picking up the threads of experiment and discovery and attempting to make something new of them. Certainly, this investigation is a crucial part of The Eleventh Hour's eclectic, intelligent theatre, and why they're one of Melbourne's must see companies.

This time, instead of reworking classic texts, The Eleventh Hour presents a new play by David Tredinnick, who is better known as an accomplished actor. *Song of the Bleeding Throat* is described as a 'burlesque', meaning its older sense of comic parody rather than striptease. And it's a fascinating beast indeed. Tredinnick is parodying ideas, in particular some of the formative nineteenth century notions behind contemporary Britain and America. His burlesque features such notables as the historian and social commentator Thomas Carlyle, his wife Jane Welsh (and their dog Nero), Abraham Lincoln, Walt Whitman, Lincoln's assassin John Wilkes Booth and the Statue of Liberty.

The text is foremost a torrent of words. Tredinnick has created a bizarrely Beckettian collage out of quotations and almost-quotations from public figures ranging from PT Barnum to Marx: statements about empire and revolution jostle with domestic intrigues, fancies, poems and obscene malapropism. The language of high oratory or Romantic poetry is continually exploded by the decay and weakness of the body: Carlyle (Richard Bligh) is tormented by his bowels, Welsh (Anne Browning) is a drug addict, Nero the dog (James Saunders) is beaten within an inch of his life, Lincoln (Neil Pigot) is dying (or dead). The only personage who seems above all this bodily flux is Whitman.

Each phrase is buffed to a dark lustre. Everyone speaks as if they all wrote out their thoughts in a goose-quill before uttering them. It's about as far as it is possible to get from the conventions of contemporary theatre: this is a text that has little truck with ideas of character or narrative. Its characters are symbols, mouthpieces, carefully constructed puppets – parodies, as Tredinnick claims. But parodies of what? There are all the obvious answers: they parody the vanity of intellectual achievement in the face of death; the selective consciousness of heart-stirring cries for liberty and revolution that ignores, say, those who happen to possess black skin; the tragic gap between ideal and reality (the play itself is prefaced by a quote from the greatest pragmatist of them all, Josef Stalin).

But most of all it seems to me that it parodies language itself. Language, which promises so much, here collapses inward on itself, revealing a pile of rubble that stinks of death, or is anerotically absorbed in the cultural body. The production often forbids us easy access to listening: Nero stutters, the Carlyles speak in Scots accents. Even its visionary clarities decay: Whitman's magnificent 'I sing the body electric' becomes a narcissistic anthem in the musical *Fame*. The only recourse at the end is the solitary voice, Whitman's 'song of the bleeding throat', which is cut off in mid-sentence.

This density of meaning and linguistic relations means that if you don't pay close attention, you will soon be quite lost. Even if you do, it's easy to feel that, as Lincoln says at one point, 'I'm trying to blaze a way through this swamp'. The weight of this orotund nineteenth century language, almost completely unleavened by contemporary brevity, often lies heavy. The danger of employing this diction is that it attenuates the work's political clout: what do all these words have to do with Now?

If it's anything, *Song of the Bleeding Throat* is an overtly political work, at once exploring and mocking the formative nationalism of our time, US patriotism. Through the figure of Carlyle, a major Romantic essayist and thinker, it picks up European revolution and imperialism, connecting these ideals to the hopes and betrayals of the brash democratic exercise in America. Yet this is an oblique tracing, more a kind of animating of ghosts which still colour the assumptions behind so much public speech.

I find myself oscillating between feeling on the one hand that the text rings its changes very successfully, and on the other thinking that all this luxuriant excess of language ends up obscuring itself, that there is, in short, too much of it. (Certainly, coming from a school that prefers poetry of the theatre to poetry in the theatre, I think there's a little too much poetry.) Its ideas are in fact often presented with an unsettling clarity, but the whole seems too much jostle. I suspect that there is a myopia of focus, an obsessive close-up attention that forgets the larger architecture of the play's argument and diffuses its point. It's common to claim that less is more, and it's not always true; but in this case, I think it might have been.

Perhaps the only director in Melbourne who could tackle a text like this is Brian Lipson, whose theatrical imagination is as baroque and elliptical as the playwright's. The production is as finely polished as the text itself: it features astonishingly disciplined and, frankly, riveting performances from its cast, although Neil Pigot as Abe Lincoln is the standout. The alienations in the text are realised in the theatre with a playful theatricality: in the first half, the three characters are formally placed as in a portrait (the staging is in fact based on a famous portrait of the Carlyles at home), with Nero – an English shepherd dog in the painting – becoming a working-class lad in a cloth cap. In the second half, in a stunning *coup de théâtre*, the entire space is reversed, and the audience finds itself looking up at the deathbed of Lincoln.

There is no moment that doesn't feel utterly worked, down to the least gesture: even the twilight shading to darkness through the windows outside. And it glints with a dark humour that segues to sheer playfulness: when Carlyle decides to light a spill from the fire, for instance, and irritably summons the dogsbody/author to crouch behind the empty mantelpiece with a lighter. There are theatrical moments which are as good as anything you'll see, seriously, but somehow it meanders, creating palpable longueurs. I kept thinking of a necklace, a string of marvellous pearls with no string. And yet, again, this isn't wholly true.

It's often very funny, but underneath the whole is a vein of pure seriousness that harks back to those twentieth century modernists, in particular the formalist experiments of Piscator and Meyerhold. Maybe my reservations exist in its timeliness. It was odd to watch this play last week, as the popular revolution in Egypt and elsewhere in the Middle East lit a more violent flame beneath the pieties that *Song of the Bleeding Throat* explores. Suddenly these ideas – democracy, revolution and their betrayals – seem invested with more urgent feeling and moment than seems adequate to burlesque. But then again, the song of the bleeding throat is precisely what is consciously elided in the play: its concern is with everything that silences that song. In any case, this is certainly an intriguing work, uncompromising and painstakingly realised, and worth seeing for that alone. Definitely not for those who like their theatre on a plate.

Theatre Notes, January 31 2011

The End

The catastrophe of the body is never far away in Samuel Beckett's writing. Mortal, decaying, risible, smelly, full of inconvenient humours and vapours and needs, human corporeality steps forward in all its poignant obscenity. It's the eternal answer to hubris, a tube of flesh which serves only to transform nutrition into dung. So too in *The End*, one of several novellas Beckett wrote in the 1940s that presage, in theme and often in phrase, many of the later works that generated his fame.

Written with Beckett's characteristic stylistic parsimony, *The End* is an exquisite work of prose. It's clearly an earlier work, since it permits itself flourishes – notably a subtext of Christian symbolism – that Beckett pared down in his later work. It shouldn't be surprising that this first person monologue translates into stunning theatre, but somehow it is: Beckett is such a purist of form that his prose gives the impression of needing nothing except the page and a reader to generate its full imaginative life. What could a performer add to this?

Robert Menzies provides one answer in this gem of a production at the Malthouse, not so much adding to Beckett as embodying Beckett's story for us. Directed with perfectly judged restraint by Eamon Flack, there is nothing here aside from the performer, the words and the dimensions of the stage. This is theatre stripped to its most essential, radiating a sternly focused power, which beautifully folds the exposure of performance into the emotional duress of Beckett's story.

The set (there is no design credit aside from the lighting, and the set was reportedly posted to Menzies) consists of a wall with a door in it and a floor on which there is marked a cross in white tape. At the beginning, Menzies enters through the door and slowly, with a sense of loathing and reluctance, makes his way to the cross and places his feet on it. Once he is on the cross, he expressionlessly examines his audience, those who have come to witness his crucifixion: at last, he speaks. Teegan Lee's minimal lighting design – there are, I think, four cues in all – shapes the space around him, at once imprisoning and exposing the actor, and at last creating a darkness without perspective in which Beckett's ghost flickers and vanishes.

The story he tells is of the adventures of a homeless man who has fallen from better days. He tells us of his peregrinations after he is thrown out of a charitable hostel, in a suit that is too small for him, his own clothes having been burnt. He has a bowler hat, a tie, 'blue, with kinds of little stars', a small amount of money. He knows that 'the end was near, at least fairly near'. He drifts through the city, recounting his various places of lodging; he is cheated by a dishonest landlady; he sits by a horse trough. He encounters his son, a businessman in the city and an 'insufferable son of a bitch'. He meets a man he had known 'in former times', who lives in a cave and offers him shelter. Like Christ, he exits the city on an ass, but instead of celebration he is greeted by small boys throwing stones.

Unable to stay in a single place for any length of time, Beckett's anti-hero ends up living in a shed in the back of a grand house, hiding in a boat he has adapted to keep out rats, and begging for a living. The story finishes with a vision of his floating downstream into the sea, crushed by the hugeness of the natural world, 'the sea, the sky, the mountains and the islands', and 'then scattered to the uttermost confines of space'.

As well as its subtextual Christ, the story echoes an ancient Irish poem, *Buile Suibhne* (*The Madness of Sweeney*), which recounts the travail of an Irish King who is cursed with insanity. Crazy with fear, he can't stay in a single spot but leaps from place to place in the wild 'like a bird', homeless and lost, and at last is killed by a cowherd as he is 'eating his meal out of the cowdung'. As the poem says, 'Wretched is the life of one homeless, / sad is the life, O fair Christ!' In *The End*, Beckett transforms this abject mythical figure into its contemporary version: a filthy, half-mad homeless man, eking out the tiny details of his life invisibly on the edge of society.

Which is no more than to say that although this is a short work, it encompasses whole worlds. Menzies' performance brings every nuance of this story into present life: its tragedy, its beauty, its obscenity, its humour. Most of the time the lighting focuses on his face and his hands, which are almost cruelly expressive. The performance gradually builds up to the desolate beauty of its finale, attentive to the crucial detail of each moment: it's Menzies at his unafraid best, straddling both grandeur and humility, pity and revulsion.

Theatre Notes, March 7 2011

Amplification / Faker

When I attend a performance, some part of my brain seems to erase any information about the show I'm about to see, even if I have read it. The one thing that seems to form expectations is the previous work I've seen by the artists involved: I have a magical ability to forget press releases completely. (It's only by dint of serious concentration that I am able to note the correct venue and time.) So it was that I watched BalletLab's Dance Massive show *Amplification* under the impression that it was a new work, and read it as an evolution of *Miracle*, which premiered in 2009.

This is, of course, totally backwards: *Amplification* is in fact twelve years old. It was choreographed long before the photographs from Abu Ghraib, long before Guantanamo and the psy-ops tortures which locked prisoners in containers and played Ravel at deafening decibels. As Phillip Adams says in his program note, he was working from a variety of genre and SF ideas: Kubrick, Frankenheimer, Lucas, and in particular JG Ballard, whose novel *Crash* is a deeply discomforting narrative about people who are sexually aroused by car crashes. For Ballard, the car accident suggested 'the portents of a nightmare marriage between technology, and our own sexuality'.

This perverse fetishisation of violence, a sexuality alienated and mediated through technology, was brought to a macabre apotheosis by the perversity of the Abu Ghraib photographs, which literally implicated every viewer in the torture of Iraqi prisoners. And it's this which gives *Amplification* its nimbus of prophecy: it's not as if that alienation was new in 2004. It's been said that prophecy is about seeing the present clearly, and in this dance Adams sees something very clearly indeed. All the same, the specificity of the images created is disconcerting: Adams' dancers are hooded, thrown naked in collapsed piles of limp limbs, locked in boxes, assaulted by deafening waves of sampled sound, all actions that seem to be the vocabulary of modern military violence.

Since this is articulated by choreography that is, often, extremely beautiful, I experienced *Amplification* as aesthetic trauma. In the opening dance the dancers' bodies became almost mechanised, their limbs unnaturally straight, creating unexpected angles and shapes, and I felt I was watching a rigorous process of objectification. This is true, to some extent at least, of all dance, but here this feeling was heightened to menace, and laid the ground for the violent images that followed.

Dancers dressed in drab, uniform-like costumes circled two others seated in chairs, their arms straight beside them as if they were restrained, and drew long lines of recording tape out of their mouths, as if they were drawing speech or entrails, winding them around their prisoners. Then one dancer flourished a pair of scissors and cut them, and there was a flash of the prisoners collapsing, before the stage was plunged into darkness. In another sequence, three clothed women, using only their legs, nudged a passive, naked male body into a box and closed the lid on him. In yet another, a pile of naked dancers – seemingly representing corpses – becomes erotically charged.

These disturbing scenes cut against others that can only be described as images of transcendence, which is where I found myself making the strongest connections with Adams' later work, *Miracle*. There is a beautiful, but overlong and overworked, sequence of movement where two bodies, brought on stage in body bags, are wound in cloths, as in a ritual of preparing a corpse for burial, and the dance ends on a strangely ambiguous resolution, all the dancers democratised by their mutual nakedness. Perhaps the most confronting aspect of this work is its eroticism, always at play in Adams' choreography: the body is a site of violent conflict, seeking escape from its materiality.

The design and sound amplify the impact of the choreography. Bluebottle's set and lighting – a raw, white stage hung with angled fluorescent lights and arc lamps – looks like a live installation by Joseph Beuys. Lynton Carr's score, performed live on turntables, begins at full throttle, sampling everything from electronic noise to snatches of dialogue from movies, then moves to a surprising lyricism and powerful moments of silence. An extraordinary work.

Gideon Obarzanek's solo work *Faker* is at the other end of the spectrum, although in its own way it is equally exposing. The conceit is simple: Obarzanek, successful choreographer, is approached by a young, female dancer, who wants him to create a work for her. Obarzanek agrees. The collaboration fails, and results in the dancer, some time later, sending an excoriating email in which she ruthlessly criticises Obarzanek's work. She claims that his exercises were such that she could 'only fail'; she says that he has no coherent aesthetic behind his work, beyond pure curiosity; she compares him unfavourably with German choreographer Tom Lehmann, claiming he is merely superficially copying his techniques, and she attacks him for his sexism and the gendered carnality of his choreography.

The stage is completely bare, a mimesis of a working studio, aside from a desk on which is a laptop computer. The structure of the work is very plain: Obarzanek enters the stage, reads us parts of the email, and then performs as if he were the humiliated young dancer, answering the unspoken question: would you put yourself through what you're asking of me? It reveals that as a dancer, Obarzanek has a considerable comic gift: some of this performance is very funny indeed.

In the first performance, she/he puts on an iPod and dances, creating a series of naïve and comic movements; in the second, she/he is asked to improvise for a stated period of time, using only movements which she/he doesn't know how to do. The third is a John Cage–like exercise in which instructions written on paper are thrown on the floor, picked up randomly and then performed in the sequence in which they fall. It culminates when Obarzanek strips to his underpants and performs a solo that he created for the woman to a lush choral score. It's the only time when stage lighting is employed, and the one thing of which she is proud in their failed collaboration. The dance itself, performed by an aging, male but still athletic body, is extraordinarily beautiful.

Out of this simplicity emerges a lot of complexity. The title alone alerts us to the perils of taking anything here literally: Obarzanek claimed in an interview that he wrote the email himself, although the dance was sparked by a real incident. If anything, this is a work of self-interrogation: aside from the final dance, Obarzanek gives no defence of himself against the criticism in the email.

Lightly, with a steady neutrality that avoids defensive heroics, *Faker* exposes the power of the choreographer, who literally shapes the dancer's body, scrutinising and exposing her; the abyss between perception and self-perception; the dilemma of creating art, of generating renewal, when the surge of youthful curiosity and passion has evaporated and a certain necessary self-deception is no longer possible. At the centre is the question of authenticity: what does it mean to create authentic art? What can truthfulness mean when all art is, by its nature, a conscious and fabricated act?

The performance ends with the chasm of self-doubt that opens in Obarzanek from a single glance of contempt thrown his way by the dancer: 'I already knew', he says. 'All that in one look.'

Theatre Notes, April 1 2011

Princess Dramas

Princess Dramas, now playing at Red Stitch, is the first play by Elfriede Jelinek ever to have been produced in Australia. And massive kudos to Red Stitch for finally giving us a chance to see her work. Jelinek – probably best known for her novel *The Piano Teacher*, which was adapted into a film by Michael Haneke – is an Austrian writer and intellectual, and a major contemporary German dramatist. She has won, for what it's worth, the Nobel Prize for Literature. She's a Marxist feminist whose work is underlaid by a continuing critique of Austrian fascism, and by extension, of the fascism which underlies Western capitalism.

However, none of these things means that Jelinek is without humour or a wicked wit: and director André Bastian gives *Princess Dramas* a grunge production that is often hilarious and always surprising. But it does ask that its audience listen in a way in which we are not often asked: here language is an autonomous entity, not an expression of character nor even of the author. What struck me first was the freedom of the writing. It's as exhilarating as reading Hélène Cixous' prose, which runs without inhibition, intelligence leaping wherever it likes, untrammelled by rule or convention. Here is a writer who feels no need to pander to anything except the imperatives of the work she is writing.

Jelinek is a bit of a leap for audiences used to the idea of theatre as an empathy machine, by which its success is measured by how much one identifies with characters. Jelinek doesn't play for feeling. Although she deals profoundly with narrative, she is not especially interested in plot, which is the least interesting aspect, after all, of storytelling. What's impossible to ignore in this is the influence of Brecht, who perhaps did more than any modern writer, through the utopia of the collective, to redefine the notion of the individual in art.

Jelinek's interrogation of language and her nearly absolute refusal of the empathically-imagined subjective self is the source of much discomfort in the English-speaking world. When she won the Nobel, outraged editorials demanded to know why an obscure Austrian had been chosen over manifestly more worthy candidates, such as Philip Roth (to be fair, Jelinek was as surprised as anyone). There's a typical 2007 response in the *New York Review of Books* (called, ironically enough, 'How To Read Elfriede Jelinek'), in which translator Tim Parks castigates her novels for their lack of authentic subjectivity.

He seems to read her novels as direct expressions of ideas or experiences, which is perilously close to assuming that Hamlet is Shakespeare. He begins the review with a conflation of the author and her narrators, and discusses her work consistently throughout the review through the lens of autobiography. (This is difficult: Jelinek herself exploits autobiography in her work, but it is surely a mistake to use it as a reference for authenticity.) At one point, he says a particular book 'might just have worked had Jelinek dedicated any energy at all to creating the dramatic encounters and characterizations that make *The Piano Teacher* such a strong novel, or alternatively if her ruminations were sufficiently coherent and convincing for us to take them seriously.' It's hard not to conclude that he has almost completely missed the point.

When Jelinek's translator, Gitta Honneger, takes him to task for ignoring all Jelinek's dramatic work, at least half her output and the source of a great deal of her fame, Parks claims that her plays – which he claims feature 'unnuanced denunciation' – are only applicable to certain very localised political struggles in Austria, disclaims any literary prejudice against drama per se (Beckett! Shakespeare!) and finally suggests that she is ultimately untranslatable. It's possible to argue that every writer, embedded deeply as she is in her own language or locale, is untranslatable; it seems absurd to single out Jelinek as especially untranslatable.

But it does expose a stubborn, even wilful, refusal to accept a central tenet of her writing; in particular, it suggests a misread theatricality in her prose. Speaking of her plays, Jelinek describes how she uses 'language surfaces' ('*sprachflächen*') in juxtaposition, in place of dialogue. Language here is a behaviour, from which meaning might be discerned only through the fractures where its tyrannies collide and break. The idea of 'language surfaces' actively refuses the depth that Parks claims is a crucially missing aspect of her writing, and suggests a more supple, less literal and crucially ironic reading of her work.

The autonomy of language is a commonplace in any engagement with modern poetry, and hardly unknown in English plays: Martin Crimp exploits the same ideas, but in a far less spiky fashion. It is an approach particularly suited to theatre, where performance is already a metaphor, where language is already a mask, already ironic, already a supple and elusive thing. What seems complex in description is, when enacted, made manifest. This doesn't mean it is necessarily simple: it forbids transparency, focusing on speech as an act rather than an expression. In *Princess Dramas*, Jelinek is especially interested in language as an imprisonment, exploring the creation of the feminine and its relationship to death in the communal psyche. She uses every linguistic resource she can, from fairytales to soap opera to philosophy, as weapons to break the prison open.

The result is an avalanche of text, dizzying, fracturing, impossible to pin down. I thought of hunting down the text before writing this review; but on reflection, I decided to attempt to think about it as I experienced it in performance, with much of it simply flying past my ears, experienced as texture as much as meaning. Inevitably, I am merely scratching the surface.

These texts, first performed in 2002, use a commonplace of feminist writing: the reworking of myth or folklore to subvert common ideas of the feminine in popular culture. Jelinek, however, is not so much rewriting the myths as empowerment, as demonstrating how profoundly their clichés infect every aspect of self. *Princess Dramas* consists of three short plays. The first two concern themselves with fairytales, *Snow White* and *Sleeping Beauty*; the final work is an extraordinary monologue by a modern-day princess, Jackie Kennedy Onassis.

All three are conversations with death. In the first two, the Princess is talking to the Prince who rescues both from sleep: the princesses here exist in a blackly ironic gap between sleep, death's counterfeit, and a waking into the happily-ever-after marriage with the Prince, which is also represented here as death. Jackie Kennedy Onassis – aristocratic, tragic, chillingly tough – compares herself to Marilyn Monroe, in whose image sex and death unite in all their seduction: Monroe is the ultimate sexualised flesh, to be inevitably consumed and discarded into her self-destruction.

Jackie escapes this fate by becoming her image: she is her clothes, impeccable, untouchable, icily self-controlled. Here fashion is not imagined as a symptom of the male domination of women, but as a weapon of survival. (This becomes most chilling in meditations on Kennedy's assassination, where his exposed brain is compared to fabric.) Its price is the dissolving of self into the abstraction of image, narcissism as brutal survival technique, that scorns the women who permit themselves to be merely victims by remaining flesh, and ultimately scorns her own body.

This suggestion of complicity makes Jelinek's feminism deeply complicated, and situates it in a much larger political argument. Rather than simply outlining the inequalities of gender, she is interested in how, as the critic Helga Kraft puts it, to 'unmask social practices as they influence the body, and by doing so... illuminate the artificiality and brutality of this process'. The yearning for power 'leads to dehumanisation against the body, against the other and the self', in both men and women.

The multiplicity of referents and the shifting vectors of the text create constant small collapses of cognition. It's text working most closely as a kind of collage, a complex tessellation of meaning that is constantly calling itself into question. As Bastian says in his director's note, the complexity of this text puts 'our relationship with language into crisis'. Language no longer behaves as a vehicle for expression, but as a kind of kind of neuroticised symptom of national (here both Australian and Austrian), ideological and personal crisis. The polarities of gender buckle under the weight of its dizzying representations: as irony piles on irony, the vacuum at its centre – the absence of a feminine self free of prior definition – becomes more and more evident. This is how Woman becomes Sartre's 'hole', the very definition of absence.

Bastian and his performers give us a suitably unreverential production which is often, as I said, very funny. Peter Mumford's design exploits every kind of kitsch, creating a picket fenced backyard that ends up festooned with washing, backed by a garage door painted with some sort of tourism ad for Austria. The casting is deliberately cross-grained and the costumes absurd. The first Prince (Andrea Swifte) is in lederhosen and an over-the-top Tyrolean uniform, while Snow White (Dion Mills) is dressed in a Disney dirndl skirt embroidered with swastikas. Genders are conventionally assigned in the Sleeping Beauty play, where the Prince is sulking in a lycra Rabobank cycling top and the be-wigged Princess gasps out her monologue between sudden collapses into catatonia.

Jackie is played by Indigenous actor Melodie Reynolds; at first we only hear her miked voice, as she stands behind a projected, shifting image of Jackie, then we see her silhouette, apparently reading from a lectern; finally we see the performer herself, but then, at various points, the text is distributed between the performers, and the performer herself is replicated in projected images. The production alienates and overstimulates in ways analogous to the text: we are literally swamped with semiotics.

I'm not sure the production is entirely successful, although the second half is riveting: you feel at times the actors are still finding a way to deal with this language, and, as I have found in this review, there is no doubt more to be said and done. But it is certainly impressive, and it's a welcome introduction to a writer who should be better known here, if only for all those uncompromising gauntlets thrown down in the face of our expectations.

Theatre Notes, June 17 2011

The Burlesque Hour Loves Melbourne

Right now, just after the winter solstice, Ms TN is struggling. The skies have been grey for too long, the news has been bleak for too long, and human beings have been stupid and destructive for too long. Nary a light gleams at the end of the tunnel, and actually doing things – like, say, getting out of bed – seems impossible and futile. Yes, I know despair is a sin – I suspect I am on my way to discovering why – but the fear of God's wrath is little use to an atheist.

Midwinter funk is an all-too-common disease. But I can recommend a very effective temporary medicine – a visit to the latest incarnation of *The Burlesque Hour* at fortyfive downstairs. The theatre is transformed by a cloud of red Chinese lanterns into a cosily tatty club that might have existed in the Weimar Republic, with nests of be-candled tables and a catwalk up the middle of the space. You can hear the buzz of conversation ascending as you walk down the stairs, and already the sad heart lifteth. *The Burlesque Hour Loves Melbourne* is a tonic for the soul: sexy, hilarious, perverse, disturbing and liberatingly beautiful.

Contemporary burlesque curated by Moira Finucane and Jackie Smith, it's an exhilarating meld of cabaret, circus, vaudeville and performance art that moves spankingly through its many moods. It's a very Australian show, and has everything I love about this culture – fearlessness, subversion, wit, mischief and intelligence. And it has a starry list of weekly guests: so far they've included Rhonda Burchmore and Pamela Rabe, and coming attractions include Phillip Adams (he of BalletLab) with an especially commissioned dance; Meow Meow, direct from the West End; Constantina Bush and the Bushettes; and Die Roten Punkte.

Finucane and Smith fans will have seen a few of these acts already: this is a kind of 'new and selected' anthology of burlesque hits, with spangles, feathers, balloons and plenty of spillage (umbrellas are provided). But I can confirm that they are even better on a return visit. There's Romeo, the leather-jacketed macho boy stripping to Chrissy Amphlett's 'I touch myself', and the Queen of Hearts, with her cloud of red balloons and her nests of nipple-needles. There's Finucane's repressed pie woman, trembling with orgasmic excitement as she stirs her finger into a meat pie to AC/DC, and spilling tomato sauce and pie innards all over her neatly buttoned uniform.

Vaudeville acts by Holly Durant, Harriet Ritchie and Sosina Wogayehu include juggling, a whip-cracking display and dance, including a dervish dance of two outrageously hairy women, an extension of an idea first performed for the burlesque by butoh dancer Yumi Umiumare. Their somehow innocent perversity recalls something of maenads or forest spirits out of a Hayao Miyazake film. And they encapsulate the polymorphous nature of this show, which is at once serious and outrageously hilarious, surface and depth, spectacle and intimacy. Many acts invert expectations, such as the incomparable

Maude Davey, stark naked aside from heels and rhinestone necklace, turning the sexual mystery of the vamp torch singer inside out by exposing everything, which somehow got funnier as the act went on.

There's a dark subtext to this show. A woman in a fur coat and sunglasses enters through the audience to Antony and the Johnsons' heartbreaking ballad 'Hope there's someone', and appears to collapse; she makes her trembling way to the back of the stage, and is then hoisted up naked, like a carcass in an abattoir, leaving us momentarily and starkly silent. Or an avatar of death parades slowly down the catwalk, draped in black fabric through which she languorously smokes a cigarette, before popping a balloon that leaks sticky strips of black tar all over her naked body.

Finucane's bizarre erotic monologue to the National Gallery's water wall is a highlight. I can't think of another performer who is able to reach simultaneously such heights of comedy and erotic extremity. Unless, of course, it's Pamela Rabe. The guest artist for this week, she appeared as a statuesque goddess in a full-length black rubber dress with buttons all down the front, and performed an extraordinary monologue. It was a collage of quotations from Frank Wedekind's *Spring Awakening* and excerpts from an ancient Sumerian poem about the Queen of Heaven, the goddess Inanna. I shall not forget (and neither, I suspect, will the two men from the audience with whom she exited stage left) Rabe declaiming: 'Who will plough my vulva!' It was breathtaking, beautiful, terrifying and absurd, all at the same time.

But maybe I laughed most at Maude Davey's astounding performance of The Angels' classic hit, 'Am I ever going to see your face again'. Davey is in heels, nipple stars, ridiculous orange ostrich feathers, spangles and not much else. I'm old enough to remember seeing an angel-faced Doc Neeson belt this one out in some sticky-carpeted pub, and I can tell you that Davey gives him a run for his money in the rock-star charisma stakes. But she is much, much funnier.

This show is all about being human: human desire and human fear and human beauty and human laughter. It's a reminder of all those complexities that get edited out of mass culture. As with poetry, these things won't make the news, but people 'die every day for the lack of what is found there'. I can't think of a better antidote to the midwinter blues.

Theatre Notes, July 8 2011

Small Odysseys

Watching Rawcus' superb new production *Small Odysseys* at North Melbourne Arts House was an oddly personal experience. For me, it was the psychological equivalent of that optical test in which, when a bright light is shone into your pupil, you see the veins of your own retina. It was as if I was watching a repatterning of some of my peak Melbourne experiences of the past few years: Ariane Mnouchkine's *Le Dernier Caravansérail (Odyssées)*, Bill Viola's *The Raft*, Ron Mueck's sculptures, the theatre of Romeo Castellucci and Jérôme Bel... even down to a recent book purchase, the haunting and comic urban miniatures of Slinkachu.

If ever there was an argument for the dependence of art on a rich soil, it's this show. It demonstrates how artists are magpies, stealing one idea here, another there, and transforming them into something completely other. Works of collage or bricolage expose this process, but all artists do it. When the original inspirations remain undigested or misunderstood, it produces more-or-less successful pastiche, the merely derivative. The process has to be equal to its sources: when it is, it creates an artwork that absorbs those earlier influences into its own concerns, throwing their illuminations into unexpected contexts. In a sweet synchronicity, I recently quoted the great literary critic Viktor Shklovsky here on just this process: as he says, 'Art cognizes by implementing old models in new ways and by creating new ones'.

This language of formal and emotional allusion is one of the ways that an artwork signals its ambitions, which is always a risky business: the bigger the ambitions, the bigger the scope for collapse. *Small Odysseys* makes its claims from its opening moments: this is epic work, seeking to give poetic shape to intimate, inarticulate moments of isolation and loneliness. Director Kate Sulan and her collaborators walk the line to create a dream-like work of theatre which is as deeply felt as it is richly imagined.

Like Back to Back, Rawcus is a company of performers with and without disabilities which collaboratively generates self-devised works. The sense of ensemble is tangible in the rhythms of the work, which are (almost) unfaltering. Perhaps one sequence extends itself too far, but mostly it steps from transformation to transformation in ways that ignite continual slight surprise, loosing time from its moorings. The performance lasts almost exactly an hour, but the concentration it quite voluntarily elicits makes this hour seem both shorter and longer: it passes swiftly, but it seems to traverse whole worlds. *Small Odysseys* is huge, both literally – it uses the vast perspectives of the Meatmarket stage to full advantage – and emotionally.

Mnouchkine's influence is perhaps the most explicit, and not only in its title: as in *Le Dernier Caravansérail (Odyssées)*, designers Shaun Patten and Emily Barrie employ miniature sets on wheels which are swept over the wide spaces of the stage: small illuminated rooms, in which we witness private moments, or islands, complete with grass, that recall the islands Odysseus visited on his long journey home. As with Mnouchkine's show, these miniature sets create a disconnect between the motion of the set and the performers which is oddly intensifying; more importantly, it generates an increasingly powerful transitoriness, a sense of how human beings exist in vast, indifferent space.

Mnouchkine used this convention to permit the swift telling of complex narratives; here, the fluidity of movement allows the performers to create poetic vignettes, images that invoke emotional states rather than stories. For some reason I can't quite trace, another artist it recalled for me was Paul Klee: maybe it was a strong sense of dream, of incongruities that create their own overwhelming emotional logic.

Mnouchkine is only one of the influences employed here – there are many others. At one point the performers recreate Théodore Géricault's famous Romantic painting, *The Raft of the Medusa*, the inspiration behind Bill Viola's *The Raft*, engaging both of the earlier works. There is minimal text – we hear one side of phone conversations, a list of questions about what it means to be lost, one performer singing lustily from the back of the space. The stage is constantly animated with an opening and closing of perspectives that moves with a rhythm like breathing. Illusions are rapidly created and as rapidly dismantled: one moment it is a sea peopled by surreal, mythically resonant islands of humanity, the next a naked, harshly lit space in which the performers stand exposed and vulnerable before our gaze. There's an honesty in this performance which allows it to escape the seductions of the merely pretty to explore a real beauty.

Richard Vabre's superb lighting design is crucial: it can blank out the stage altogether by blinding us with a bank of yellow lights, give us a haunting glimpse of a ship with a lighted prow gliding far in the distance, or set us in a moment of complete everydayness by locating a performer in a corridor of light. And the emotional texture is extended by Jethro Woodward's encompassing sound design, which reaches from lush lyric to harsh percussion.

Within this complex construction, the performers move like voyagers, always the central focus. It is probably closest to dance theatre – there is in fact is a powerful dance sequence, in which gestures are picked up and repeated by an increasing number of performers – but it's not purely anything. What's most interesting is a gathering sense of the individuals who made this piece, a sense of personal investment, that is released by the show's formal shaping. (This is the quality that made me think of Jérôme Bel). Its lucid focus on human desire and longing makes *Small Odysseys* deeply moving. It's probably one of the most beautiful works of theatre we'll see this year.

Theatre Notes, July 20 2011

Pina

I've never seen a work by Pina Bausch. As with those of us who come too late, who miss the boat, who weren't there, my knowledge of her work with Tanztheater Wuppertal has been limited to the scraps you gather together – critical books, photographs, videos, reviews, the descriptions of friends, even the traces of her influence in the work of others. I have built a patchwork Bausch, intuiting the language of this choreographer, whose work galvanised modern dance and theatre, from the traces left behind. It's never as good as being there. It never will be.

Wim Wenders knows this. His beautiful documentary film *Pina* is all about absence: most signally, the absence of Bausch herself, after her sudden death in 2009, five days after being diagnosed with cancer, and just as she and Wenders were planning to make a film about her work. It is not a biography of Bausch, so much as an invocation of her work and her company. Among improvisations made for the film by the different dancers, we are shown some of her most famous dances, including three iconic pieces from the 1970s – *Le Sacre du Printemps,*

Kontakthof, and *Café Müller* – and a more recent work, *Vollmond.*

Wenders opens with an evocation of a virtual theatre, in which 3D technology permits him to open up illusory spaces and perspectives to give the spectator something like the shape of Bausch's choreography. As he begins, with scenes from *Kontakthof,* the 3D illusion is heightened, emphasising its artifice to a degree that I found discomforting. The powerful illusion of depth, of the rounded presence of dancers, made clear what was missing: the bodies of the dancers themselves.

These dancers were creatures of light, phantoms who are exact in every visual degree; but in watching dance, I suddenly realised, other senses are also employed, subliminal animal senses that track physical weight, the smell of sweat, disturbances in the air, perhaps even changes in heat. The lack of these other stimuli was at first alienating, then strangely revelatory: the absence of the dancers' bodies was sometimes as strong a feeling as the loss of Bausch. This is, in a real sense, a posthumous film: it's a tribute to a choreographer who is dead, recording performances that have long vanished from the air.

What's beautiful is how conscious Wenders is of these limitations. He knows very well that he can't reproduce the experience of performance, so he doesn't attempt to: from the beginning, his framing of the documentary makes this very clear. He subtly highlights what is missing, and then translates dance into the language of film, the language of light and shadow and illusion. Sometimes this is stunning; there's a particular moment when, as audience members, we stand between curtains at the edge of the stage, looking in at the dancers. He films dances on stage (without too many close-ups, a particular bugbear of mine in filmed performance), and places them also in different contexts – the industrial streets of Wuppertal, a quarry, a modern building that appears to be a glass gallery in the middle of a spring forest.

Wenders uses minimal documentary footage of Bausch herself; the major sequence is a moving black and white film of her role in *Café Müller,* which she danced with her eyes shut. He is, quite rightly, more interested in her work than her life. Her work, you feel, left her naked enough; and her recondite presence in the fleeting glimpses we are offered radiates a powerful sense of privacy. She is mainly remembered through her dancers, who are filmed in front of the camera, their faces mobile with thought, as a voice-over of their reminiscences plays against their silence. (In a couple of cases, the dancer remains speechless.)

The film is not merely a tribute to Pina: it is also, with an increasing freight of emotion, a tribute to the company she made, the dancers who worked with her, in some cases for decades, attempting to realise her vision. They were, as becomes increasingly clear through the film, her collaborators, offering their ideas and feelings and wit as well as their skilled bodies to her work. As much as anything, this is a film about relationship: it permits us an insight into the profound relationships between these artists, and how these emerged into some of the most influential dance works of the past 30 years.

What I wasn't prepared for was the overwhelming emotional power of Bausch's dance. For all the difficulties of performance on film, this is where Wenders triumphs. All her dancers speak about the feeling of Bausch's work, of her scrupulous, pained search to create a language that could express and embody the inexpressible. 'Words can only invoke', said Bausch. 'That's where dance comes in... ' A dancer said of Bausch: 'She danced as if she had been risen from the dead... in her pain and loneliness'. In *Pina*, you can see that quality for yourself. I don't know how the precise gesture of a hand, the angle of a head, a leap, a step, can so surgically open the latent grief and love in your own psyche, but this is what Bausch's choreography does. I was floored by the immediacy and beauty of her language, the fluency and toughness of its emotional economy.

It's not surprising to learn that Wenders was a close friend of Bausch's. Without resorting to the vulgarity of declaring it, this film is made with a great deal of love. It's a lament and celebration, an invocation and farewell. Wenders never intrudes: he stands modestly behind the scenes, enabling us to see what he so admired in his subject. Like Bausch, with the maximum of tact and the minimum of fuss, he manages the translation of feeling into his own medium. It's a marvellous film, and essential viewing for anyone with even the slightest interest in contemporary dance.

Theatre Notes, August 7 2011

Namatjira / Rising Water

The notion of 'authenticity' in art has whiskers all over it. Art, by definition, is artifice, mimicry, representation: at its most achieved, it can perhaps aspire to be authentically fake. It's entirely possible that the rest is marketing: celebrity didn't just start with Paris Hilton, after all. This generates one of the central paradoxes of art: what makes art matter, to those who encounter it as well as those who make it, is a quality that can best be called truthfulness. It's that quality, wherever it exists, which calls up the immediate sense of recognition that makes a work resonant. It goes through you, like wine through water, and changes the colour of your soul.

It is a quality at home in any form, and therefore as indefinable as it is recognisable. I've found it in work as diverse as the alternative realities of Ursula Le Guin or the astonishing visual poems of Cy Twombly; in HD's reconstructed etymologies or Beckett's astringent theatrical sculptures or, most recently, in Antonio Tabucchi's novels. It's in Fernando Pessoa's multiple identities as much as in the passionate fakeries of Picasso's paintings. This quality might, as Viktor Shklovsky hints, come down to something as simple as the changes registered in a work of art, its movement from one state to another, mimicking similar psychic and physical states within wider human experience. Whatever it is, it is experienced as a sense of truthfulness: and in a work of art, no matter how difficult or tragic the truth might be that it communicates, that is a joyous experience.

Authenticity and truthfulness are not the same thing, although they're often confused. While truthfulness emerges from within the work itself, authenticity is a kind of certificate, an extrinsic guarantee that the work is, in some way, 'genuine'. In literature, for example, the author is often the guarantor, feeding a public hunger for the authentic that somehow elides the whole question of fictional truthfulness or even imagination. This is, of course, the primary reason for literary hoaxes like Helen Demidenko or Norma Khouri.

Namatjira, which opened last week at the Malthouse after a hugely successful Sydney season at Belvoir St, plays authenticity against truthfulness in deeply revealing ways. I haven't seen a lot of Big hArt's work, but it's an exemplary maker of community theatre, and one of the most interesting companies working in Australia. I first encountered

Big hArt with the production *Ngapartji Ngapartji*, which featured in the 2006 Melbourne Festival, and later saw a moving documentary on their community work in the Northcott Housing Project in Sydney, which resulted in a Sydney Festival performance called *Sticky Bricks*.

Big hArt's headline festival performances are the publicly visible part of much larger long-term community engagements. *Namatjira*, which narrates the story of the hugely popular Aboriginal painter Albert Namatjira, is one aspect of a community project in Hermannsburg, Central Australia, which, as the program note explains, 'is designed to leave lasting legacies beyond this touring performance'. It's this profound level of engagement which gives the production its sense of authenticity: for example, this story is told with Namatjira's grandchildren, Kevin and Lenie Namatjira, on stage. They are both painters themselves, and throughout the show, with fellow painters and family members Elton, Hilary and Kevin Wirri, work on the massive chalk drawings of country, representations of Namatjira's own paintings, that constitute the background of the set.

Such careful signals of a work's authenticity can set off all sorts of warning signals. When work like this is presented in the privileged, middle-class setting of a theatre, it risks being merely worthy, served up with a sense of piety that replaces vitality and, worst of all, art itself. I don't deny there's an element of piety somewhere in the work, as well as in its reception, but mostly this is exploded with comedy, the mischievous parodying of precisely those careful contemporary proprieties. Big hArt are upfront about seeking connection with their audiences, and, in their oscillation between these contradictory qualities of truthfulness and authenticity, this is what they achieve. The key is the art.

Namatjira, written and directed by Scott Rankin, is a supple mediation between the artifice of theatre – highlighted in the charismatic central performance of Trevor Jamieson, the major narrator, and his offsider Derik Lynch – and the realities that the story of Namatjira reveals, signalled by the presence of his inheritors on stage. Into this are layered the mediations of painting itself. The performance unfolds in what is effectively a giant, dynamic work of visual art.

As the audience enters, Robert Hannaford is hard at work on stage, painting a portrait of Trevor Jamieson, who sits patiently as the artist darts back and forth from the canvas to his palette. This is an allusion to Sir William Dargie's famous portrait of Namatjira, but it's also, quite clearly, a portrait in its own right of the actor who is playing Namatjira. Before a word is spoken, we are already in a complex world of representation.

The performance modulates into song and music – lush choral songs from the Lutheran Mission, country and Western parodies, and Genevieve Lacey's haunting recorder compositions, played live on stage. It's a contemporary take on old-fashioned storytelling, and irresistibly seductive: within ten minutes, Jamieson has his audience eating out of his hand.

The story itself is a fascinating fable of colonial Australia, at once tragic and hopeful. It starts with Namatjira's parents and his childhood on a Lutheran Mission in Central Australia, his meeting with his friend and mentor Rex Battarbee, and his decision to begin painting to feed his rapidly growing family. Then there's Namatjira's extraordinary fame and wealth at a time when Aboriginal people were still considered part of Australia's flora and fauna, and his subsequent exploitation. He was the first Aboriginal given citizenship, although this 'honour' was conferred so he could be taxed.

There are also the various rip-offs – his desperate selling of his copyright, his unsuccessful bid to buy a cattle station – which demonstrated that, for all his fame, he was still a second-class citizen. And there was his old age, culminating in the humiliation of his unjust imprisonment to hard labour after an alcohol-related crime in his community for which he was considered responsible, and which broke and killed him.

The show is careful to pay attention to complexities: Namatjira was a victim of the conflicts that resulted from his stepping between both cultures. Here the depth and complexity of personal relationships are set against the blank impersonality of institutional racism: the friendship of Rex and Albert and their mutual exchange of knowledge becomes a glimpse of a lost possibility that the company itself seeks to resurrect in its work. It's not so far from what historian James Boyce described as 'indigenising', a process in which a white underclass learned from black knowledge. It created a new way of living in this country, and was often violently repressed by colonial authorities. In the utopian space of theatre, this possibility is ignited as a hope for something better.

The word is never said, but *Namatjira* is an enactment of reconciliation. For one thing, it's a show consciously directed towards a white audience. White attitudes to Aboriginality are gently mocked, but this is never alienating; instead, mischievously, it invites its audience into its world. The fact that the production manages to do this without a trace of false sentiment, moralising or special pleading is a tribute to how artfully its makers step through the political minefield of this kind of community-based work. It's feel-good theatre that generates an answering goodwill in its audience, a sudden generosity of possibility. And that's a rare thing to witness.

Tim Winton's first play, on at the MTC, is another vision of Australia. *Rising Water* is in its own way as artfully positioned as Big hArt's. Let's make no mistake: both these productions are unashamedly directed at mainstream audiences, and in their own ways are equally manipulative (as all art, in fact, is). But *Rising Water*, like Winton's novels, carefully shows us the Australia we would like to imagine, or at least, would like to talk about over our dinner tables. The artfulness here, rather than disarming me, made my teeth ache.

Rising Water is set on Australia Day, on three boats moored at a Perth marina on which live three different middle-aged characters, Col (Geoff Kelso), Baxter (John Howard) and Jackie (Alison Whyte). They all have secrets which are gradually revealed through the show. They are all stuck in the backwater of their lives, wondering how to go on. They all represent various aspects of Australia, or the Australian character, with various nationalistic tics going on in the background. Variously, they provide occasions for critiquing contemporary materialism, via WA Inc or the rapacious consumerism of suburbia, or nationalism, or change.

There are some secondary characters, played by Stuart Halusz, and a mysterious boy (Louis Corbett) floating around in a boat, whom at first I thought was a Ghost of Childhood Lost or somesuch, until in the second act he turned out to be a character too, with his own monologues. And lastly there's the young British backpacker (Claire Lovering) who sparks the action of the play. Foul-mouthed and drunk, with 'Pogrom' (the name of a band, apparently) tattooed on her back, she represents what has happened to the Mother Country.

It feels like a thoroughly colonial work, in a way that *Namatjira* – which is wholly concerned with colonisation – totally manages to avoid.

Even its diction seems like a colonial derivation of something else. Perhaps Winton's attention to a certain idea of authentic Australianness means it never feels quite truthful. Among other things, the play is about nostalgia, but at the same time the writing itself seems to be crippled by nostalgia. It is curiously old-fashioned, like a play written about fifty years ago.

The structure consists of dialogues punctuated by long reflective monologues, with moments of theatrical poetic usually signalled by the presence of the Boy. Winton gives us a kind of cod Tennessee Williams with Australian accents, only without the Williams pathos and passion. Most of the time, it's clear that this is a novelist's play: the language tends to the descriptive rather than performative. There's not a lot of sense that language is an act, a necessary understanding for writing in the theatre. This transformation does occur sometimes in Winton's dialogues, and when it does, the difference is palpable.

Kate Cherry's production is a suitably lyrical rendition in a minor key, with silhouettes of masts against a changing sky and the water itself represented by a highly polished black floor. The central performance, John Howard's Baxter, is hugely enjoyable, and makes the most of the text. Baxter is in fact the only character to whom anything happens; everyone else just witnesses it happening to him, doing a kind of psychological striptease along the way.

Given my reservations, and they are considerable, *Rising Water* wasn't nearly as bad as it might have been. For all its dramaturgical vagueness and its pandering to the dinner-party-fodder aspect of culture, I feel a bit eccentric for confessing that I was sitting there thinking, well, at least the man knows how to write a sentence. There are a few playwrights who could learn that skill to their benefit.

Theatre Notes, August 18, 2011

Ganesh Versus the Third Reich

I've been dithering over this post for days, trying to find a way in to writing about this extraordinary show. As with Back to Back's *Food Court*, which remains one of the most compelling experiences I've had in a theatre, *Ganesh Versus the Third Reich* (at Malthouse Theatre as part of the Melbourne Festival) takes an idea which initially appears to be very simple, and then, with cumulative force, systematically unpicks every expectation that you might have formed, until the psyche finds itself at such a point of vulnerability that you are suddenly confronted with – what? The Human Condition? Your own existential solitude? The naked soul as Foucault imagined it, criss-crossed and scarred by the traces of power and authority?

One of the problems in discussing Back to Back, the little theatre company from Geelong that could, is that it creates experiences that defeat description. Outlining a production's shape gives an idea of its characteristics, its morphology, if you like; but this morphology doesn't explain the vitality that inhabits the work. I feel, even more than usual, as if I were attempting to invoke an entire life, with all its incidence, richness, mundanity, conflict and beauty, by dissecting a corpse.

Bruce Gladwin and his collaborators make a work that can only happen in a theatre. It can't be translated into another medium, because it exists so fiercely in its transient present, in the particular moments in which it's witnessed by the particular people who happen to attend. Its transformations are a kind of alchemy, a human magic that ignites in the shifting relationships between the performers and the audience. It's at once transparently simple and profoundly complex.

As those who have followed the mild controversy that greeted its publicity will know, *Ganesh versus The Third Reich* is, in part, a fable about how Ganesh, the elephant-headed Hindu god, travels to Nazi Germany to wrest back the swastika from Hitler. A major god in the Hindu pantheon, Ganesh is the deity of obstacles: he not only removes them, but will place them in situations that need to be checked. One of his lesser aspects is as lord of letters and learning, an avatar of stories (which is why I have two small brass effigies of Ganesh on my desk).

Ganesh's aspect as remover of obstacles must have special significance for a company in which most members are disabled. And Back to Back's decision to interrogate Hitler reminds us that, well before their plans to eradicate Jews, homosexuals and Roma and Slavic people, Nazi Germany targeted its disabled population. In 1939, the state systematically began to murder people with mental and physical disabilities, labelling them 'unworthy of life', with estimates of deaths varying from 200,000 to 250,000. These murders were the experimental laboratory for what later became the death camps: Auschwitz-Birkenau, Belzec, Chełmno, Majdanek, Sobibór and Treblinka.

Given such a dark subtext, not to mention the questions of cultural appropriation in employing the figure of Ganesh, it's unsurprising that the company discarded their initial idea for *Ganesh Versus the Third Reich*. 'We knew our narrative was morally fraught', says Bruce Gladwin in his program note. 'Over time our thinking shifted. Our self-imposed censorship – our reasoning that we should not create the work – became the rationale for bringing it to life.'

What is presented instead is a double reality. We see the actors – Mark Deans, Simon Laherty, Scott Price and Brian Tilley – and director David Woods creating their Holocaust fairytale. When we walk in, the stage is a working studio littered with tables, ladders and other miscellaneous mess, with a row of huge curtains tied up at the side of the stage. As the performers argue in a desultory fashion, the director comes in and takes charge.

These glimpses of rehearsal are punctuated by scenes of theatrical spectacle, in which the semi-transparent plastic curtains, painted with silhouetted outlines of trees, houses and other illusions, are drawn across the stage. They are backlit, so performers can be seen in silhouette as well, or are used as a screen for shadow puppetry. The shifts from mundane reality to fairytale are swift, signalled by sound and lighting, and completely transform the stage, so that you are plunged wholly into mythic realities and just as suddenly, almost with a sense of bereftness, dragged out of them.

What is hard to explain is how this rhythm of contrast intensifies into a shattering potency during the show. As in *Food Court*, the work is an ambush: gestures and relationships which seem of merely mundane importance, or which begin as comic confrontations, inexorably gather emotional force. Subtly and incrementally, connections begin to accrete between the two storylines; for example, David plays Mengele, the Nazi doctor who conducted horrific experiments on, among others, disabled children, and David's very correct treatment of his actors begins to collect sinister undertones.

Perhaps part of this sense of ambush is in how lightly these connections are drawn. The rehearsal scenes are leavened by absurd comedy: Simon, for instance, complaining about his part as one of Mengele's experimental subjects – 'It's hard being a Jew'. They argue, passionately, about the issue of appropriation. There are sudden and confronting gestures towards the audience: David flinging his hand towards us, as if he is addressing a bank of empty seats, claiming that the audience is just coming to watch 'freak porn'. As the arguments between the performers intensify, his contempt becomes double-edged, and you begin to wonder if the person most interested in 'freak porn' is David himself.

When these arguments explode into violence, the effect is devastating and shocking: the disparate elements and themes of the production suddenly fuse in a wholly unexpected way. The final image is unforgettable. David, tired of his job, tired of these freaks, is left with Mark, who has been the silent focus of many of the cast's arguments. Mark's mother will pick him up later. David, using all his professional skills in people management, deals with the annoyance of Mark by suggesting that they play hide and seek.

Mark hides under the table; David, pretending to look for him, picks up his things, and leaves the room. As the light closes in on him, Mark remains crouched under the table, wriggling with delight at the game, waiting to be found. Even thinking of this moment shakes my heart. It's not simply that this disabled man has been carelessly abandoned by someone who should know better. It's how this apparently trivial gesture becomes, in the deepest and most vulnerable echo chambers of the consciousness, a metaphor for the betrayal of all human hope.

This shows the power and ambiguity, also, of what Back to Back do to the notion of performance. David Woods is the only actor without disability, and his is, in the conventional sense, a brilliant performance. There is no question, at any time, that the rest of the cast isn't making a performance: this is the company's counter-argument to the bitter notion of their being 'freak porn'. But these actors bring another edge, a sense of perilous exposure that is intensified under Gladwin's impeccably sure direction. I can't think of another company which so foregrounds the knowledge that this work is being made, in each moment, before our eyes: it is a great part of why the audiences becomes so deeply involved.

Back to Back have never had any truck with 'special' treatment: their work has a harsh honesty that makes it impossible to patronise. But they also specialise in moments of breathtaking beauty that assert the sheer power of their skills. There are images I won't forget: the impossible poignancy and strangeness, for example, of Ganesh, dressed in a business suit, standing before Hitler, who is played by Simon in a ridiculous knitted Hitler costume. Or an evocation of Indra's net, when a back curtain of stars was lifted to reveal a blazing light, like a sunrise. I've never seen anything like this show, because only Back to Back could make it. They are, simply, our most important independent theatre company.

Theatre Notes, October 7 2011

Return to Earth

I walked out of the opening night of Lally Katz's new play *Return to Earth* with my stomach in a knot. Readers, I have seldom seen a production which was so utterly wrong. It's wrong from the ground up, wrong from the first moment, and goes on being wrong all the way through to the end. Every flicker of life in this play is wrestled to the ground and throttled to death.

Any text, if it's at all interesting, invites a multiplicity of interpretation, and it's always possible merely to disagree with a take on a play. In this case, the wrongness goes beyond disagreement to a fundamental misunderstanding of the very being of the writing, to the point where the play itself is terminally obscured. It can happen to any play – I've seen it done to Shakespeare. It's as if a mistaken decision were reached early in the process, and every step afterwards led inexorably to doom. How this happened with the cast and production team that director Aidan Fennessy had to hand is a case study in artistic car crashes. On paper it's impeccable, some of the best talent that our theatre has to offer.

I should say that I am already familiar with this play. Back in 2008, I was one of three judges who unanimously gave *Return to Earth* a RE Ross Playwrights' Award for further development. The following year I saw it read in Hobart as part of Playwriting Australia 2009, and saw no reason to revise our judgment that this was one of Katz's best plays so far. Not that it's visible in this production; if I hadn't read the text, I might have thought it one of her worst.

Katz's early work, from the closely observed suburban absurdity of *The Eisteddfod* to the wildly theatrical dislocations of *Lally Katz and the Terrible Mystery of the Volcano*, created a riveting tension between a stern, even cruel emotional truthfulness and the dizzying vortex of her imaginative world. As her work has developed, from plays such as *Goodbye Vaudeville Charlie Mudd* to *A Golem Story*, the writing has become sharper: more theatrically crafted, less anarchic. But those desolating absurdities remain at the centre of the work: an obsession with death, loss and love, refracted through a self so splintered it can be scarcely said to exist. Katz is, crucially, a playwright of surfaces: her characters are performances of themselves, role-players in the most profound sense, and the emotional abysses that open beneath their emptiness and lostness can be vertiginous.

Return to Earth is an apparently simple fable that preserves Katz's unstable realities, but here locates it firmly in a – supposedly – naturalistic suburbia. There's not much in the way of plot. Alice (Eloise Mignon) returns home to her family after an unspecified time away, searching desperately for something real. Her parents Wendy (Julie Forsyth) and Cleveland (Kim Gyngell) welcome her home with claustrophobic solicitude.

Alice attempts to reunite with an old childhood friend Jeanie (Anne-Louise Sarks), reconnects with her widowed brother Tom (Tim Ross) and her terminally ill niece Catta (Allegra Annetta) and has an affair with local car mechanic Theo (Anthony Ahern), a man whose skin is disconcertingly covered with shellfish. Alice finds she can save her niece's life by donating a kidney, but at the same time discovers that she is pregnant, which means the life-saving operation can't be done. Her niece dies, but Alice has her baby. Finally she tells her mother where she has been – in outer space, where she has lost her self but discovered the marvellous.

What counts is the slippages and ellipses in the texture of the play, how it lurches from apparently banal reality to strangeness in the space of a sentence. The result can be, as in Jorge Luis Borges' story *Tlön, Uqbar, Orbis Tertius*, an increasingly disturbing feeling of the known world losing its moorings, becoming strange and perilous. In this production, we get quirky instead of strange, and emotional insight becomes mere whimsy.

Alice is played as terminally naïve: there is no sense of interstellar alienation in her performance, no sense of almost irretrievably damaged adulthood. Her unvarying tone sets the pitch for the rest of the performances: somehow these characters, despite everything that happens in the play, are curiously static. The performances are generalised caricatures, rather than detailed investigations of emotional states. Claude Marcos' design, an abstract revolve mimicking a planetary system with a diorama of a night-time suburb in the background, exacerbates the problems: the actors all seem lost in the space. The set almost acts as a spoiler, leaving nothing to reveal about Alice's travels: we know from the beginning that she has been in outer space. Everything looks slick, but feels empty.

The major problem in this production is that the play's emotional realities have been flattened or simply avoided; certainly, I very seldom felt any emotional connection with what was happening on stage. Once or twice – interestingly, when the everyday realities were allowed to play without an overlaid theatrical self-consciousness – you could feel a flicker of life in the text, but otherwise its comedy and poignancies are all but destroyed. One feels that the MTC has tried to 'make sense' of Lally Katz, closing up the centrifugal polarities of her work in the process, when her real gift is to use emotional truthfulness to destroy such enclosing rationalities. Without that truthfulness at its heart, the felt realities of loss and lostness, the play makes no sense at all.

Theatre Notes, November 15 2011

Oráculos

After I left Teatro de los Sentidos' *Oráculos* last night, I wandered back to my hotel room through the Perth streets feeling as if my skin were luminous, as if I moved through the luscious darkness like a soft, cool flame. It was the kind of night when the air is exhausted after a day of brutal heat and now wants only to touch you tenderly. And, as is often the way when I am away from home, my own exhaustion rose up out of me, up to the surface of my skin, but now it evaporated, along with all my anxieties, all my dreads and fears. For those moments, I was simply present. I couldn't tell whether I was wholly empty or wholly full: perhaps I was both at once, in that state in which plenitude and poverty meet in the possible.

I had been treated gently. I had been invited by many hands that beckoned out of the shadows, and I had been given a key and led to a door. The door opened me back to my present, out of the dark labyrinth of memory. I could have stayed there, in the labyrinth: it contained my childhood, but it was a childhood transfigured, made into a thing of wonder, leached of hurt. It is easy to remember the wounds, those defining scars that make us who we are. It is less easy to remember the small moments of joyous pleasure: standing on dead leaves in your bare feet, dry sand between your toes, the warm, live smell of yeast as you push the heel of your hand into bread dough, the dry liquidity of wheat as it runs through your fingers. They arrive in little shocks of sensual recognition as you move, your arms outstretched to guide you through a warm, blinding blackness, a soft labyrinth. Sometimes you stand, sometimes you stumble, sometimes you crawl. A light blooms and you turn and follow. Here, you are your own oracle.

The condition of entrance is that you must ask a question. I had a question, but it is personal.

❖ ❖ ❖

Teatro de los Sentidos is a company from Barcelona that, under the artistic direction of Enrique Vargas, has pioneered the art of immersive theatre over the past two decades. Their particular area of research is the poetic of the senses and body memory: the environments through which the traveller moves in *Oráculos* are designed to resonate within each participant. I'm quite sure that each person's experience of this work is entirely unique. Much of the theatre occurs in your own head: the complex, dimly-lit designs, the playful eroticism, the carefully placed sensual triggers, are all invitations to interior experience, reinforced by the darkness and silence out of which they emerge. Participants enter the labyrinth one by one: you are taken by the hand and led through it, but it is essentially a solitary journey.

Oráculos occurs inside an old building in an unremarkable suburban street. You enter the shopfront and inside are other... (pilgrims? witnesses? 'Audience' seems simply the wrong word for this experience...) Inside are others, waiting their turn to enter. Everyone is quiet, everyone seems patient. After a time, a man takes you by the hand and leads you outside, around the side of the building and up a fire escape. He tells you that you must ask a question, and waits while you think of it. Then he points you to a door, and tells you to knock. Soon someone answers, and you enter.

I have absolutely no idea how long I spent there: it must have been about an hour. What I entered was a fantastic world, structured by the Major Arcana of the Tarot: each encounter is a theatrical realisation of a different card. Early on, you are shown a miniature landscape, in which your life is depicted as a river winding down to the sea: you are asked to point to where you are in the landscape, and then you are given a card which you wear around your neck. My card was the thirteenth card of the Major Arcana, Death: the card of transformation. It was so appropriate that I wondered if everyone was given the same card, although I can't imagine that they are.

The trust you feel in the total darkness is astonishing. Although I might as well have been blindfolded, I never felt unsafe. The labyrinth guides you by touch to different rooms, where different things are happening. Most are populated by a half-seen person, who might silently point you to a chair and ask you to grind wheat into flour, or plant a seed in a miniature pot. One man, after carefully arranging your pose, takes an image of your shadow. Maybe you will dance.

One you encounter with no light at all: your hands blindly reach out and touch naked skin, long curly hair, the swell of a breast. She guides you, through a complex spiral dance, to a deeply padded coffin: you stand inside and slowly it tips backwards, so you are lying down, suspended in space, curiously weightless because you can see absolutely nothing at all. Some, like The Lovers – a white maze of lacy nightdresses hung on a clothes line, which brushes your skin as you walk through, or The Moon, a plank bridge over a small pond in which a crescent moon is reflected – are sculptures through which you simply pass. Each environment is full of details that I wish I had looked at more closely: tiny objects, empty picture frames, mirrors, toys, intricate machines which you activate with a ball-bearing or a ladle of sand, books, images, structural plans.

Another defining image is the seed, a grain of wheat. As you make your way through, this seed is planted and grows into a seedling, which becomes wheat, which you take to grind into flour. For me, the seed was the tangible symbol of my question. At the end, you find yourself in a room with lamps and chairs, where you might sit for a long time; you are given fresh hot bread and a cup of tea, and invited to write about your journey. There is home-made paper, which feels a little like very thin unleavened bread, and a board to rest it on, and a pencil. I wrote something down, but I don't remember what it was.

You need that transition, a space of time in which to return to the surface levels of the world.

There were moments when I realised that I was entirely happy just where I was, in this suspended, gentle, questioning, absurd universe. It is a profound world, which reaches into the places that language cannot express. Inside it is everything you want. It doesn't exist, but it is real, and you take it away with you afterwards.

I know the resonances for me were so powerful in part because I was a country child. I went barefoot all summer, and had to make bread every week. I spent a lot of time looking at moonrise through trees, or out in the bush making houses out of branches. I am so urban now that even if I haven't forgotten these things, I had forgotten their sleeping power within me. The poet Yves Bonnefoy said once that ritual is always an enactment of origin in the present: I think this is how *Oráculos* worked for me. Death is never simply an ending: and sometimes ending means that you have to go back to the beginning.

❖ ❖ ❖

When I was back in my hotel, I wrote down some images so I could remember them:

> The journey from the mountain to the sea.
> The seed.
> The paper boat and the joker.
> The scales.
> The lovers. The caress. Lace.
> The devil.
> The rope and the candle and the dark forest.
> The moon and the uneasy water.
> The wheat. The flour. The dough.
> The naked woman and the coffin.
> Always the seed that is growing.
> The shadow that is me.
> The hand that touches mine.
> The voice touching my ear.
> The chicken.

The basket of bread.
The shoes and the houses.
The door.

I didn't write down Death, although that was my card. I underlined 'The door' three times.

Theatre Notes, February 22 2012

Welcome to Thonnet

For the past couple of weeks, the Melbourne International Comedy Festival has crashed over our fair city like a tidal wave, dragging the crowds and a bunch of increasingly exhausted critics out into the extraordinarily beautiful autumn evenings. But your humble blogger has remained at home, deaf to the siren call of comedy: far be it from me to 'discourage earnest conversation', as psychiatrist Brendan Flynn suggested is the dark heritage of festival time. Flynn would approve of me: I have resolutely remained in my dour study, turning my face from the trivial levity of the light-hearted, to defend Melbourne's beetle-browed reputation as 'a home of original ideas'. But at least I now know who to blame for the sad state of our public discourse: it's those damn comedians.

And so it would have remained, gentle reader, had not rumours come my ears of a show called *Welcome to Thonnet*. Playing at the Northcote Town Hall, it is written and performed by Martin Blum. Blum is a very interesting actor: along with talents like Hayley McElhinney and Dan Spielman, he was one of the twelve original members of the STC Actors Company, resigning a couple of years later to travel overseas. The show has been assisted by various other intriguing names: its co-devisors include Chris Ryan, of *Thyestes* and *Wild Duck* fame, and Bojana Novakovic (*The Story of Mary MacLane, By Herself*). Govin Ruben, who's designed lighting for Hayloft and Black Lung, is production designer and provides some incidental performance. In short, all these seemed sufficient reason to wash my inky hands and venture off into the balmy night.

I returned home shaken, to recover from one of the most uncomfortably hilarious hours I have spent in the theatre. Blum is a fearless actor, and his monstrous creation, YA author Ray Living, demonstrates his courage: I haven't been on this kind of razor edge since seeing Howard Stanley's brilliant *Howard Slowly* shows in the 1980s. *Welcome to Thonnet* is pitiless: its cruelty plays on the abyss between self-perception and the perception of others that makes David Brent in the UK edition of *The Office* so toe-curlingly compelling.

The unassuming room in the Northcote Town Hall is a perfect setting for the show's conceit. Ray Living, unsuccessful author, has decided to attract the notice of publishers and other important people who might promote his career: and to this end he is launching his new book, *Welcome to Thonnet*, on the unsuspecting public. He has a lectern plastered with posters of himself and a planned evening of entertainment which includes a rendition of Green Day's 'Good riddance (Time of your life)' on acoustic guitar.

He emerges from backstage with his authorial persona intact, if somewhat shakily nervous (he takes a call on his mobile because it might be, he says, from a publisher, only to find that it's his mum). He has some photographs of himself that he's happy to sign 'for a gold coin donation': although they all look the same, they have 'different expressions'. Eager for feedback, he offers paper and pencils so the audience can note down their responses. We are given to understand that, but for the blindness of the publishing industry, we would be confronting one of the stars of teen fiction.

Even in the opening moments there's a hint of creepiness: his imagined conversation with a lonely teenager has a sweaty touch of predatoriness. The full horror doesn't really begin to dawn until he reads an extract from his first book, a sci-fi piece, he explains, about aliens and spaceships. It's floridly pornographic, and Mr Living, all eagerness to please, is staggeringly unaware of its inappropriate nature.

Things only get worse as he turns to his new masterpiece, *Welcome to Thonnet*: a tale about a 17-year-old schoolboy who is (as he confesses coyly) perhaps a little like himself. The hero's name, Jay Giving, rhymes uncomfortably with Ray Living: he is a kind of pornographic Mary-Sue, a character invented by the author as a wish-fulfilment fantasy. Eventually it becomes clear that Living is a convicted paedophile, who is violating the terms of his parole.

Living's fantasies are increasingly outrageous, and he becomes at once increasingly pathetic and increasingly sinister. Blum pushes the limits of the author's self-delusion to almost unbearable heights of embarrassment. What scrapes most deeply, as it's so immediately recognisable, is Living's impregnable faith in his own talent, in the face of all the evidence against it.

Blum's performance is so convincing and detailed that, on its outing last year at the Melbourne Fringe, one reviewer seemed to take it straight, criticising Blum for his bumbling around on stage. 'Awkward, why yes it was, I smiled out of tact and ended up looking at the floor to avoid feeling bad every time a bead of sweat slid down Blum's glistening forehead.' A backhanded compliment if ever there was one. Awkward it is: not because the acting is bad, but because it's so uncompromisingly good. And it's deeply, sharply funny. Not for everyone, and it comes with a strict R18+ rating: but for those who like edge on their comedy, a must see.

Theatre Notes, April 7 2012

Olive as tragic hero

To anyone familiar with Australian theatre, Ray Lawler's 1950s play *Summer of the Seventeenth Doll* is a monument: the most famous Australian play ever written or produced. Like many monuments, it generally stands unnoticed in the background, covered with dust and sundry pigeon droppings, and every now and then it's dusted off to remind us about the achievements of Australian culture. As I said in a review of Neil Armfield's recent Belvoir St production, which I saw at the MTC earlier this year:

> One of the paradoxes of art is the uneasy legacy of success. As soon as a work is labelled a 'classic', it becomes curiously invisible: it transforms into a monument, cobwebbed by all the extraneous things its success now symbolises, and the energies that made it a success in the first place are polished away by the pieties that must now attend it. *Summer of the Seventeenth Doll* is a good example: a fixity in the Australian theatrical universe, a symbol of nationalistic pride, it too easily becomes a thing instead of an act. It even has a nickname: *The Doll*.

The significance given to *The Doll* as a unique, groundbreaking Australian drama, the 'Great Australian Play', has meant that it has been largely read through a lens of cultural identity, which I think has inadvertently obscured some of its interesting aspects. I agree with everyone, however, that it's a thoroughly Australian play. Its cultural status has also obscured other plays of the time that might have an equal claim to attention. All the same, it deserves its place in theatre history. I don't believe it's a great play – Australian playwrights have arguably written works of greater theatrical and literary significance. Even in its own time it broke little new ground: it opened in London the week after the premiere of John Osborne's *The Entertainer*, which starred Laurence Olivier. Next to *The Entertainer*, *The Doll*, as a well-made three-act play, appears a little old-fashioned.

But it is churlish to deny that *The Doll* remains a compelling drama 60 years later: it's a realist tragedy that still has the capacity to strike home. If anything makes a classic, it's the ability of a work to remain vivid, a quality of suppleness that allows it to speak to us powerfully in times different from those in which it was written: and *The Doll* certainly qualifies.

Lawler's play has suffered from its classic status, as much as it has benefited from it: the nimbus of nationalistic pride, and especially the masculine ethos that goes with that, has tended to obscure its more interesting aspects. Armfield's magnificent production earlier this year revealed it to be a play of more complexity and genuine power than is usually assumed. I hadn't seen it, or thought about it much, since I saw the 1978 MTC production in high school: for me, as for many others, it was a dusty part of our theatrical heritage, an achievement worthy of genuine respect, but perhaps not of huge intrinsic interest. Armfield's production reminded me, first of all, just how well-written it is: it's an impeccably structured play without one ounce of fat, in which every utterance works inexorably towards its shattering climax.

The other thing that struck me was that in Olive, then played by Alison Whyte, we saw a protagonist every bit as tragic, every bit as iconic, as Willy Loman in Arthur Miller's *Death of a Salesman*. For me, Olive is the central character – hers is the desire which holds the dream together and which, finally, destroys it. Although the tragedy in the play belongs to all the characters, it belongs most of all to Olive.

Lawler's story of itinerant cane cutters who migrate to Melbourne every summer for the lay-off is a parable of fantasy coming into brutal collision with reality and, like all tragedies, a meditation on mortality.

For sixteen years, Roo and Barney have returned to their lovers Olive and Nancy, for a white-hot summer of love in the Carlton boarding house run by Olive's mother: each year Roo brings Olive a kewpie doll, as a token. But now Nancy is gone: she has married a bookshop owner and settled down. Olive, refusing to face the implications of Nancy's desertion, has roped in her barmaid friend, the respectably widowed Pearl, to take Nancy's place.

When the boys arrive, it's clear that all is not well: Roo is broke, and his and Barney's relationship simmers with unsaid hostilities. These have been catalysed by the arrival of a young ganger, Johnnie O'Dowd, whose youthful virility shows Roo that he isn't the man he once was. As the play continues, the fantasy crumbles under the sceptical eyes of Pearl: against Pearl's sardonic observations, the other observer, Bubba, a young girl who lives next door, asserts the reality of the romance. Roo gets a job at a paint factory, and finally, in the shattering conclusion, proposes marriage to Olive: a proposal that she rejects in horror. In the final scene, Barney and Roo, both broken men, leave the house forever.

The Doll employs an Australian idiom that has largely vanished from our cities, with the broad vowels and supple, ironic wit that later became caricatured as the 'larrikin' or the ocker. In Lawler's hands it's plain and unexaggerated, the speech of working-class people. The play's three-act structure is similarly unadorned. Armfield's stripped-down production exposed the bones of the play, and showed what it always has been: a startlingly well-written text, of its time and place, but resonating beyond them.

As John McCallum notes in his book *Belonging: Australian Playwriting in the 20th Century*, *The Doll* was 'the first professionally produced Australian play outside the commercial theatre to receive any serious professional support and backing'. He argues, rightly I think, that much of its subsequent success was in luck and timing. It's worth remembering the fate of Oriel Gray's *The Torrents*, which, with *The Doll*, was joint winner of the Playwrights Advisory Board's play competition. In fact, the judging panel considered *The Torrents* 'the more complete play': but Gray's work, without the support of a production, sank into total obscurity.

This illuminates a major aspect of theatre writing, which doesn't apply to works such as poems or novels: playwrights must have a theatre to write for, and a play isn't complete until it's produced on stage. This makes a play an impure art form, as it necessarily becomes the point of focus for a range of other disciplines that together produce the finished (or, perhaps, to steal a phrase from Duchamp, the 'finally unfinished') work of art.

Because of this, there's been a lot of discussion in recent years on whether plays can be considered 'proper' literature: if the text is subject to such instability, to the rigors of interpretation and reinterpretation through the visions of directors, designers, actors and musicians, can it really be thought of as literary art? Some playwrights, inverting the literary snobbery too often directed against their art form, themselves resist the idea that plays are literature. Myself, I don't see the argument: to me it makes no sense at all to deny that plays are literature, especially in an Anglo culture which considers its greatest literary genius to be Shakespeare, and which traces its roots back to Aeschylus. You can read plays, just as you can read other books, and they exhibit all the qualities we expect from other literary writing: formal curiosity, style, intellectual and emotional engagement. Well, at least good plays do.

No matter how good they are, playwrights need a theatre to write for, and in the 1950s it scarcely existed. *The Doll*, with its unapologetic Australian vernacular, its invocation of the bush legend and its contemporary urban setting, burst on the scene in 1955 with stunning effect. According to critic Katharine Brisbane, it was a household name within a year of its premiere.

Most of all, *The Doll* was rapturously received as a 'mature' play, a statement that Australia was, at last, 'growing up' and asserting its unique identity in the world. This, of course, was reinforced when it went on to a highly successful London season. It was even made into a Hollywood film starring Ernest Borgnine, which I'm told is best forgotten. When it opened at the Elizabethan Theatre in Sydney in 1956, Lindsay Browne in the *Sydney Morning Herald* struck the note:

> This fine play, untranslatably Australian in all its accents, gave Australian theatre goers the chance to feel as American audiences must have felt when O'Neill first began to assert American vitality and independence in drama, or the Irish must have felt when Synge gave them *The Playboy of the Western World*. This was real and exciting Australiana, with Australian spirit springing from the deep heart of the characters, and

never merely pretending that Australianism is a few well-placed bonzers, too-rights, strike-me-luckies and good-Os.

J. Griffin Foley in the *Daily Telegraph* wrote similarly: 'It has happened at last – someone has written a genuine Australian play without kangaroos or stockwhips, but an indigenous play about city dwellers.' (Indigenous, of course, was used differently then.)

As those reviews make clear, *The Doll* was lifted up on a burgeoning nationalism, a hunger to assert Australian identity unapologetically in the face of our colonial heritage. John McCallum traces the various readings of the play: as he says,

> *The Doll* is so well-known, and has been written about so widely, that it is difficult to discuss it without cliché or, more importantly, without supporting one or more of the standard critical perspectives. Is it a socio-cultural document of its time or an individual drama of personal interactions? Is it a story of the failure of childish illusions or a proud assertion of a new vision? Is it a hard-nosed study of a new urban Australia or a sentimental elegy for a lost past?

In 1978, Katharine Brisbane wrote that it was a play about growing up, locating its meaning firmly as a statement about Australia's national identity. 'It is about growing up and growing old and failing to grow up: and the study throws into relief not only the failures of a dilapidated Melbourne household, but the character of a nation.' She placed it in context of a struggle for national cultural identity: in the 1950s, as Brisbane puts it, Australians had 'a yearning to mix on terms of equality with those older civilisations thousands of servicemen had glimpsed during the War'. She said that Lawler had 'unconsciously drawn upon the major themes of our literature: man pitting his strength against nature, mateship and freedom and alienation in the itinerant life this vast country offers, rugged individualism and the resilient humour that shrugs off despair. He presses these country-bred virtues into a new, urban context and gently questions them one by one, finding behind the sun-blessed strength a tragic lack of spiritual resource.'

This points to a common interpretation of the play as a 'tragedy of inarticulacy': as Brisbane says, one of the qualities of the play is 'the economy with which [Lawler] expresses the inarticulate nature of the characters and the way the deprivation of language is related to a deprivation of spirit and intellect'. I would take mild issue with this: Lawler's characters all seem to be, on their own terms, perfectly articulate to me. I'm troubled about the class judgment implied here, since these inarticulacies are seen to be the result of being uneducated, working-class characters: it's perilously close to saying that the inability to express feelings means that those feelings don't exist. Lawler certainly positions the unseen Nancy as smarter, a woman who is forever reading books and who escapes the impending doom of the lay-offs by marrying a bookshop owner. But I'd suggest that there's a profound ambivalence here. One thing underlining this ambiguity is the fact that it's the very articulacy of these characters that allowed them to create their alternative reality: the myths that they have constructed around their relationships crucially depend on the imaginative capacities of language.

Olive heroicises the image of rural masculinity symbolised by Roo and Barney: as she says, for years they have flown down from the north, 'two eagles flyin' down out of the sun'. She vividly portrays them to Pearl as the epitome of untrammelled, sexual force:

> Nancy used to say it was how they'd walk into the pub as if they owned it, even just in the way you walked you could spot it. All round would be the regulars, soft city blokes having their drinks and their little arguments, and then in would come Roo and Barney... She always reckoned they made the rest of the mob look like skinned rabbits.

Just as it's language that builds the myth, it's language that ultimately tears it down. Now nearing their forties, Roo and Barney both find, to their bafflement and anger, that they are no longer young, that the youth and vigour which they took for granted has deserted them. But it takes Pearl's innocent laughter at Barney's toast to 'glamorous nights' to rip away the final rags of the illusion. Roo is prepared to cut his cloth to his new circumstances, and gets a regular job, just like the soft city blokes, readying himself to make an honest woman of Olive. Barney, once the epitome of sexual charisma, finds himself mocked by the women who once succumbed to his charms. The quintessential henchman, Barney shifts his loyalty to the new alpha male, Johnnie O'Dowd.

Reading the critiques of *The Doll* now, it's striking how the action of the play is critiqued primarily through its male characters: Olive's desires and struggles are seen as subordinate, certainly secondary, to the drama of the men. In 1987, Jane Cousins wrote that 'Roo is the term of reference and Olive merely the site at which his new identity is to be confirmed'. Certainly, the final image is the play is of the two men leaving together, after a sudden, 'uncharacteristic' gesture of genuine friendship from Barney, in which he touches Roo's shoulder and gently leads him away. Here the glossy ideal of mateship that the two men supposedly embody is stripped of its mythos, and reduced to a single moment of insight and compassion. I'm not sure that this gesture really legitimates, as Cousins claims, 'a nostalgic return to [the] imaginary unity [of the outback hero]': it's far too ambiguous. In its unexpected tenderness, it could be seen as the introduction of a feminine understanding into the aggressively masculine ideal of mateship. It's certainly an image of overwhelming defeat.

The character who is most invested in the ideal of the lay-off is Olive herself: she is the person who passionately resists change, and who will destroy everything rather than compromise her dream. Olive is a huge role, both emotionally and in terms of her presence on stage: we see her well before Roo and Barney, she drives the action, and the dramatic climax belongs to her.

Why does Olive so passionately resist Roo's offer of a wedding ring? Lawler himself, implicitly rejecting the grander notions that he was making a narrative of Australian identity, said that he thought *The Doll* was simply a play about 'alternatives to marriage'. With this in mind, it's worth looking again at the relationships portrayed in the play.

Olive has mostly been seen as the foolish, immature woman, clinging to unrealistic dreams. Joy Hooton places her with the infantile feminine imaginary, 'seduced by an illusion'. Brisbane says of the famous scene in which Olive rejects Roo's proposal of marriage that 'it is a woman's response that is needed here – but Olive in Roo's care has never grown to womanhood. She wants, not marriage, but her girlhood restored.'

Cousins considers Olive as a site of feminine resistance and conflict in the constitution of a national character, and concludes:

> this requires an analysis of the formal constraints within which the attempt to change the meaning of the dominant [bush] image of national identity led to the staging of contradictions within this figure as a conflict between the 'masculine' outback and the 'feminine' city... Critics have hailed *The Doll* as the agent of a positive transformation of the 'national character',

but this character (secure within its humanist and phallocentric frame) remains predictably unified, univocal, and gendered masculine.

I read *The Doll* rather as a critique about the difficulty of sustaining equality in sexual relationships in a society in which roles for men and women are rigidly defined. The dream that is destroyed is a dream – Olive's dream – of equality. Behind this is a hint of another Australia, one that in the late nineteenth and early twentieth century bridged the urban and rural divide. This is the Australia that was thought of as the 'working man's paradise', in which the rural shearing unions were as crucial to social progress as the building unions in the cities; the country that was the first to introduce the eight hour day and only the second to give (white) women the vote. I think it's not too much of a stretch to read *The Doll* as an elegy, not for the 'bush', but for this egalitarian vision: it's a portrayal of how this idea of Australianness began to vanish after World War II, when working-class aspirations began to give way to the middle-class values espoused by Pearl.

It's certainly uncontroversial to say that the conflicts in *The Doll* are driven by socially gendered constraints, symbolised most powerfully by the marriage which the major characters have rejected. But if we take Olive to be an active protagonist, rather than a passive reflector of the men, it seems to me that Olive isn't rejecting the 'feminisation of the outback hero' so much as demanding those outback freedoms for herself. She seeks to reconstitute those freedoms in an urban context, making herself a 'mate' as well as a lover. When she hears that Roo is broke, she says aggressively 'What's wrong with me? I'm workin', ain't I?' Roo, defending his masculine pride, tells her he won't bludge off her, and insists that he will get a job: but Olive herself has no problems at all with the idea that he might be financially dependent.

Olive's resistance to marriage has been taken to be a proof of her refusal to 'grow up': it's seldom been seen as a resistance that goes to the heart of her autonomy as a woman. At the end of the play, in a brief but significant moment of rapport, Roo says to Olive: 'Y'know, a man's a fool to treat you as a woman. You're nothin' but a little girl about twelve years old.' Olive's response is to refer to her job: 'Try telling that to the mob on a Saturday night.' Roo insists: ''S true, all the same', and then attempts to persuade her to take the day off work. It's an offer that Olive tellingly refuses.

Olive is usually taken at Roo's estimation, but seldom at hers: in her own eyes, she is an independent working woman. If she marries, she loses her freedom: she becomes indeed the dependent female that she's ironically been often considered in criticism. By entering marriage, she gives up her name, her autonomy and especially her financial independence (in the 1950s, married women lost their jobs, just as Nancy has had to leave the bar to be with her bookshop owner). For Olive, this means giving up her life. With Roo away for seven months of the year, she can have her cake and eat it too. The lay-off, she tells Pearl, is 'not just playing around and spending a lot of money, but a time for livin'. You think I haven't sized that up against what other women have? I laugh at them every time they try to tell me. Even waiting for Roo to come back is more exciting than anything they've got... '

This statement has usually been taken as an assertion of Olive's dependence on Roo, rather than an expression of her independence. Yet when it comes to the crunch, Olive gives up her man, but she won't give up her job. Our last sight of her is after the dream has crashed: in a magnificently melodramatic moment of renunciation, Roo kneels down and tells her, 'This is the dust we're in and we're gunna walk through it like everyone else for the rest of our lives!' Olive reacts with physical anguish, 'doubling over herself on the floor as if cradling an awful inner pain'. What she is mourning is her sexual life, which is now over: the trade-off that women must make, choosing between autonomy and sexuality, is inescapable. Perhaps the worst possibility of all is that the equality she thought she possessed never really existed. That's the real betrayal in Roo's proposal: to him, she is only a little girl. In the face of this, stumbling with shock, she does the only thing left to her: she picks up her bag and goes to work.

In *The Doll*, Lawler puts both masculinity and femininity under the burning glass. The roles evaporate in the heat of the drama and reveal desperate people seeing through a glass darkly, aware of how they are trapped, but unable to do anything about it. None of the characters is socially conventional, but for all their refusal of their allotted roles – as dutiful working husband or suburban wife – they remain trapped: Roo and Barney in their limited ideals of manhood, Olive and Pearl in different imprisonments of femininity. Their tragedy is that in the society in which they live, there is no escape for them: the only alternative to accepting the deathly conventions they have abjured all their lives is absolute loss. I think that central dilemma is the reason it remains such a powerful play today.

Australian Literature 101 lecture series, Wheeler Centre, April 2012

The Histrionic

The Malthouse/Sydney Theatre Company production of Thomas Bernhard's 1984 play *The Histrionic* is, apparently, the first professional production of Bernhard's work anywhere in Australia. The transparency of Daniel Schlusser's triumphant production makes you wonder what the problem was: why did we have to wait so long? *The Histrionic* is so manifestly a brilliantly written play, gripping from its beginning to its extraordinary final moments. It's outrageous, sadistic, hilarious, brutally bathetic, playfully and powerfully theatrical. In the most expansive sense of the word, it's an entertainment, exploiting every trick in the theatrical book: but here Bernhard employs entertainment as a depth charge, to destroy the submarine walls of our self-regard.

The Histrionic premiered nearly three decades ago. I'm well used to the fact that most significant playwrights, especially those outside the Anglosphere, are largely invisible in our mainstage culture – where are our professional productions of major contemporary dramatists such as (to stick with the Europeans) Jon Fosse, Elfriede Jelinek, Biljana Srbljanovic, Falk Richter? – but for some reason this delay struck me. If anything demonstrates the narrowness of our mainstream culture, it's this kind of catching up after the fact. It's not as if myopia is limited to overseas writers: we had to wait longer than three decades to have Patrick White's *The Ham Funeral* professionally produced in Melbourne, and his plays are still thought of, even by people who ought to know better, as lesser achievements than his novels. The luminously unconventional, the intransigently theatrical, the poetic, the rawly intelligent, even the beautiful, have more often than not been marginalised in Australian culture.

Nowhere do our colonial petticoats show more than in Australia's anxious love for authority. In our culture, genuine artistic originality, with its unsettling combination of disrespect for authority and serious respect for its own antecedents, can only figure as an embarrassment. It has no visible means of support, no legitimisation beyond its own artistry. In a colonial culture, the fear of being thought 'wrong' overwhelms all other possibilities of reception. It even muffles outrage: the response to too many of our most interesting artists has been the white noise of silence. Bernhard is the model of another possibility, and this production of *The Histrionic* is one of several events that suggests that doors long sealed shut may now, very slowly, be creaking open.

Thomas Bernhard was no stranger to outrage: no writer was more embarrassing to his own culture. Shortly before Bernhard's death, President Kurt Waldheim – at the time enmeshed in controversy over his wartime service in the Wehrmacht in Eastern Europe – called his play *Heldenplatz* (Heroes' Square) a 'crude insult to the Austrian people'. It was also a crude insult to Waldheim, whom Bernhard denounced in the play as a liar. Bernhard made himself a scandal: as one of Austria's most important postwar writers, he's impossible to ignore, and yet his life's work was an attack on his homeland. His insults continued after his death: one of the provisos in his will was a ban, until copyright expires, on any Austrian production of his plays. I'm not sure we could sustain such a figure here; the only writer who remotely approaches this kind of ambiguous cultural position is Patrick White, and the comparison is an uneasy one.

Bernhard was obsessed with the moral catastrophe of Austria, and in particular its denial of its Nazi past. The scar of Nazism runs through all his work, as it runs through European history: it's the giant faultline on which Europe's pretensions to civilisation crumbled into barbarism. Bernhard's response was to become histrionic (a *theatermacher*, a 'scene maker'). In all his work, from newspaper articles to plays to novels, he excoriated Austria as a gallery of grotesques: hypocrites and fools, liars and murderers, 'a nation of six and a half million idiots living in a country that is rotting away'. Yet Bernhard's role was curiously ambiguous. As his biographer, Gitta Honneger, acutely points out: 'As energetically as he dramatised himself as the unwanted outsider, he constructed himself as the penultimate insider… The renegade son laid claim to a cultural nobility Austria had forfeited.' And, she added, pointing to Bernhard's qualities as a literary actor: 'Such a feat required a brilliant performer… '

Given this, it's impossible not to see Bruscon, the central figure in *The Histrionic*, as a kind of grotesque self-portrait. Like Bernhard, Bruscon is both writer and actor: he is the fleshly embodiment of ambiguity and contradiction, the one who contemplates and the one who enacts. And he is high culture personified: he is, as he tells us, 'the greatest nationally recognised performing artist / In this nation's history'. He even has 'the piece of paper, the medal' to prove it. The play is basically a monologue: Bruscon is surrounded by a cast of unfortunate witnesses and enablers who act as the brunt of his abuse and sadism. For Bruscon they are the admiring, uncomprehending masses, the anti-talented slaves to his talent, the necessary ears for his long lament.

The conceit is this. Our hero (Bille Brown) has arrived at the Black Hart inn in the tiny pig-farming hamlet of Utzbach (280 people). He is on tour with his family theatre company, his son Ferruccio (Josh Price), his daughter Sarah (Edwina Wren) and his consumptive wife Agatha (Jennifer Vuletic). But here in Utzbach, Bruscon is casting pearls before swine: the performance of his masterpiece *The Wheel of History* – an allegorical absurdity featuring the great figures of history, from Napoleon to Stalin – is threatened by the local fire chief, by the incompetence of his actors, even by the fact that in the Black Hart the staff is busy with Blood Sausage Day. Bruscon bullies the landlord (Barry Otto), the landlady (Kelly Butler) and the landlord's glaucomic daughter Erna (Katherine Tonkin). Almost all of the supporting cast suffers from injury, illness or deformity: Otto's landlord has so many tics and twitches he is almost a blur; Ferruccio's hand is broken after a third-floor fall sustained on the way to the toilet; Madame Bruscon is suffering from a malady of the lungs which makes her particularly allergic to the stench of pigs. Bruscon himself is, of course, a monster.

Every line in the play is shot through with a corrosive irony and ambiguity. Bruscon is ridiculous, patently pathetic; his play, as we see it through his descriptions and rehearsals, is a nonsensical, ahistorical fiction in which every fact is comically wrong. He insists that every picture is taken out of the hall, aside from a cobwebbed portrait of Hitler. 'Everyone here is Hitler', he tells his son. 'So leave the picture here / As a reminder.' He is the model of misogynist, patriarchal tyranny: in a disturbing scene with his daughter, he tortures her until she informs him that he is the greatest actor that ever lived. And yet his criticisms are deadly serious, and hit home: 'There was once a forest / Now there's a quarry / There were once wetlands / Now cement works / There was once a human being / Now there's a Nazi... '

The declension in each case is from organic complexity to brutal simplicity, the reduction of things and people to objects of use. And this is where Bruscon's contempt attains the 'cultural nobility' that Gitta Honneger says Bernhard claimed for himself: it is the sour lees of the never-realised ideals of the Enlightenment, the remains of the respect for complex human possibility, now destroyed beyond the hope of its even being perceived. That's a lament by no means confined to 1980s Austria: this reduction to use is the machinery which is most powerfully at work in our contemporary world. Just as the Nazis burned people in their ovens, our reductive vision is reducing our living planet, forest by forest, to ash. It's no accident the landlord's daughter is half blind.

And yet, just as he embodies the desolate remnants of high culture, so Bruscon gives us its culpability and complicity. Like everyone else, he is Hitler. The central moral question of Western culture after World War II, as rehearsed through thinker after thinker, from Steiner to Adorno, from Handke to Jelinek to Fassbinder, was how one of the most evolved cultures in world history spawned the genocidal atrocity that was Nazism. It's a question that Bernhard presents, without giving us an answer: and it's a question that, rather than retreating into the shadows of the twentieth century, strikes hard now.

The Histrionic is a satire on many things, but perhaps first of all it's a satire on history itself. At its centre is the play that we never see performed. *The Wheel of History* is, as Bruscon informs us, a comedy that comprehends all of human history, but all we get to see of his masterpiece is Bruscon himself. To complicate his ambiguity, Bruscon becomes, to borrow a distinction from Walter Benjamin, at once symbol and allegory. He combines the particular aspects of symbol and the general aspects of allegory: he is an individual with a specific historical biography, and an abstract embodiment of the vicious futility of a tragic history.

Writing about German tragic drama, or *Trauerspiele*, in his essay Walter Benjamin said:

> Everything about history that, from its very beginning, has been untimely, sorrowful, unsuccessful, is expressed in a face – or

rather in a death's head. And although such a thing lacks all 'symbolic' freedom of expression, all classical proportion, all humanity – nevertheless, this is the form in which man's subjection to nature is most obvious and it significantly gives rise not only to the enigmatic question of the nature of human existence as such, but also of the biographical historicity of the individual. This is the heart of the allegorical way of seeing, of the baroque, secular explanation of history as the Passion of the world; its importance resides solely in the stations of its decline. The greater the significance, the greater to subjection to death, because death digs most deeply the jagged line of demarcation between physical nature and significance.

Bruscon is Bernhard's death's head, marking the stations of History's decline. We are here to witness his crucifixion.

'Allegories' as Benjamin said in the same essay, 'are, in the realm of thoughts, what ruins are in the realm of things'. In Bernhard's world, the disaster has already happened: we stand in the ruins of culture, surrounded by the rubble that is all that remains of its vainglory. When we walk into the Merlyn, we encounter Marg Horwell's set, which is an apparently structureless space littered with absurd kitsch: gigantic plaster statues of eagles or neo-classical hands, overblown paintings casually leaning against the wall, bare rostra strewn with sawdust or crumbs that an automatic vacuum cleaner, buzzing to and fro, is vainly attempting to clear. The landlord's family is lounging about doing nothing in particular; Madame Bruscon stalks on, wearing an inhaler and dragging a suitcase. Nothing happens, aside from the casual markings of insignificant activities, until Bruscon arrives to prickle the cast into guilty activity as he surveys the scene with contempt. 'My God... complete cultural wasteland...'

Tom Wright's translation is robust and theatrical, with a hint of Australian colloquialism that serves this production well: terms such as 'proletarian' have been transposed to 'suburban' or 'battlers', subtly habituating the text to local conditions without any crass parallelism. Schlusser's production strings this text across the stage with an apparent artlessness, and makes it resonate.

There's been a lot of discussion recently about auteur theatre, not much of it to the point, which makes Schlusser's arrival on the main stage of particular interest. For years he has been creating some of

Melbourne's most essential theatre. So far his most interesting work has been investigations of classic plays – *Peer Gynt*, *A Doll's House*, *Life is a Dream* – which have been meticulously undone and represented in a kind of radical uber-naturalism. In *The Histrionic*, Bernhard has written a text in which everything is already dislocated: Schlusser's job is to enable the process of decline, as it occurs before our eyes. What is perhaps most striking about this production is how, while it is unmistakeably a Schlusser production, it exposes the essential modesty of his practice.

The nature of the play is, in fact, particularly suited to Schlusser's performance-centred approach. Almost all of the text belongs to Bille Brown, who gives what must be the performance of his life. He is all the colours of the histrionic, with the deeper black of sorrow rising up within his acting like silt, until he is trapped in a final, tragically absurd stillness. The rest of the cast, all six of them, are dim foils to Bruscon's brilliance. Yet even when they aren't directly involved in scenes, we are aware of their constant, uneasy presence about the stage: they labour awkwardly to clear the dance hall of its rubble, picking up gigantic props and putting them down pointlessly elsewhere, involving themselves in inscrutable tasks that engage all their attention.

This is choreographed with a precise sense of rhythm that works contrapuntally to Brown's central drama. The result is a performative richness that emerges, paradoxically, from the deliberate visual poverties of the stage. It means that when the production shifts to full-blown theatricality, as it does towards the end, this movement has a sense of evolution, rather than appearing out of nowhere: in the background, the theatricality has already been sketched for us.

The usual criticism of auteur theatre is that one only sees the director's ego at work. This production is saturated with the director's vision, but in performance his hand becomes almost invisible. What we witness is the enabling of performance, which itself reveals the living tissue of the text. It's exhilarating to see a play of this intransigent quality given such an intelligent, unapologetic production. Unmissable.

Theatre Notes, April 18 2012

Persona

> It may sound banal, but the most important thing, both in film and in the theatre, is the human being – the study of human beings. What you want above all, whether you are doing film or theatre, is to make the audience experience the result as something absolutely alive. The most important thing of all is to create a reflection of reality – to capture a heightened intensity, a distillation of life – and to guide the audience through that magical process.
>
> Of *Winners and Losers*, interview with Ingmar Bergman

> What I have written seems more like the melody line of a piece of music, which I hope with the help of my colleagues to be able to orchestrate during production. On many points I am uncertain… I therefore invite the imagination of the reader or spectator to dispose freely of the material that I have made available.
>
> Preface to the script of *Persona*, Ingmar Bergman

Persona is one of Ingmar Bergman's most enigmatic films. The idea is notionally very simple: an actress, Elisabet Vogler, falls silent in the middle of a performance of *Elektra*. She resumes the performance, but the following day refuses to speak at all. Doctors can find nothing wrong with her, physically or mentally: it seems that she has simply chosen to be mute. Her doctor decides that she should spend the summer at an isolated house with a nurse, Sister Alma. Elisabet never speaks. Alma never stops speaking. The result is a film that investigates profoundly, and often cruelly, the nature of performance as an existential state of being human.

To attempt to remake *Persona* as a work of theatre is surely the definition of risk: certainly, director Adena Jacobs and the Fraught Outfit team at Theatre Works can't be faulted on their ambition. Such an adventure could so easily end up being a bad imitation, with the haunting performances of Liv Ullmann and Bibi Andersson inviting invidious comparison. Yet, miraculously, Fraught Outfit has taken up Bergman's invitation to 'dispose freely' of his material, translating it into another form, and, crucially, into an autonomous work.

Persona is signally not an adaptation of Bergman's film. Instead, Jacobs and her collaborators have worked directly from his script, building the theatre from the ground up. The script is slightly edited, and the show is shorter than the film – 70 minutes as opposed to the film's 85 – but the text is all Bergman. The theatre, however, is all Jacobs: and it is arrestingly pure theatre. Fraught Outfit creates the kind of experience that is almost impossible to describe: it's so experientially involving that the ending comes as a shock, as you find yourself surfacing out of the heightened reality of the work.

It left me with the weirdly exhilarating feeling that, without quite knowing what had happened, some kind of inner transformation had taken place while I had been watching it. Perhaps Cathy in *Wuthering Heights* most memorably describes this sense of untraceable change: 'I've dreamt in my life dreams that have stayed with me ever after, and changed my ideas: they've gone through and through me, like wine through water, and altered the colour of my mind... ' Sometimes art does something similar. But it does make it difficult to write about.

The simple premise of Bergman's film, an almost absurdly formal conceit of one character speaking while the other is silent, creates a drama of such complexity and ambiguity that it never seems quite graspable. Alma takes Elisabet's silence as an invitation on which she projects her fantasy of the perfect listener: she exposes her loneliness, her fears, her shames, and, in a famous monologue, an orgasmic moment of happiness. Then she reads a letter in which she discovers these intimate revelations are, for Elisabet, an amusing diversion. 'I have her confidence and she tells me her troubles large and small. As you can see, I am grabbing all I can get, and as long as she doesn't notice it won't matter... '

After this moment of betrayal, it becomes clear that Elisabet, who seems at first be to be a passive and benign receptor, is really a predator. As she hungrily absorbs Alma's confessions, she is practising a form of identity theft. Gradually, Alma becomes the blank cipher on which Elisabet can project identities – wife, mother, actress – which she finds too painful to endure. Alma isn't strong enough to resist her, and the two women merge into a single, disturbing, conflicted self.

In Bergman's film, this instability, even vertigo, of performance is heightened by the alienation of the medium itself. Bergman never lets the audience forget that they are watching a film, a representation of reality, rather than reality itself. Halfway through, the projector seems to burn up the negative, and then the film reconstitutes itself; the screenplay finishes with the instructions: 'The projector stops, the arc lamp is extinguished, the amplifier switched off. The film is taken out and packed into its brown carton.' Likewise, Jacobs never lets us forget that we are watching a work of theatre.

What this production exposes is Bergman's essential theatricality, a quality always present in his cinema and, given that he worked extensively as a theatre director, in his life. The realism of cinematic settings is here replaced by theatrical framing. Dayna Morrissey's elegant design exploits the size of the Theatre Works stage, with a defined white floor split by a white curtain that is the width of the space. Backstage is a simulacrum of a Swedish holiday house seen through large paned windows, also curtained, that are framed with blond wood. This creates a flexible playing area that permits both a naked, unadorned stage, when the front curtains are closed, and an almost naturalistic set that opens up distance. The design creates theatrical analogues, if you like, for the close-up, medium shot and long shot.

The play moves between perspectiveless close-up in front of the curtain and stylised but naturalistic distance. As the drama turns towards the surreality of dream, these conventions merge and dissolve and reconstitute. The other aspects of the design – Danny Pettingill's lighting and Russell Goldsmith's extraordinary sound environment – heighten its sense of intense but unstable realism. Something interesting is going on here with time as well – both in the duration of the performance and the passing of time in the drama (the action occurs over a summer): it collapses into a series of distinct sequences that operate like the elisions of dream or memory.

The design frames performances of extraordinary rigor and intelligence. Meredith Penman as Elisabet begins as a glamorous cipher, a beauty in gold silk whose impassivity is rippled briefly by private laughter, hidden from the nurse, that hints at the cruelty that is to follow. She performs the consummate actor, whose anguish is that she knows, unlike Alma (Karen Sibbing), that while all her behaviour is a performance, the pain that drives it is real. Sibbing's Alma is a masterpiece of subtle layers. At the start of the play she speaks almost as an automaton, her self hidden in her role of nurse. She warms through her intimacy with Elisabet, illuminated by her joy that, at last, someone cares enough to listen to her. After Elisabet's betrayal, she is almost numb with fury and impotence and, more deeply, a sense of panic that she has lost herself.

One of the most disturbing moments in the film occurs in a dream sequence in which Elisabet's husband, Mr Vogler (played here by Daniel Schlusser), addresses Alma as his wife. Jacobs reimagines this scene as a raw and desperate sexual encounter which is at once blackly, hilariously grotesque and deeply sad. The physical presence of these three actors is compelling and unfaltering, their portrayals precise and starkly unsentimental; but what drives deep into perception is the felt experience of pain that inhabits each performance.

This was a show that I couldn't fault in any of its particulars, and which as a whole manifests a lucid complexity that is rare in any medium. Subtle, detailed and truthful, this collaboration transfers the mystery at the heart of Bergman's film intact, while entirely remaking it. As I said, miraculous.

Theatre Notes, May 24 2012

On the Production of Monsters

The art of light writing, as playwrights like Oscar Wilde demonstrate, is a serious business. Writing a light play about serious business is even more serious. The danger is that 'light' – which is not, by any means, a synonym for 'slight' – can so easily become banal or substanceless or, worst of all, indigestibly soggy in the middle. It requires a quicksilver theatrical wit, faith in the intelligence of the audience, a lot of writerly tact and, perhaps most of all, the ability to keep contradictory impulses in dynamic suspension. You can see all these qualities at work in Robert Reid's *On the Production of Monsters*, now playing in the Lawler Studio at the Melbourne Theatre Company.

Set in the cafes and offices of inner-city Melbourne, *On the Production of Monsters* exploits hipster urban chic even as it pokes fun at its absurdities. The elegant conceit is that each scene is a dialogue between different characters, all of them played by the same two actors, Virginia Gay and James Saunders. The plot revolves around the young couple Shari and Ben, uber-cool Melburnites who, following the unwritten laws of hipsterdom, recognise the hip in everyone but themselves. They are sweeter than they realise, basically well-intentioned and harmless. Reid is interested in how these two are transformed, through an innocent mistake, into the favourite monster of the tabloids: child pornographers.

The play opens with Ben and Shari breakfasting in a cafe, tallying up points for hipster-spotting while they sip their coffees. Ben works in a call centre for the local water authority, where he embarrassedly fends off awkward advances from his supervisor. Shari, a keen environmentalist and aspiring artist, is seeking funding for a project which will see children from local schools clearing rubbish from the banks of the Merri Creek. When she is interviewed by an ambitious young reporter from the local newspaper, she forwards him an email leaked by Ben, which has the minutes of a meeting from the water authority. Unfortunately, Ben has also forwarded a photo of a naked and possibly underage girl which his boss has sent to him as a coarse attempt at seduction.

The reporter is much more interested in the nude photo than the minutes, and the story rapidly escalates to a national scandal about child pornography. In this, Reid is consciously echoing the scandal that erupted around Bill Henson in 2008. Just as the offending Henson photograph was discovered not to be obscene at all (and was in fact rated PG by the Classifications Board), so here the photograph isn't child pornography, although the question of its obscenity is left open. The play's concern is really with the unstoppable machine of manufactured public outrage.

Step by step, we watch Ben hang himself. At his boss' request, he even erases the evidence that would prove his innocence. The personal fallout is devastating. Labelled a paedophile by the media, Ben loses his job and, the public taint now indelible despite the lack of a conviction, any prospect of a career. Worst of all, he begins to question his own motivations. Shari loses her Merri Creek project, which goes on without her, and breaks up with Ben. The damage spreads even to the lawyer who decides to represent Ben, who finds her practice disastrously depleted by her public defence of a widely exposed paedophile.

One of the virtues of *On the Production of Monsters* is the modesty of its pretensions. Reid draws no morals and refrains from lecturing; rather, he works his themes subtextually beneath a finely detailed, and often very funny, surface of dialogue. The story is told elliptically in a series of scenes that, not unincidentally, create a slyly hilarious portrait of twenty-first century Melbourne, in much the same way that *Seinfeld* sketched 1990s New York. Nothing is overwritten, and there's a lot of play in the language that is beautifully picked up by the actors. What comes into precise focus is the human mundanities and complexities that exist beneath the stark judgments of sensationalist headlines.

None of the characters is innocent nor, importantly, without innocence. In leaking confidential minutes to his girlfriend, for instance, Ben is hardly in a position of moral superiority. Shari is a fantasist, exploiting the kindness of strangers to compensate for her nagging sense of insignificance. Ben's boss, a woman with the sensibility of a brick, manipulates him easily, and gets a promotion while his career spirals into disaster: yet beneath her brash exterior, she is palpably lonely and insecure. The subtleties of Melbourne diction, from the Werribee office manager to the lisping innercity primary school teacher, are all richly written, deftly avoiding cliché. If this play weren't so accurate and astringently intelligent, it might all be too cute for words.

As with the play, director Clare Watson and her design team unashamedly place the action in a very local here and now. The action moves swiftly and lucidly, and never quite in the way you might expect. The production is driven by two excellent performances that particularly shine in how Gay and Saunders sketch the fragility and need in the relationship between Ben and Shari. The comedy is sharp but surprisingly gentle, and the production generates a subtle but insistent emotional texture that culminates in a deeply moving, and wordless, final scene.

Andrew Bailey's ingenious traverse set is a highlight: the initially bare stage has a wealth of pop-up props that the actors assemble for each scene, so by the end the stage is littered with the detritus of the action. Like many others, I couldn't help having a closer look as I left the theatre at the iconic Melbourne imagery embedded inside it: the Melways beanbag, Banksy's parachuting rat (now sadly destroyed), the inevitable glasses of latte. This is the kind of play which makes it difficult to deny the real pleasures of recognition, but its charm relies on the characters it draws for us; local colour is stroked in as unobtrusively as a samovar in *The Three Sisters*. It adds up to a gem of a production, a work in which an unassuming integrity shines in every decision.

Theatre Notes, May 31 2012

Next Wave: Monster Body / Dewey Dell / Justin Shoulder

Over the past few years, I've lost count of the number of columns I've read which lament the Youth of Today. Pundit after pundit has informed me that young people, Generation Whatever, are spoilt, self-obsessed, materialistic and non-political. This always makes me think of the poet Kenneth Rexroth, who as a fascinated elder statesman was one of the first people to chronicle the youthful counterculture of the 1960s. Back then, as Rexroth reported with constant surprise, newspaper columnists also regularly lambasted the apathetic, non-political, self-obsessed youth of the day. *Plus ça change, plus c'est la même chose...*

Like Rexroth, I think that underneath the surface, something interesting is stirring in Generation Youth. Of course, as in the 1960s, the majority of the population observes the status quo: what matters is the critical mass of those who don't. It doesn't take an especially sharp observer to see the symptoms of a new political urgency occurring everywhere: the raw protest of the Occupy movement through 2011, the resurgence of feminism and Marxism, the resistances against increasingly repressive regimes worldwide in Egypt, Yemen, Bahrain, the responses to increasing environmental crisis. As with the apocalyptism of the Cold War, coming out of the birth of the nuclear bomb and the disaster of the Vietnam War, there is a sense of global crisis driving politics now. And, as it was back in the 1960s, you'll only find the surface reflected in the news.

Given the tumultuous events of the past couple of years, it's unsurprising that much of the work in the Next Wave festival harks back to the art of the 1970s. The difference between what's going on now and what happened then is that this is a generation that knows what has already happened: it's perhaps the most historically self-aware generation we've had, with more access to more information than at any point in human history. At its most shallow, this results in the pomo irony of the hipster. But, as performance art works like Atlanta Eke's *Monster Body* or Justin Shoulder's *The River Eats* demonstrate, this awareness of the past can lead to something altogether more interesting.

Monster Body is a pitch-perfect work that examines the inturning grotesquerie of the female self as it deals with the image of the feminine. We enter the Dance House theatre, harshly exposed by fluorescent lighting, to find Eke, naked except for a rubber lizard mask, standing on a box made of mirrors, rotating a hoop on her hips. She stands there for ages as the audience sits and settles, totally exposed and yet, because her face is covered, totally hidden. Her body trumps her identity, is the whole of her identity, and she gazes out on us through the eyeholes of the mask with the anonymous face of a reptile. It's an image that somehow has the impersonal, stark impertinence of Manet's Olympia.

What follows is a series of sequences that riff off various representations of the nude, both historical and contemporary. There's the disciplined, angular control of a ballet dancer, who utters inarticulate growling screams; the nude of a thousand *Playboy* centrefolds, posing in a puddle of her own urine; an infantile cartoon bunny with a grotesquely large head, poignantly waiting as a motorbike whizzes back and forth, always a little sinister, never arriving; perhaps most confrontingly, five naked female dancers bopping along to Beyonce in Abu Ghraib black hoods, which managed to be outrageous, excessive, disturbing, absurd and bizarrely joyous all at once. At various points the leaky female body is cleaned up by a man in a biohazard suit.

Eke's images balance disturbingly between comedy, disgust and eroticism. So much of this show was funny. The point where people stopped laughing was when Eke put on a flesh-coloured body suit and filled it with pink water balloons – analogues of breast implants – turning her body into a misshapen, lumpy monster. She then took it off over her head like a reptile skin, so it seemed that her head was eaten by this other body. The image recalled the obscene surrealism of Hans Bellmer and his mutilated mannequins, and was as viscerally disturbing. A fascinating, deeply absorbing and intelligent work, driven by a profound anger, that was performed with outstanding poise.

The big talk of Next Wave was *The Exchange Program*, two evenings of performance presented by Italian theatre artists Dewey Dell ('the Castellucci kids') and Sydney performance artist Justin Shoulder. I only made the second program, which made me very sorry I had missed the first. Dewey Dell are second generation artists, the children of Romeo Castellucci and Chiara Guidi, directors of Societas Raffaello Sanzio. Comparisons are probably inevitable, but it's clear that Dewey Dell, although they create the same kind of resonant theatrical ambiguities as their parents, are making a different kind of work.

Grave is a new piece, performed with local artists, which is as driven by anger as Eke's work. Picking up on images from contemporary horror films, Dewey Dell create dark, ambiguous dance theatre. It expresses a dead, chaotic urban world possessed by zombie ideas, ideologies long emptied of their significance; but underneath this is an irrepressible feeling of immanent life, imprisoned and rebellious, flashing out from beneath the undeadness.

It opens with a figure drawn from the Japanese horror film *The Ring*: a girl whose face we never see, because her long hair completely covers it. This is genuinely spooky: the low lighting at first made it seem that the lone figure at the back of the darkened stage had no head at all, as her white hands crawl up the wall blindly searching for something. For us? She lurches towards us with a sense of blank menace but also, perhaps because she is physically present, a feeling of vulnerability. There's a brief interlude of colour as a bizarre clown figure, whose costume I am unable to describe, emerges from backstage, a historical memory perhaps of commedia dell'arte.

Then, like denizens from some surreal underworld, the other dancers enter the stage, strangely lit by lights concealed in the backs of their costumes, zombies who transform into, well, not-zombies. The final extraordinary image, the shadow of the first dancer's hair lit from behind and projected into the wall like a veil or a curtain, seemed an image of hope. I have no idea why: perhaps it was the sense of the organic nature of the hair, which suddenly was alive and real, an expression of life. Perhaps it was because the image created was of a threshold, an opening into something new.

Constantly inventive and surprising in its movement, sound and design, this was a work that left me feeling exhausted. It's a measure of the attention it involuntarily elicits, but also of the violence you feel is contained in the work, not quite articulate, but always there. I'm sure everyone there made their own meanings from what was presented, but the images on stage were all tightly focused and totally specific, created with the discipline that permits such images to go straight into your subconscious and resonate with multiple possibilities.

Justin Shoulder's *The River Eats* – brash, colourful, funny and spectacular – was a brilliant foil to *Grave*. On reflection it had a similar trajectory, a journey from the alienations of urban technology to a contemplation of and return to the natural world, enacted here through a superb performance of display. Again, I don't know how to describe the costumes. The show began with a kind of pink animal, a heart-like creature the colour of fairy floss, with naked legs and bottom painted pink. It was marching across the stage to harpsichord music, like a clockwork toy. Then the costume was serially discarded to reveal the clown Pinky, in huge pink wig, body paint and sequinned g-string, bowing and primping before a soundtrack of tumultuous applause. The soundtrack ceased, and he kept bowing to the silence, suddenly poignant and bereft and absurd.

Then Pinky was on Skype, waving at three huge projections of himself, who were all waving happily back, holding a birthday cake. Sequence followed dazzling sequence, projected image and costume melding into each other, all focusing on the gorgeously costumed figure of Shoulder. Pinky draws from pop culture referents – pornography, the internet, music videos – creating unsettlingly bizarre and funny images (at one point we see a butterfly made of dildos). But this is a performance of transformation: we watch the emergence of something other, the creature OO: an elaborate, atavistic figure, half animal, half god, that is an expression of harmony and, perhaps most surprisingly of all, of the natural world. *The River Eats* is a beautiful exploration of the estrangements of desire, the hunger towards wholeness that inhabits the divided self, that is at once wholly contemporary and yet reaches back to impulses much more ancient than our civilisation. Truly astonishing.

Theatre Notes, June 4 2012

Queen Lear

For the first thirty seconds I thought we were in for something special in the Melbourne Theatre Company's *Queen Lear*. Robyn Nevin in the titular role, regally costumed in red, is lushly illuminated backstage studying her face in a mirror, a cameo blooming out of impenetrable darkness. Four corridors of light delineate the borders of the stage and she paces them slowly, marking out her realm. It is arresting and bold theatrical image-making. But almost nothing in this production bears out the opening promise. Misled, misconceived, misdirected, *Queen Lear* is almost baffling.

There's absolutely no reason why Nevin, one of our most majestic actors, should not play this towering role. What's much less clear is why Lear therefore had to be a woman. In Benedict Andrews' sublime *The War of the Roses*, Cate Blanchett and Pamela Rabe played Richard II and Richard III without changing the sex of the role: as I said at the time, 'we are made pricklingly aware that Richard is an actor, a player who is, moreover, a woman, Pamela Rabe, who after the play is over will walk off the stage, strip off her costume and take a shower. This double consciousness of performance is a particularly Shakespearean trope, and Andrews has exploited it to the hilt in *The War of the Roses*.' The playing of the kings by women in that case heightened Shakespeare's essential theatricality, and brought the question of gender into intriguing play.

Here the assumption seems to be that feminising Lear has only a superficial effect on the play's meaning: as in a Lego set, all you have to do is take out the boy toy and stick in the girl toy. Since *Lear* is, among many other things, a profound study of patriarchy, one would expect that changing the sex of the title role might have been thought through a little more. Afterwards, seeking some clues, I read director and dramaturge Rachel McDonald's note in the program. It opens with a bald statement: '*King Lear* is a political story that also deals with revelation, reconciliation and the infinite'. The 'infinite'? O-kay…

McDonald then drags us through some pop psychobabble ('in dysfunctional relationships, we often fall into the roles of Bully, Rescuer or Victim. In this play we watch characters continually rotate their way through this Drama Triangle'). There's reference to single-parent families – Gloucester and Lear – and 'abusive parenting'. We are told that 'Lear's gender is almost irrelevant. The play doesn't concern itself with gender issues... ' And then, confusingly: 'Our female Lear is not gender-neutral casting: we are not side-stepping the issue of gender. We are embracing it, imagining the story as written for a woman in the first place.' What we have, according to McDonald, is a 're-focusing' of the story, with a bad mother instead of a bad father.

I really don't know where to begin with this, but it's fair to say this note reflects the production. *Lear* might not be about 'gender issues', but gender plays into it all the time in complex and often ambiguous ways. Lear's gender isn't irrelevant: he is a king, an absolute patriarch, in a society that is absolutely patriarchal. This is a crucial aspect of his relationship with his daughters: Richard Eyre's domestic 1998 production, which focused on the family drama, drew this out brilliantly.

Moreover, you can't help reflecting that if Shakespeare had written Lear as a woman, it would have been an entirely different play. In Shakespeare's time there was a notable queen, Elizabeth I, a politically brilliant tyrant who retained power by the expedient of not marrying: unlike her unluckier cousin, Mary Queen of Scots, she knew very well that marriage would signal the death of her authority. Instead, she played her sex as the Virgin Queen ('Better beggar woman and single than Queen and married', as she famously told William Cecil). Queen Lear, the mother of three daughters, would be a very different creature to King Lear, the father. Imaginatively wrenching *Lear* into a story about a bad mother is by no means impossible, but it requires a deal more intellectual finesse than is on show here: such a central change has domino effects throughout the drama, and almost none of these is addressed.

McDonald's editing of the play is injudicious, to say the least. Much of this production makes no sense because important plot points (most grievously, the marriage of Cordelia to France and their subsequent invasion of England) have been cut altogether. Without the political framework of war, the treatment of Gloucester is reduced to reasonless sadism: we have no idea why he should be tortured. More significantly, the Fool – a role absolutely crucial to the central meanings of the play – is removed altogether, to be replaced by a series of appearances by the three daughters in ghostly nightgowns, voicing Lear's inner doubts.

The usual doubling is the Fool and Cordelia (in Shakespeare's play, the Fool mysteriously disappears after the storm scene, and we never hear what happens to him). In their mutual vulnerabilities and honesty, Cordelia and the Fool illuminate the humanity in Lear's psyche, its absence early in the play, and its revelation later: distributing the Fool between Cordelia, Regan and Goneril, and cutting Cordelia's story, completely dissipates the power of these roles. For these and other reasons, Lear loses her crucial moments of empathy, which in turn deprives the significant turns in the play – the prayer during the storm scene, or her reconciliation with Cordelia – of their potency.

The production itself is a startling instance of meaningless overdesign. Niklas Pajanti's palette of absolute darkness and focused illumination is gorgeous, but Tracy Grant Lord's set is strangely bitty. Its main feature is golden chains descending from the ceiling: these are mostly used as prop carriers, so random objects (a bicycle, or a cage, or a landscape painting that presumably represents the realm) can be lowered. A lot of the time the chains just get in the way. As the play progresses, some of them keep falling, with a liquid sound, so their links pile up on the stage, but this didn't happen to all of them, which I found curiously irritating. I spent some fruitless time trying to work out what they meant: were they, for example, the chains of power? If so, what did that mean?

Stage right is a weird phallic construction which seems merely superfluous. It rises and falls, sometimes acting as a plinth for a chair or a vision of the Fool, or as a fountain. I don't at all understand the convention of the costumes, which shift between Ruritania-style braided uniforms to contemporary dress to 1940s formal glamour to, I don't know, some kind of Slavic steampunk. Why is Edgar (Rohan Nicol) in preppie bicycle shorts, and why is it necessary for him to remain half naked as Poor Tom in the final fight with Edmund, when he is supposed to reveal as Edgar? Everything opens and closes and goes up and down, but nowhere is there any sense of a unifying vision.

It's not all bad news. In a plethora of performances that all seem to be from different productions, Robert Menzies' Kent is a beautiful and moving portrayal, and one of the few instances where the changing of gender makes sense: his loyalty to Lear is illuminated by a passionate, unspoken love. Greg Stone's wheelchair-bound Albany likewise makes strong work of a role that's often primly wishy-washy. In the second half, in scenes between Gloucester (Richard Piper) and Edgar, or Gloucester and Lear, there are flashes of what might have been: the poignancy of some of the greatest scenes ever written start to register, and you begin to see how changing the sex of Lear might have brought something new to the role.

Nevin's Lear is always virtuosic, but is so badly let down by the lack of a thought-through framework that her character remains cold and unmoving. In particular, too often the nuance is missing in an insistence on her femininity: ironically, she is at her best when she is arrogantly royal, or humbly human, without reference to her femaleness. Alexandra Schepisi in the crucial role of Cordelia is hampered because we have no idea what happens to her after Lear banishes her and consequently little idea of who she is, but it has to be said that her performance is utterly flat.

The mother/daughter relationships between Goneril (Geneviève Picot), Regan (Belinda McClory) and Lear never sparked for me. These are the central relationships in this reading of the play, and yet somehow, despite fine efforts, they never made emotional sense. Picot was not always audible either, despite being miked. I suspect the problem here is in dozens of tiny details: would Queen Lear really be carousing with her soldiers? Can Lear's speech about the sulphurous devilry of female sexuality really transfer with proper force to feminine self-hatred? How much sense does it make for a queen who has been shouting throughout the play to say 'Her voice was ever soft, / Gentle, and low, an excellent thing in woman'? Wouldn't an aging, tyrannical queen jealously eye the youth and power of her daughters? And so on.

That these questions insist themselves demonstrates that 'embracing gender' in the interpretation of this play is no simple thing. At the centre is the question of transgression: the rebellions of Regan and Goneril against their father have the more force in this hierarchical universe as they are transgressions against male authority. Lear's blind confidence in his authority is a very masculine entitlement: no woman in a position of power would be so cavalierly unaware of the consequences of relinquishing it. This is absolutely embedded in the play, for good or ill, and you can't solve that problem by ignoring it. If the production itself had not been so incompetent, perhaps we could have been beguiled into ignoring these questions, but the absurdities are overwhelming. The buck stops with the director here: this is a text that deserves a lot more respect. God, as Flaubert once said, is in the details.

Theatre Notes, July 13 2012

Queen Lear: the perfect storm

The reaction to *Queen Lear* has been a perfect storm. This hotly anticipated show, one of the prestige productions of the Melbourne Theatre Company's year, was always going to be in the headlines. Robyn Nevin playing one of the great roles in the canon, changing Lear's sex along the way, was a publicist's dream.

The bad side of such attention is that any failure occurs in a harsh public glare. Early reviews – Chris Boyd in the *Australian*, Cameron Woodhead in the *Age* and myself on my blog Theatre Notes – agreed that the show failed in important ways. We also agreed that the major problem lay in its direction, although we differed on details. Boyd, Woodhead and I have a history of vocal disagreement, and this unusual unanimity of response was duly reported in the *Australian*.

None of those reviews was kind – although all of them noted virtues in the production. But I simply don't recognise the bloodbath director Julian Meyrick described yesterday. Slamming Melbourne critics, he writes in sensational terms: 'Why… is reading the 20-odd reviews for *Queen Lear* like swimming in a sewer? A tsunami of diatribe condemns the production in lurid tones, while individual malfeasants are fingered with the glee of a Bloody Assizes.'

Gracious. Really?

Like Meyrick, I've followed the critical response to *Queen Lear* closely. There has been every kind of reaction, from print reviews in the daily paper, to blog reviews, to tweets from audience members. And these responses, as is to be expected, in fact canvass a wide range of opinion.

In the case of *Queen Lear*, the critics – again unusually – seem in harmony with the majority of popular opinion. The controversy isn't, for once, about disagreement. Perhaps it's this atypical alignment of opinion that leads Meyrick to his histrionic excesses: it looks as if the critics are ganging up on a young director. We're not: we're just doing our job, which is to write about what we saw in a theatre.

I'm all for critical responsibility, which means, before anything else, critical honesty. Sometimes that honesty will be hard for the artists who made the work. Sometimes I too think that critics permit snark to overcome their better judgment. No-one is above criticism, and that includes critics.

Meyrick's certainly saying nothing new. Critics have been rude about theatre since well before Ibsen's *Ghosts* was excoriated as an 'open sewer' by London critics in 1891. Sometimes, as with *Ghosts*, history proves them wrong; but they're proved right just as often. Many shows are justly forgotten.

What's puzzling is that, while attacking 'bi-polar' critics, Meyrick makes a very confused critique of something he calls the 'blogosphere'. For one thing, online theatre writing encompasses a great deal more than blogs. There are online magazines like *Australian Stage Online* or *Time Out*, online discussion in mainstream newspapers, twitter, blog comments and so on. It's a complicated virtual world out there. And Meyrick finds himself all at sea.

The reviews online have in general been kinder than the newspapers. For example, Andrew Fuhrmann, theatre editor for *Time Out Melbourne*, gave the show four stars and claimed it was the best Lear seen on stage in Melbourne for a decade. Anne-Marie Peard on *Sometimes Melbourne* blog describes Nevin's performance as a 'Lear like no other'. And so on.

Despite this, Meyrick points the finger at the 'blogosphere' as being the place where the most vicious criticism exists: 'Its cobble-close association with radio and print reviewing has led to a bleed-through of toxic behaviour: disinhibition; mixing substantive opinion with scurrilous attack; lack of gravitas; lack of social responsibility.'

I suspect – it's difficult to be sure, because Meyrick is very unclear – that he is particularly referring to the very lively discussion thread underneath my blog review, where most of the debate about *Queen Lear* has taken place.

That thread broke all previous records, logging 100 comments by the end of the opening weekend. I can't remember a similar fuss about a particular production, ever. The discussion has included critics, audience members and all sorts of interested others in a frank and sometimes chaotic exchange of opinion.

Theatre Notes is an open forum, and that means that all sorts of people with all sorts of levels of knowledge post there. I moderate with as light a hand as possible, trying to ensure that passionate debate doesn't descend to flame wars or libel, but I can't force everybody who posts there to make sense, or to have a degree in Shakespearean studies. It's a place where anyone who's interested can contribute to the discussion.

I think it's a sign of cultural health if critics, audience members and artists freely exchange ideas and opinions. Such debates are distinct from reviews themselves, something that Meyrick doesn't seem to understand: they are the conversation that continues after the judgments made in a review.

Meyrick seems to think that this debate is a terrible thing. There is a sneaking sense in his article that the unwashed masses are banging on the doors of the theatre. Yet if anything is to mitigate what he condemns as the 'wall-eyed certainty' of critics, it is the possibility of having their judgments publicly challenged. In our theatre culture, this happens all the time on blogs.

In his concern for *Queen Lear* director Rachel McDonald – a concern with which even critics empathise – Meyrick forgets an important point. Audience members are paying up to $99 a ticket for this show.

Are they expected to hand over their money and stay silent? These days, they don't. They tweet. They comment on blogs and write what they thought. They might even start their own blog.

For better or worse – and often it's been a great deal better – this conversation is the critical landscape now. It's no utopia, but I have no nostalgia for the days when a review was the end of the discussion. That, more than anything else, encouraged the kind of critique Meyrick claims to be against.

He finishes his incoherent call for critical responsibility with the observation that 'Behind [critics] stands a changing media and cultural landscape they seem not to understand – and perhaps do not want to'.

I'd say it's pretty clear that the person who doesn't understand the changing landscape is Meyrick himself.

The Australian, July 25 2012

Top Girls

I was completely unprepared for the emotional impact of watching Jenny Kemp's brilliant production of *Top Girls*. It was as if an abscess of grief and anger were lanced deep inside me: all the things I already know, that are reconfirmed in the media every day, in casual conversation and trivial encounters, in a lifetime's experience of being a woman, were given form and focus and represented anew. It's a long time since I've read or seen this play, perhaps the most famous of Caryl Churchill's extraordinary *oeuvre*, but as Kemp and her team so lucidly demonstrate, it remains as powerful as it was when it was first performed in the 1980s, at the height of Thatcher's Britain.

Most of all, *Top Girls* released an overpowering sadness. To be a woman in a male-dominated world is to be the second sex: millennia of cultural conditioning can't be overthrown in a generation, or even in a century. And what this play argues, with unwavering pitilessness, is that the subjugation of women can't be separated from the subjugation of class. It's a play driven by the 'shuddering horror' described in a letter to her lover by Rosa Luxemburg, which the British poet Keston Sutherland recently quoted in a paper on 'Revolution and Really Being Alive':

> [T]his feeling of shuddering horror does not let go of me… Especially when I lie down to sleep, this fact [of my mother's death] immediately arises again before my eyes, and I have to groan out loud from pain. I don't know how it is with you but I don't suffer mainly from longing anymore and I don't suffer on my own account, but what makes me shudder every time is this one thought: what kind of life was that! What has this person lived through, what is the point of a life like that! I don't know of any thought that is so dreadful for me as this one; I feel as though it would tear me apart if I began to think about it, and yet it comes to me under the most surprising circumstances, at any moment.

There's some dialogue in the second half of *Top Girls* that so precisely echoes Luxemburg's letter, that I wonder if it is one of the seeds of the play itself. *What kind of a life is that?* And the passion and horror of this question tears apart the shallowness of popular critiques of feminism. It's all too easy for the Western middle-class – and especially for men and women who argue that feminism is over, that women are quite equal enough – to ignore the poverties that the West has outsourced to so-called 'developing' countries, and even to ignore those that exist closer to home. Yet these poverties – physical, economic and intellectual – exist everywhere, inflicting their damage on millions of lives. And, as study after study has shown, it is women who bear the brunt. What can equality possibly mean if the glamorous boardroom success of a few does nothing to change the lives of the many?

Churchill exposes these questions with a text that remains formally audacious, and which made me reflect how slight are the ambitions of most contemporary plays. She combines a sense of total formal freedom with an almost icy control of her metaphors. I've noticed before that Churchill's work has an odd effect: it's only at the end that everything suddenly slots into place. It's as if she is building an architecturally impossible arch, which may fall down at any moment: and then, in the final moments, she places the keystone, and all at once the structure reveals itself as clear and formally irreproachable. It's this almost magical reflexiveness, a mixture of complete imaginative freedom and stern dramaturgical and stylistic discipline, that makes her one of the major English language playwrights of the past half century.

Her formal ingenuity also allows Churchill to suspend meaning, so that her work never falls into trite didacticism. For Churchill, a play is a form that releases ideas, rather than encloses them in a moral homily. As with many of the most exciting playwrights, this can make her a challenge to present on stage: a director looking for a 'message' will inevitably make the play less than it is. Jenny Kemp's direction, however, is equal to the text. I can't imagine a better production.

As is well known, the first half of *Top Girls* is a fantasy dinner party, arranged by Marlene (Anita Hegh) to celebrate her promotion as a corporate executive. She invites a number of women, real and legendary: Lady Nijō (Li-Leng Au), Imperial concubine and Buddhist nun; Isabella Bird (Margaret Mills), Victorian traveller; Dull Gret (Sarah Ogden), the subject of a painting by Brueghel; the apocryphal Pope Joan (Maria Theodorakis); and Patient Griselda (Nikki Shiels), who arrives late, the fairytale peasant girl married to a prince, who demonstrates inhuman loyalty in some inhuman testing of her fidelity. The setting then shifts brutally to Thatcher's Britain, where a non-chronological story about Marlene's work, and in particular her relinquished daughter Angie (Eryn Jean Norvill), open up the wounds of class and sex, exploring the same ideas in contemporary terms. In a way, the effect is quite simple: the mundane encounters of the everyday are opened out into a historical perspective, complicating both.

Dale Ferguson's design and Richard Vabre's lighting exploit the potentials of the Sumner Theatre better than anything I've seen there yet. The design elements are simple and few, but all of them feel essential. And as we might expect with Kemp, there are some breathtaking visual transformations.

Kemp introduces the play with a brief glimpse of Marlene, daydreaming at her desk as she reflects on her promotion, with the brutalist cityscape of modern London illuminated behind her: a conceit that means Marlene summons the fantasy dinner, with its dreamlike elements emphasised by a rabbit-headed waitress. Halfway through the dinner party, as the tone darkens, a silvery curtain descends, enclosing the cast in a fairytale forest, which then itself reddens to a depiction of hell. The office scenes take place on a broadly lit stage, every detail exposed under a wide light; the final domestic scenes, in contrast, are given us as a pool of naturalistic detail on a huge, dark stage. When actors walk off, they disappear into the shadows.

The show is punctuated by glimpses of Elizabeth Drake's various compositions, placed with absolute tact to heighten particular scenes or dialogue, or to orchestrate the transitions between scenes. This also heightens the sense, which is foregrounded by the crossing dialogue, that Churchill writes her plays with the ear of a composer, attentive to the rhythms and sounds of spoken utterance as much as to its meanings.

But the emotional weight of the show relies on the ensemble cast, led by Hegh's spikily assured performance of a woman grappling with the price of her success. Kemp has gathered an impressive cast, and there are no small performances here. As the production cumulatively builds its complexities it gathers power, racing to the devastating final conflict between the two sisters, Marlene and Joyce (Maria Theodorakis): the sister who escapes her destiny in the underclass, the sister who remains. The performances are nuanced with great delicacy, switching between heightened theatricality and heightened realism, comedy and sorrow. The only criticism, and in the face of the wider achievements it's minor, is the odd wavering accent.

It shows what happens when great contemporary writing meets imaginations prepared to take it on its own terms. You get theatre that wakes you, intellectually and emotionally. You get theatre that questions instead of confirming the status quo. You get theatre that matters. *Top Girls* is indisputably the highlight of the Melbourne Theatre Company's main stage season this year.

Theatre Notes, September 16 2012

Some notes on Orlando

White. No colour, every colour; plenty and absence at once. The empty page awaiting inscription, the page which may be shredded or burned. The colour of milk, the colour of semen, the colour of fertility. The imaginary of European Empire, the sterile fictions of race, purity, virginity. The hymeneal bride, the *deuil blanc* of mediaeval mourning. The colour of deep freeze, of immobility, of the Great Frosts of Elizabethan London, when the river Thames was sheeted with ice eleven inches thick. Arsenic. The nuclear heart of a star, the colour of absolute cold. The colour of The Rabble's *Orlando*.

In Kate Davis' design, the Tower Theatre stage at the Malthouse is a shallow pool of white liquid, enclosed above by a low ceiling outlined by lights, and backstage by a huge mirror. Before the actors appear, it is absolutely still: it seems a solid white floor, a sheet of ice. As the actors wade ankle-deep through the liquid (milk? semen? both? neither?), the surface becomes a chaos of ripples, their white costumes become sodden. It is impure, this white.

The imagined shade of absolute clarity. The white-out of a snowstorm, in which everything is obscured.

❖❖❖

It's certainly been an interesting, if not especially edifying, fortnight for women. A popular resurgence in feminism, which in Australia has remained largely beneath the radar, collided head-on with the received wisdom of mainstream political commentary. Julia Gillard's Question

Time speech in which, turning on a rhetorical sixpence, she took Tony Abbott's hypocritical borrowing of feminist feathers and shoved them so far down his throat that he choked, became the focal point of a blizzard of debate. Suddenly sexism and misogyny were the words of the moment. Feminism? Not so much.

On one side, a phalanx of mostly – but not exclusively – male pundits claim that, in calling out the misogynist attacks that have attended her leadership of the country, Gillard herself is being sexist: playing the 'gender card', she is taking unfair advantage of her sex to wrongfoot the leader of the Opposition. In other words, the real victim of Tony Abbott's sexism is… Tony Abbott. On the other, the uncritical ra-ra-ra for Gillard as feminist hero ignores her policies: the implications, for instance, of her decision – on the same day that she made her viral speech – to join forces with the Opposition to vote in significant cuts to the income of sole parents, a decision which disproportionately affects women. Feminist? How much?

Of course there has been insightful comment, but most of the ensuing discussion left me depressed and bored. A snowstorm indeed, in which the genuine grievances of women were whited-out by a trivialising rhetoric that stands complacently on the assumption that women are a 'minority'. Covertly or overtly, the rational desire of women to be treated as human beings is characterised as 'female unreasonableness': worse, serious issues of public policy – abortion rights, for example – somehow became equated with mentioning mussels in public. The misogyny in Australian political debate – and its first cousin, homophobia – bared its teeth, calling on every possible hypocrisy to conceal its vicious defence of its own privilege. It's all so familiar. It's all so deadening.

And then you go and see a show like *Orlando*. It's not that a work like this makes everything better; it manifestly can't. It's not that it teaches you anything that you don't know; it doesn't. It's that it *is* something. An uninhibited howl of laughter. A scream of grief. A forthright act of unshamed beauty. Female desire in all its violence, perversity and monotony, its repetitive assault on the self, its redemption, its dolour, its breathtaking, liberating lust for life. *Orlando* is, most of all, a work of theatre: a performance that explodes, with the white-hot fission of its full meaning, into the present moment.

❖❖❖

I haven't read Virginia Woolf's *Orlando* since my early twenties, and have only the vaguest memory of the text. I wondered whether to re-read it after seeing The Rabble's show, but decided that I'd rather simply respond to the show: this so clearly isn't an adaptation of the novel, however much it riffs from Woolf. The Rabble steals *Orlando*'s central conceits – the ageless lover of Elizabeth I who lives through several centuries, changing into a woman along the way – and its characters: Orlando (Dana Miltins), and her lovers Nicholas Greene (Syd Brisbane) and Sasha (Mary Helen Sassman). These become the occasion for a new work of theatre.

The Rabble's production, created by Emma Valente and Kate Davis, constructs a collage of words and performance and sound. The text includes passages from *Orlando* and *The Waves*, original poems (mostly by Emma Valente), writings from Emily Dickinson, Gertrude Stein, Elizabeth I, a translation of Sappho by the Elizabethan poet Ambrose Philips. But for all its textual richness, this performance is generated as much by gesture, sound and visual cues as it is by language. The novel is literally a pre-text for three extraordinary performances.

There are long silences, longueurs stretched almost to the point of breaking – most cheekily when Orlando, newly translated into the female, waits as a kettle boils for a cup of tea. There are sudden, overwhelming eruptions of sound: heavy-metal music, piano solos, the unbearably amplified and repeated shattering of glass, always the sound of water. There are sumptuous visual plays of light, as when Orlando, lying corpse-like in a sea of milk, dissolves into an image of the Milky Way.

There is no easily discerned dramaturgical shape, no gradual rise of tension to the expected orgasmic climax: in fact, it's only in the final moment of the performance that its intentions become clear. Theatrical tension is wound up, climaxes and retreats, again and again: desire is met, sated, withdrawn, over-stimulated to the point of irritation, delicately teased to reawakening. You could perhaps evolve a theory of how feminine sexual response is expressed as dramatic energy in *Orlando*, in direct argument with the singular dramatic release of a masculine theatre. It's very tempting, in fact, to think along those lines. But it would likely be dodgy, and could diminish and enclose much of what is interesting here. The Rabble are working in recognisable traditions of avant-garde theatre, and their challenge is as much towards the commodification of meaning as it is to gendered expectations of form or content.

Nevertheless, in the centre of *Orlando* is the question of gender.

Male has always been the default neutral gender of human. It remains radical for women to claim this default status: woman is a special category of (hu)mankind, confined and defined by her body. This is why women are thought of as a 'minority' in patriarchal society, despite the fact that women slightly outnumber men: in the imaginative economy of gender, a woman can never represent the universal. She can never simply be a person: she is always, whatever she does, a cunt with a person attached. If she steps up to claim her personhood, she is expected to speak for women. It is permissible – nay, it is imperative! – for any prominent woman to symbolise all women; in this way, as is the case with 'minority' races in a white-dominated culture, she is denied the ability to symbolise all people. Personhood – the ability to universalise humanity in a particular individuality – is withdrawn from her. A man can be an individual man, since he can also be a neutral symbol of humanity, speaking of and for all of us. A woman is never a neutral person. She is a woman.

For the representative artist, this is truly a horned dilemma. And this crisis of representation spawns the man who is a woman who is the multiply gendered, multiply conditioned, historicised, atemporal self, all at once. This is where Orlando comes in.

As it were.

❖❖❖

Obscenity can be sexist, but it is not in and of itself sexist. It might just be sex. It might just be absurd.

> I want the penis when I am waiting
> When I am waiting now I am thinking of the penis
> I am thinking of the penis riding a horse
> When I am cold I am hoping the penis will come
> The penis will make me warm
> The penis makes me penis
> I am penis
> Penis penis
> Penis me please penis
> Penis please penis my penis

> Penis the penis in the penis penis
> Penis put penis penis in my penis penis

It might allude to the Galenian idea that the vagina is an inverted penis: inversion, perversion, transexual, transgressive: Orlando. It might be Dada soundpoem nonsense sense. It might be a straightforwardly joyous expression of sexual desire. It might, in the mouth of Mary Helen Sassman, acquire an outrageous Russian accent. She might be eating an apple at the time. I might not have been able to stop laughing.

❖ ❖ ❖

But these complexities – the breakages enacted for us, the confusions and violences and comedies of desire – condition a longing that is nothing to do with gender. All these selves, all these costumes, all these histories and literatures, are the veils which obscure ourselves from ourselves. The great beauty of Woolf's writing is given its due in the long final monologue, in which Miltins, abject, exhausted, soaked, in the androgynous costume of a dunce, arrives in a place where identity fails, where there are no selves, no names: only the body, breathing and speaking; only the joyous and painful details of life, its mundanity, its terrifying beauty. It is now, as we are watching. Suddenly we know it is now.

Theatre Notes, October 17 2012

Pompeii, LA

> From medium to medium, the real is volatilized, becoming an allegory of death. But it is also, in a sense, reinforced through its own destruction. It becomes reality for its own sake, the fetishism of the lost object: no longer the object of representation, but the ecstasy of denial and of its own ritual extermination: the hyperreal.
>
> *Symbolic Exchange and Death*, Jean Baudrillard

America is burning. In Declan Greene's new play at Malthouse Theatre, *Pompeii, LA*, there is no reality except death. Everything that exists is simulation: LA is the imaginary city whose representation has become so much more real than the city itself that it has devoured its original referent. The City of Los Angeles evaporates in the toxic dream-machinery of Hollywood: all that remains are the volatilised hallucinations of corporate capital, in love with its own terrors, which it stages again and again on the dreaming screens of the American Empire. Earthquake, volcanic eruption, environmental desertification, murder, accident, psychic breakdown, economic disaster, the annihilation of meaning. *What are you so afraid of?*

Pompeii, LA is Greene's most ambitious work yet. Here are obsessions familiar from his earlier work – the apocalypse of the individual in *Moth*, the B-grade Hollywood camp of *Little Mercy*, the self-consuming fetishes of twenty-first century trash culture of *A Black Joy*. Greene's discontinuous text is rendered through the spectacle of Matthew Lutton's direction to create a work of theatre that compellingly expresses, through a glass darkly, the present cultural moment.

In the opening sequences, reality shifts from scene to scene, even from sentence to sentence, generating an increasing sense of vertigo as it becomes clear that there is no original 'reality' from which these scenes depend, no ground on which this narrative can stand. The scenes are all 'backstage', at first posing as the banal realities behind the fantasies of Hollywood: Judy Garland (Belinda McClory) in her dressing room with her make-up artist (Anna Samson); a cast rehearsing a scene from a disaster movie, in which one of the stars (Luke Ryan) storms out.

Yet these scenes quickly lose their moorings: the make-up artist tells us a story about returning home to her murdered boyfriend (is it real or a story from television?); an older actor who has 'paid his dues' (Greg Stone) enacts an uneasily hilarious monologue about love with a horrific subtext of paedophilia, which ends with him grotesquely kissing a television. Actors change costumes in front of us to become other characters, reality retreats into an infinitely receding hall of mirrors. Each moment is serially revealed as fantasy, leaving the audience nowhere to rest. The only thread linking these scenes is a constant iteration of dread: *What are you so afraid of?*

This apparent chaos nevertheless has a strange sense of continuity, the source of which only becomes clear in its second half. *Pompeii, LA* is in fact a dance of death. This is not the logic of surreality but of hyperreality, the term Jean Baudrillard coined in the 1970s to describe a world in which representation no longer bears any relationship to the real. This hyper-mediated universe of representation, generated and brought to critical mass by corporate capital, references only itself. As 'signs are exchanged against each other rather than against the real', it creates a catastrophe of value. You can see the symptoms of this catastrophe in political discourse around climate change, for example, where what matters is not scientific evidence but the power of rhetorical assertion, or in the dazzlingly absurd spectacles of the recent US election, which perhaps reached their apotheosis when Clint Eastwood harangued an empty chair at the crucial moment of the Republican National Convention.

In *Pompeii, LA* the reality under question is that of the individual, the defining myth of contemporary America. Greene portrays this self as a collection of traumatised fragments, coming to life like zombie memories of half-forgotten television shows that have colonised the space where meaningful relationships might once have existed. At the last the individual coalesces as a shattered body necrotising in a hospital, trapped in a materiality emptied of meaning, and especially of any meaningful relationship. Staging these ideas as live performance, rather than through the all-consuming seduction of the screen, makes their dislocations and cruelties coldly articulate.

As Greene and Lutton explain in their joint program note, the Hollywood child star super-narrative (enacted through the lives of Judy Garland, Jonathan Brandis, Macaulay Culkin, Lindsay Lohan and so on) is the embodiment of the cannibalistic fetishes of capital. 'A young life [is] enumerated as pure capital, inflates rapidly, then declines just as fast… ' And this itself becomes representative of the excesses of Western consumerism, 'a livelihood inflated to the point that it can no longer support itself'. The desertification of the real is dramatised in the ultra-commodification of the individual, sacrificed for our mass pleasure on a billion screens. In the spectacle of these celebrity implosions, we see the flickering reflections of our own emptied, commodified selves.

For all its complexity, the play is boldly and simply structured: it moves from the sinisterly apocalyptic world of the hyperreal, understood afterwards as a nightmare of the traumatised unconscious, to the desert of the real, rendered as hyper-naturalistic, fragmentary scenes in a hospital. The two halves of the play are divided by the spectacle of a smashed red Porsche, being inspected by traffic police as they photograph the wreckage and remove the mess. As with everything in this production, we only witness the aftermath of disaster. The worst has already happened.

The unnamed child star (David Harrison) only comes fully into focus as a character in the final scenes: in the first half he is mainly a peripheral dogsbody, lurking at the edges of his own nightmare. The other actors now become the faces around him in the hospital: a doctor (Tony Nikolakopoulos), a nurse who photographs herself with the sleeping actor, a man dying in the bed next to him. His reality is an anguish of pain, terror and loneliness as his body deteriorates, punctuated by the artificial days and nights of hospital routine.

The performances, in particular Belinda McClory and Greg Stone's, are riveting, at once grotesque and naturalised, finding the more-than-real extremity in the stereotypes they are portraying. Lutton's production is impeccably orchestrated, exploiting David Franzke's sound design to shift seamlessly from dramatic time to simple duration, as when we watch actors sweep shattered glass up on the stage. Nick Schlieper's design meets the boldness of the writing, sweeping from the spectacular to the intimate, and uses the space of Merlyn as well as anything I've seen there. It's dark, pitiless theatre, obscenely and bathetically comic, that enacts how apocalyptic America plays out its neuroses through the spectacle of the individual.

Theatre Notes, November 25 2012

On the Importance of Being Seen

Late last year (2012), I closed my theatre review blog, Theatre Notes. It was the first theatre blog in Australia, and one of the longest-running anywhere. I expected a measure of dolour and dismay when I announced my decision; I didn't expect what actually happened. I was swamped by hundreds of tributes, private and public, that left me stunned and, quite genuinely, humbled. It was like being at my own funeral, without the inconvenience of having to die first. And it told me things about the blog that I never knew while I was writing it.

Theatre Notes was an attempt to change the conversation. Miraculously, it did.

Since I closed the blog, there's been a lot of discussion on the place of criticism, especially for an ephemeral art form like performance, and how it can be financially sustained in the new, bleak media landscape. That's an important debate, especially for the younger generation of critics now emerging online; but it has nothing to do with why I started the blog, or why I decided to close it. Theatre Notes wasn't funded and was never dependent on institutional support; that was a very conscious decision on my part. What I valued above all in that writerly space was my autonomy, and I was very willing to pay for my freedom.

As a former journalist, I couldn't but be aware that the blog was a small part of a massive revolution, the rise of digital culture and the breaking of print's monopoly on the world of public ideas. It was a blog that took, if anything, a rather old-fashioned view of criticism, and exploited the new freedoms of the internet in order to explore it. It began on an impulse: I was at home, manacled to the desk writing a novel, and I was broke and bored with myself. And the thought lit up in my head: why not start a blog for theatre reviews? So I did.

I wasn't a newcomer to theatre criticism. For three tumultuous years in my late twenties, I was the Melbourne theatre reviewer for the weekly national magazine *The Bulletin*. My time there included a high-profile banning by the Playbox Theatre – I even made *60 Minutes* as an archetypal bitch critic – for my 'vitriolic' reviews. I had discovered what turns out to be an unquenchable passion for the performing arts, but I didn't much enjoy my notoriety. I resigned, disillusioned, in 1992, and for the next decade worked as a full-time writer, mostly concentrating on poetry. As I said in a lecture delivered to students at the VCA in 1993, thinking back to my time at *The Bulletin*: 'Nothing is as deadening as apathy. Nothing is as savage as pettiness called to question. Nothing is as unanswerable as wilful ignorance.'

In 2004, when I began Theatre Notes, I had little idea what had happened in Australian theatre in the twelve years since I'd given up criticism. There weren't many ways of finding out, either (which highlights the archival importance of performance criticism): aside from mostly unilluminating print reviews, the only really useful source was *RealTime*, a pioneering print and internet journal that has covered innovative performance for fourteen years.

My personal knowledge was mainly confined to my involvement in founding the Keene/Taylor Theatre Project, a poor theatre collaboration between director Ariette Taylor and my husband, playwright Daniel Keene. It opened in 1997 with unfunded productions in the Brotherhood of St Lawrence warehouse in Fitzroy, with people queuing down Brunswick Street to see actors like Patricia Kennedy, a very young Dan Spielman, Greg Stone, Malcolm Robertson, Helen Morse and Paul English in some now legendary performances. The KTTP was playing the Sydney Opera House within two years, and within five years had reached the end of its lifespan, winning the Kenneth Myer Medallion for the Performing Arts along the way.

I have no doubt that the KTTP was one of the unconscious models behind Theatre Notes. It was a concrete demonstration that you could begin with nothing but a burning faith in the possibilities of art, and it could drive through to anywhere you liked. You don't have to ask permission; sometimes asking permission is the last thing you should do. Still, I had no expectations; I didn't know whether anyone would read my blog, or even be interested.

As it turned out, over the next eight years people were interested. Much of that comes down to pure chance: I was the right person in the right place at the right time. The first reason was the poverty of theatre coverage. As a battle-scarred veteran of Melbourne theatre once commented to me, back in his day the most you could expect as a response to your work was a few indifferent paragraphs in the *Age* and, at best, a small but thoughtful notice in the *Melbourne Times*. Then it fell into a memory hole and was never heard of again. The high concentration of media ownership in Australia – the highest in the Western world – meant that there were very few outlets for critical response. There was a gap, a hunger for thoughtful, long-form, immediate response that reached beyond the standard consumer review, that was screaming to be filled. I was very conscious of that lack, and I intended Theatre Notes to address it.

The other reason is more interesting. In the end, a critic is only as good as the work she writes about; and I was fortunate enough to find the work. Although I didn't know it, as I was having my private light-bulb moment in my study Melbourne theatre was about to change out of recognition. In 2004 the Playbox Theatre, the second largest theatre in Melbourne, was artistically moribund, playing to houses of around 30 per cent capacity. And in one of the most significant appointments for Australian theatre in the past decade, the board called in Michael

Kantor, a freelance director-about-town, and Stephen Armstrong, a producer with a track record ranging from independent theatre to a tenure at the Sydney Theatre Company, to be respectively artistic director and executive producer. Digging into energies always present but long marginalised, they proceeded to redefine the mainstream Australian stage.

Looking back now, it's impossible to over-estimate the importance of this change. Work that had for years been the province of the 'fringe' – working, like the KTTP, in found spaces or tiny theatres, with perhaps a distant prospect of a moment in the spotlight before it vanished – was invited onto the main stage. Artists who had been dismissed by the overwhelmingly conservative culture – seen at best, when they did flicker into visibility, as anomalies – were centre stage, with the resources they needed to realise their possibilities. This resonated far beyond the newly named Malthouse Theatre itself: young independent companies had something to aim for (or to react against, an equally important dynamic). And audiences who thought the theatre on offer on the main stages was as outdated and dusty as a Remington typewriter woke up.

When the Malthouse launched its first show in 2005 – a double bill of Patrick White's *The Ham Funeral* and an adaptation by Tom Wright of Daniel Defoe's *Journal of a Plague Year* – I wrote with excitement and relief:

> It is a breath of fresh air to see mainstream theatre with ambition and intellectual clout, and that takes itself seriously as an art. I have no doubt this shift in artistic direction will generate a lot of controversy; Helen Thomson's bitterly hostile reviews in the *Age* this week are probably symptomatic. I also have no doubt that this new phase at Malthouse is the best thing that's happened there in the past decade; and as a theatre goer, I am hoping that this is only the beginning of a more generous imagining of the Australian stage. [*See the full review on page 24*]

This hopefulness turned out to be no chimera: between 2004 and 2010 the assumptions that underlaid mainstream theatre were turned upside down, and independent theatre flowered into a remarkable renaissance. Of course, this kind of shift never happens without resistance. In Australia, the reluctance to embrace new work can be particularly vicious: the new might fight its way to the front, but staying there is quite another question. There are too many to cite, but a telling example is when Jim Sharman took over the State Theatre Company of South Australia, renaming it the Lighthouse Theatre. He employed an extraordinary ensemble cast that included Geoffrey Rush, Robert Menzies and Kerry Walker and premiered plays from Patrick White, Louis Nowra and Stephen Sewell, in seasons that are now the stuff of legend. The Lighthouse also lasted only from 1982–83. And although its legacy still resonates through the culture – for one thing, it kickstarted the distinguished career of Neil Armfield, who later took over Sydney's Belvoir St Theatre – it's impossible not to look back and see it as an opportunity lost, a possibility that briefly flared and died.

I could see this repressive mechanism at work in the consistent press attacks on the Malthouse's programming policies (and on other institutions that were bringing welcome vitality to the culture, such as Kristy Edmunds' Melbourne Festivals, or some of the more outrageous young companies that were emerging in Melbourne). There was, as I saw at the time, no reason why the same fate as attended the Lighthouse might not happen to the Malthouse. But this time a radical reimagining didn't fail of its promise; and the internet, by providing a public space for alternative views, was an important part of that. The monopoly of opinion was over.

As a young theatre critic I had often been baffled by the apathy or outright hostility that usually greeted what for me was the most exciting work. I didn't believe it was a conscious conspiracy, by any means, but I had already noted how indifferent criticism could erase accomplishment, rebuke the new for challenging received wisdom, and assert authority in order to forbid discussion. Theatre Notes, and the blogs that sprang up in the following years, began a conversation that invited difference, that spurred interest, that argued fiercely and (at its best) without rancour about ideas, aesthetics, politics. And gradually, instead of being the only public truth available, the authority that trumps all others by virtue of its mass exposure, the conservative mainstream pundit became what he actually is: only one voice among many.

From the beginning Theatre Notes was militantly against the silencing of art and debate, the insistence on 'business as usual' which had characterised, with a number of notable exceptions, the generality of Australian arts criticism and sometimes arts institutions themselves.

There have always been critics who saw their task to be critical advocates or purveyors of ideas – Katharine Brisbane, co-founder of Currency Press and one of the most passionate campaigners for new Australian theatre through the 1970s, is a case in point – but they were rare.

More common was the kind of critic who believed himself to be the final word on a show, holding himself above the audience and pronouncing judgment from on high. Such judgments were held to be unchallengeable: the critic was the ultimate authority, and the childlike artist was presumed to be unable to make critical judgments of his own. For such critics, the only thing that counts is the imprimatur of approval or rejection. Yet that imprimatur remains the most boring aspect of reviews. The distinguished American critic and theatre practitioner Robert Brustein – one of the major influences behind Theatre Notes – described this well during a roundtable on criticism, 'The Critic as Thinker: A discussion at the Philoctetes Centre of New York City':

> The task I set for myself was to put theatre into a context and try to see how this or that play fit into our particular time, our particular society, our particular culture, our particular political life, and how it reflected on that… And more and more, I found myself subordinating the judgment that was so necessary to criticism, and that we're all looking for: Does he like it? Does she hate it? When I read criticism, I find that to be the least interesting part. I began to call that 'Himalayan criticism' after Danny Kaye – when he was asked whether he liked the Himalayas, he said, 'Loved him, hated her.' (Laughter.) It's essentially what we've all been practicing – Himalayan criticism.
>
> Especially when I began practicing as a director – as an artistic director, an actor, a playwright – I knew that that kind of criticism did me no good whatsoever. I was trying, really, to find what it was that was helpful and useful, without in any way deferring or cheating or cheapening or lying. I wanted to see what it was that could possibly help a theatre artist to advance. And so I thought my most important function as a critic was to try to find out what these artists, if they were artists, were trying to do, and then to see whether they did that successfully. But at least to try and find out what the intention was before I rejected it.

This was exactly what I attempted to practise: a criticism which employed my knowledge and experience as a writer and sometime practitioner in the theatre, in order to form a response that was 'helpful and useful'. It carries an important rider: 'helpful and useful' doesn't mean being 'kind' or 'supportive'. Often it can mean the reverse: unwarranted praise has no place in rigorous criticism and is of no use to anyone, artist or audience. Flattery has always seemed to me, equally as much as gratuitously snide contempt, a mark of disrespect; it betrays that you are not taking the work seriously. Of course all artists desire to please their audience, but for most, myself included, what matters a great deal more than praise or blame is that someone perceives, with accuracy and insight, exactly what you did.

For me, the biggest lesson of Theatre Notes was that, just as indifferent criticism can be disabling, good criticism can be enabling. It carves out cultural space, makes connections, suggests further possibilities, opens generosities of perception. Often I thought I was only stating the obvious, looking at what was in front of me. What I only partially realised, although I understand this from my own experience, is how important stating the obvious is: how much it matters for a work to be seen, for its virtues and problems to be considered in the terms the work itself presents. As the blog evolved, I began to understand that a responsible criticism is one that refines that simple act of recognition and carefully articulates it for readers. Whether the upshot is positive or negative, it is this dynamic perception that makes criticism an empowering and creative act. And it's the only thing that makes criticism, which the Italian poet Eugenio Montale so gracefully names 'the secondary art', worth doing at all.

Kill Your Darlings, Issue 13, April 2013

The Cherry Orchard

I can only hope that this lucid, pitch-perfect production of *The Cherry Orchard* shines through the miasma of controversy that has recently surrounded its director, Simon Stone. Controversy might be a great way of generating headlines, but it's also a smokescreen that can effectively obscure an artist's work. And this production is work worth noticing. It's a revelatory investigation not only of *The Cherry Orchard*, but of the dramatic machinery that Anton Chekhov employed with such mastery.

Someone in the Melbourne Theatre Company should have stayed Stone's hand and prevented him from billing *The Cherry Orchard* as 'by Simon Stone, after Anton Chekhov'. Unlike Stone's reimagining of Henrik Ibsen's *The Wild Duck*, which barely contained a line from the original play, this version of *The Cherry Orchard* is certainly by Anton Chekhov.

The billing has sparked a deal of talk about Stone's arrogant dismissal of playwriting, and in this case is markedly misleading. What illuminates this production, in all its aspects – from Alice Babidge's starkly elegant design, to the beautiful ensemble performances from an outstanding cast – is a profound fidelity to the original play. The only substantial change is the dropping of some very minor functionary characters.

Chekhov's tragicomedy about the passing of the decadent Russian gentry is translated, virtually line by line, into modern Australian idiom, suspending the action in a reality that is not quite contemporary Australia and not quite pre-Revolutionary Russia. In this theatricalised medium, aspects of both realities exist side by side, anachronisms intact. We witness Chekhov's characters trembling on the cusp of catastrophic change. The play opens and closes in the nursery of the old mansion, surrounded by the discarded toys of a childhood that soon will be erased forever. The whole is woven together by its attention to emotional detail: the focus is firmly on the actors.

This is reinforced by Alice Babidge's set, a white, doorless three-sided box in which every object and every movement is mercilessly exposed. A black scrim descends soundlessly between acts, as if a wing of night were falling on the characters, and the four acts are signalled by projections onto the scrim: Spring, Summer, Autumn, Winter.

Stone's style of heightened naturalism is peculiarly suited to Chekhov, who advises us in *The Cherry Orchard* that 'You shouldn't go to the theatre. You should look more often at yourselves'. It's fair to take this as a instruction to the spectators: Chekhov wanted his work to embed itself in his audience's lived reality.

His pitilessly clear insight into how tragedy is inseparable from life's comic trivialities reflects Oscar Wilde's observation that 'the real tragedies of life occur in such an inartistic manner that they hurt us by their crude violence, their absolute incoherence, their absurd want of meaning, their entire lack of style'. Art has long fooled us that tragedy is noble: Chekhov believed no such thing. And so we have, unfolding before us, the clumsy, unfinished business of human longing and unsatisfied desire, irredeemable sadness, irrevocable choices gone awry, the anguish of nostalgia, the whole messy deal of human mortality.

The production fascinatingly exposes Chekhov's writing. Although Lopakhin (Steve Mouzakis) is, for example, now a nouveau riche developer of shopping malls and Ranevskaya (Pamela Rabe) a hanger-on to the hippy counterculture, although the language is precisely contemporary with nary a sniff of a samovar, the rhythms and dramaturgy of the play are preserved intact. And you realise that it's these bones that create the play's emotional machinery.

The complexity at work in the characters is explored by the cast with finesse and truthfulness. There is no weak link among the actors: every performance has its moment of emotional nakedness, reflecting Chekhov's refusal to condemn any of the characters he created. Gayev (Robert Menzies) and Ranevskaya, the brother and sister whose inability to grow up ensures the destruction of their estate, are portrayed in all their shocking carelessness and pathos, victims of their blank refusal to perceive the disaster that threatens them.

And you see just as clearly those who are victims of their blithe privilege. Lopakhin, the former underling made good, who barely got through school and was beaten by his illiterate father, both longs for that privilege and desires to destroy it. Mouzakis' performance is outstanding: Lopakhin, the vulgar, clownish butt of the family jokes, is portrayed with an empathy which makes his final scene with Varya (Zahra Newman) completely heartbreaking. But perhaps it's the ancient family retainer Firs (Ronald Falk), forgotten and abandoned in the nursery, who most stays with you.

It's a production which leaves you with a strong aftershock, as the subtextual tragedy rises cumulatively through its comic surface. The most striking quality is its air of lightness and transparency: *The Cherry Orchard* reaches its emotional peaks without cheating, simply permitting them to emerge. There are no grand directorial gestures: this is an elegant and simple frame in which the action of Chekhov's play is boldly brought to life. Stunning.

The Guardian, August 15 2013

Roman Tragedies

In the twenty-first century, we are all connected all the time. As we sip our morning coffee, we scroll through the morning's litany of disaster on our smart phones, email a colleague in London, joke with friends, check the weather. The news quacks in the background: riots in another city, revolution, politics, death and scandal. Toast burns in the kitchen as the world burns outside.

The genius of Ivo van Hove's *Roman Tragedies* is how it brings the contemporary quality of simultaneity to Shakespeare. The six-hour marathon begins with stripped-back versions of *Coriolanus* and *Julius Caesar*. In the so-called Roman plays, Shakespeare moves his focus from what Jan Kott calls the 'demonic history of the royal' that drives the History plays to the wider politics of the Roman Republic. This is a more contemporary arena of struggle between the patricians, the Roman nobles, and the plebeians, the people. The first two plays set up a compelling reality in which, surprisingly but convincingly, the doomed passion of *Antony and Cleopatra* plays out as an erotic fantasy of sex, power and death.

The stage is designed as an anonymous hotel lobby, which, like the Roman Senate or the Forum, is a contemporary interface between public and private space. This is a visual language familiar to everyone who watches press conferences on the news: anonymous beige couches, tables loaded with microphones, huge lampshades dangling from the ceiling, everywhere television screens with scrolling CNN footage, a coffee bar discreetly to the side. The performance extends to the foyer, where there are more screens, more bars. The auditorium doors are never shut. An LED display suspended on stage runs headlines and instructions: the audience is exhorted to tweet their responses to the show, and even given a dedicated wifi feed (ROMAN TRAGEDIES).

It all seems at once distracting and deeply familiar. And then, with an assault of drums and cymbals that vibrates through your bones from BL!NDMAN, the percussion group that plays live in front of the stage, the show begins. Coriolanus' mother Volumnia (Frieda Pittoors), seen at once in close-up on the big screen front stage and live on stage, speaks with bloodthirsty relish about her son's military victories. There's no way not to pay attention.

For the next six hours, *Roman Tragedies* switches between riveting scenes in which Shakespeare's dramaturgy is stripped down to its lean and hungry essence, and the 'scene changes', when, with no moment of transition, the lights come up, elevator music starts playing and the master of ceremonies gives the audience information about the performance. Each change is timed precisely, counting down to the moment when, bang! the action begins again.

During the first scene change, we're invited to go up on stage whenever we like, to sit on the couches and buy drinks from the bar. At once half the audience moves onto the stage and becomes an instant forum crowd, peering curiously at the protagonists, chatting, buying coffee. I found I didn't want to sit on the stage, although I sat in different places in the auditorium in the course of the evening: the *mise en scène* as seen from the front was too gripping. But it was fascinating to see how the movement of people throughout the show added to its feeling of immediacy, the sense of multiple lives surrounding and amplifying the lives we witness in dramatic relief before us.

Events are given as television news interviews or press conferences, with details of Roman history (wars, rivalries, imperial campaigns) scrolled rapidly across the LED strip to background the action. Roman headlines are mixed with headlines from tonight's news. There is a sense of spectacle, of the audience at the Colosseum waiting for blood, which is underlined by text that flashes up at intervals: FIVE MINUTES TO THE DEATH OF CORIOLANUS, or 75 MINUTES TO THE DEATH OF JULIUS CAESAR.

The adaptations of *Coriolanus* and *Julius Caesar* are clean, fast and surprisingly faithful, filleting out the significant dramatic moments in the plays. They're translated into contemporary Dutch by Tom Kleijn and then back into contemporary English as surtitles projected onto the screens. We lose the rich Elizabethan English of Shakespeare – but surprisingly, not much of it. The metaphors are all there, colloquialised perhaps but as powerful as ever. There's no attempt to update the story: this is Rome, with its bloody factions, conspiracies and murders. Each death is photographed like a crime scene, flashed up on the screens for our voyeuristic pleasure.

If it wasn't for the performances, all this could be so much technological bling, but *Roman Tragedies* is ensemble acting at its best. Van Hove has an extraordinary cast, and we see them at once in close-up, with the faux intimacy that attends the celebrities that live on screen in our lounge rooms, and with the presence of charismatic stage actors. It seems wrong to pick out particular performances, as you end up wanting to namecheck everyone in the cast, but there are stunning performances from Gijs Scholten van Aschat as Coriolanus, the soldier schooled in the black and white ideology of military service, fatally lost in the treacherous dissembling of city politics; Alwin Pulinckx as Brutus, the honest man betrayed by his own ideals; Helene Davos as Portia, lying distraught on a couch, playing the dialogue of her maid and herself in a terrible moment of psychic breakdown.

The sheer detailing of this production, the thought that rifts every decision, is impressive. There's an entire subtext of gender: the Roman Senate, both Republican and Imperial, is the very definition of patriarchal structure, underlying the bases of our own institutions. Van Hove subtly weaves a critique through the show, often casting against gender – Octavian, for instance, is a woman. The Roman ideal *virtus*, the virtues of manhood as personified in Coriolanus – valour, courage, honesty, rectitude – is contrasted first with the doublespeak of the Senate, and finally with the rebellious sensuality of Cleopatra. No judgment is made: all these multiple points of view exist on stage at the same time. Judgment is a question for us, the audience.

By the time we reach *Antony and Cleopatra*, we are versed in the conventions of this production and have internalised its language. The audience is now familiar with Antony's history, and knows the story of the end of the Roman Republic, which immediately precedes Antony's war with Rome. The stage is set for the telling of *Antony and Cleopatra*, maybe the most thrilling production of this passionate, amoral love story that you are likely to see, in which two wholly selfish and obsessed people destroy the lives of everyone around them. (As they are kings and queens, that really does mean everyone.)

Productions of *Antony and Cleopatra* so often stumble fatally on the absurdity of the plot. I mean, the woman kills herself with *asps*. Van Hove plays it straight, even down to a real snake. Cleopatra, played by Chris Nietvelt, is utterly charismatic: played on the edge of extremity, wilful, utterly uninhibited, vulnerable, sulky, every inch a queen, it's easy to see why Antony can't resist her. Antony (Hans Kesting), shameless womaniser, reckless soldier, magnetic, ambitious and treacherous, is played with a passionate complexity, shifting between indolence, passion and rage.

For the final 60 minutes the audience is sent back into the auditorium, but the connection between the action on stage and the audience is now intimate. The result is electrifying, its extremities raw and immediate. There's no point where you question the characters; their passions play out before us, raw and immediate. Even though we're now merely witnesses to the events on stage, the theatre remains porous, open to our everyday realities.

When Antony's general Enobarbus (Bart Slegers) betrays him and absconds to the Roman camp, he runs outside the theatre and plays his final scene in the street, before bewildered Adelaide Festival crowds, as we watch live video footage on screen. It's at once comic and horrible. And when Cleopatra howled in grief at Antony's death, all the hairs on my neck stood up: it was a representation of pure agony. For all the mediations presented in the production, this is total theatre, miraculously unmediated, Shakespeare remade as our contemporary again.

ABC Arts Online, March 1 2014

Hedda Gabler

Gender is so hot right now. If gender is, as is often claimed, a performance, then theatre is the place, *non pareil*, to explore it. And theatre is exploring it, for good or ill: in the past few months, I've seen at least half a dozen productions which feature cross-gendered casting or some kind of gendered critique.

There's nothing new about this: from the playful subversiveness of Shakespeare's cross-dressing heroines in plays like *The Merchant of Venice*, *As You Like It* or *Twelfth Night* to the stylised camp of Oscar Wilde to Robyn Archer, theatre has exploited the fluidity of identity in performance for centuries.

Some of the present popularity of gendered critique follows the mainstream success of queer theatre Sisters Grimm, the brainchild of Declan Greene and Ash Flanders, which produces a razor-sharp, hilarious trash camp that comments on racism and colonialism as well as gender. Their shows were the vanguard for a rash of cross-gender casting, not all of which have been as incisive or radical as Sisters Grimm.

As with cross-racial casting, it isn't enough merely to be 'gender blind': the representation of sex on stage must be contextualised thoughtfully if the result isn't to end up as ultimately conservative as the attitudes it supposedly critiques. Too easily cross-gender casting can become a pantomime of attitudes that never actually asks its audience to think.

And sometimes the most interesting critiques can simply not register. This is a dilemma very familiar to feminist artists, or to anyone whose work steps outside received wisdoms, the wider, unquestioned matrix of assumptions through which art is perceived. It's an issue quite aside from the perceived success or otherwise of a work.

How possible is it to *see* art that is genuinely radical, genuinely questioning; or does it inevitably become, as it's absorbed into the wider cultural discourse, somehow invisible? This question has been bothering me for several reasons, but seeing Adena Jacobs' production of *Hedda Gabler* near the end of its run at Belvoir St snapped it into focus.

This production has been controversial for the casting of Ash Flanders, co-founder of Sisters Grimm, in the title role. Like Sisters Grimm, but using very different means, Jacobs is interested in using theatre as a means to expose the paradoxes and imprisonments of gender. She takes a naturalistic play – in fact one of the iconic naturalistic plays – and directs it as a heightened and stylised work of anti-naturalism. This production overtly forbids any kind of easy identification or empathy with Hedda. As with Thomas Ostermeier's Schauhbüne production, which generated a similar affectlessness, we are given a slick, cool portrait view of bourgeois aspiration and anomie.

I loathed the Schaübuhne production with a passion, and wondered if I might feel the same about this one. Instead, I found it fascinating, and left unsettled and disturbed, feeling it was maybe the cruellest interpretation of Ibsen's classic that I had seen. The major difference is in Jacob's quietly brutal investigation of the mundane objectification of women: and in particular, how that causes women to objectify themselves, at the expense of their entire sense of self.

Even on its own terms, I'm not sure that the production entirely works – I had a nagging feeling from about halfway through that there was a missing dimension. It's a vague sense that a problem – the yawning abyss that exists at the heart of the objectified woman – had been clinically exposed, without its being quite solved in its theatricalisation. And no, I don't mean this as a question of the quality of the performances, which I thought were outstanding. It's more about a layer of intellection.

What's certain is that afterwards I couldn't stop thinking about this deeply uneasy, horrifyingly bleak interpretation of Ibsen. The intelligence that drives it is undeniable. The production seems to work backwards from Hedda's suicide, with every action intended to illuminate as lucidly as possible that final, irrevocable act. This gives the show a sense of unity of action, and particularly a metaphorical unity, that is compelling to watch.

Many critics, perhaps expecting a reprise of Flanders' performance of femininity in *Little Mercy*, were baffled by the casting. Chris Hook in the *Daily Telegraph*, for instance, said that 'subverting gender seems to serve no discernible purpose'. Others objected to Flanders' affectless performance, to his blunt refusal of depth and empathy, and more broadly to the production's lack of realism. That both of these decisions are, quite clearly, deliberate seems to have prompted almost no-one to ask why they were made.

The real insightfulness in Jacobs' production is how she removes, unobtrusively but tellingly, the sociological anachronisms that bedevil contemporary revisionings of Ibsen's script. Traditionally, Hedda is interpreted as bored, destructive and empty because she is trapped by stifling social conventions. She has no agency. In this production, highlighted by some sharp dramaturgy that cuts Ibsen's play to the bone while remaining startlingly faithful to its action, Hedda has a very twenty-first century sense of agency: all her choices are, on the surface at least, her own. She is trapped by her own choices, her own complicities.

It's interesting, for instance, that this version has preserved the maid, Berte, who is often dropped in contemporary adaptations. Played by Branden Christine, Berte is the one character that doesn't desire anything of Hedda; when Berte shares a cigarette with Hedda, it is a brief moment of companionship, interestingly free of the power plays that exist in all Hedda's other relationships. As a black, lower class servant, Berte's desires and agencies are invisible to the other characters, but this erasure means that she is also, paradoxically, the freest character in the play. Nobody looks at her, so she is free to see.

In this production, Flanders' performance of emptiness – a performance that, as the *Telegraph* reviewer notes quite accurately, is a 'wall, into which the rest of the cast drive at full speed' – is not at all about a man playing a woman, or even a man playing femininity. Jacobs is playing up Flander's androgeneity: he is neither male nor female in this role, as we see when he stands naked, looking out of the audience, deliberately unsexed, completely desireless. He is a human being neutered by patriarchy.

Yet the display of desire is all there. Flanders' flesh is constantly exposed, a decision which becomes progressively more uncomfortable. It calls into question the unquestioned and ubiquitous exposure of female flesh – is it uncomfortable because Flanders is male, and makes little effort to conceal that he is? If a woman were so constantly on display, would anyone bat an eyelid? Is the exposure of female bodies anything to do with actual desire?

Hedda is all surface, the sum of all the reflections projected upon her by the other characters. She has chosen, out of vanity, material ambition and, finally, boredom, to be the object that the other characters desire her to be. As a result, she has destroyed her own desires. She is so alienated from them that she no longer knows what they are, and can only envy and despise the desires of others – her husband, her aunt, Løvborg, Thea. The person who perceives Hedda clearly is Bracks, played brilliantly, without a skerrick of redemption, by Marcus Graham: and because he is a man, he has the upper hand and the ultimate power.

Ash Flanders' Hedda is a metaphor, placed, like Marianne Moore's imaginary toads, into a real garden. She is the extremity of a woman who plays by the rules of patriarchal femininity, the trophy wife that Tesman (Tim Walters) wins. This delights his aunt Julia (Lynette Curran), who sees the marriage as a sign of Tesman's social and career success, the manifestation of her ambition for him. Like Thea (Anna Houston), Løvborg's (Oscar Redding) lover and amanuensis, Julia can have no ambition for herself.

In the competition of patriarchal femininity, Hedda is the alpha female, to whom everyone defers. But she has nowhere to put her ambition. It can only resolve into a desire to have power over others, as the alpha male does: but as a woman who has chosen this confining mode of femininity, she has queered her own pitch.

The price is self-erasure: she has nothing beneath the reflection, no inner life of her own, no purchase on selfhood. She cannot conceive that she is capable of a meaningful act: that is the true meaning of Lovberg's accusation that she is a coward, and also why she insists that he make that meaningful act for her with a 'beautiful' suicide. In the end, the only thing she can create is utter negation: her suicide is not an act of defiance, but the recognition and logical end of all the choices she has made throughout her life.

This is a production, in short, that makes sense only if you take it out of the frames it is critiquing. The unsexing of Hedda Gabler – performed neither as man nor a woman, but as a construction of reflections – is read back into the binary expectations it is critiquing, and its larger meanings are obscured, or in the most egregious instances, not even noticed. Peter Gotting's review in the *Guardian* is among the most obvious examples of this: Gotting refers to 'genderbending', but at no point even attempts to consider what 'genderbending' might mean, beyond a buzzword indicating some kind of camp. Instead, he startlingly claims that, as she is reinterpreting a classic, Jacobs is aping a male director, Simon Stone, although Jacobs' subtle directorial intelligence has little in common with Stone's flamboyance.

In the *Australian Book Review*, Ian Dickson thunders: 'Is Hedda simply a psychopath, a narcissist with a tendency towards melodrama, or is she a captive of her era, a woman of strength and intelligence whose fear of scandal has condemned her to a limited, meaningless existence and has warped her judgement? Neither of these questions is answered or indeed even asked in the train wreck that calls itself *Hedda Gabler* at the Belvoir.' Hedda is supposed to be a product of nineteenth century society, he says, 'trapped by social convention', which becomes meaningless when she's made contemporary. Again, Dickson simply doesn't register the ways in which a contemporary Hedda might be trapped, nor that this production is asking another kind of question, about how the insidious forces of patriarchy distort and ultimately destroy a woman's inner self.

These responses may reflect the feeling I mentioned earlier, that there's a layer missing in this production. But all the same, the questions raised in this *Hedda Gabler* seemed brutally obvious to me. It suggests some of the difficulties of remaking and restaging gender for women and queer artists when most of the modes of critique are themselves deeply inflected by gendered assumptions: the constant frustration of being read through a matrix which erases the very point the work is making.

ABC Arts Online, April 1 2014

Hipbone Sticking Out / Team of Life

For this year's Melbourne Festival, both Big hArt and Kage offer shows created by working with specific communities – in Big hArt's case, the Aboriginal community of the Pilbara town of Roebourne, and in Kage's, Sudanese refugees and young Aboriginals.

Big hArt's *Hipbone Sticking Out* is gobsmacking in its ambition and its achievement, a landmark work of Australian theatre that writes its own rules (and then breaks them). And Kage's show, which encloses itself in a therapeutic technique designed to help traumatised refugees, ends up, despite moments of brilliance, being merely well meaning.

Community theatre foregrounds theatre's essential utopianism. Every work of theatre is, in essence, a social microcosm, as a bunch of disparate people collectively attempts to create a common vision. As in life, sometimes this works brilliantly, and sometimes it doesn't. In the case of community theatre, the work extends into a specific community with the ambition of generating social and individual change that extends beyond the life of the art itself.

Hipbone is one aspect of a four-year-long engagement with the people of Roebourne, the Yijala Yala Project, a multiply-pronged community project that in particular is directed at young at-risk Aboriginals. It's a work of so many dimensions that it's hard to know where to begin.

Hipbone Sticking Out is a rough translation of Murujuga, the Ngayarda language name for the Burrup Peninsula in the Pilbara, site of more than 10,000 rock engravings or petroglyphs that date back 30,000 years. It's also the location of Roebourne, the township where, in September 1983, 16-year-old John Pat (played here by young

Nelson Coppin) died in the police lockup, his brain swelling fatally after a violent confrontation with police. His death sparked the 1987 Royal Commission into Aboriginal Deaths in Custody.

If he were still alive, Pat would now be 47 years old. Trevor Jamieson plays Pat's 47-year-old self, the ghost of what-might-have-been, as he meets Pluto (Lex Marinos), the Roman King of the Underworld and judge of the dead, in the two hours before his death. Pluto is also, as it happens, the god of wealth, especially mineral wealth found underground.

It's a truism that the clearest view of a power structure is always from the bottom, from the point of view of those whose lives are at the mercy of its whims. Big hArt writer and director Scott Rankin, in collaboration with Roebourne's Aboriginal community, takes this notion and runs with it.

The first act is a wickedly funny pantomime of the history of colonisation, witnessed by both John Pats under the guidance of Pluto. When we walk into the theatre, the scrim has a gigantic representation of Brueghel's epic painting *Orpheus in the Underworld*. It's kindly explained to us that in order for white people to relate to Aboriginal stories, it's best to have some kind of European model. What follows is a mischievous meta-theatrical mashup of Bach, Smetana, Britney Spears, Gilbert and Sullivan and many others, often sung in Aboriginal language. The theatre is hilarious; the stories it tells – of slavery, dispossession, disease, exploitation and slaughter – are not so funny.

The second half narrows its focus to Roebourne, and addresses contemporary ills, such as the Northern Territory Intervention and the alienations of young Indigenous people, now properly seen as the latest in a long narrative of dispossession. The huge cast includes Roebourne people, and the night I went, John Pat's mother was in the audience. The picaresque parody shifts to a grim countdown to a boy's death, a death that has been transformed into a symbol of the dispossessions of racism and colonialism, but which is nevertheless the real death of a real person, who is still mourned almost three decades later.

That *Hipbone* manages to keep all these different levels of reality present on stage at the same time is its astonishing achievement. It's extraordinarily generous theatre: funny and tragic, tough and tender, unsentimental, angry and heartbreaking. The show generates its complex emotional impact from its very literal enactment of *maragutharra*, the Yindjibarndi word for 'working together', and it's explicitly addressed to a white audience. It says, this isn't our history: this is *your* history. And it is, told as clearly and passionately as I've seen.

Kage's *Team of Life* is wan in comparison. The show emerges from a program of the same name developed by David Denborough, the brother of Kate Denborough, artistic director of Kage. The Team of Life therapy uses narrative-based techniques, and in particular sporting metaphors, to help young refugees, particularly former child soldiers, as they adjust to Australian society. The show itself incorporates young Indigenous people, and uses the common languages of soccer and Australian Rules football to generate a metaphor for an integrated community.

Kate Denborough's strength is in creating expressive physical movement on the borders between dance and theatre. The opening is thrilling: a recorded monologue is broadcast in darkness, a stark narration of David Nyuol Vincent's experiences as a child soldier in Sudan. A spotlight snaps open in the huge space of the Merlyn, illuminating a young woman (Kiki Kuol) reading a newspaper. She's joined by a young man (David Nyuol Vincent), who takes off his sock. Together they screw up the newspaper and stuff it into the sock, which is skilfully transformed into a soccer ball. This the cue for a dance sequence, in which sport movement is integrated into dance, with some awesome soccer skills.

The set is dominated by three shiny four-wheel utes, which attract the eye but end up just being stage furniture since they are never used, and a caravan front stage, which is the set for the domestic sub-story that punctuates the more abstract movement. On the plus side, this sub-story occasions some spine-tingling singing from Kutcha Edwards. On the downside, these dialogues, written by David Denborough, are clumsily integrated with the dance, and in their banality sometimes get perilously close to the 'poverty porn' that is mercilessly mocked by Trevor Jamieson in *Hipbone*.

The particularities and complexities of the issues of Indigenous dispossession, child soldiers and refugees are blurred into a feel-good plot in which everyone ends up watches the Grand Final together. We are reminded that 'it's more than just a game'. At the end, I felt all the issues the show intended to address became subordinate to the therapy. It's hard to entirely dislike a work so overtly well-meant, and it has undeniable moments of brilliance; but *Team of Life's* splintered focus and clumsy dramaturgy ultimately betray its own intentions.

ABC Arts Online, October 20 2014

Cut The Sky

There's no getting around the fact that climate change is the issue of our time. It's a problem that encompasses every facet of our lives, from our domestic habits to global politics. One of the reasons why it's difficult to process, quite apart from the difficulty of extending our individual senses of mortality to imagining our extinction as a species, is its complexity.

Everything that climate change touches is complex: the science, the politics, the economics, the contradictory collective and individual responses of human beings. Addressing the challenges and uncertainties of climate change in a work of art demands a concomitant complexity. Not to mention a great deal of ambition.

So all respect to Broome-based dance company Marrugeku, which tackles climate change head on in its most recent work *Cut The Sky*, which premiered at this year's Perth Festival. *Cut The Sky* frames its argument through an Indigenous perspective, articulated through the poems of Edwin Lee Mulligan and its focus on the 1979 Noonkanbah protests, when the US company AMAX, escorted by hundreds of police, forced its way through Yungngora community pickets to drill for oil on sacred land.

As I walked out, I thought I had seen nothing like it; but it's difficult to describe precisely why this is so. Cross-disciplinary collaborations are common in theatre, and it's not remarkable that dance, video, poetry and song should all collide in a single work.

Cut The Sky is, like climate change itself, at once local and international, and this concept is embedded in the collaboration itself. The creative team stretches to Belgium, with associates of Belgium's les ballet C de la B as core creators. As well as Marrugeku's Rachael Swain (concept and direction) and Dalisa Pigram (concept and choreography), there is choreography from Serge Aimé Coulibaly and dramaturgy (Hildegard De Vuyst). The influence of les ballet C de la B is clear in the vocabulary of the dance, a theme of neurotic, broken movement that expresses human and environmental damage.

There are original songs from soul singer Ngaiire and Indigenous songs as well as covers from Nick Cave and Buffalo Springfield, sung live with thrilling effect by Ngaire Pigram in a poison green corset. The video design encompasses the literal – broad sweeps of country, the devastation after a cyclone – and the poetic. There is the speaking of poems, direct and honest recitations from Edwin Lee Mulligan that weave traditional knowledge with contemporary anxieties. And, of course, there's superb dance.

All these elements – popular and high art, literal and poetic, Indigenous and European – are jammed together into a breathtaking 70 minutes, each at once clashing against the others and creating electric connections. The transition from one mode of performance to the next is often jarring, even deliberately crude, but it's always exciting. If it's true, as Peter Brook said, that theatre is about contrast, then this show is as theatrical as it gets.

It's performed on a set by Stephen Curtis which gives the sense, like the workaday costumes, of being put together from materials to hand. The set is bare aside from a gas pipeline thrusting up from the floor of the stage. Backstage is hung a huge length of fabric, its folds visible, which serves as a screen for projections.

The dance moves through five acts, beginning, like *The Tempest*, in the middle of a storm. It moves back and forward in time, touching on conflict with mining companies, the destruction of fauna and abnegation of the marginalised, the perfidy of a state that demands that its subjects trust it, while at the same time betraying them.

The intellectual frame is provided by Indigenous mythmaking that warns of the terrifying ambiguity of the natural world, which both gives and destroys. It leads to an astonishing finale that evokes both catastrophe and plenty. I was surprised at the end when only six cast members took their bows: they had so filled the stage with their presences that it seemed there must be more. Exhilarating and original work.

ABC Arts Online, March 6 2015

MTC Neon (Shit and We Get It) / Birdland / Love and Information

Sometimes you need reminding.

It's been a while since I walked out of the theatre with that surge of white hot elation that tells you that you've just seen something amazing. Making theatre is such a complex tissue of variables: so many people, so many ideas, so many aspects of craft and art must integrate in an instant of time, their presences at once autonomous and collectively coherent, that sometimes it seems a miracle that theatre occurs at all.

I hadn't realised how much I had missed that excitement until I saw the Melbourne Theatre Company's production of *Birdland*, Simon Stephens' dark parable about celebrity and the neoliberal self, at the beginning of June. An astonishing text, an intelligent, felt production, remarkable performances: the recipe for great theatre is, after all, quite simple. But then it kept on happening.

June was a stellar month in Melbourne theatre. Against the gloomy backdrop of the worst crisis to face Australian culture in decades, it was as if theatre artists decided to pull out all stops and demonstrate exactly what is threatened. The truth is that we have something remarkable here: a passionate artistic community and an engaged culture that every now and then produces extraordinary work that illuminates the joys and terrors of our times.

One hesitates to use the word 'excellent' these days, but if excellence is what we're striving for, then our theatre is doing something right. June saw four first-class productions that demonstrate the range, skill and commitment of Australian theatre-makers. There were two productions of major British plays – Simon Stephens' *Birdland*, directed by Leticia Cáceres at the Melbourne Theatre Company, and Caryl Churchill's *Love and Information*, directed by Kip Williams for Malthouse/Sydney Theatre Company. Both of them are about as good productions of these texts as you can imagine, and made me think wistfully of how comparatively poor we are at supporting local writers in our theatre.

And then, as if on cue, along came the two final productions of the Neon Festival of Independent Theatre: Patricia Cornelius' elegantly raw, poetically devastating *Shit*, brilliantly directed by Susie Dee, and the exhilarating wit and anger of Elbow Room's *We Get It*. No, it's not as if we don't have the writers. We do. And sometimes they do get the productions they deserve.

❖ ❖ ❖

Birdland is a contemporary version of Bertolt Brecht's first play, *Baal*. In Brecht's play, which remains disconcertingly cruel almost a century after it was written, the myth of male genius is stripped of its romanticism and exposed as an amoral, thoughtlessly exploitative, relentlessly misogynistic narcissism. Stephens follows the Rake's Progress of Brecht's play, but situates his rock star Paul in the context of a morally bankrupt Europe in which the only value is money. It's an argument that has particular poignancy in the midst of the Greek crisis.

Paul, played by Mark Leonard Winter, is the direct product of neoliberal nihilism. Early in the play he's interviewed by a journalist and explains, with a kind of ecstasy, that the significance of his music can be measured exactly by how many people are prepared to pay for it. The seduction of this brutal reduction of human experience to abstract numbers is the abyss that underlies the action of the play. As a star that sells out stadia, who can command his every whim, from women to peaches, Paul needs no justification.

Through a series of swiftly enacted, fluid scenes, we witness his cruelties, his boredom, his betrayals, until at last he is himself betrayed by the values he himself upholds and epitomises. But there is no pat moral at the centre of this play, more an appalled witnessing of a particular phenomenon. Perhaps what's most uncomfortable about Paul is his intelligence, the perceptiveness that permits him to be so exquisitely cruel. The writing is scarifyingly free, rising from intimacy to heights of poetic grandeur with a sense of impeccable sureness.

Its various levels of speech and its shifting realities makes *Birdland* a challenging play to produce, but Cáceres and her team are equal to it. The centre of its achievement is Mark Leonard Winter's icily mercurial performance as Paul, as astonishing a feat of acting as I have seen. But he is the centre of a faultless ensemble: Michala Banas, Bert LaBonté, Socratis Otto, Anna Samson and Peta Sergeant, playing various roles, the mirrors through which we see the damned emptiness of Paul's existence.

Every aspect of the production – lights, costumes, sound – is unobtrusively stylish. Marg Horwell's set is a rehearsal room, creating a fluid, spare space in which banal objects are constantly repurposed, and which foregrounds it as a work of theatre. Cáceres direction moves quickly and lucidly, establishing its language of movement early, so the play is at once lifted out of naturalism into the poetic. It's the most searingly intelligent production of a text I've seen this year.

Or so I thought until the following week at the Malthouse, when I saw Kip Williams' production of Caryl Churchill's 2012 play, *Love and Information*, now playing at the Sydney Theatre Company. This again is a challenging text on the page: it's written as a series of more than 70 modular, self-contained scenes, arranged in seven acts. The director can shift the order of the scenes inside each act, but the order of the acts is set. There is another series of sixteen optional scenes that can be included if desired.

At 76, Churchill remains at the top of her game. *Love and Information* feels breathtakingly contemporary, a textural portrait of human consciousness in the speed of modernity and the age of instant information. We are, as one scene which lists the alphabetic code of DNA underlines, analogues of information of all kinds. Given the fragilities of memory and communication, what is relationship? So what is it, this thing called love? How do we know it?

Each of these scenes is a glimpse of the ordinary: a conversation at a party, in a restaurant, between couples, between strangers. A couple only consist of a single line of dialogue. These are glimpses across imposed divisions of class, race and sexuality – one of the reasons this production feels so contemporary is its glancing senses of the diversity of human beings. The achievement of Williams' direction is, again, how the fluid intelligence of the ensemble – the cast and the production crew – meets Churchill's writing, generating a cumulative poetic resonance around the trivial bafflements of our lives.

It's performed at lightning speed by an extraordinary ensemble – Marco Chiappi, Harry Greenwood, Glenn Hazeldine, Anita Hegh, Zahra Newman, Anthony Taufa, Ursula Yovich and Alison Whyte – on a bare stage furnished with moveable white blocks. What makes this production compelling is its painstaking detail. Each scene generates its own biography in seconds, in the details of costumes and props and performances, creating the sense of a larger narrative before and beyond it. The production has the sparkle of constant ingenuity, and moves seamlessly from the comic to the beautiful to moments of unbearable poignancy. Chiappi's portrayal of a man in the grip of Alzheimer's, for instance, just breaks your heart.

Patricia Cornelius' latest play, *Shit* (which opened the following week), is a study in contrast. Cornelius is a stalwart of independent theatre, as is her long-time collaborator, the criminally underrated Susie Dee. In *Shit*, they offer us a raw, powerful play, an excoriating examination of the intersections of class and misogyny. It's a companion piece to Cornelius' lauded play *Savages*, which looked at relationships between men, and for my money is the more refined work.

As with *Savages*, Cornelius employs choral dialogue and repetition to create a compelling poetry out of the speech of the everyday. It opens, characteristically, with a comic dialogue about the semiotics of the word 'fuck'. It's a commonplace that swearing means a diminishing of consciousness: Cornelius calls this into question in a very Australian way, demonstrating how meaning exists in usage, and how vocabulary and lack of education is no indicator of intelligence. It also introduces the aggression and defiance of her three characters, Billy, Bobby and Sam, played by Peta Brady, Sarah Ward and Nicci Wilks.

These women are trouble. It's clear that they have been in trouble all their lives, beginning with being born. A narrative begins to emerge through a series of scenes: we understand that they are in prison for a crime they committed together, that they have bounced from foster homes to institutions and back again, that they have all been sexually abused.

We aren't asked to pity them: it is very clear that these women don't pity themselves. Their defiant inexcusability is part of the reason why this play, for all its bleakness – and it is very bleak, refusing any consolation – is paradoxically exhilarating. It's at once a fierce denunciation of the damage of a society in which femaleness is rendered as second class, forcing the sexual competitiveness that causes women to destroy each other, and a celebration of human resistance.

Susie Dee's production, designed again by Marg Horwell, energises the text, emphasising its poetic diction with an abstract and muscular physicality. The stage is dominated by a giant wall, pierced with three windows, which stands forestage. We can see backstage via a huge convex mirror, like those seen on railway platforms. It creates a brooding sense of claustrophobia and permits the performance to move lithely from private to public spaces, and from interior and heightened language to more naturalistic dialogue. The performances themselves are full on and abrasive, almost amounting at times to an assault. You walk out feeling as if you haven't quite breathed for the duration of the show.

Shit is a show impelled by anger, alive to the structural injustices of the society in which we live. So too, in a very different way, is the final show of the MTC's Neon season, *We Get It*. This, by independent company Elbow Room, is co-written by Marcel Dorney and Rachel Perks, and co-directed by Dorney and Emily Tomlins, who also offers a central performance. As with all the theatre I've discussed, it's characterised by dynamic, supple and uncompromising intelligence.

The first half hour is laugh out loud funny. It exploits the template of reality television, revisiting the manipulative tropes we know and love/hate so well: the humiliating exposure, the gross exertion of power, the crass appeal to audiences. I particularly enjoyed the opening, a witty inversion of the male gaze. Emily Tomlins, in an intimidating blonde wig, high heels and white suit, is the host, haranguing her five finalists. Maurial Spearim, Amy Ingram, Kasia Kaczmarek, Tamiah Bantum and Sonya Suares are competing to perform one of five classic female monologues (written by men): Antigone, Medea, Lady Macbeth, Nora Helmer and Blanche DuBois.

The contestants are put through their paces in a series of humiliating scrambles in which they are asked to rank themselves according to increasingly insulting criteria: 'Most Neurotic', 'Most Likely To Hang Herself'. They are asked intrusive questions that they are supposed to answer in character, but which begin to blur the borderline between character and actor. In the solitude of a *Big Brother* 'diary room' they perform monologues to the camera which are projected on stage, and which have a desolating personal edge. And, one by one, they each get to perform their chosen scene from a classic play.

What gets exposed, with a sense of real weight and complexity, are the structural inequalities that underline our society. Sexism and racism are pitilessly excavated through the trivial behaviours and mediated representations that reinforce them. Gradually the misogynistic and racist frame of the reality show begins to disintegrate. Emily Tomlins finally rebels against the earpiece that silently instructs her, refusing her complicity in this cruel reality, prompting one of the show's highlights: a monologue in which she is stripped both literally and metaphorically naked.

Perhaps most subversively of all, the monologues are performed with real skill and feeling, opening up the teasing ambiguity of performance: these imaginary women might reinforce all kinds of stereotypes about the female sex but within them, if it is unleashed, exists a genuine possibility of revolt. The final monologue, from *Antigone*, is performed by Indigenous actor Maurial Spearim, who comments kindly, when told that the play is 2,500 years old, that she is a fan of 'new theatre'. It becomes a stirring speech against the endemic injustices against Aboriginal Australia.

We Get It is a passionate, smart and surprisingly raw attack on a society in which inequalities of sex, race and class structure almost every aspect of our lives. Its savagery reflects the invisible brutalities we encounter every day, directly and indirectly. Its makers decline to provide any answers: the hope is in the vision of these five people at the end, standing in front of us as themselves, for the moment liberated from the labels that enclose and inhibit them. Its invitation is that we cease our own enabling collusions. It's political theatre at its best.

ABC Arts Online, 14 July 2015

Antigone

Last month, a grim drama played out on the Habur border between Turkey and Iraqi Kurdistan. Amid simmering tensions between Ankara and the Kurdistan Worker's Party, a truck carrying the bodies of thirteen Kurdish men and women killed fighting Islamic State was refused permission to cross into Turkey, where grieving relatives were awaiting to bury their dead.

In searing 50 degree heat, distraught families protested against the government for ten days, until finally the government relented and let the truck through. 'I want my son to have a grave', said Abdurrahman Pusat, the father of one of the fighters. 'He is a citizen of Turkey and not any other country.'

The passions unleashed on that border are a contemporary enactment of the conflicts of Sophocles' tragedy, *Antigone*. Here, written in new blood, is the profound need to mourn the dead, pitted against the stark authority of the state; the questions of what it means to be a citizen, and what it means when citizenship can be revoked, even in death. The Turkish opposition leader might have been quoting Antigone herself when he said, 'People have the right to demand respect for their dead, no matter how they have died.'

Two millennia after it was written, *Antigone* remains a strange and terrible story, shocking in the brutal simplicity of its argument. The sister wants to bury her criminal brother, but the state forbids her: in choosing to defy the state, she destroys both the state and herself. But given its contemporary resonances, it's no wonder that this story is enacted over and over again.

This year I've seen two very different renditions, both written by classicists: Adena Jacobs' production at Malthouse Theatre, adapted by Jane Montgomery Griffiths, and Anne Carson's translation for Ivo van Hove's production, which I saw in Paris at the Théâtre de la Ville and which recently played at the Edinburgh Festival.

Carson's is a close rendering of Sophocles written especially for van Hove, while Montgomery Griffiths has adapted the play into a tautly poetic contemporary text; but both productions summon this ancient tragedy into the present. In both cases, the artists were prompted to re-enact the play by the violence of contemporary events: in van Hove's case, the death of a member of his company in the shooting down of MH370 over Ukraine; in Montgomery Griffiths', the dark dehumanisation of the police state that increasingly defines global politics.

For all their differences, they have striking similarities. Both highlight the play's original function as a moral and legal argument between opposing, irreconcilable forces. The old truism of tragedy is that it is a clash of right against right, but by the end of both nights I felt I had witnessed the clash of wrong against wrong, the outlining of a human dilemma made intractable by the authoritarianism of patriarchy.

Both Carson and Montgomery Griffiths underline the play as a condemnation of the very premise of patriarchy. Antigone (Juliette Binoche in van Hove's, Emily Milledge in Jacobs') is loyal to her treacherous brother, but in her defiance is the narcissism of martyrdom, an extremity nourished by a society in which her own sex has no authority outside the imprimatur of her male relations. Both productions draw Creon as the ruthlessly authoritarian CEO of Thebes Inc. And both emphasise the slow-burning rhythms of ritual, gathering up the emotional weight of tragedy to spill its power into the present.

But in other ways, they are night and day. In Carson's version, the indictment of patriarchal authority is written with a classical clarity: to be bested by a woman is, to Creon, the very definition of a threat to state power. Montgomery Griffiths recasts Creon as a female Leader, folding the character of Creon's wife, Eurydice, into the body of the king, which makes the argument darker and more ambiguous. The Leader is an Athena figure who has rejected the Furies – the matriarchal goddesses who pursued Orestes with the laws of blood vengeance – and has donned the rational armour of the patriarchal state. Think Margaret Thatcher, Julie Bishop, Hilary Clinton.

Ivo van Hove's actors play across a stage decorated like a hotel foyer, the anonymous luxury of contemporary power. Above the stage hangs a disc, both a sun and a moon, which every now and then cusps into eclipse. The bare backstage is a screen on which play unfocused projections of wilderness, or urban landscapes, or even, at one stage, home videos. The colours are desert, sun-drenched, dry and sterile. In contrast, Adena Jacobs' stark set, broodingly lit by Paul Jackson, emerges out of darkness. Above a sterile, grey floor looms a ship's container on stilts, the office of a detention centre. Van Hove gives us the sumptuous costumes of power, while Jacobs shows us the ugliness of its guts.

And there's a significant difference in how they treat the relationship of past and present. Hove runs the classical play in parallel with the present on the ahistorical space of the stage: the production, through its design and performance, does the work of bringing Antigone and Creon's tragedy ever closer to the present, until it unites in a postscript which opens up from the play's action into a bird's eye view of a contemporary city projected on the back wall as the actors dissolve from their characters into anonymous, mundane tasks – washing up, typing letters, answering phones – in the foreground.

Jacobs' approach pushes the tragedy at once further into the past and more brutally into the present: past and present at once rupture and illuminate each other throughout the performance, enacting these ancient arguments with a visceral force that makes it impossible not to feel their pertinence to now. It's almost operatic, driven by music as well as text.

Two passages are sung in the original Greek, scenes of spine-chilling beauty that emerge from the terrible action on stage to bring us as close to the experience of classical Greek tragedy as we are likely to get. Jethro Woodward's brilliant score is as much a player as the actors themselves, making sound a material thing: its pulsing percussion and tense lyric cuts against breathing silences. It's a fierce, unforgettable production. I'm quite sure I didn't move for the duration of the show.

And for me, it's Jacobs' production that will linger in the memory, and which most truly cuts tragedy back to the nightmare of history, then and now. Here the gods are absent. In Sophocles' play, the gods are the engines of destiny, the dispensers of capricious justice, the transcendent poles of morality. Without them, human justice has no higher authority; it hangs in an abyss, to be argued out in an unforgiving court. Their only hint is in the scraps of sung Greek, but the gods summoned in those poems are hidden from us by language and time; they are echoes that ring obscurely through a dark present, as does the play itself.

Next to this stern invocation, van Hove's production looks a little sentimental. The body of Polynices is rather thanklessly played by a pretty actor who has no other role, and a long passage where Antigone pours libations and strews earth on her dead brother is a kind of lyrical nostalgia. The play ends with Creon's grief, deleting the Chorus' final homily: in his sorrow is a hinted redemption, even hope: he has learned his lesson, perhaps, and will go on to be a wise tyrant. Montgomery Griffiths' much more radical rewriting gives us no such redemption. Her Creon goes the way of Jean Anouilh's retelling, with Creon getting on with the business of state. 'They say it's dirty work', says Anouilh's Creon. 'But if you don't do it, who will?'

Jacobs' production, with its emphasis on the body – rotting in death, suffering in life – has no tint of nostalgia. It reminds us that in the centre of the tragedy of *Antigone* is the body. It opens with a functionary (Josh Price) slowly stepping down a flight of ugly steps, a naked body over his shoulders, which he casts onto the ground. We don't know if it is Polynices or Antigone: it becomes clear, when she stands and speaks, that it is both of them, that Antigone has already folded her brother's death into her living flesh.

In David Greene's standard translation of *Sophocles*, the body of Polynices is left 'moist and naked' for the scavengers of carrion. Jacobs and Montgomery Griffiths insist that we are aware of this decay and liquefaction: the body oozes, its borders porous, like the threatened borders of the state. Even the stage liquifies as we watch, a dark trickle of fluid – blood? tainted water? – deepening as the bodies mount. This production insists on the reality of those bodies in the truck in Habur: it summons the stench of death, the rawness of grief, the unhealable wounds that are everywhere about us.

At the beginning of the play neither Antigone nor Creon hold any doubt of her rightness: they are mirrors of each other. But both of them are forced to face the abyss that their certainties conceal. The Leader, claiming to protect her state above all else, destroys her own son, her lineage and her future. At last, neither a mother nor father, driven beyond the possibility of language, she runs in a blind panic, tearing at her clothes, until she is on the verge of collapse. And then, slowly, resolutely, she again dons the patriarchal armour of her role. But now, as she speaks her law, it is emptied of meaning: the state is merely an exhausted repetition that upholds only itself.

Antigone has a parallel fate. Rejecting her sister, her only living sibling, for her dead brother, she is rebuked for her extremity, for only seeing things in black and white. She also endures her certainties collapsing into their own contradictions. 'I am', she says, as she faces burial alive in Anne Carson's version, 'a strange new kind of in-between thing'. In Jacobs' production, this liminal state is translated into an awful image: a torturer is to harvest her body parts, so she will live on in others despite her own death. This, the destruction of all symbolic order, all certain borders, is the true horror.

There is no stable identity anywhere in this production: all bodies are porous, 'in between', ambiguous. Her eyes excised by the torturer, Antigone becomes not only her father Oedipus, his eyes plucked out so he does not have to see his own fate, but the blind prophet Tiresias, who foretells Creon's bleak future. She turns a bandaged face that recalls the classical tragic mask and then sings, in ancient Greek, Antigone's lament before she is walled-up alive. The final image is her body, swinging in the air.

We are left in the ruins of patriarchy, without gods, without justice. It is this dissolution of certainty, the dissolving of bodies corporeal and politic, that is the source of terror: the terror of the rebel who defies the laws of the city; the terror of the state, the torturer slyly obliterating the body in pain, destroying even language itself; the terror of the self undone by death. Somehow this production touches that source, leaving it open. It's great, unforgiving theatre, that looks the horror of our times squarely in the face.

ABC Arts Online, September 1 2015

Asking For It: A One-Lady Rape About Comedy Starring Her Pussy and Little Else.

Of all the stereotypes of feminists bandied about – the hairy legs (often very guilty), the man-hating (#notallmen) – the one about feminist humourlessness puzzles me most. Sure, feminists tend to find things like family violence, pay disparity and intimate partner murder distinctly unfunny. And of course there are feminists who don't have a funny bone in their bodies. But compared to the number of Men's Rights Activists who appear to have had an irony bypass at birth – by definition, all of them – they are a distinct minority.

In my experience, feminist women are very funny indeed. Since 1600, when the Venetian poet Moderata Fonte asked in disbelief why anybody would believe anything male historians said about men or women since men 'never tell the truth, except by accident', wit has been a significant part of a woman's armoury against sexism.

Adrienne Truscott, half of the cabaret duo Wau Wau Sisters, is no exception. From the moment she first appears, naked from the waist down, in three improbably blonde wigs, denim jacket and high heels, her daffy persona is planting comedic depth charges. This is a show that takes no prisoners, and yet, at the same time, it's curiously gentle.

As the title indicates, Truscott is talking about rape. She begins brashly: 'Hands up anyone who has been raped!' Of course, despite the statistical likelihood that there will be women who have been sexually assaulted in the audience, no-one stirs. 'Ok. Hands up anyone who has raped!' Again, the statistical likelihood is that the audience would include a rapist. But this time the question has knives.

As the American humorist Erma Bombeck once observed, 'There is a thin line that separates laughter and pain'. A lot of women's humour emerges from the anguish of sexual violence, both overt and covert. The pain of women has very often been erased from comedy, where women, in a heavily male-dominated industry, have been the traditional object, not the subject, of jokes. Think of the endless punchlines about mother-in-laws, nagging wives, dumb blondes. And nowhere is this more clear than in the debate around rape jokes.

Truscott's show circles around the debate that occurred when US comedian Daniel Tosh 'joked' how hilarious it would be if a woman audience member who objected to his comedy were gang raped by five men 'right now'. The subsequent furore shaped the debate as humourless PC feminists seeking to censor the free speech of comedians.

But, as Truscott argues in this show, this is the wrong framing. Of course a large part of comedy is crucially about trampling on taboos: but the defining aspect of comedy is that it is funny. It's supposed to touch the sweet spot in our anxieties and release as actual laughter.

And maybe, just maybe, it isn't that edgy or transgressive to echo the misogyny embraced by politicians such as Republican Todd Akin, who notoriously claimed women don't get pregnant if they are 'legitimately raped' because 'the female body has ways to try to shut that whole thing down'. (Like ducks, apparently.)

The most telling aspect of Tosh's joke is that it isn't remotely funny. Nor, if the YouTube videos I've watched of Tosh's 'edgy' humour are anything to go by, are the rape jokes that prompted the woman's objections. The debate about rape jokes might be more accurately characterised as an argument about lazily using offensive stereotypes for cheap shock value. And something more sinister: the tacit acceptance of sexual violence against women.

Truscott has a sequence where she imagines raping a man after slipping him a drug ('Such hard work, you guys!') which is equal parts hilarious and horrifying, and which illustrates the brutal transgression and erasure of rape as effectively as anything I've seen. The men next to me were shifting a little uncomfortably, but women were in stitches. Maybe the projection of this act onto a male body by a woman was too outrageous; maybe it brought home what those anodyne words 'date rape' might actually mean.

But it's all done, paradoxically, with the lightest of touches. Truscott's faux-naïve persona lets her get away with the most outrageous of transgressions: she's an entirely likeable stage presence. And she's funny because she's reaching into actual pain, opening it up so we can laugh, rather than using comedy as a means to anaesthetise ourselves against it. Maybe it's not, as Truscott says, the ideal show for a first date, but it's the kind of show you wish everyone could see. Especially men.

ABC Arts Online, 11 September 2015

Watching Xavier Le Roy: Self Unfinished at Dancehouse, Melbourne

Here is a man. He wears a grey shirt, trousers, sneakers. He sits, his hands flat on the table in front of him, like a man who is tired after work. He might be any middle-class, middle-aged white man, slender, greying, tall. His hands are precisely placed. He is very still.

He bends his torso forward over the table, making a noise with his mouth as if he is a child being a plane or a truck, and stops abruptly. He moves closer to the horizontal, until his nose almost touches the table, making the noise again. He is a machine at play. His elbow goes up and down. He stands up and walks, each movement angular, articulated, each movement with its different pneumatic sound. When he moves his head, he beeps like a backing truck. He is absurd. He is very serious. He is very funny. I want to laugh but nobody is laughing.

He walks to the ghetto blaster and presses the button. Silence. Somewhere outside the theatre, a little distance away, a dog is barking.

Here is a man. He is walking backwards, very slowly. He makes no noise now. He creates an anatomy of walking, lifting his heel, placing down his toe. He is very precise.

He stands, facing the white wall. He is very still. His ears. His back.

He walks to the ghetto blaster and presses a button. Silence. The dog is still barking. Birdsong. Traffic. Someone in the theatre laughs.

Here is a man. He takes off his grey shirt over his head. Underneath is a black t-shirt. He lifts it up over his head as if he is stripping it off, but when it covers his head he stops. He is trapped in his shirt. He bends over until his hands touch the ground.

He slips off his shoes.

Here is a man folded in half. Now he is two pairs of legs, connected by a naked torso. The legs walk, all four of them, every movement articulate. This animal is blind. A long, preposterous man creature. It stands up and feels its way across the back wall with its feet-hands. Is it looking for something? How can it find anything, with no head? It crawls under the table and kicks off the table top. It kicks over the chair.

Here is a man. He pulls down his black t-shirt over his legs. It is a long, black, stretchy dress, quite elegant. He sits down and crosses his legs and rolls on his back. He grasps his feet with his hands. He is not a man, he is a knot. He rolls his torso upside down and tucks his head out of our sight. He wriggles off the dress. He rolls off his underpants.

There is a mole right in the middle of his back. His skin is flushed with physical strain. This is a naked man, but he is not displaying his nakedness. It is simply unclothed flesh. He has no head that we can see.

Here is a man, but we are no longer sure if it is a man at all. We know it is a man but our perception keeps tripping over him. Living flesh, skin, limbs. Fists that look like alien faces. What is the difference between an arse and a shoulder? What are legs if you walk on your neck? It's a huge, plucked turkey, its wings splayed out. No, it's a swaying torso with the feet of a child. It's a lump of flesh with no face. It creeps like a mollusc, a new eyeless flesh species. It's alive.

Finally the man unfolds himself. Red pressure marks on his shoulders, his neck. Weals.

Here is a man who is getting dressed. His jeans, his shirts, his shoes. He reassembles the table. He sits down. He walks. He lies down. He sits at the table. He walks. He lies down. He sits at the table, very still. Days pass before our eyes.

Here is a man who is alone. He is very still. He is very precise.

He walks to the ghetto blaster and presses a button. Diana Ross.

He walks out, fast, free.

Miscellany, Tumblr, December 5 2015

Miss Julie

Strindberg. How do you solve a problem like August? In his own time he was considered extreme. When Strindberg gave *Miss Julie* to his publisher Joseph Seligmann in 1888, Seligmann insisted it be cut to make it more palatable for the Swedish public. The play wasn't published uncensored until 1984. In the nineteenth century, *Miss Julie*, a chamber play in which the daughter of an aristocratic estate is seduced by her father's valet, was thought scandalous for its frank articulations of sexual desire, bestiality and menstruation. (Strindberg may be the only canonical playwright to mention periods.)

Now, of course, sexuality isn't nearly so scandalous. These days Strindberg is on the nose because of his toxic misogyny. There's no avoiding it, in his writing or in his life. Strindberg's relentless misogyny makes Michael Meyer's excellent biography miserable reading. In his attitudes to the 'woman question', Strindberg was influenced by Darwinism and, of course, Nietzsche, but he gave these ideas his own pathological spin.

Strindberg's contempt for the 'inferior' sex, his envy and hatred of the power that he claimed feminine weakness and manipulativeness exercised over the trammelled strength of men, is uncomfortably reminiscent of the kinds of statements you find from Men's Rights Activists in the less savoury corners of the internet. And exactly as with its twenty-first century manifestations, Strindberg's misogyny was a reaction to contemporary feminism, the 'new push' by women for equal rights.

Miss Julie is a case in point. Strindberg describes his nominal character as a 'new' creature, 'a half-woman born of a half-woman'. By this he means that Miss Julie is the daughter of a feminist, a woman who cuckolded her aristocratic husband, made the estate a laughing stock by reversing gender roles among their servants, and finally burned down her own house in revenge for her slave status as a wife. Miss Julie and her mother are in fact prototypes of that bogeywoman beloved by MRAs, the man-hating feminist.

In this, as in so many other ways, Strindberg was an uncannily prescient forerunner of modernity. If he were merely a misogynist, he wouldn't be worth remembering; but he was also a visionary theorist of theatre. He invented chamber theatre, a reaction against the artifice of the Romantic theatre that dominated Europe in his day. His notion of 'intimate theatre' is what we think of now as standard: small audiences, intimate performance, emotional and behavioural truthfulness. Reading his endless notes, letters and theoretical speculations, you are constantly struck by his restless insights, many of which remain cogent more than a century after they were written. And his plays still exert a dark fascination.

So, to return to my original question: how do you solve a problem like Strindberg? Well, you don't do what Kip Williams does in his production of *Miss Julie* for the Melbourne Theatre Company: scrub him clean and render him up as Mr Nice. Strindberg was many things, horrific and wonderful, often both at once: but never nice.

Barry Jacobs, one of Strindberg's many translators, says implacably: 'There can be no excuse for literary translators who themselves distort Strindberg's text in an attempt to clarify the subtext… or to force their own interpretation onto the original.' Yet this is precisely what has happened in this production. Williams' interpretation distorts *Miss Julie* so egregiously, it makes you wonder why he wanted to direct the play in the first place. It transforms a vicious play about class and sexuality into a variety of soft porn.

On paper, this is a production with all the right ingredients. Williams is one of Australia's most talented young directors, seen most recently in Melbourne with his startlingly intelligent production for Malthouse/Belvoir of Caryl Churchill's *Love and Information*. He's backed by a design dream team: lighting by Paul Jackson, sound design and composition by THE SWEATS, set and costumes by Alice Babidge. These are some of the best people in their fields, and the result is sumptuous. I spent much of the show admiring Jackson's lighting, which is no less than exquisite.

The casting is equally impressive, with Robin McLeavy, Mark Leonard Winter and Zahra Newman, again some of our best performance talent, as, respectively, Miss Julie, Jean and Christine. There's no doubt they give of their best, but the energies they generate on stage are fatally compromised, most notably by a bowdlerised text which attempts to make Strindberg's misogyny more appetising for contemporary audiences.

It's a production marked by half-baked decisions. The action takes place in an uber-naturalistic nineteenth century kitchen that's enclosed in a perspex box, surrounded by the amorphous black space of the rest of the stage. When the play opens, the kitchen is hidden by a huge screen, on which is projected the introductory moments of the show. At first it appears to be a prerecorded movie, but when the screen lifts, to settle above the set, we realise that the action is being filmed live by half-seen cameras moving outside the box. This video plays continuously through the show, creating a doubled performance, projected and live.

After Benedict Andrews and Simon Stone, glass boxes and filmed action are pretty much clichés of the wunderkind director doing the classics. Used well, these tropes can contribute powerfully to a troubling and alienating sense of voyeurism. Andrews' 2007 production of *The Season at Sarsaparilla*, for instance, put screens either side of the stage, which flickered into our consciousness to show distorted, oblique close-ups of the actors in intimate moments: staring into the bathroom mirror, doing the washing up.

In this case, the video seems to be serving a reductive idea of naturalism. With few exceptions, it simply gives us another view of the action in close-up; when the actor has her back to us, for instance, we are able to see her face. Rather than heightening the power of the performances, the effect is to draw the focus away from the warm bodies on stage, diminishing their presence (quite literally: the actors seem tiny in relation to their bloated projections). And it adds little to our understanding.

It seems to me a profound misunderstanding of Strindberg's naturalism, which was a philosophy as much as a stylistic intention. The video acts very much as the 'misconceived naturalism' that Strindberg himself condemned as mere 'photography which includes everything, even the speck of dust on the camera lens'. He specified that the design for *Miss Julie* should be 'impressionistic', because being unable to see all the action 'creates the opportunity for surmise, that is to say, stimulates the imagination to complete the picture'. There is little opportunity for surmise here: everything is laid out plainly for our inspection. Especially, and most deadeningly, our moral stance in relation to the action.

As practised by Strindberg's contemporaries Ibsen and Zola, naturalism was a revolutionary philosophy which sought to illustrate how human behaviour is a product of heredity and environment. *Miss*

Julie is perhaps the play where Strindberg most explores the notion of naturalistic determinism, in which these factors operate in lieu of fate. Both Miss Julie and Jean are shown to be the decadent products of their gender and class. Jean, the son of a peasant, is the up-and-coming capitalist, ambitious and predatory, seeking to replace the aristocracy. Miss Julie, ruined by her feminist upbringing, the scion of a degenerate upper class, disastrously betrays both her feminine nature and her class. Each, as they say in the play, is as bad as the other.

Strindberg loaded *Miss Julie* with contradiction, calling it a 'naturalistic tragedy'. This label has much the same intention as Wordsworth and Coleridge's groundbreaking Romantic publication 'Lyrical Ballads', jamming together two contradictory traditions to create a new artistic tension. Naturalism claims that human behaviour is determined, while tragedy turns on the exercise of free will. And this contradiction is part of the energy behind the action of the play, in the shifting dominance between the two major characters, and in the complex movements of Miss Julie's final decision to suicide.

None of this tension is present in the production. In lieu, we get some anachronistic and gratuitous profanity. It's a superficial gesture that is emblematic of the whole, in which the economical sadism of the text is diluted by crude rewriting. Subtext is brought to the surface, giving us explanations about class or gender which operate as essayistic and, it must be said, banal commentaries on the action. This also has the effect of making these characters more self-aware, as if they're moral allegories rather than characters driven by forces they barely understand. The worst example is the new coda, in which the maid Christine exhorts Miss Julie not to choose the dark side.

Of course it is possible to do violence to the classics and produce new insights. Daniel Schlusser's radical adaptation of *A Doll's House*, for instance, recuperated the original surprise of Ibsen's ending, 'the door slam heard around the world', by staging the bowdlerised ending in which Nora returns. But this kind of transformation requires an agonistic intellectual engagement with the text that Williams' production signally avoids.

It's a waste of the talent that is gathered on this stage. *Miss Julie* is *about* misogyny: to soften the play's ugly heart, to creep pusillanimously around the wounds of class and gender that drive it, is the worst sort of pandering. Perhaps if those questions were dealt with head-on, we might emerge with some insight into the class and gender divisions that bedevil our society now. Without that engagement, why program this play at all?

Australian Book Review, April 16 2016

Neon Festival

Last Friday saw the opening of *The Sovereign Wife*, the final work in the Melbourne Theatre Company's bold foray into independent theatre, the Neon Festival. By noon on Saturday, the show's festival run was sold out. The only hope now to see the anarchic trash camp of Sisters Grimm is a waiting list, or perhaps a season extension.

It underlines the success of Neon. Over ten weeks, the MTC's Lawler Studio has been hosting five of Melbourne's leading indie companies, with a wider program of free masterclasses and public conversations taking place in the Southbank theatre. The result has been 'Bizarro World': the MTC, long a byword for theatrical conservatism, is suddenly a hub for some of the most challenging and exciting new work made in this city.

Neon has enlivened a main stage year which has so far been unusually lacklustre for fans of contemporary theatre. Aside from Neon, the MTC, as is its remit, has presented a conventional season, sneaking in interesting, off-beat plays like Nick Payne's *Constellations* among big-ticket items such as the National Theatre of Great Britain's hugely enjoyable *One Man, Two Guvnors* or an underwhelming production of *The Crucible*. But, as the Neon Festival throws starkly into relief, the real disappointment is down the road, at the Malthouse Theatre.

As the city's second company, the Melbourne equivalent of Sydney's Belvoir St Theatre, the Malthouse is the natural home for new or risky performance. You always expect some dross among the gold, but this year something is badly askew. From the disastrous opening show, a remount of Stephen Sewell's *Hate*, to a second-rate work from Chunky Move in *247 Days*, to the badly judged *Dance of Death*, to the awkwardly adapted Soviet-era play *The Dragon*, the last six months have struck a succession of dud notes. It's been the poorest run I can remember since the Malthouse rebranded itself in 2005.

The quality work at Malthouse has, tellingly, come from small independent companies. Larissa McGowan's dance *Skeleton* was a bright spot during Dance Massive. In the past couple of weeks, two independent remounts – Fraught Outfit's exquisite *Persona*, part of the main stage season, and Sydney-based US-A-UM's *Lord of the Flies* (which opened Helium, the Malthouse's own independent season) – totally outclassed the in-house work. It's no coincidence that they've played to the fullest houses. One can only cross fingers for the remainder of this year, which includes highly anticipated premieres from Back to Back and Michael Kantor.

That independent shows book out demonstrates, if nothing else, that Melbourne audiences have a keen appetite for the formally adventurous, intelligent work that characterises the best of the independent scene. Perhaps this isn't surprising: Melbourne theatre's great strength, from the days of the APG and the Pram Factory, has always been in small collectives. The relationship of these entities to the major institutions in many ways defines the health (or otherwise) of the broader culture.

Neon brought to the MTC a kind of theatre previously unimaginable within its portals. It's been a fascinating ride. From the first two productions – the Daniel Schlusser Ensemble's *Menagerie* and Fraught Outfit's *On the Bodily Education of Young Girls* – the standard has been extraordinarily high.

All the Melbourne companies featured in Neon have things in common – most obviously, a desire to question theatrical conventions, but also a deep engagement with the constructions of gender. But what's been most striking is how different each production has been. After the large casts of the first two shows, The Hayloft Project's *By Their Own Hands* was an exercise in distilled simplicity. Conceived, written, directed and performed by its two creators, Anne-Louise Sarks and Benedict Hardie, it strips bare the mechanics of theatre and lays them out before us with icy clarity.

By Their Own Hands is three distinct tellings of the tragedy of Oedipus. In the first part, the two performers enter, introduce themselves and invite the audience to join them on the bare stage, immediately shifting the expected relationship between watchers and the watched. What follows is the plainest of storytelling: they narrate the bones of the Oedipus story, picking members of the audience out to symbolise different characters – Oedipus, Jocasta, various palace functionaries, Tiresias. Already in this retelling are hints of what has most characterised Hayloft's work to date, notably in the hit *Thyestes*: a fascination with the mundane, unremarked moments between the dramatic climaxes of high tragedy.

In part two the audience returns to its chairs, and the events of Sophocles' play (*Oedipus the King*) are re-enacted as a series of highly stylised mute tableaux. Everything is exposed: we see the actors put on costumes, prepare props, rearrange the stage. These are moments that are off-stage in the play: a brief, vivid glimpse of a wedding, Anne-Louise Sarks as Jocasta meticulously washing the blood from her newborn baby, or a startling moment of erotic intimacy between Jocasta and Oedipus. Most disturbingly, Jocasta hangs herself: even though we watch as Sarks laboriously dons a harness, which is visible throughout the scene, it generates a stomach-tightening anxiety.

The final section is a series of apparently artless and comic conversations between Hardie and Sarks, spoken into two microphones front stage. Here a couple, whom we know to be a contemporary version of Jocasta and Oedipus, discuss the fears and desires of parenthood. The show narrows down to the moment of horrified realisation, that they are at once lovers and mother and son. At the end, language breaks down completely, and we are left with a sobbing moan in the darkness.

The story – given to us, from Sophocles to Freud, as the tragedy of Oedipus – becomes also the tragedy of Jocasta. Jocasta is usually presented as a mere function of Oedipus' suffering: here she has autonomy, as the other half of the story. There's a lightness of touch in the staging that belies its ultimate emotional impact: it's as if, by the end of the performance, your mind has deftly woven together the different elements of storytelling employed in the three parts, bringing them all devastatingly to bear on the final, wordless horror of recognition. Elegant, spare and very beautiful.

Next were The Rabble, who had a hit at last year's Melbourne Festival with their extraordinary take on Virginia Woolf's *Orlando*. The Rabble's creators – designer Kate Davis and director/writer Emma Valente – have long been notable for their imaginative theatricality, which has drawn comparisons with the surreality of Romeo Castellucci's Soc`ietas Raffaello Sanzio, and over the past couple of years their undoubted talent has begun to snap into sharp focus.

For Neon, Valente and Davis adapted Anne Desclos' 1950s bestseller *Story of O*, written as an erotic letter to her lover, the writer Jean Paulhan. I revisited the *Story of O* just before I saw this show, and was taken aback by how confronting Desclos' narrative of self-annihilation remains. It is also, unlike The Rabble's take on it, almost entirely humourless: a Sadean imagining of ecstasy as a means of enlightenment, in which the erasure of the self through sexual humiliation becomes a metaphor for spiritual liberation.

It is also impossible to read outside the lens of gendered expectations, especially the erasure and abuse of women by patriarchal society. The Rabble's solution to this is to have their cake and eat it too: they perform the story, following its inexorable arc to inhuman depersonalisation, and frame it in a queered critique which suspends judgment. Judgment is the audience's business, as was clear in the preview, when reportedly almost a quarter of the audience walked out: but after opening night, *Story of O* seemed to find its place (or perhaps people who read its extensive warnings notice). People still walked, but not en masse, and the season was extended after the show sold out.

Unsurprisingly, *Story of O* generated a hugely divided response. I'm with those who found it stunning, perhaps The Rabble's best show to date. It's a markedly thoughtful work, opening with a lecture from Sir Stephen (written and played by Jane Montgomery Griffiths) which traces the etymology of 'pornography'. 'In English there is no word erotographia – I write my desire,' she says. 'In English, rather, we have the word porn-o-graphia – I write the body of the whore... Consequently, we inscribe our desires on the body of the prostitute, the harlot, the tart, the slattern, the ho... '

This lecture situates *Story of O* not only as fantasy, but as a gendered linguistic creation, conditioned by language itself, in which the phallus is not the cock, but 'words penetrating us and fulfilling our desires'. The word is the medium of transformation. Interestingly, Desclos' dark fantasy is only represented by the action on stage: there's surprisingly little from the book in the text, which is a collage of original writing by Emma Valente and Montgomery Griffiths and excerpts from the Marquis de Sade and surrealist poet Renée Vivien.

Kate Davis' design invokes the peculiarly French romanticism of Desclos' book: the stage is dotted with carousel horses, and the floor is covered in a thin layer of flour, and scattered with flowers. The all-powerful phallus is subversively represented by a series of differently sized rolling pins, at once a symbol of feminine domesticity and also, in countless traditional jokes, the weapon of choice for the shrill housewife. When O (Mary Helen Sassman) is finally masked as an animal, she becomes not an owl but a unicorn, the mythical beast that is a symbol of purity, a favourite emblem of internet kitsch and here, also, a feminised phallus. The ambiguity of the images is reflected in the performances, where the notion of fantasy becomes blurred: these are real bodies before us on stage after all, unmediated by film or imagination.

It's a cumulative, deeply complex work, impeccably performed and directed, that switches on a dime from the confronting to the absurd, the distressing to the hilarious. In exploring these disturbing sexual fantasies, it raises intriguing questions. In her brilliant analysis of Sylvia Plath's poetry, *The Haunting of Sylvia Plath*, Jacqueline Rose suggests that losing the capacity to tell the difference between fantasy and reality may be a psychic injury that makes it impossible to acknowledge trauma, and thus to heal it. Perhaps at its heart, *Story of O* is an argument against the misogynistic literalisation of porn that characterises so much contemporary culture: an attempt to release the liberating energy of desire itself.

The Neon Festival finishes, fittingly enough, with a darkly celebratory piss-take of all things Australian from Sisters Grimm. Co-written by Declan Greene and Ash Flanders and directed by Greene, *The Sovereign Wife* is an unruly epic melodrama in which some of our favourite nationalistic stereotypes are taken apart and exploded as offensively as possible. Here we see our favourite clichés as we have never quite seen them before: the heroic miners of the Eureka Stockade, the faithful Aboriginal farmhand ('his skin was black, but his heart was white, and that's what matters most', as Slim Dusty sang in one of his most famous songs), the lost child, the unforgiving Australian landscape.

Sisters Grimm have generated a loyal following over the past few years for their anarchically funny queer theatre, in which gender is relentlessly foregrounded, inverted and deranged. Here they've broadened the lens, critiquing the racist stereotypes of white colonial culture. Their inspirations range from the early melodramas of Charles Chauvel (as seen in films such as *Jedda*, which promises 'the magic of the native mating call!') to Baz Lurhmann's *Australia*. They do this most obviously through some gloriously inappropriate casting, in which race and sex in this multiracial cast are blithely ignored. Felix Ching Ching Ho, a small woman in a fake beard, plays a true-blue digger in Act I and the faithful Aboriginal farmhand Bill in Acts 2 and 3. Tiwi Islander Jason De Santis plays Irish working-class criminal Joe Stockley in a blond shock wig. And so on.

The Sovereign Wife is not only epic in ambition: it's also, at almost three hours, epic in length. The whole is framed as an extended flashback, beginning as journalist Murphy (Ash Flanders) arrives at a country motel, researching a goldfields memoir by her ancestor Moira O'Flaherty. We follow the fortunes of O'Flaherty (played successively by Genevieve Giuffre, Ash Flanders and Jason De Santis) as she arrives with her no-good husband Connor (Paul Blenheim) at the Ballarat goldfields, sets up a general store and then, through some wilful plot machinations, loses her gender-dysmorphic daughter Abigail (Peter Paltos) when Abigail's horse bolts into the desert.

On opening night, notably in Act 1, it sometimes lacked the pinpoint accuracy that characterises the best of Sisters Grimm's apparently DIY theatre, but this didn't stop it from being outrageously funny. The comedy comes with a sting in the tail. There are moments when the stereotypes portrayed so wilfully here make you wince: they can cut very close to the bone and leave ambiguous the question of why you might be laughing.

The white Australia portrayed here remains as colonised as it ever was in the days of the British Empire, a bricolage of cultural signifiers that ultimately add up to a grinning vacancy. The show has four endings, all of them versions of the contrived Hollywood/soap opera reconciliation. One is a celebration of complacency, as our heroine Moira finally arrives in heaven (contemporary Melbourne) and is applauded for finally 'giving up fighting'. Ouch.

What holds it all together is the quality of the writing: as with all parodies, Greene and Flanders pay tribute to melodrama as much as they satirise it, generating moments of genuine pathos amid the chaos. But above all, it's deliriously fun. As I said above, *The Sovereign Wife* is sold out: but watch out for a season extension. If the standing ovation on opening night is anything to go by, you'll have to be quick.

ABC Arts Online, July 16 2016

Australia's leading Artistic Directors should embrace both positive and negative criticism

Critics. Who cares what they say? Paid-up members of an elite that swigs chardonnay for breakfast, they blag free tickets to expensive shows, only to write sneering takedowns of work over which artists have wept tears of blood.

According to their critics, reviewers are the headlice of culture, a scabrous itch that justifies itself as public discussion. They consider themselves superior to the honest punters who really support the arts, who put their money where their mouth is. Critics are mediocre wannabes who failed at art and were forced into the stalls, their essaying motivated by envy. What gives them the right? Why is their opinion so hallowed?

Over almost three decades of working as a theatre critic, I've heard most of the insults. And I confess, there are times when critics can make it difficult to defend our profession. Criticism is a broad, and very argumentative, church.

Opera Australia artistic director Lyndon Terracini certainly appears to have little regard for criticism. Last week he purged OA's media list and refused complimentary tickets to Sydney critics Harriet Cunningham and Diana Simmonds for writing negative critiques of the company's direction. Why should he facilitate the enemy?

To which my answer is: as a cultural leader, it is Terracini's job to facilitate the enemy. As an outstandingly well-paid executive of a flagship performing arts company, I'd consider that one of his duties is to foster Australia's cultural richness. In fact, given the public money that flows into OA's coffers – around $25 million a year in government funding – Terracini's responsibility to the wider culture is particularly acute.

One fundamental aspect of that richness is the cultural debate that surrounds art. It is perhaps no accident that the criticism that has got under Terracini's skin raises questions about his cultural responsibilities.

OA might argue that they are, indeed, fostering critical conversation. Last year they offered 'professional development opportunities' for a 'critic-in-training'. This inevitably raises alarm bells: should performing arts companies be training their own critics?

The decentralisation of arts commentary that arrived with the internet means that it's now standard for main stage companies to run in-house blogs, with interviews and articles about their shows. Some court reviews from punters, or as the Melbourne Festival did a few years ago, run their own reviews alongside the independent and mainstream media offerings. It can feel queasy, even for a commentator like me, who believes passionately in the importance of dialogue between critics and artists (and that artists have every right to take issue with critics).

So why should OA hand out comps? Surely anyone can purchase a ticket and criticise as much as they like, especially now we have the internet on every computer? Yes, indeed. But the convention is – as it has been for decades in Australia – that companies give complimentary tickets to critics.

This might not be ideal, but it is the standard. No professional critic I know regards free tickets as perks. Comps are the condition of being able to do the job at all: newspapers don't pay for tickets and, if asked to do so, might simply cease the minimal arts coverage they already do. There's no way anyone without a large private income could afford to see the three shows a week a critic averages, let alone a freelancer scraping a marginal living, or a blogger who is not being paid for her work at all. And in this digital age it's freelancers or bloggers who do the bulk of performing arts commentary.

The withdrawal of comps from particular critics breaks the unspoken convention that these tickets are given with the understanding that the critic is free to respond as freely as he or she likes. It singles out particular critics for punishment, with the aim of intimidating the rest. This has often been a successful ploy – Australian performing arts companies have an inglorious history of banning or secretly pressuring publications to sack troublesome critics – but it doesn't make it any less contemptible. Both things happened to me when I was a young critic writing for the Bulletin in the early 1990s.

The result of these pressures has too often been a timid and compliant critical culture. The obverse of this phenomenon, which is about reducing criticism to a branch of public relations, is something companies are quick to protest: uninformed and shallow reviews. If companies wish to benefit from an informed, vital and engaged critical culture, then they are obliged to put up with the rough as well as the smooth. Nobody's saying they have to like it.

If particular reviewers are targeted for writing negative critique, any commitment to free and open critical discourse becomes deeply questionable. The implication is that only tame critics who toe the company line are acceptable.

Australia, unlike Britain and the US, has never had highly paid arts critics: even back in the good old days before the internet, there was no such thing as a full-time theatre critic on any of Australia's daily papers. Our media institutions seldom put a high value on cultural debate, unless it happens to be a scandal. But this doesn't make a diverse, robust and honest critical discourse any less crucial to the creation of a vital culture.

The truth is that critics, despite their willingness to foist their thoughts on the general public, tend not to be the caricatures of popular imagination. Rather, they are like most arts workers: poorly paid enthusiasts, doing a demanding (and often singularly thankless) job that requires a high level of skill and experience for very little remuneration.

As the distinguished Mexican poet Octavio Paz said of literature, without criticism you don't have a culture; you just have a bunch of books. It's criticism that illuminates relationships, that makes connections, that generates love of an art form, that hails the shock of the new. Without informed criticism, no matter how annoying it might be to our cultural leaders, Australian culture would be much poorer. That's why Terracini should swallow his ego and take negative criticism with public grace. It's his job.

ABC Arts Online, January 6 2015

Assemblage #1, Matthew Day

I don't know what you're about to see.

I know it will have certain shapes, certain colours, certain sounds, perhaps certain smells. It will occur within a landscape mapped out in a room, scattered with a miscellany of objects – fruit, items of clothing, construction materials. As with all landscapes, what happens within it occurs in time, and is unpredictable. Someone moves through a landscape and changes it, and is changed by it.

Matthew Day offers us two possibilities of engagement. In one, we sit and watch a fifty minute performance. In the other, a three hour performance, we may walk in and out at will, investigate a reading room, behave as we might in a public space. In both performances, the doors are open.

Like all performances, it's an invitation. It asks for our attention. Perhaps it asks whether this is a performance at all, since Matthew Day may be responding purely spontaneously to the materials he has assembled. There may be movements that appear like a concentrated impulse of the moment, introduced as casually as the way we might unconsciously brush a fly off our face, that blur the borders of finished and unfinished.

The finishedness of all art is an illusion, after all. It is always, as Marcel Duchamp said of *The Bride Stripped Bare*, 'finally unfinished', a process that has reached a temporal pause. Day offers us a place of suspension between before and later, a chance to inhabit the ambiguity of the present.

A man walks into a space, and his presence in that space gradually transforms it. Our presence in that space transforms him. He is very alone: he has only his materials to play with, the curiosity of his body. We are here to observe him. He has his thirst and his hunger, his bananas and Berocca, his costumings of masculinity, his Bunnings building materials, his blankets and caps, his precarious contructions. He is a little comic, a little sad, joyous, fragile. He is constantly struggling against gravity, which never goes away, but which may grant him some respite.

Or perhaps not. I don't know what you are going to see.

Day resists representation, but a human being on a stage is always a metaphor from the moment he or she appears, in those ambiguous moments when we begin to understand that a performance is taking place. A metaphor is something that is at once literally and figuratively true. It is about likeness. He is like us, and he is unlike us, both at once. A metaphor is not an illusion. It is a moment of disruption in which relationships are created between things that are like and unlike each other, an instability created in our perception. A moment of what Day calls 'subtle incitement'.

There is no illusion in this performance. The process of making it is absolutely apparent: everything we see is made before our eyes. The artist turns on the sound. The artist controls the light. The artist manipulates objects. Nothing is hidden, and everything we see is ordinary.

Mystery hides inside the ordinary. The unsensational, the apparently transparent, holds within it the fascination of the unknown. If we release our constant, panicky demands for crude sensation, perhaps we can sit inside the ordinariness of ourselves and be surprised. Perhaps this possibility of ordinary mystery is a place of radical importance. Perhaps it is something that that we must decolonise from consumability. Perhaps we should pay attention to the silence – the sadness, the delight, the desire, the mystery – that exists inside us all.

Do we pay attention? How do we pay attention?

Program note, Dancehouse, November 2016

The Book of Exodus: Part One

One of the reasons I enjoy writing about live performance is its unique challenges. I am a profoundly word-centred person: written language has been, for as long as I can remember, the first thing I reach for when I wish to express myself. And yet performance always exceeds language: it is at once word embodied as action, and presence that can't be contained by words. Writing about performance is by definition a dance with failure, an attempt to translate the untranslatable.

Some shows highlight this struggle more than others. Fraught Outfit's *Book of Exodus: Part I* (at Theatre Works in Melbourne), co-created by Adena Jacobs and Aaron Orzech, brings the paradoxes of performance into sharp relief: the past, as embodied and inscribed history, playing out in a wholly absorbing present; a mostly wordless play that interrogates one of the most significant texts of Judaic culture. It feels particularly challenging, as if language itself has been erased in the process of the show and must somehow be resurrected in a new form.

Any text that claims to be artistic exceeds itself. Like poems and novels, even the most conventional plays carry within them the realm that exists beyond language. And perhaps, as is demonstrated by the millions of words of exegesis that they spawn, nothing is as excessive as religious texts. The inherent instability of meaning in written language is intensified, or perhaps made obvious, when a text is embodied in the flesh of actors and realised in three dimensions.

Exodus is the first instalment of the final part in Fraught Outfit's *Innocence Trilogy*, with part two coming in October. The trilogy began with a coolly intelligent interrogation of Frank Wedekind's *On the Bodily Education of Young Girls* and continued with an extraordinary adaptation of *The Bacchae* for the 2015 Melbourne Festival. All of these shows are acute and powerful examinations of patriarchal power, performed mostly by children.

Even though, like the previous shows, *Exodus* has little text, it is heavy with the word. This is true even of the least representational performance – abstract dance, for instance, has the shadow of language in the process of its creation – but subtext in this show is almost everything.

It begins with a stage that evokes the stillness after catastrophe. When the lights go up we contemplate in silence a set by Kate Davis (lit by Emma Valente) made entirely of styrofoam: a high white wall at the back, with a rectangular floor knee-deep in broken styrofoam that defines the playing space. It's like the ruins of a city, or the floor of a stony desert.

Two young children (on the night I saw it, Sol Feldman, 8, and Tarana Verma, 11) rise from beneath the rubble masked and cloaked as an old woman (Feldman) and an old man (Verma). The old man hobbles to a video camera at the side of the set, which projects into the back wall, and instructs the old woman to show her arm (a long red scar), her legs (another scar on her ankle), her back (another). The wounds of slavery. 'Show me your gold', he says, in the voice of a young girl. The old woman mutely displays her gold bracelets, her earrings, and puts them aside. And suddenly Auschwitz is chillingly present.

The children are clearly following rehearsed actions, but they aren't 'acting' in any conventional sense. They enact the plagues of Egypt as a game of doctor and nurse, the building of the Tabernacle with a gingerbread house, their play heightened by a various score by Max Lyandvert. They're as often comical as serious. The effect is completely compelling, winding you in past the noise of conscious thought to some deeper place, so that the end of the show comes as a shock. At just over 50 minutes it's short, but I would have sworn it was no longer than half an hour.

The sole text in the performance is Yahweh's grim instructions to the Jews in Egypt, to sacrifice the paschal lamb in order to escape the plague that will kill every firstborn in the kingdom. The children we are watching are both survivors and victims, bound to a jealous and vengeful God, the uber-patriarch who first seeks to demonstrate his power, not only over his enemies, but over his own people. The presence of the children on stage mutely poses the questions: How are these things inscribed upon childish bodies? How are children to understand the suffering and crimes of history? How much is memory itself a reproduction of violence?

The show doesn't attempt to answer these questions. Rather, it brings them to the surface of your mind, delicately and even playfully, in a way that is profoundly unsettling. The fusion of literal presence and allusive meaning becomes more complex as the show progresses, but always remains poised on the fulcrum of ambiguity. At one moment we are watching children playing with paint, but this is also a video of dead children sprawled in the ruins of a city, perhaps Palestine, perhaps Syria, that maybe we saw yesterday.

Feldman and Verma are strikingly able and autonomous performers, but their solitude on stage, exposed before the gaze of the audience, gives their presence a heightened sense of fragility. I don't think that quite accounts for the resonance of *Exodus*, which reaches inward, evoking memories of childhood, and outward through histories and the present in multiplying ripples. It leaves you speechless, and then forces you to speak in order to understand what just happened.

The Monthly, June 6 2017

Macbeth

Shakespeare's plays are meant to be vulgar. So Simon Phillips' astoundingly vulgar production of *Macbeth* at the Melbourne Theatre Company isn't, at least on the face of it, out of step with the spirit of the play.

Elizabethan theatre existed in a weird bubble between royal privilege and low origins: protected by the Crown, it was under constant attack by clerics until the Puritans succeeded in closing theatres by edict in 1642 for promoting 'lascivious Mirth and Levity'.

'Do [theatres] not induce whoredom and uncleanness?' thundered Philip Stubbes in his 1583 pamphlet, *Anatomie of Abuses*. 'For proof whereof mark but the flocking and running to Theaters and Curtains, daily and hourly... to see plays and interludes, where such wanton gestures, such bawdy speeches, such laughing and fleering, such clipping and culling, such winking and glancing of wanton eyes... is wonderful to behold.'

There's a lot of room in Shakespeare for the popular, even for crass extravagance, and *Macbeth* is indeed wonderful to behold. Phillips gives us extravagance in spades, with a Macbeth-as-superhero production that leaves no stage effect unexplored, no prop unhefted, no nonsensical climactic punch-up unpunched.

Calling Jai Courtney back to the stage to play Macbeth after six years' absence making his name in Hollywood movies such as *Terminator Genisys* and *Suicide Squad* needn't be merely a cynical, if extremely successful, ploy to sell tickets. What Shakespeare can't be is bloodless, and this production is as bloodless as any CGI explosion dreamed up Marvel or DC.

Teasingly, there's also a nagging sense of what might have been. Phillips' most successful Shakespeare, his 2010 production of *Richard III*, married Phillips' undoubted theatrical flair with a deeply intelligent, passionate performance by Ewen Leslie. It made exhilarating theatre. For *Macbeth* he has a cast that includes Robert Menzies (Duncan, the Porter) and Jane Montgomery Griffiths (First Witch). It is cast – very successfully – across race, with Rodney Afif, Kamil Ellis, Shareena Clanton and Khisraw Jones-Shukoor playing various roles.

This casting creates a sense of depth and human variousness that is left sadly unexploited. You get glimpses: Menzies playing the Porter is one of the few occasions where the language comes alive, and the murder of Lady Macduff (Clanton), staged in a contemporary domestic setting complete with children's drawings on the fridge, is the only time that the horror of Macbeth's tyranny comes home. A little more attention to meaning and performance and a little less to overdressing the spectacle, and this *Macbeth* might have been magnificent, instead of magnificently terrible.

An odd literalness haunts this production. For example, Macbeth, in riding boots and nineteenth-century military jacket, meets his hoodied ice-addict murderers in the royal stables to arrange the death of Banquo (I suppose because of the line, 'Ride you this afternoon?') Presumably because Macbeth references dogs – 'in the catalogue ye go for men; / As hounds and greyhounds, mongrels, spaniels, curs… are clept / All by the name of dogs' – Macbeth picks up two dead dogs, quite clearly fluffy toys, that happen to be hanging around and petulantly casts them to the floor.

This entirely meaningless gesture left me wondering why there should be dog corpses in the stables (horses get agitated around dead things). Literalness is catching, and often distracting. In another scene, the otherwise puzzling presence of a glamorous kitchen sink on stage seems to be explained by Macbeth's need to wash his hands of Duncan's blood. Likewise in the sound design: when the owl is mentioned, as it is mentioned often, the soundtrack obligingly gives us a shriek. The mention of horses signals neighing. And so on.

On the plus side, there's lots of fire on stage – burning cars, candelabras – and every word is audible. Courtney makes a decent if monochromal Macbeth, a bluff career soldier led astray by his hyper-ambitious wife (Geraldine Hakewill). For all the glamour on show – Hollywood gowns, luxury dining rooms and bedrooms – there's little sense of the erotic between the couple, their passions stated rather than communicated. But maybe they were just squashed by the score that inevitably swells to signal every emotional moment.

This lack of erotic frisson points to the real vulgarity of the production. Vulgar is derived from *vulgus*, meaning 'the common people', which over the centuries has come to mean obscenity and coarseness, or a lack of good (upper-class) taste. In culture, this has led to a continuing tension between 'high' and 'low' art. The critic Erich Auerbach, in his heroic work *Mimesis*, contends that all Western culture has been about the dialogue between these different modes of representation.

Shakespeare's vitality comes essentially from his marrying of the 'high' and the 'low', the melding of courtly sophistication with the sensual immediacy of the everyday. What we get in this production is a meeting of the culturally vulgar – the superhero movie – with the aesthetically vulgar – an empty excess not unreminiscent of Trump's America. The gestures towards contemporary relevance – hoodied murderers, homeless witches in abandoned cars, militarised violence – exist as decoration, stylistic flourishes that amount to a theatrical version of *Zoolander's* egregious fashion label 'Derelicte'.

The warmth of human feeling that is the gift of vulgarity is, aside from glimpses such as the Porter's scene, mostly absent; but so too is the feeling that emerges from a rigorous attention to, for example, the poetic of language.

Instead of emotional engagement, you get Ian McDonald's score. It's the obligatory ear-numbing soundtrack that blasts through every interminable superhero climax, covering up all the holes. After two hours of this sensual assault you walk out limp with aural fatigue, having felt nothing at all.

The Monthly, June 14 2017

The Real and Imagined History of the Elephant Man

The story of Joseph Merrick, popularly known as the Elephant Man, has a huge absence in its centre: Joseph Merrick himself. Ever since his death aged 27 in 1890, imagination has rushed to fill in that missing subjectivity.

The latest offering is Tom Wright's *The Real and Imagined History of the Elephant Man*, which has been given an overwhelmingly beautiful production by Matthew Lutton and his team at Malthouse Theatre. The design and performances are astonishingly good, and Wright's text, an episodic series of vignettes that create, as is promised in the title, an imagined biography of Merrick based on some of the known facts of his life, is lyrically written and theatrically intelligent.

Merrick is performed by Daniel Monks, himself disabled, and the four other actors, who play multiple roles, are cast with an eye to difference from the white male norm of Enlightenment-era Europe. They are all female, Paula Arundell is a woman of colour, and Emma J Hawkins is short statured.

Daniel Monks, dignified, resistant, is on stage for almost the entire show, the vulnerable centre of our attention. Around him, Paula Arundell, Julie Forsyth, Emma J Hawkins and Sophie Ross enact a huge cast of characters, spinning their performances on a dime to create a hallucinogenic parable. There are moments of enormous beauty and grace in both the production and the text, and Arundell's performance – beguiling, powerful, icily precise – is alone worth the price of the ticket.

They're backed by a superb production team. Marg Horwell's design, with the help of Paul Jackson's atmospheric lighting, uses the barest essentials – geometric light screens, billowing smoke, a few props and items of furniture – to evoke Industrial Revolution Britain on a bare stage. Jethro Woodward is one of the best sound designers in our theatre, and has created a textured, evocative score.

And yet. And yet. For all the care of its framing, I was left with a nagging question: at what point, in even the best-intentioned critiques, does art unwittingly reproduce and confirm the very attitudes it is critiquing?

There are elements in *The Elephant Man* that have uncomfortable reverberations with the furore around South African artist Brett Bailey's *Exhibit B*, which recreated the popular 'Human Zoos' of the late nineteenth century. As one of the young black performers asked of Bailey, 'How do you know we are not entertaining people the same way the human zoos did?'

It's hard not to feel that this 'real and imagined history', a brave attempt to step through the voluminous literature that has grown around Merrick – medical reports, books, plays, films – is merely, again, erasing Joseph Merrick.

What we know about Merrick has been mediated through others from the beginning. The most influential publication is Ashley Montagu's 1971 book *The Elephant Man: A Study in Human Dignity*, which inspired most of the subsequent plays and films.

Montagu resurrected an obscure 1923 narrative, part of a longer reminiscence, by the Victorian surgeon Sir Frederick Treves. This is the tale that's become familiar: the tragedy of a beautiful soul trapped inside a monstrous body. 'I supposed that Merrick was imbecile and had been imbecile from birth', writes Treves, after graphically describing the horrors of Merrick's body. 'That he could appreciate his position was unthinkable.'

To Treves, and later to Montagu, Merrick is primarily an insoluble medical problem that poses a moral lesson on the persistence of the human spirit. Montagu's account, like Treves', is deeply sentimental, but that obscures the obscenity of how Merrick is transfixed in what Foucault called the 'medical gaze', which diagnoses, defines and imprisons him. We see endless descriptions, coroner's reports, accounts of reactions to his hideousness: but we hear very little of Merrick himself.

What Merrick ultimately becomes in these accounts is a mirror for the kindness of the privileged: not only the medical profession, which charitably rescues Merrick from a life of degradation in sideshows, but his wealthy benefactors. In an appendix, we are told of Lady Dorothy Neville, whose 'sympathy was so awakened on his behalf that she offered him a cottage on her estate for some weeks, on condition that he did not leave it until after dark'.

Wright's text attempts to be an unsentimental correction to this narrative. It's not so much a biography of Merrick as a theatrical critique of the impact of industrial capitalism on the human body, how it literally inscribes itself on the bodies of workers and turns the human being into stereotypical norms. Enlightenment medicine and science, in their passion for categorisation and measurement, are shown as major mechanisms of this social conformity.

Wright attacks head-on the narrative of disinterested medical kindness, suggesting that hospitals were created more for the benefit of those outside them than those inside. In a particularly confronting scene, he exposes the sideshow aspect of medicine, where Merrick was displayed as a medical freak (Merrick later refused to take part in these expositions).

Wright's point is that the supposed 'kindness' of the charitable doctors is as inimical to Merrick's humanity as the showmen who exploited him. In Treves' account, medical enlightenment rescued Merrick from a horrific life – abandoned by his family, rejected by society and forced to exist as a sideshow exhibit – to give him haven in London Hospital, where he became a magnet for high society ladies, even royalty, anxious to demonstrate their capacity for compassion.

In a supposedly autobiographical pamphlet, Merrick's account differs in several ways from Treves: for example, he presents his sideshow career as his own decision. In a 1923 letter, Merrick's former manager Tom Norman ('65 years a Butcher, Farmer, Showman, Auctioneer'), indignantly corrected some of Treves' assertions of mistreatment, claiming that 'the big majority of showmen are in the habit of treating their novelties as human beings, and in a large number of cases as one of their own, and not like beasts'.

Norman's account is no doubt as self-interested as Treves': but it raises the possibility that Merrick's immurement in hospital, so much less offensive to the middle-class norms of the time, was more exploitative than his sideshow career. Before freak shows were outlawed in Britain, driving the circuit to the continent to find work, Merrick was able to save 50 pounds – a fortune for a working class man. According to Norman's letter, he refused charitable donations, saying 'We are not beggars, are we, Thomas?' It may well have been that Merrick felt that earning his keep in a freak show was more dignified than subsisting on charitable donations from the rich and curious.

Other accounts of circus 'freaks', such as circus performer Daniel P Mannix's *Freaks: We Who Are Not As Others*, suggest there might be some truth in this. 'A good freak is so important that usually the concessionaire won't allow him to appear in the pit with the other acts', says Mannix. 'The crowd must pay an additional fee to see him, often much more than they paid to see the rest of the show.' Mannix's book talks of people cruelly treated at home and in society who found community, the dignity of earning a good wage, and even happy marriages on the freak show circuit, and who were miserable when they were confined to institutions when freak shows were outlawed.

This possibility is never touched on in the show, no doubt because freak shows do cause moral revulsion. But it means that, despite the production's careful framing, Merrick's autonomy is unimaginable. Merrick is presented equally as the helpless victim of the society in which he lives and of his body, which becomes a palimpsest for a more abstract notion of nature. Until his final speech, when Merrick tells his carers that they are the real monsters and escapes the hospital, he remains almost completely a cipher. For the entire middle of the play he is traumatically mute and isolated, and is wholly defined and measured by the words and gestures of those who surround him.

When Merrick finally rebels, he claims himself as a body continually evolving into its own being to become a different species, a 'species of one'. And while, on the one hand, I can read here the Romantic embrace of difference that's seen in, say, Gerard Manley Hopkins' 'Pied Beauty'; on the other, Wright flings Merrick out of the human race altogether, as a vision of post-humanity. It's hard to imagine a more thorough Othering.

As a result, we are mere witnesses to Merrick's suffering, and as audiences are not asked to think much further than Lady Dorothy Neville's 'awakened sympathies'. This discomfort, of remaining within a matrix of thought that itself limits the possibility of what is being perceived, persisted after the show. How do we think outside the systems in which we are conditioned to live?

It's worth pondering how Back to Back Theatre, in their own confronting examinations of disability, manage to avoid this trap. *Ganesh Versus the Third Reich*, for instance, was an examination of eugenics which powerfully knitted mundane personal interactions with the horrific history of Nazi murders of the disabled. In *Food Court*, they enacted one of the most viscerally powerful theatrical representations of bullying and abuse I have witnessed.

In Back to Back's work disabled bodies are, of course, on display: but the medium of theatre is used to excavate all the dimensions of what that display means. The experience of being disabled is always at the centre. The company exploits voyeurism, sometimes shockingly, but as audiences we are unable to distance ourselves, intellectually, emotionally or historically, from our complicities in the production of that voyeurism. This is because the autonomy of the disabled performers is embedded in the conception and process of Back to Back's shows.

One of Back to Back's mechanisms is to continually remake the aesthetic through which they present their stories. They create beauty and then they destroy it, using that aesthetic radicality to destabilise our default frames of perception. *The Elephant Man* goes part of the way but, for all its virtues, not far enough: it's still looking out of the intellectual frame of those grave Victorian doctors, disinterestedly pondering the nature of humanity through its freakish monstrosities. Perhaps, in the end, this show is too beautiful.

The Monthly, August 18 2017